FROSTBORN:
THE DRAGON KNIGHT
Frostborn #14

Jonathan Moeller

Book Layout © 2017 BookDesignTemplates.com

Frostborn: The Dragon Knight / Jonathan Moeller. -- 1st ed.
ISBN 978-1544191980

To the readers of the Frostborn series

Everyone you meet is fighting a hard battle.

—PLATO

OTHER BOOKS BY THE AUTHOR

CHAPTER ONE

GATE

Six hundred and seventeen days after it began, six hundred and seventeen days after the day in the Year of Our Lord 1478 when blue fire filled the sky from horizon to horizon, Ridmark Arban tumbled through gray nothingness.

At least, he thought he was falling.

He could see nothing around him but sheets of gray mist, rippling and undulating. For a moment, he thought that the strange gate had sent him falling from the Tower of the Keeper to his death in the gardens below, but the ground did not rush up to meet him. He remembered what Morigna and Mara and Antenora had told him about the threshold, the place between the worlds, and wondered if he had stumbled into it.

Yet the sensation of falling lasted for only a moment.

There was a pulse of white light ahead, growing brighter and brighter.

The gray mist washed away, and Ridmark felt solid ground beneath his feet. He stumbled a few steps, using the staff of Ardrhythain to catch his balance.

He was no longer in the Tower of the Keeper.

In fact, unless Ridmark missed his guess, he was nowhere near Tarlion.

2 · JONATHAN MOELLER

He was standing on a broad, stony beach, the rocks beneath his boots worn smooth from centuries of waves. Beyond the beach stretched a vast expanse of water, the waves splashing gently against the shore. A large quantity of driftwood lay scattered across the stony shore, and Ridmark saw more branches bobbing in the waves.

Atop the waters, perhaps fifty yards from the shore, stood the wall of mist.

Ridmark had never seen anything quite like it. The wall of rippling mist rose so high its top vanished into the hazy sky overhead. There was a light breeze coming off the lake, cool and moist, and it ought to have sent the mist flowing towards the shore. Yet the gray wall did not move from its position, rippling in a way that had nothing to do with the wind.

It had to be magical. Mist did not act that way naturally. Calliande ought to know...

Ridmark stiffened with alarm. Where was Calliande? She had been with him when that strange gate had opened, as had Third. Both women had been pulled into the gate with him. Though now that Ridmark thought about it, he suspected that Third had managed to escape. He recalled seeing a flash of blue fire the instant before he had jumped into the gate after Calliande. Perhaps Third had been able to get away before the gate had drawn her here.

Wherever this place was.

A sense of disorientation threatened to overwhelm Ridmark. The spirit of Morigna had been waiting for him in the Tower of the Keeper, as had the woman from his strange dreams, the woman gowned in fire. He had been suffering from strange dreams for the last several months, losing all memory of them when he awakened, but when he had stepped into the Chamber of Sight in the Tower of the Keeper, the memories of those dreams had returned in a storm.

God and the saints, what did it mean? Third had suspected that the sword of the Dragon Knight had been hidden in the Tower of the Keeper. Had the spirit of the sword been calling to Ridmark in his dreams?

He pushed all the questions out of his mind. For the moment, they weren't important. What was important was finding Calliande, and then figuring out where they were.

Ridmark turned in a circle and then started down the beach. Beyond the shore, the ground rose into a dense forest, the trees thick and old, their trunks dotted with moss. A stillness hung over the shore and the forest, and the stony beach seemed deserted.

"Calliande?" called Ridmark.

No one answered him save the echoes of his own voice.

Ridmark frowned, slung his staff over his shoulder, and lifted his bow, setting an arrow to the string. Just as well that he had been carrying all his weapons when he and Calliande had stumbled into that strange gate. Of course, if life had taught him anything, it was that keeping weapons close at hand was always a good idea. He had been carrying his weapons when he had asked Calliande to marry him.

A flicker of dread went through him as scanned the beach and the trees. Was Calliande hurt? He had followed her through the gate, and his landing had still been rough. It would have been easy to lose his balance and strike his head on the rocky ground.

Even as the thought passed his mind, he saw a flash of green on the beach far ahead.

Calliande had been wearing a green dress.

Ridmark broke into a run.

About a hundred yards later he found Calliande. She lay motionless on her side, her eyes closed, the staff of the Keeper a few feet from her outstretched hand. There was blood on her temple, and for an awful instant Ridmark was certain that she was not breathing. Something squeezed inside his chest, and he remembered Aelia falling in her own blood on the black and white tiles of the great hall of Castra Marcaine, remembered finding Morigna dead in the keep of Dun Licinia...

Then Calliande took a breath, and a flood of relief went through Ridmark.

He went to one knee next to her. "Calliande."

She didn't respond. Ridmark turned her head to the side as gently as he could manage and saw a cut on her left temple. It wasn't deep, and the blood had made it look more serious than it really was. Likely she had fallen and hit her head when the gate had deposited them here. There was some bruising as well, and he felt a small lump beneath her blond hair, but he didn't think that she had cracked her skull. She ought to wake up with a nasty headache, but she would be fine.

Calliande shivered, and her blue eyes opened. They were unfocused and confused.

"Ridmark," she murmured, and then she fell unconscious again.

Ridmark squeezed her hand, then looked around and thought about what to do.

He had no idea where they were, and he didn't recognize the lake. All he knew was that he didn't smell any salt, so they weren't near the western or the southern seas. Perhaps the Lake of Mourning near Caerdracon and the Northerland? Or maybe the Lake of Battles near Coldinium? He didn't know, and with the wall of mist blocking his sight, he couldn't make a guess. Right now, he needed to focus on the problem of survival. It had been nearly nightfall when he and Calliande and Third had entered the Tower of the Keeper, and the gray sky had darkened steadily as Ridmark had searched for Calliande.

Though as he considered it, Ridmark realized that he had seen this stony beach before, even if he didn't know where it was.

It had appeared in one of his dreams with Morigna's spirit, where she had warned him (however obliquely) that the Weaver and the Sculptor had disguised themselves with false faces and were hunting Calliande. Did that mean the beach was somewhere in the

Wilderland? The shore of some lake that Morigna had visited before she had met Ridmark?

At the moment, it didn't matter. Before long night would fall, and he and Calliande would be alone and without supplies in a strange country.

The first thing to do was to find a suitable campsite. He didn't dare leave Calliande alone for too long, so someplace on the beach would have to do. Ridmark picked a spot about fifty yards away at the edge of the forest. It ought to be sheltered from the wind, and the trees were thinner there, meaning he would have a better chance of spotting anyone who tried to approach.

Ridmark stooped and lifted Calliande with a grunt. She was heavier than she looked, largely because years of campaigning had left her with more muscle than a woman her size usually had. It had been a challenge not to stare at her when they had first met, or when she had been forced to remove all her clothes to enter Dragonfall in Khald Azalar...

He put all those thoughts out of his mind. He hadn't been with a woman since Morigna had been murdered, and his desire for Calliande might cloud his judgment at a dangerous time.

Ridmark carried Calliande to the campsite, then hurried back and retrieved her staff. Once she awakened, the first thing she would do would be to reach for her staff. He wrapped Calliande in her cloak, cleaned the cut on her temple, and then started gathering driftwood for a fire as the shore darkened. Before long, he had a sufficient pile of driftwood, and a few sparks from his axe's blade and a piece of flint got a fire going. It crackled merrily, and Ridmark appreciated the new heat. It wasn't exactly cold here, but it wasn't warm, either. For that matter, perhaps the fire would draw the attention of boats upon the lake, or someone traveling through the forest.

It might also draw the attention of enemies, so Ridmark sat on a log facing the fire, placed his bow upon his knees, and set an arrow to the string.

Then he waited, alternating between watching Calliande and scanning the trees and the beach as the light faded away.

Third must have gotten away from the rift. Else she would have found him by now. Perhaps it was just as well that she was still in Tarlion. Someone had to tell High King Arandar what had happened. For the Keeper of Andomhaim to disappear on the eve of the army's march to face the Frostborn would be a devastating blow to morale. Calliande had been with the army during the campaign across Caerdracon, and without her help, they would not have been able to defeat Tarrabus Carhaine and the Enlightened.

And without her, the army of Andomhaim and its allies had no chance against the Frostborn.

Ridmark had to ensure her safety, and he had to get her back to Tarlion. For once, the necessary thing to do and the desires of his heart were in harmony.

It was a pleasant feeling. It didn't happen all that often.

A flicker of motion caught his eye.

Ridmark remained motionless, but turned his eyes, watching the movement. A moment later a wild turkey ambled into sight, pecking at the ground, followed by a half-dozen other turkeys. At least he and Calliande would not go hungry tonight.

Slowly, calmly, he slid another arrow from his quiver, setting it next to his leg. A few deep breaths to steady his hands, and he snapped his bow up, releasing one arrow and then another in rapid succession. The first arrow pierced a turkey's chest, and so did the second. Both turkeys fell dead to the ground, and the remainder fled into the forest, squawking and clucking.

Ridmark nodded to himself in satisfaction, checked on Calliande once more, and got to his feet. He retrieved and cleaned his arrows, and then carried the dead turkeys to the beach, pausing long enough to check the direction of the wind. The smell of blood might draw predators, and he would clean and prepare the turkeys downwind of the fire.

He had spent years surviving alone in the Wilderland, and preparing game was something he had done many times before. With his dagger and dwarven axe he cleaned and gutted the birds, and found driftwood branches to serve as crude spits for the meat. Once he had the meat cooking over the fire, he dumped the offal and the remainder of the carcasses in the lake, washed his hands in the water, and went to tend to the meat.

Calliande stirred and tossed, her eyes darting back and forth behind closed lids. Ridmark hoped that meant she would wake up soon. Maybe the smell of cooking turkey was helping to draw her awake. They had been going to attend the High King's feast in the Citadel of Tarlion. Then Ridmark had asked her to marry him, and their minds had been on other things than food.

He looked at her, smiled, and then turned his attention back to the spit, rotating the meat to make sure it cooked thoroughly. Undercooked bird meat was a superb way to get sick, and the last thing he and Calliande needed was an illness while in this unknown country...

A flicker of motion behind Calliande caught his eye.

Ridmark didn't move. Yet he kept watching the rocky beach behind Calliande. For a few moments, nothing happened, and he began to suspect that his eyes were playing tricks on him.

Then he saw the flicker again. Only this time it was more of a ripple, like the air rippling above hot stones on a sunny day. The sun had gone down, and it wasn't nearly hot enough for anything like that.

Ridmark had seen a ripple like that before.

His mind went cold, and he set aside his bow. It would be useless. Instead, he gripped his dwarven war axe in his right hand, the bronze-colored haft cool and hard against his fingers. The dwarven glyphs carved into the blade glimmered with sullen, fiery light. With his left hand, he grasped the spit, turning it some more, pretending to frown at the fire as he watched the rippling distortion.

It moved closer and closer in silence.

Ridmark took a deep breath, tightened his grip on the axe's haft, and jumped to his feet.

One step took him around the fire. With the next he jumped over Calliande where she lay, raising the axe over his head. Ridmark brought the axe blade hammering into the rippling distortion. He felt the impact as the axe sank into something hard, the blade rasping against bone.

There was a tearing, metallic shriek of rage, and the urvaalg appeared as it abandoned its camouflage.

Like all the other urvaalgs Ridmark had fought and killed over the years, the urvaalg looked like a twisted hybrid of ape and wolf, its gaunt body covered in stringy black fur, its talons and fangs like daggers, its eyes like hot coals. Urvaalgs were immune to weapons of normal steel, and one urvaalg could wipe out an entire troop of men-at-arms. Fortunately, Ridmark had guessed right, and his dwarven axe had sunk deep into the urvaalg's neck, black slime bubbling from the wound. Ridmark ripped the axe free and struck again, and his blow took the urvaalg's head off. The creature's body slumped to the ground, black slime pumping onto the stones.

Ridmark whirled and shifted his axe to his right hand, yanking his black staff free with his left hand. The symbols carved into the staff of Ardrhythain started to glow as he did, responding to the presence of dark magic nearby. That only served to confirm Ridmark's suspicions.

Urvaalgs always hunted in packs.

He caught the rippling distortion from the corner of his eye and threw himself to the side. An instant later a second urvaalg came into sight, its claws rasping against the ground. The creature pivoted with inhuman grace and came at him, but Ridmark had anticipated the movement. He swung his axe with his left hand, and the blade crashed into the urvaalg's jaw, reducing its head to bloody ruin. The urvaalg let out a metallic, bubbling scream, and Ridmark swept his staff at the creature's legs. The weapon landed with a bone-thudding crack, and the urvaalg stumbled. Ridmark swung the axe at its neck, and this time the blow was lethal.

The second urvaalg slumped to the ground, dead, and Ridmark turned again, seeking for a third urvaalg. It was possible that only two urvaalgs had attacked, but the creatures preferred to hunt in larger packs. But with nightfall, Ridmark had a harder time seeing the telltale ripples of an urvaalg using its stealth ability. He turned again, his eyes scanning the darkness...

The ripple was right in front of him.

Ridmark tried to raise his axe, but he was too slow. The impact of the urvaalg knocked the weapon from his grasp, and the urvaalg's bulk drove him to the ground, the breath exploding from his lungs. The urvaalg bore down on him, its claws raking against the dark elven armor sheathing his torso, its jaws yawning to crack his skull like an egg.

Ridmark still had a grip on his staff, and he snapped the weapon up before him, holding it horizontally before his face. The urvaalg's jaws snapped shut, intending to bite the staff in half, but the staff once carried by the high elven archmage Ardrhythain had endured far more potent forces. The urvaalg's fangs did not even scratch the black wood, and Ridmark shoved, forcing the urvaalg's head back. The urvaalg tried to release the staff from its jaws, but Ridmark had shoved it too far forward, and the creature could not get its teeth free. Ridmark shoved again, and the urvaalg reared back, just enough that Ridmark could draw back his legs and kick. His boots hammered into the urvaalg's midsection, and Ridmark twisted, flipping the creature off him.

He surged back to his feet just as the urvaalg attacked, black claws slashing and black fangs snapping. Ridmark retreated several steps and then struck back, landing several blows in rapid succession with the staff. The impacts landed hard, and the urvaalg flinched from the strikes. Yet while the staff could harm an urvaalg, it was difficult to land a killing blow with the weapon. Ridmark needed his axe.

Unfortunately, he was not sure where his axe had landed.

The urvaalg lunged again, trying to drive Ridmark out of the circle of light surrounding the campfire, and Ridmark swung the staff. The side of the weapon caught the urvaalg's jaw, and the creature's head snapped back, though not hard enough to break any bones. The urvaalg crouched, burning eyes fixed on Ridmark, and as it did, he saw the glint of metal behind the urvaalg.

His axe lay on the stones there.

Ridmark threw himself into a furious attack, striking again and again with a rapid flurry of sweeping blows. None of the blows were meant to hit or even harm the urvaalg, but the creature had learned that the staff could hurt it, and the urvaalg retreated step after step. At last Ridmark had advanced enough that he could take the risk, and he struck again, dropped his staff, and seized the axe with both hands, swinging it and straightening up with the same motion.

It was just in time. The urvaalg bounded forward, jaws yawning wide, and Ridmark buried the axe in its chest, the blade sliding between two of the ribs. The creature's weight pressed against Ridmark, forcing him to take several stumbling steps back, and he felt the reek of rotten meat coming from the urvaalg's gaping jaws.

He twisted to the side, ripping his axe free, and the urvaalg fell forward, landing hard. It started to rise again, but Ridmark brought the axe down on the top of its head.

There was a crack, and the urvaalg fell limp to the rocky ground.

Ridmark wrenched the axe free, retrieved his staff, and stepped back, his heart hammering in his chest. He looked towards Calliande at once, but she was unharmed. None of the urvaalgs had reached her.

He turned around again and saw the blue light in the darkened forest.

For an instant, he thought that Third had indeed been pulled through the rift, or that they had landed in the territory of the

Anathgrimm and that Queen Mara had found them. But Mara and Third traveled in pulses of blue fire, and this light was steady. It reminded Ridmark of the blue fire that the Warden and the Sculptor had used in their spells, the ghostly blue light of dark magic.

He hurried to the fire, putting himself between Calliande and the light.

A moment later, the creature glided from the forest.

It stood about seven feet tall, and it wore blue armor like Ridmark's. Unlike Ridmark's dark elven armor, the creature's armor was ornate, adorned with elaborate reliefs and scrollwork. A winged helmet of blue dark elven steel covered its head, and in its armored right hand, it carried a longsword of the same metal.

The creature's face was the grinning skull of a long-dead dark elf, and the blue light came from its eyes.

It glided forward, floating a few inches off the ground, and Ridmark felt the icy weight of the undead thing's attention. The creature said something in a musical-sounding language that Ridmark did not know, and he remained motionless. The undead thing regarded him for another moment and then started speaking in the orcish tongue, though the words were archaic.

"You have slain my hounds, churl," said the creature.

"Then you should not have set them to hunt me," said Ridmark.

"Do not think that the high elves can save you," said the undead dark elf. "Our power is greater. The shadow of Incariel has made us strong. They cling to their feeble superstitions. We shall triumph, for with the shadow of Incariel we shall make ourselves the gods of this world."

"A man I knew said much the same," said Ridmark. "It didn't end well for him."

"Bah!" rasped the creature. "Mortal dog! Perish!"

The undead thing raised its armored left hand, blue fire blazing to life around its fingers. It was casting a spell. Ridmark sprinted forward and struck with his staff, and the weapon landed on the creature's hand, snapping its arm to the side. The spell unraveled, but the undead creature attacked with its sword, and Ridmark got his axe up to block.

Soon he found himself on the retreat. The undead thing was fast, quicksilver fast, and unencumbered by the necessity of breathing. The sword flashed back and forth before Ridmark, and he had to devote his entire attention to his defense. Staff and axe blurred before him, deflecting the undead creature's thrusts and swings, but Ridmark could not find a way to land a blow on the creature. A few times he jabbed the staff through the creature's guard, but the staff rebounded from the plates of dark elven armor. Unless Ridmark thought of something clever, the creature was going to wear him down.

The beach lit up with dazzling white light.

Both Ridmark and the creature froze with surprise, and then a shaft of brilliant white fire passed through Ridmark and drilled into the undead creature. The flames did no harm to Ridmark. If anything, it felt pleasantly warm. But the creature shrieked as the fire burned into it, and the undead thing ripped apart in a spray of yellowed bones and blue armor. The armor clattered away in all directions against the stony beach, and the sword fell with a ringing clang.

Ridmark turned and saw that Calliande had gotten to her feet, the staff of the Keeper blazing with white fire in her right hand. Her face was tight with concentration, her blue eyes narrowed.

"It shouldn't get up again," said Calliande. Her eyelids fluttered as she drew upon the Sight. "And I don't think there are any others nearby." She looked at him, and concern flooded her face. "Are you all right? Are you hurt?"

"No," said Ridmark. "That cut on your temple…"

She made a dismissive wave. "It should heal shortly."

"Good," said Ridmark, walking to join her. "Calliande, where are we?"

She grimaced. "Ah. Well...it's a long story. Morigna was right about me."

"How so?" said Ridmark.

"I might have been overly clever."

CHAPTER TWO

SUMMONS

Arandar Pendragon, the High King of Andomhaim, knew that there would be hard fighting ahead. Tomorrow the host of Andomhaim would march against the Frostborn. Thanks to Calliande and Ridmark, allies would join them, but even the combined forces of Andomhaim, the dwarves, the manetaurs, and the Anathgrimm might not be enough to turn back the tide of the Frostborn.

He knew he might be marching to his death and the destruction of Andomhaim.

Tonight, though, Arandar would celebrate his victory.

It really wasn't his victory, he knew.

It belonged to the tens of thousands of men who had fought and struggled and died outside the siege walls that Tarrabus Carhaine had raised around Tarlion. It belonged to the Swordbearers who had dueled the Enlightened of Incariel in the final moments of the battle. It belonged to the nobles and the knights who had organized and led their men into the fray, who had kept their commands intact in the chaos of the battle. It belonged to the Magistri who had labored to heal the wounds of the battle, saving many men who otherwise would have perished from sword and spear and arrow.

So tonight, he would let the city of Tarlion and his army celebrate. They had set out to reunify Andomhaim under its lawful High King, and they had done so against long odds. The Frostborn were invading from the north, and Imaria Shadowbearer was still free and spinning her webs of evil. Arandar might lead the realm of Andomhaim to its final destruction, and that thought weighed heavy upon its mind.

Tonight, though, he could not let any of that show. Tonight, he must play the victorious High King, leading the chief nobles and knights of the realm in the feast. The High King could not show doubt or hesitation or weakness to his lords and knights, and Arandar would not rob his men of the joy of their victory.

Nevertheless, a sense of doom weighed upon him.

So, he was not entirely surprised when the alarm bells started ringing out.

Arandar sat at the high table in the great hall of the Citadel of Tarlion, the ancient seat of the High Kings of Andomhaim. The hall was as large and wide as the Great Cathedral of Tarlion in the city below the Citadel, and its windows of stained glass showed scenes from both the scriptures and the history of Andomhaim. Hundreds of knights and lords sat at the tables below the dais, eating and drinking. The food was not rich, but thanks to the granaries of Taliand and the supplies they had taken from the men of the former Dux Timon Carduriel, the food was plentiful.

The old proverb always said that hunger made for the best spice.

Around Arandar sat the chief lords and knights who had followed him – Dux Gareth, Dux Leogrance, Dux Kors, Dux Sebastian, and Prince Cadwall, along with the three kings of the baptized orcish kingdoms and the Masters of the Two Orders. A chair had been left empty for Calliande, who Arandar suspected would arrive shortly. He had seen her talking to Ridmark before they had left the Great Cathedral for the Citadel.

Though come to think of it, maybe they wouldn't be along shortly. Arandar had seen the way that Ridmark and Calliande had been looking at each other before the battle. She had been in love with

Ridmark for years, and perhaps Ridmark had finally worked through the various griefs that had both driven him to bold deeds and led him to keep Calliande at arm's length.

Perhaps Ridmark and Calliande were off somewhere celebrating the defeat of Tarrabus Carhaine in their own way.

Of course, even that reminded Arandar of his own duties. His son and heir Accolon was safe in Nightmane Forest, as was his daughter Nyvane, but now that the Enlightened were defeated Arandar could summon them to his side. He would have to arrange for marriages for his children, suitable marriages that would strengthen the realm and ensure that Accolon one day would have heirs of his own. Arandar supposed that he had better remarry himself to establish better ties with the nobles, and perhaps to have additional heirs if any tragedy should befall Accolon.

And, truth be told, it would be nice not to sleep alone any longer.

More and more, such thoughts pulled at him. From what he had seen, the women of Tarlion had been very grateful to those who had lifted the siege, and he was the High King of Andomhaim. It would not take much to persuade a woman to spend the night in the bedchamber of the High King, though guilt tugged at Arandar at the thought. The Dominus Christus had said that a man had ought to lie only with his own wife, and Arandar himself was the result of one of Uthanaric Pendragon's dalliances.

On the other hand, Arandar's wife had been dead for years. And they all might be dead in another month.

An army of pages and squires moved through the great hall, pouring wine for the nobles and knights. Soon Arandar would lead them in a toast, and then the Duxi and the Comites would have toasts of their own. Many a lord and knight would set out from Tarlion tomorrow with a sharp hangover, but there were worse things.

Sir Gavin and Antenora stood behind Calliande's empty chair, talking in low voices. Gavin had become a fine young knight, and he had been in some of the hottest fighting in the battle. Antenora waited next to him, a dark shadow in her long black coat and hood. She and Gavin seemed close, and Arandar was not sure that he approved. A young man like Gavin needed a young wife. Antenora was ancient, and cursed with dark magic. She was more undead than truly alive.

Still, given the dark days to come, perhaps they ought to find their joy where they could.

"This is good wine," said Prince Cadwall, taking a sip from his goblet.

"Aye, my lord Prince," said tough old Corbanic Lamorus, the Constable of Tarlion who had held the city against a year of siege. "You're fortunate there was any left. Had Tarrabus's men broken into the city, we would have drunk it all to deny it to him."

"Very sensible," said Leogrance, calm and patrician as ever.

Dux Kors let out a booming laugh. "It is an excellent wine. Almost as good as the wine we drank when we took Castra Carhaine from the usurper's dogs. Sitting in Tarrabus's hall and drinking Tarrabus's wine, aye, that was a splendid feast."

"Though sitting in the High King's hall with the usurper defeated," said Dux Gareth, "is the finest feast of all."

"Agreed," said Arandar. "We…"

Right about then, the alarm bell started to sound.

The conversation ceased, and the knights and nobles looked around. The bell sounded as if it was coming from somewhere in the city below, deep and clanging and dolorous. Arandar frowned. Had the sentries upon the walls of Tarlion seen enemies approaching? Had the Frostborn acted already? Or were some of the remnants of the Enlightened launching an attack? Most of the Enlightened had been killed or had surrendered, but a few had escaped and might have been stupid enough to attack.

"That is not the sentry bell," said Corbanic, frowning. "I've…never heard that bell before, come to think of it."

"Nor have I," said Arandar, alarm turning to puzzlement. He had grown up in Tarlion. He knew what the city's bells sounded like, both the bells of the church and the bells and horns and trumpets of the sentries upon the walls. "The magical defenses of the city, perhaps?"

"Lord Corbanic and I disarmed those," said Master Kurastus, the Master of the Order of the Magistri. "With the Enlightened broken, it no longer seemed necessary to keep the wards against dark magic active."

"And that's not the magical defense of the city," said Corbanic, getting to his feet with a growl. "I know what that bell sounds like, my lord King. That bell...damned if I know what it is."

There was a flicker of blue fire at the far end of the hall, and a sudden commotion from the knights and lords there. Arandar just had time to glimpse a dark figure glimmering with blue fire, and then it vanished.

Only to reappear before the high table.

The woman was tall and lean, paler than normal, with thick black hair and the pointed dark elven ears of her father's blood. Her eyes were as black as her hair and were usually as cold as a winter night. She wore close-fitting dark armor of some dark elven material, and always carried a pair of short swords of dark elven steel at her belt. Threads of blue fire pulsed and glimmered beneath her skin, fading away as she caught her breath. The nobles around Arandar shifted. They were always unsettled by Third, but there was no denying that her skills had helped win the battle against Tarrabus.

"Lady Third," said Arandar.

Third bowed to him, the movement always seeming correct but somehow mechanical. Of course, Third was the half-sister of the Queen of Nightmane Forest, and under no obligation to bow to him or to anyone else.

"High King," said Third. "The alarm bell. It is ringing from the Tower of the Keeper."

Arandar frowned. "The Tower?" That was impossible. The Tower of the Keeper had been sealed since the last Keeper had disappeared centuries ago.

Except that Calliande had been that Keeper. She had sealed the Tower, and then put herself to sleep below the Tower of Vigilance. If anyone could open the Tower, it would be the Keeper of Andomhaim herself.

Arandar looked at the Keeper's chair, and suddenly he knew exactly where Calliande and Ridmark had gone.

"They have opened the Tower, haven't they, Lady Third?" said Arandar.

"They have," said Third. "I fear it has gone ill. There is some sort of magical defense around the Tower that has been activated, and..."

Arandar rose to his feet. "I wish to see for myself."

In short order, the squires had horses saddled, and Arandar rode from the Citadel. He had given orders that the feast should continue in his absence, though he imagined that the festivities would be rather subdued. Or the knights and lords would continue drinking with enthusiasm. Arandar rather hoped they would.

There might not be another chance.

Third accompanied him on horseback, as did Gavin and Antenora. Both the Swordbearer and the Keeper's apprentice had appointed themselves the Keeper's bodyguards, and both were furious with themselves for letting the Keeper go into danger. Kharlacht of Vhaluusk, Brother Caius, and Camorak went with Arandar as well. Kharlacht and Caius had gone with Arandar into the dangers of Urd Morlemoch and Khald Azalar, and they were trustworthy companions. Camorak was a drunkard, but he had been a reliable man-at-arms in the service Dux Kors for years, and he was now a capable healer of the Magistri. Master Kurastus of the Magistri accompanied him, along with Master Marhand of the Swordbearers and Sir Constantine Licinius and Sir Valmark Arban.

The High King of Andomhaim could not do anything alone.

Given the number of people who wanted to kill him, it seemed wise to travel with well-armed companions. Though if it came to a fight, Arandar was not helpless himself.

The sword hanging on his left hip guaranteed that.

He had carried the soulblade Heartwarden for years, but Excalibur felt different. For one, the blade was a little shorter and a little thicker, reflecting the ancient designs of swords upon Old Earth. For another, the sword's presence in his mind felt different. Excalibur was a soulblade, but it had possessed magic long before Ardrhythain had reforged it into a soulblade. Heartwarden had burned with rage whenever confronting a creature of dark magic. Excalibur did the same, but the sword also had a sense of stern implacability, of an unyielding tower of iron. It put Arandar in mind of a stern but fair magistrate sitting upon his curule chair and issuing judgments.

Perhaps that explained why Excalibur's magic allowed the sword to cut through nearly anything. The sword cut through flesh and bone and steel with equal ease. If Arandar had wanted, he probably could have used Excalibur to slice a tunnel through the walls of Tarlion.

The horsemen rode from the courtyard of the Citadel, down the ramp that encircled the stone crag upon which the fortress stood, and into the Forum of the Crown, the Great Cathedral of Tarlion rising on one side and the Castra of the Swordbearers on the other. From there they circled around the Citadel and rode down the Via Ecclesia until the Tower of the Keeper came into sight.

All the while, that strange bell tolled.

And as the Tower came into sight, Arandar realized that something was indeed wrong.

The Tower of the Keeper had been a place of silent mystery all his life. Its grounds stood behind a low wall of white stone, the Tower rising from a copse of ancient oak trees. The Tower itself was a slender structure of white stone, topped with a dome of greening copper several hundred feet above the ground. Mist had always wreathed the woods at the Tower's base, and more mist had concealed its windows. Anyone who ventured into the grounds of the Tower, even the most powerful and skillful Magistri, disappeared at once, reappeared unconscious on the street a few blocks away, and did not wake up again for a day and an hour. The Tower had been a mystery that no one could solve, but it had been a harmless mystery. It never hurt anyone, and only those who dared to venture within its grounds were subject to its power.

Now gray light flashed up and down the Tower's length. The mist in the windows rippled and lashed. The mist in the trees flowed in thick, ragged curtains, and the trees themselves seemed to stir, their heavy branches whispering as the leaves brushed against each other.

"Master Kurastus," said Arandar.

The old Magistrius bowed his head and cast a spell, his eyes narrowed as he concentrated. Then his head snapped up, his eyes wide, his mouth open in surprise behind his white beard.

"Your Majesty," said Kurastus. "The magic within the Tower...it has always been there, but it has been dormant. Yet something awakened it." He frowned and gestured, white light seeming to flicker around his fingers. "And...I think there is a magical gate of some kind within the Tower. A world gate? No, something else..."

The bell clanged three more times in rapid succession.

Then the Tower seemed to fall asleep.

The ripples of gray light vanished. The mist stopped writhing, and settled back to its slow, steady swirl through the oak trees. The windows of the Tower were once again concealed with the mist, and the bell fell silent.

Kurastus cast another spell. "I think...the Tower is dormant once more, my lord King. The magic around it feels the same as it always did. I am uncertain of what has transpired."

Arandar looked at Third. "My lady, I think you had better tell us what happened."

Third nodded. "The lord magister and the Keeper were alone in the Great Cathedral, and then they both started to hear the heartbeat."

"Heartbeat?" said Caius, edging his horse closer.

"A heartbeat," said Third. "Evidently since the Tower of the Keeper came into sight from the siege camps, both the Keeper and the lord magister have been hearing an identical heartbeat inside of their heads from time to time." The others shared a look. "Additionally, the lord magister has been suffering sharp nightmares for the last year, nightmares that he always forgot on awakening. The Keeper believed the source of the dreams and the heartbeat was in the highest chamber of the Tower of the Keeper, though she was not sure."

"How could she not be sure?" said Constantine.

"The Keeper evidently removed her memory of the Tower, just as she removed her other memories before going into the long sleep," said Third. "She feared that Tymandain Shadowbearer or one of the Enlightened might be able to gain access to her memories and therefore obtain a powerful weapon to use against us."

"Go on," said Arandar. "What happened when you went to the Tower?"

"The Keeper was able to enter, for the magic yielded to her, and the lord magister and I went with her," said Third. "As we climbed the Tower, her fear increased, and she almost turned back from the highest chamber. I began to suspect that the Keeper had concealed a weapon of great power within the Tower."

"What was in the highest chamber?" said Arandar.

"Two spirits," said Third. "One was a woman gowned in fire whom I did not recognize, though her features seemed to shift between those of Calliande, the lord magister's late wife, and the sorceress Morigna. The other spirit was that of Morigna herself."

"Morigna?" said Kharlacht, startled. Arandar recalled that Kharlacht had always gotten on well with Morigna, though Arandar himself had found her caustic and unpleasant and possibly dangerous. "How is that possible?"

"I do not know," said Third. "Morigna's spirit said that she was sorry, and then a gate opened. It pulled the Keeper through it, and the lord magister jumped after her. I would have followed them, but the gate closed the minute he passed through. By then, I suspected the Tower's defenses were returning to life, so I used my power to escape and warn you." She shrugged. "That is all I know on the matter."

"Master Kurastus?" said Arandar. "What do you make of it?"

"I do not know, your Majesty," said Kurastus, shaking his head. "The Keepers of old kept many secrets that they did not share with the Magistri. The Keeper Calliande has shown powers and abilities beyond the reach of the Magistri. Perhaps this is another such power."

"I have a possible explanation," said Third.

"Please," said Arandar. Third was older than anyone here, apart from Antenora, and thanks to her long centuries in service to the Traveler, she likely knew more of the ancient lore of the world than many others.

"I believe," said Third, "that the gate took the lord magister and the Keeper to the hiding place of the sword of the Dragon Knight."

Silence answered her.

"What makes you believe that, Lady Third?" said Kurastus at last.

"The balance of probability points in that direction," said Third.

Marhand snorted. "A scholarly answer."

"But a true one, Master Marhand," said Third. "Consider. During the first war against the Frostborn, the Keeper and the Dragon Knight led the armies of the nations to victory against the Frostborn. The Keeper realized the Frostborn would return one day, and so put herself into magical sleep to await their return."

"She recovered her memory at Dragonfall," said Caius. "Her powers, and her memories."

"But she did not recover any memory of the Tower of the Keeper, or what had happened to the Dragon Knight after she went into the long sleep," said Third. "This suggests that the information was dangerous, and she dared not have it fall into the hands of Shadowbearer."

"Lady Third is right," said Kharlacht. "I was there when the Keeper awakened. Tymandain Shadowbearer captured her with my cousin Qazarl's help, and he asked her about a staff and a sword. At the time, I did not understand the significance of the question, but the staff was obviously the staff of the Keeper. The sword must have been the sword of the Dragon Knight."

"Or was he asking about a soulblade?" said Marhand, his doubt plain. "The Gray Knight slew with him a soulblade. He would have been wise to fear them."

"But he did not, Master Marhand," said Constantine. "I was there for that battle. Tymandain Shadowbearer did not fear us at all. Perhaps he should have because his pride and cruelty allowed Lord Ridmark to slay him with a soulblade. But it was plain that while he feared Calliande, he did not fear any of the rest of us."

"But he would have feared the sword of the Dragon Knight," said Arandar. "It helped defeat the Frostborn the first time."

"Precisely, lord High King," said Third. "Therefore, logic dictates that since the Keeper knew the sword would threaten Shadowbearer, she needed to hide it away from him. Yet she also knew she might need the use of the sword if the Frostborn attacked. If the Frostborn returned, the Keeper would almost certainly go to

Tarlion at some point. I conclude that the Keeper worked her spell so that her memory of the Tower of the Keeper would return after passing the gate of Tarlion, and the heartbeat was a compulsion to go to the Tower. Once she was there, the gate opened and drew her and the lord magister to the place where the last Dragon Knight had concealed the sword."

"It is a good argument," said Marhand at last.

"Very well-reasoned, Lady Third," said Kurastus.

"Thank you," said Third.

Kurastus blinked. "By chance, have you read the writings of Aristotle on logic in his book the Organon? I think you would find his discussion on the syllogism in Prior Analytics to be fascinating..."

"Perhaps there will be time for that later," said Arandar. Kurastus was a good man and a powerful Magistrius, but if left unchecked, he could lecture on his beloved ancient Greek authors for hours at end. "Right now, we must assume that the Keeper and Lord Ridmark have departed to find the sword of the Dragon Knight. At the very least, that is what we shall tell the rest of the host."

"We will?" said Gavin. Next to him, Antenora looked displeased. Likely she wished to have accompanied the Keeper. "But we're not entirely sure."

"No," said Arandar, "but that is what we will assume. I had hoped to have the Keeper with us when we marched against the Frostborn. Her powers would have been useful, and her presence would have heartened the men. We laid siege to Tarrabus for weeks before she arrived, and with her help, we broke the usurper."

In truth, Calliande's absence troubled him more than he wanted to show in front of the men. The Keeper's aid had been invaluable, both at Dun Calpurnia and during the long campaign across Caerdracon, and again during the battle before the walls of Tarlion. Without the Keeper's aid, they would not have won the battle at Dun Calpurnia, and they might have been defeated by Tarrabus Carhaine.

What would happen when they faced the Frostborn without her?

Perhaps she and Ridmark would be able to return before the army faced the Frostborn in the Northerland, but Arandar did not like marching without the Keeper.

Nevertheless, he had no choice.

"It seems plain that the Keeper and Lord Ridmark went to secure the aid of the Dragon Knight," said Constantine. "They have done this sort of thing before. They departed to win the aid of the dwarves and the manetaurs, who even now march to fight the Frostborn."

Caius frowned. "Do you think she means to make Ridmark into the new Dragon Knight?"

Kharlacht shrugged. "Someone has to wield the sword. Given that most of us would be dead if not for Ridmark Arban, it may as well be him."

"But the sword of the Dragon Knight carries a heavy price," said Caius. "It holds the power of the ancient dragons, and grants mastery over all forms of fire, or so the lore of the stonescribes claims. Yet it is also said that the sword exacts a grim price upon anyone who carries it."

Marhand snorted. "As if the Gray Knight isn't already adept at inflicting grim prices upon himself."

He had a point.

"Very well," said Arandar. "We cannot let this change our plans. The army must march tomorrow to join our allies in the Northerland. We shall announce that the Keeper and Lord Ridmark have gone to find the Dragon Knight and recruit him to our cause, just as Ridmark found the Keeper."

"That…seems dishonest, somehow," said Gavin.

"It's true as far as we know," said Caius. "And the High King must tell the army something. If the army's morale cracks even before we depart Tarlion, it could be disastrous."

Gavin still looked unsettled, but he nodded.

"I should have been with her," said Antenora, her raspy voice heavy with self-rebuke. "I should have accompanied her into the Tower. I should have insisted…"

"As should I," said Third. She shook her head with a grimace. "If I had known the rift would close so quickly, I would have tried to follow. My sister asked me to look after the lord magister. But I fear both he and the Keeper have passed beyond our reach, Antenora. They must look after themselves. We can best aid them by ensuring the High King's army is victorious until they return."

"Agreed," said Antenora, though she did not look pleased.

Arandar was not pleased himself, though for a different reason. Still, what was done was done. The aid of Ridmark and Calliande would have been invaluable in the battle to come, but if they had to fight without the Keeper and the Gray Knight, then they would fight.

And perhaps Third was right, and Calliande would return with the Dragon Knight to fight the Frostborn. The first Dragon Knight had been named…Kalomarus, yes, that was it. The histories that Arandar had read had spoken little of his powers, save that he was a fell warrior without peer, and he had been able to command the fires of the dragons, whatever that meant. Given the ice magic of the Frostborn, a little dragon fire would not go amiss.

"We should return to the feast," said Arandar. "I suppose we ought to announce that the Keeper and Lord Ridmark have departed to bring the Dragon Knight to our aid. We might as well get the bad news out of the way."

"Agreed, your Majesty," said Marhand. "But perhaps Lady Third is correct, and it will not be bad news."

"No," said Arandar. "We…"

Antenora was frowning again, but this time she was looking at the sky, and a puzzled expression went over her gaunt face.

"Lady Antenora," said Arandar. "What is it?"

"I...do not know," said Antenora. "The Sight is stirring, but overhead. There is..."

She frowned again, and then her yellow eyes went wide, the symbols upon her black staff blazing into fiery light.

"Beware!" said Antenora. "The enemy comes! Beware!"

Arandar looked up, wondering if Soulbreaker had returned, and then he saw the frost drake diving towards them, its jaws yawning wide.

The creature's body was the size of an ox and armored in silvery gray scales the color of ice. Its vast wings were like sails, its serpentine neck the length of a tree, and its eyes burned with blue fire. The gray-armored shape of a Frostborn warrior sat upon its back, one hand holding leather reins, the other raised to cast a warding spell. Around the drake flew dozens of the blue, insect-like shapes of winged locusari scouts.

The Frostborn had come at last.

The drake's jaws yawned wide, and a blast of freezing mist burst over its fangs.

ICE AND FIRE

Gavin looked at the sky in shock, surprise dulling his reactions for a critical moment.

It was impossible. The Frostborn were in the Northerland, fighting the Anathgrimm and the men-at-arms holding Castra Marcaine in Dux Gareth's name. That was hundreds of miles away. Not even the Frostborn could have learned of Tarrabus's defeat so quickly, and not even the Frostborn could have covered hundreds of miles of terrain in a few days.

Then Gavin realized that the Frostborn needn't have bothered.

There had been frequent reports of frost drakes and locusari scouts ranging out of the Northerland and overflying the lands of Andomhaim. The Frostborn atop the frost drakes and the locusari scouts accompanying their masters had never engaged in battle, and they had only been content to observe. It was possible that the Frostborn knew more about what was happening in Andomhaim than the men of Andomhaim knew about events in the Northerland.

And if a Frostborn scout had seen the defeat of Tarrabus Carhaine, if they had seen the ascension of a new High King, if they had seen Arandar ride with a few knights and Magistri to look at the Tower of the Keeper...why, a bold Frostborn scout might have decided to take a calculated risk of ridding Andomhaim of its new High King in one sharp blow.

All that flashed through Gavin's mind in an instant.

In the next moment, he yanked Truthseeker from its scabbard at his side, the blade shining with white fire. The other Swordbearers were following suit, and both Camorak and Kurastus were casting spells, but it was too late. The frost drake had them dead to rights, and Gavin had seen the killing power of the frost drakes' breath at Dun Calpurnia and Dun Licinia. The Swordbearers might be able to protect themselves, but anyone else would be frozen to death when the freezing mist touched them.

Fortunately, Master Kurastus was faster.

The old Magistrius shouted and raised his hands over his head, his fingers glowing with white fire. An instant later a dome of flickering white light appeared above the horsemen as the frost drake breathed its chilling breath. The plume of white mist struck Kurastus's warding spell and spread over it in a half-dome, the white mist hardening into a layer of jagged ice. Had that freezing mist touched a living man, it would have encased him in a layer of ice, sucking away his life and warmth in a few moments.

Kurastus shouted and shoved his hands, and the half-dome shattered, the frozen shards spraying across the street and tumbling into the woods surrounding the base of the Tower of the Keeper. Antenora thrust her staff, and a gout of fire streaked across the night sky, striking the side of the frost drake. The creature shrieked and clawed higher into the air, and banked away. Antenora's spell had hurt it, but the creature was still capable of fighting, and the Frostborn upon its back might be able to cast spells.

It would come around for another attack.

Before it did, the locusari struck.

They descended in a blue blur, gossamer wings blurring. The locusari scouts were the size of large dogs, albeit large dogs with foot-long blades attached to their segmented forelimbs. The creatures looked sort of like blue grasshoppers with eyes like faceted jewels, though Gavin had never met a grasshopper capable of killing a man, and the locusari were brutally efficient killers.

He leaped from his saddle, Truthseeker blazing in his right fist, and his blow cut a locusari in half, the two halves bouncing away across the street and leaking an odd yellowish slime in their wake. Another locusari came at him, and Gavin whipped Truthseeker around, the soulblade bisecting the creature's head. The locusari managed to make a disgruntled buzzing noise, and then it fell dead at his feet.

He did not bother to reclaim his saddle. A Swordbearer always fought better on foot, since a soulblade's strength and stamina did not extend to a Swordbearer's mount, and a man on horseback was at a disadvantage when fighting winged locusari anyway. The others had fought locusari before as well and had dismounted, raising weapons and shields. Gavin reached up to the saddle of his horse and yanked down his dwarven shield from its straps, grateful that he had taken the time to bring it along.

"Swordbearers!" said Arandar. "Defend the Magistri! Lady Third, please return to the Citadel and sound the alarm. It seems the city is under attack already."

Third nodded and vanished in a flare of blue fire, and as she did, Gavin caught a glimpse of another silver-gray shape flying over the city, illuminated in the silvery glow from the Tower of the Moon. It was a second frost drake, and it was flying towards the northern wall of the city. Had the Frostborn launched a serious attack already? Gavin couldn't imagine how they had gotten a substantial force this far south so quickly...

Then another attack came at them, and Gavin had to fight for his life.

It started with another blast of freezing mist from the frost drake. Kurastus cast his warding spell, holding the deadly mist at bay with his magic, and shattered the resultant wall of ice. As the ice fell, the locusari swooped in to strike again, their wings buzzing, their scythed forelimbs slashing. Gavin killed one with a sweep of Truthseeker and caught the attack of another upon his shield. The dwarven shield clanged beneath the scythed forelimbs, and Gavin shoved. The locusari buzzed away, its flight wobbling, but before he could kill the creature Valmark Arban split it in half with a blow from his soulblade.

Gavin found himself fighting alongside Sir Constantine as he had a score of times before. They had fought alongside each other against Tymandain Shadowbearer and at Dun Calpurnia and during the campaign in Caerdracon, and by now he knew the older Swordbearer's instincts and patterns. Gavin caught a blow on his shield, and Constantine thrust with Brightherald, skewering the locusari. Constantine deflected a strike on his own shield, and Gavin killed the attacking locusari, yellow slime spattering across his blue armor.

In the distance, he heard a deep bell booming out from the Citadel. Third must have found someone in authority, most likely Corbanic Lamorus, and sounded the call to battle. Of course, half of the knights and the lords were well on their way to becoming drunk, and Gavin wondered how well they would be able to fight.

The frost drake swooped around for another attack, jaws yawning wide. Master Kurastus started to cast his warding spell, but this time Antenora struck first. While the battle had been raging around her, she had been casting a spell, a sphere of fire spinning over the end of her staff as she gripped it with both hands. The symbols upon the black staff blazed brighter and hotter, and the sphere had grown larger and larger as it whirled over the end of her staff. Now the sphere was about twice the size of Gavin's head.

Antenora thrust her staff, and the sphere leaped from the end of her staff and soared through the air.

The frost drake had already begun its attack dive, and it could not change direction. Antenora's sphere slammed into the Frostborn upon the creature's back and exploded in a blaze of flame. The frost drake screamed in agony and climbed higher, wings lashing at the air as flames burned on its neck and shoulders. The blast ripped the Frostborn from his saddle, and the gray-armored warrior plummeted to the ground, wreathed in Antenora's elemental fire. The Frostborn struck the street outside of the Tower of the Keeper with a crash. The blue fire within the warrior's crystalline skin pulsed and went out, leaving only a giant body wreathed in fire.

"Good shot!" said Gavin.

Antenora smiled at him as the frost drake fled away to the north. It made her look younger, less weary. In Thainkul Morzan, one of the Sculptor's urshanes had presented itself to Gavin wrapped in an illusion of Antenora, or at least Antenora as the woman she would have been if the curse of dark magic had not bound her for the last fifteen centuries. When Antenora smiled at him, he could see glimpses of that woman.

He wished he could have kissed her at that moment. Well, he could have kissed her, but she would not have felt it.

Blue fire swirled next to Arandar, and Third returned, breathing hard.

"The Constable has sounded the alarm," said Third, looking around. "There have been sightings of other frost drakes circling over the city. I saw them myself as I traveled here. Five or six in total, I think, all ridden by Frostborn and all accompanied by flights of locusari scouts."

"A raiding party, then," said Arandar.

"Or a test of our defenses," said Marhand. "To see how we react."

"Lady Third," said Arandar. "Go back to the Constable, please. Tell Corbanic to employ the siege weapons we prepared earlier." Third nodded and vanished again. Her power to travel in the blink of an eye made her very dangerous, but Gavin had never considered its potential utility as a method of delivering battlefield messages.

"We seem to have driven off the enemy," said Kurastus.

"Only this group," said Arandar. He looked to the north, and Gavin saw another frost drake flying low over the northern ramparts of the city. "To the northern gate, quickly. Some of the new ballistae will be there, and hopefully, we can employ them against the frost drakes."

The frightened horses had scattered, but not far, and soon they were riding in haste for the Forum of the North and the city's northern gate.

Arandar heard the city rousing itself for battle.

Blasts of trumpets came from the Citadel and the gatehouses, calling the men-at-arms and the city's militia to their posts. He supposed it made sense for the Frostborn to launch a raid on Tarlion tonight. With Tarrabus defeated and the Enlightened broken and the Frostborn hundreds of miles away in the Northerland, the men of Andomhaim had won themselves a brief respite.

Or so they had thought.

Arandar was alarmed, but he was not surprised.

He had known this day would come, and he had thought about it during the campaign across Caerdracon and the siege of Tarrabus's army. If they were victorious, they would have to face the Frostborn, and the Frostborn had a massive advantage that the men of Andomhaim could not match.

Specifically, they had creatures that could take to the air.

The locusari scouts were bad enough. They were not that dangerous as combatants, little better than skirmishers, but they could stay in the air for hours, and they made highly effective scouts. The Frostborn had always known exactly where Uthanaric Pendragon's army was and had arranged themselves accordingly. The frost drakes were even worse. They carried a Frostborn warrior, and the Frostborn could bring powerful magic to bear. Even without that danger, the freezing breath of the frost drakes was a deadly weapon.

Arandar had feared that the Frostborn could simply loose a half a hundred frost drakes at his army and rain their icy breath down until the host broke and ran. Fortunately, Calliande had fought the Frostborn long before he had been born, and she had talked about a method of fighting the frost drakes. The armies at that time had constructed lightweight siege ballistae, small enough that only two men could move and operate them, but powerful enough to punch through the armored scales of the frost drakes. The design wasn't useful for siege warfare, so after the defeat of the Frostborn, the light ballista had fallen out of favor.

Arandar had ordered his blacksmiths to start constructing the weapons, and men-at-arms and militiamen to train in their use. There had been a thousand other more pressing tasks during the campaign in Caerdracon, but the weeks of the siege of Tarlion had given the blacksmiths time to catch up, and the finished ballistae and their bolts had been distributed throughout the host.

He only hoped there had been enough time to train in their use.

They reached the Forum of the North, the broad market square below the city's northern gate. Statues of long-dead knights and lords and Magistri dotted the square, and already companies of militiamen were hurrying in response to the alarm. Unfortunately, that did little good. Already Arandar saw a half-dozen pillars of ice scattered throughout the forum, each one holding a dead militiaman who had been caught in the breath of the frost drakes.

There was a roar from overhead, and one of the frost drakes swooped down. Arandar saw the harsh blue-white glow of the eyes of the Frostborn riding the creature, saw the white mist start to swirl behind the drake's fangs.

Antenora was already casting. A fireball leaped from the end of her staff, hurtling into the sky, and slammed into the Frostborn. The blast knocked the Frostborn warrior from the saddle to land in the Forum, while the frost drake screamed in rage, banked to the north and flew away.

The landing had not killed the Frostborn, and the warrior rose to his feet, reaching over his shoulder for the hilt of his greatsword.

He was only ten yards away. The Frostborn warrior stood eight or nine feet tall and wore armor the gray of hard ice. His skin was like crystal, and fiery blue light flowed through his veins. Beneath his bladed helm, his eyes burned with a blue-white light, and Arandar felt the cold radiating from the warrior.

The Frostborn warrior lifted his right hand, blue fire and white mist swirling around his armored fingers as he began casting a spell. Arandar raised Excalibur, preparing to charge, but Antenora acted first. A gout of fire lashed out and hit the Frostborn, and the warrior staggered back, the fire chewing into the gaps in his armor. The spell ended, and the Frostborn began casting another spell, but Arandar was already charging.

The Frostborn warrior raised his greatsword to block, but Excalibur sliced through the sword without slowing. The greatsword fell in two pieces with a ringing clang, and Arandar drove Excalibur to the hilt into the heavy armor. The Frostborn staggered, falling to his knees as the blue fire that seemed to serve as the blood of the Frostborn sprayed from the wound in the crystalline skin.

The Frostborn fell dead, and Arandar turned to see another wave of locusari scouts drop from the sky. He rushed to join the fray, slashing and stabbing with Excalibur, and he fought his way to the side of Constantine, Valmark, Marhand, and Gavin. Together the five of them formed a pillar of defense, the Magistri casting spells to augment their strength and speed. Caius and Kharlacht fought side-by-side, Caius smashing locusari with his war hammer and Kharlacht cutting them in half with his greatsword. Blue fire swirled, and Third flung herself into the battle, her short swords blurring as she struck.

A few moments later the surviving locusari took back to the air, rushing to rejoin their masters.

"High King," said Third, catching her breath. "The Constable sends word. Men trained in the new siege weapons are joining the battle."

Even as she spoke, Arandar heard the rasp of wheels against the paving stones and turned to see two men-at-arms in the colors of the House of the Licinii rushing to join them, pulling a two-wheeled cart.

A small ballista rested in the back of the cart alongside a stack of iron bolts.

Gavin alternated between watching the sky and looking at the men with their odd siege weapon.

Arandar had ordered them built during the campaign across Caerdracon, and Gavin had seen a few of them before he had left with Calliande to find Ridmark. He hadn't been sure what the ballistae could do against a creature as powerful as a frost drake, but Calliande had said that the weapons had worked during the last war, and Gavin supposed that the Keeper knew her business.

Six men had joined the High King's party, each pair of men pulling a cart with one of the ballistae. The siege weapons looked like oversized crossbows, with a metal bow mounted on a wooden stock, and the entire weapon had been affixed to a swiveling metal stand that allowed it to aim in any direction, even straight up. The bolts for the siege weapons had been based on the design of the javelins the legions of the Empire of the Romans had once used in battle, with a sharp iron head and a shaft of softer metal that would bend and make the weapon difficult to remove from its target.

The men had loaded their ballistae and were aiming them.

They would get the chance to use them soon enough.

Another frost drake swooped towards the Forum of the North, its jaws opening wide, white mist swirling behind its fangs. A Frostborn warrior rode the winged creature, one hand grasping the leather reins, the other drawn back to cast a spell.

"Release!" shouted Arandar, pointing Excalibur at the frost drake.

All three ballistae fired at once.

Master Kurastus had started casting his warding spell, but it proved to be unnecessary. One of the bolts missed the descending frost drake, but the second punched into its side, and the third pierced the drake's left wing, pinning it to the creature's body. The frost drake let out a startled scream of pain, and the blast of freezing mist lashed across the air without harm. The drake's right wing flapped at the air, trying to recover its balance, and the creature spun out of control and crashed to the ground.

"Go!" said Master Marhand.

Gavin charged, Truthseeker raised, Kharlacht and Caius and the Swordbearers following him. The Frostborn had been knocked from his saddle by the crash and started to rise, white mist swirling around him as he cast a spell, but Antenora struck first. Her whirling fireball shot past Gavin, and the explosion of flame engulfed both the Frostborn and the side of the frost drake. The Frostborn fell to the ground, engulfed by magical fire, and the frost drake screamed in pain again.

The creature started to rotate its head to bring its killing breath to bear, but the Swordbearers struck first. Gavin plunged Truthseeker through the drake's armored hide and between its ribs, the blade seeking its lungs. A terrible chill radiated from the frost drake, and the creature shuddered as Truthseeker wounded it. Valmark, Constantine, and Marhand attacked the drake's neck, and soon they had its head off, its blood spilling across the ground and hardening to ice.

The drake shuddered once more and went still.

Gavin supposed that those ballistae had been a good idea after all.

"Come," said Arandar. "This battle isn't over yet."

###

The fighting was over by midnight, and Arandar stood on the rampart overlooking the northern gate, gazing at the ruins of the siege walls.

They had killed five more drakes, the ballistae shooting them down from the sky and sending them crashing in ruin into the streets, and finally the raid had ended. The remaining Frostborn on their drakes had turned and flown away to the north, accompanied by the surviving locusari scouts.

The men of Andomhaim had won this first skirmish, but there were far sharper battles to come. Arandar worried about the effect it would have on the army. They had thought Tarlion safe from the reach of the Frostborn, at least for now, but the Frostborn had just proven them wrong.

He worried about what other tricks the Frostborn might have to play.

A boot rasped against the stairs, and Arandar turned as Corbanic Lamorus and his son Sir Cortin came to the ramparts.

"I have the final numbers, lord King," said Corbanic. "Ninety-seven dead, and about that many more wounded. The Magistri think that all the wounded will recover."

Arandar scowled. "A bitter exchange, given that we only slew eight Frostborn and their drakes."

Corbanic shrugged. "It is, but from what we've seen of the Frostborn, it seems the Frostborn themselves are the nobles, and the medvarth and the locusari and the khaldjari and the others are their commoners. Better to kill one Frostborn than a dozen locusari."

"Aye," said Arandar. "I'll make sure at least a dozen of the ballistae are left here, and that your blacksmiths are shown how to make more. I suggest you train the garrison in their use. Even after the army has departed, the Frostborn may decide to make raids on Tarlion again."

Corbanic nodded. "Then you still intend to march tomorrow?"

"This raid has changed nothing," said Arandar. "Our allies are struggling against the Frostborn, and now is the time to strike."

Because if the Frostborn could attack this far south, how much longer would before they could bring their entire host against the walls of Tarlion? How much longer would they remain bottled up in the Northerland?

Arandar feared that it might already be too late.

CHAPTER FOUR

PREPARATIONS

Calliande had a thunderous headache.

She must have hit her head harder than she had thought because the effort of summoning the fire to destroy the undead dark elf had only exacerbated her headache. Someone had already done a good job of cleaning the cut on her temple. That must have been Ridmark. Calliande could also smell cooking meat from the campfire, which meant she had been out for long enough for Ridmark to clean her wound, go hunting, kill some birds, and cook them.

And it was all her own fault.

"I might have been overly clever," said Calliande.

There was an understatement. Damn it all, Morigna had been right. Calliande tended to make her plans too complicated, and this time, it had come back to haunt her.

Worse, it had come back to haunt Ridmark.

To her immense relief, he was not hurt. He looked tired, and he was breathing hard from his combat with the undead dark elf and the urvaalgs. God and the saints, if he had been hurt because they had stumbled into her long-forgotten plan…

Calliande drew a deep breath, intending to explain.

"Wait," said Ridmark. "You had better check for any other urvaalgs or," he looked at the scattered bones and blue armor plates, "or whatever that was."

"Undead dark elf," said Calliande. "Like the ones we saw near Urd Morlemoch. There have been hundreds of battles here over thousands of years."

She focused her mind and drew on the Sight, sweeping it over the shore and the trees as she sought for enemies.

At once she saw the magical power around her, old and ancient and strong. A mighty warding spell maintained the wall of mist that encircled the island, and the Sight itself scattered against the mist, blocked by its power. Over the island, Calliande saw the echoes of thousands of ancient spells of terrible power, spells with the power to rip down mountains and tear open chasms. Here and there the Sight glimpsed other creatures of dark magic moving through the trees, or other undead wrapped in necromantic magic, but none of them were approaching.

For the moment, they were safe.

Yet beyond that, beyond the creatures and the undead and the spells, Calliande glimpsed a colossal wall of warding spells in the center of the island, magic intricate and powerful beyond her understanding.

"There aren't any enemies nearby," said Calliande.

"Good," said Ridmark. He stepped closer and looked at her head. "That cut…"

"It's already healing," said Calliande. Healing magic was far less effective when cast on herself instead of someone else, but it would still work in time. A few hours would suffice to take care of the cut on her temple and the lump on her head. "Ridmark, I think we had better talk."

"Yes," said Ridmark. He led her to the fire. "Are we anywhere near Tarlion? We ought to get back as soon as possible."

Calliande swallowed as she sat on a log. "I am afraid that we are as far from Tarlion as humans have ever gone in this world."

He frowned. "Then where are we?"

"We are on an island in the center of the Lake of Ice beyond the northern reaches of the Wilderland," said Calliande.

His frown sharpened. "Does that mean..."

"Yes," said Calliande. "We are only two or three days away from Cathair Solas, the last city of the high elves on this world."

Ridmark considered that for a moment, then reached over and withdrew two skewers of meat from the campfire.

"I think," he said, passing her one of the skewers, "that you had better tell me the whole story. And I think we should eat, because I suspect that we will be on our way to Cathair Solas tomorrow."

Dread pulsed through Calliande at the thought of Cathair Solas.

Of what awaited her there...and what would likely await Ridmark there.

"Yes," said Calliande. "I can remember it all now. When we entered the Chamber of Sight in the Tower of the Keeper, all the memories returned."

She took a bite of meat, chewed, swallowed, and started to speak.

"A long time ago," said Calliande, "during the first war with the Frostborn, we were losing. The Frostborn were too powerful and too methodical. They were slowly pushing their way out of the Northerland, and they overran Caerdracon and conquered half of Khaluusk. The men of Andomhaim and our allies fought well, but...it was not enough. The Frostborn could bring reinforcements through their world gate at will. It might take them a few decades to grind us down, but sooner or later they would triumph. We needed help."

"So, you went to Cathair Solas," said Ridmark.

"It seemed the best course," said Calliande, remembering those desperate days. "It had been done before. When the urdmordar laid siege to Tarlion five hundred years ago, the Keeper at the time traveled to Cathair Solas to ask for aid from the high elves. In response, Ardrhythain agreed to the Pact of the Two Orders, which created the Swordbearers and the Magistri. With the help of the Two Orders, the High King was able to break the siege and defeat the urdmordar."

"What happened when you went to Cathair Solas?" said Ridmark.

"The High King agreed to my plan," said Calliande. "I left Caerdracon with an escort of a hundred knights, fifty of them Swordbearers. They were led by a knight in the High King's service named Kalomarus. He wasn't a Swordbearer, but he was a veteran of the wars, and he knew how to lead men in battle. The Frostborn tried to stop us, and we fought our way loose and into the Wilderland. From there, we faced all the other dangers of the Wilderland...the creatures of dark magic and the dvargir raiders and all the others. That was the first time I faced Rhogrimnalazur, you'll remember." Ridmark nodded. "The survivors and I fought her creatures as we passed Urd Cystaanl, and we barely got past."

"Then this is about the Dragon Knight, isn't it?" said Ridmark. "Third was right. You went to Cathair Solas to summon the Dragon Knight."

"Yes," said Calliande, "but that came later. I didn't even know the Dragon Knight existed at the time. I just hoped that Ardrhythain and the high elves would be willing to help us as they had helped our ancestors. By the time we crossed the Lake of Ice and reached the gates of Cathair Solas, there were only eight of us left – me, Kalomarus, and six of the Swordbearers."

"What happened then?" said Ridmark.

"I asked Ardrhythain for aid," said Calliande, rubbing her forehead as the sharp memories cut into her mind. She had been desperate and frightened, knowing that appealing to the high elves for aid had been a gamble. "I told him of the Frostborn, and Ardrhythain agreed to help us. He told us of the Dragon Knight. Long ago, dragons ruled this world but departed when the time of the elves came. The elves interred the bones of the dragons in Dragonfall, lest someone abuse their power."

"I remember," said Ridmark.

Calliande nodded. "The dragons left a sword for the elves to use, a sword that contained their power. The warrior who carried this sword was the Dragon Knight and could wield the might of the ancient dragons. In the high elves' long wars against the dark elves and the urdmordar, the Dragon Knight had been their paramount warrior and their champion, but no high elf had wielded the sword since before Malahan Pendragon came to this world with our ancestors."

"Then he gave you the sword of the Dragon Knight," said Ridmark.

Calliande grimaced at the painful memory. "No. Not quite. He gave us the chance to wield the sword."

"The chance?" said Ridmark. "There was a trial?"

"Of a sort," said Calliande. "The sword...it has to be mastered. I don't know exactly how. Each one of the knights lifted the sword and tried to wield it, and it rejected them. Or they failed the trial. The sword burned their hearts out of their chests. Kalomarus was the last one to try. He started at the sword for hours, gripping it with both hands. I thought it drove him mad, and he ranted and raved and screamed at the walls. But he held out, and he mastered the sword. He and I left Cathair Solas, and we returned to join the men of Andomhaim and our allies. The sword of the Dragon Knight turned the tide. As the Dragon Knight, Kalomarus could command fire, and he set the swords of the army ablaze with elemental flames that the Frostborn could not stand. It also let him control distance and time. He could open gates and travel hundreds of miles in an instant, and he could freeze time for a few moments, allowing him to strike down his foes while they were immobile."

"Useful," said Ridmark.

"It was," said Calliande. "It let us push the Frostborn back to Black Mountain. I forced Tymandain Shadowbearer to abandon his gate, and I destroyed the soulstone powering it. The Frostborn were defeated, and I thought we could live in peace."

"Then you learned that Shadowbearer had corrupted your apprentice," said Ridmark.

"Yes," said Calliande.

She wasn't hungry, but she forced herself to finish the meat. Ridmark was right. She would need her strength for the days ahead.

"But we knew about the Dragon Knight," said Ridmark at last, tossing his emptied skewer into the flames. "We didn't know what happened to him after you went into the long sleep."

"No," said Calliande, "but we do now."

"Go on," said Ridmark.

"I made my plan with Kalomarus," said Calliande. "The Tower of Vigilance, the Order, all of it. We knew Shadowbearer would return, that he would try to bring back the Frostborn. I would go into the long sleep beneath the Tower, but Kalomarus would return to Cathair Solas, to bring the sword back to the high elves. But just as I would need to stop the Frostborn, we both knew Andomhaim might need the Dragon Knight again. If the Frostborn returned, we would need the Dragon Knight's power to drive them back."

"Then you planned to find the sword if necessary," said Ridmark.

"Yes," said Calliande. "I removed my memory of the sword and placed it within the Tower of the Keeper, but the spell would summon me when I drew close enough to Tarlion. That was the heartbeat that we heard, the memory calling me to the Tower. The minute I stepped into the Chamber of Sight, I remembered what Kalomarus and I had done."

"And what did you do?" said Ridmark.

"Kalomarus used the power of the sword to create a gate leading from the Tower of the Keeper to the island of Cathair Solas in the Lake of Ice," said Calliande. "If the time came, if I thought we needed the sword of the Dragon Knight, I would use the gate and retrieve the sword and choose another Dragon Knight." She shook her head. "I was a fool."

Ridmark blinked. "Why?"

"Because I thought that when I recovered my memories and realized that I was the Keeper," said Calliande, "I would return at Tarlion at once to present myself to the High King. I didn't anticipate the possibility that I wouldn't come to Tarlion for nearly two years."

"No plan of battle survives the first meeting with the enemy," said Ridmark.

"Aye," said Calliande. "And I've spent centuries teaching that to myself, it seems."

They sat in silence for a moment, and Ridmark asked one of the questions that she had been dreading.

"Morigna's spirit," he said. "Why did I see her in the Tower of the Keeper?"

"You had been dreaming of her, hadn't you?" said Calliande.

Ridmark snorted. "More like she had been inserting herself into my dreams. I suppose she was stubborn enough that even death itself could not keep her from having the final word."

Calliande laughed a little. "That she was. She was in my dreams as well."

"She was?" said Ridmark, giving her a sharp look. "What did she say?"

"She warned me that you were in danger," said Calliande. Was he angry? Sad? She could not tell. "She said that I would have to save you."

"And you did," said Ridmark. He poked at the fire with Ardrhythain's staff, stirring the coals. The heat of the flames did nothing to the staff. "From my wounds in the Stone Heart."

"Aye," said Calliande, though she did not think that was what Morigna had meant.

"I wish you would have told me," said Ridmark.

"I...I should have," said Calliande. "I didn't know what to say. How would I have told you? 'Good morning, Ridmark. I'm in love with you, and by the way, the spirit of your slain lover has appeared in my dreams.'"

Ridmark grunted. "That would have been a strange conversation. Much like this one."

"I'm sorry," said Calliande. "I should have told you." She hesitated and took his hand. To her great relief, he did not pull away. "It was selfish of me. I...I just did not know how you would react."

"Badly, probably," agreed Ridmark. "Maybe it was for the best." He squeezed her hand. "The other woman. The one gowned in fire. Did you know who she was?"

That was the second question that Calliande had dreaded. "Tell me about your dreams."

"There was a hall of white stone," said Ridmark. "An old knight sat on a throne, a sword across his knees. Maybe it was Kalomarus himself for all I know. Morigna was there, warning me about the woman gowned in fire. She said that the woman was calling to me, that she was summoning me, and that the woman gowned in fire would destroy me if she could."

"Oh," said Calliande, the dread increasing.

"You know who it is?" said Ridmark.

"I cannot be sure," said Calliande, "but I think the burning woman that you saw is the spirit of the sword of the Dragon Knight."

"It can talk?" said Ridmark.

"Is that so surprising?" said Calliande. "You said you had talked to that taalkrazdor in Khald Tormen, and to Excalibur before you used it against Tarrabus. Magical weapons have a will and a mind of their own, and the sword of the Dragon Knight is more powerful than any other weapon on the face of the world."

"Then why is the spirit of the sword talking in my dreams?" said Ridmark.

Calliande took a ragged breath, trying not to let her fear show. "Because...I fear that means the sword has chosen you."

"Chosen?" said Ridmark.

"I don't really understand the process," said Calliande. "Kalomarus refused to speak of it. But the seven knights who had reached Cathair Solas with me the first time...I think the sword chose all seven of them. Of the seven, Kalomarus was the only man strong enough to master the sword, or to resist its strength."

"Then it seems clear what we must do," said Ridmark.

The dread in her sharpened. "It is?"

"We must go to Cathair Solas," said Ridmark, "and I must take up the sword of the Dragon Knight."

"Ridmark," said Calliande, her voice rasping a little. She forced moisture into her throat. "It might kill you. It might drive you insane."

"Morigna said that," said Ridmark. "She said the sword would destroy me if I let it."

"Yes," said Calliande. "This might have been a mistake. Perhaps we should leave at once and try to find a way back to Andomhaim..."

"No," said Ridmark. "We cannot. If I can take the sword of the Dragon Knight, that will give us a powerful advantage against the Frostborn. You said it yourself – Kalomarus and the sword allowed you to turn the tide against the Frostborn during the last war. Tomorrow morning Arandar is going to march to join the Anathgrimm and the dwarves and the manetaurs, and they will need all the help we can bring them."

"And I am not there to help them," said Calliande, another stab of guilt going through her. God and the saints, what a fool she had been. What a proud, arrogant fool, thinking to arrange events that would happen centuries after she should have died. She ought to have been with the army of Andomhaim as it marched against the Frostborn.

Instead, she was here…and she might watch Ridmark die as he tried to claim the sword of the Dragon Knight.

Her folly might get him killed.

"You cannot save Andomhaim alone," said Ridmark. "You gave them the chance to fight for themselves. And perhaps we can do more for them yet. Once before the Keeper and the Dragon Knight saved Andomhaim. Maybe they can do it again."

"Perhaps," said Calliande. She took a shuddering breath, trying to calm herself down. The sword of the Dragon Knight might kill Ridmark. But he might die fighting the Frostborn, just as he might have been killed a dozen other times during their travels together.

But none of those times would have been the result of her plans. She didn't want him to become the Dragon Knight. She didn't want him to expose himself to the danger.

But he was right. Their duty demanded it.

"Do you know the way to Cathair Solas from here?" said Ridmark.

"Yes," said Calliande. "We just head inland and go uphill. The city is in the center of the island. It…is something of a majestic sight. It is hard to miss."

"We'll set out tomorrow, then," said Ridmark.

"You're very calm about all this," said Calliande.

Ridmark shrugged. "After all the things I've seen in the last two years, traveling hundreds of miles in the blink of an eye and seeking a relic of legend seems…less remarkable than it should be." He snorted. "Though since I met Ardrhythain and went into Urd Morlemoch when I was eighteen, perhaps I ought to say the last twelve years."

They sat in silence for a while, watching the crackling fire.

"Ridmark," said Calliande at last.

"Yes?"

She took a deep breath. "Are…we still betrothed?"

He looked at her in surprise. "What?"

"I made a grave mistake," said Calliande. "It almost got both of us killed. And it might get you killed yet if you take the sword of the Dragon Knight and it burns out your heart." For a moment, the present and her grim memories fused into one, and she seemed to see Ridmark with flames burning out the center of his chest. "And it would be my fault. My arrogance brought us here. And my foolishness might get you killed…"

"Stop," said Ridmark.

She fell silent, swallowing the last sentence halfway through.

"No one can see the future," said Ridmark. "Not even the Keeper of Andomhaim."

"I should have been able to realize what would happen," said Calliande.

"The fact that Andomhaim survived at all," said Ridmark, "and that it is ruled by Arandar and not the cult of the Enlightened is because of you. The fact that the dwarves and the manetaurs are marching to aid the Anathgrimm and Andomhaim is because of you. Perhaps your plans did not always go as you wished, but the reason we have not been defeated is because of you."

"Well," said Calliande. "You had something to do with it. Maybe I did all those things, but I couldn't have done them if you hadn't stopped Qazarl and the Artificer and the Warden and Tymandain and the Weaver and God knows how many others from killing me."

"No," said Ridmark, and he laughed a little. Calliande blinked in surprise. He laughed so infrequently that it always caught her attention when he did.

"What's funny?" she said.

"We've had this conversation before," said Ridmark. "But usually you're the one telling me not to blame myself for what happened to Aelia and Morigna."

Calliande sighed. "The shoe really does pinch upon the other foot."

"It always does," said Ridmark.

"What changed, then?" said Calliande.

"You have more responsibility now," said Ridmark. "Which means you have more things you can blame yourself for, even if they are not your fault."

"I knew that," said Calliande. "But...what changed with you? You're different now, Ridmark. Ever since Khald Tormen."

He considered this for a while. "You did, I suppose."

"Me?"

He nodded. "I wanted to get myself killed over Aelia. I wanted to kill Imaria and the Weaver and Tarrabus because of Morigna, and I didn't care if I got killed doing it." His eyes met hers. "But I had to think about what that would do to you." He shrugged. "I suppose in time one learns to live with sorrow. It never really goes away. But it just becomes part of you. And other things deserve your time and attention. Maybe it took me eight years to learn that. Or meeting you."

They sat in silence for a while, the only noise the crackling of the flames and the quiet rush of the lake against the stony shore.

"Then," said Calliande, swallowing, "we are still betrothed?"

Ridmark blinked, smiled, and then leaned down and kissed her. "Yes. If I had been able to work my will, we would have been wed by now."

"Oh," said Calliande. "Good. I...thought you might be angry. I just never have been betrothed before."

He lifted his right arm around put it around her shoulders. Calliande hesitated, and then leaned against him, her cheek resting against his shoulder. The idea of sheltering in his strong arms was a pleasant one. The fire was warm, and with Ridmark's arm around her, she could almost forget that they were far outside the boundaries of Andomhaim, that deadly peril lay before them.

Almost.

"This is nice," murmured Calliande.

"As pleasant as it can be, given where we are," said Ridmark.

"Yes," Calliande conceded. "But if I must be here, I am glad to be here with you."

He kissed the top of her head, and a flush of warmth went through her. Calliande was tired, so tired, of being alone. She had been the Keeper for a long time and had carried that burden by herself. She hadn't realized how much she had wanted...

What, exactly? A lover? A husband? Certainly, there had been opportunities to have lovers if she had really wanted to do so.

No, she decided. What she wanted was Ridmark Arban. She wanted him, or no one.

They sat before the fire for a while, and then Ridmark lifted his arm from her and stood up.

"I will put some more wood on the fire," said Ridmark, "and then take the first watch. You should get some sleep."

"Maybe I should take the first watch," said Calliande. "I've already slept, and you fought the urvaalgs."

"Hitting your head and falling unconscious is not the same thing as sleep," said Ridmark, "and if it comes to a fight, it would be better for you to be rested. Your magic can deal with the undead and creatures of dark magic far more quickly."

That was a good point. He tended to be right about things like this.

"True," said Calliande. She stood up, stretched, and then lay down near the fire, wrapping herself in her cloak as Ridmark threw more wood into the flames. "Please wake me if anything happens."

"I will," said Ridmark. "Sleep well."

For a minute, she considering inviting him to join her. They were betrothed, after all, and a few hours ago, she had been certain the night would end with Ridmark taking her virginity. But she was exhausted, the stony ground was uncomfortable, and it was cold enough here that the thought of taking off her clothes made her shiver, and not in a pleasant way.

Later. There would be time later.

But what if there wasn't going to be a later?

No, Ridmark was right. Best to rest while she could.

Calliande closed her eyes, consciously relaxing her mind and will. It had been a long and exhausting day even before they had come here, and she felt fatigue coming up to swallow her. Falling asleep would not be hard.

Her eyelids fluttered, and for a moment she saw Ridmark standing by the fire, watching the forest for any sign of enemies. The firelight played over him, throwing stark shadows on the folds of his gray cloak.

For a terrible instant, she thought she saw his heart burning within him, just the way the hearts of those six knights had burned centuries ago when the sword of the Dragon Knight killed them.

It was only a trick of the light, but the dread followed her as she fell asleep.

CHAPTER FIVE

THE ORDER OF THE INQUISITION

The next morning, the host of the realm of Andomhaim marched from its camps outside Tarlion.

Arandar had entertained the faint hope that he would awaken to find that Calliande and Ridmark had returned, perhaps with the sword of the Dragon Knight in their possession. The hope proved unfounded. There was no sign of either the Keeper of Andomhaim or the magister militum of Nightmane Forest, and the Tower of the Keeper remained sealed.

Andomhaim would have to go to war without its Keeper.

Arandar waited atop his horse, flanked by the Swordbearers and Magistri of his bodyguard, and watched the army gather itself into a massive column for the march north along the Moradel road. Dux Sebastian Aurelius and some of the men of Caertigris went first to scout the way and screen for enemies. The men of Caertigris grew up in the saddle, hunting the game of the western plains of their lands, and were the best scouts and light cavalry in the host of Andomhaim. They would scout the way and hopefully report if they saw any foes approaching the army. The Enlightened had been broken, but Arandar would not put it past the dvargir to make trouble, or bold raiders from the Wilderland and the Deeps.

After the scouts came the bulk of the army, the men-at-arms and militiamen who made up the infantry, followed by the proud warriors of the three baptized orcish kingdoms. The knights came next, flying the banners of their lords in a blaze of color. At last came the vast bulk of the army's baggage train, thousands of wagons laden with supplies, their wheels creaking as their oxen dragged them forward. More of Dux Sebastian's scouts hung back to guard the supplies since the baggage train was the most vulnerable part of any army. Poor Sir Joram Agramore had been busy in his capacity as the army's quartermaster, and regular supply trains from Taliand, Calvus, and Caerdracon would help feed the host of Andomhaim as it marched north. Fleets of barges recruited by Sir Tormark Arban would row up the Moradel as well, carrying the crops of southern Andomhaim.

Arandar hoped that would be enough. The campaign against the Frostborn might take years, even if they were victorious, and with so many men in the army, there might not be enough hands to work the fields or to fend off opportunistic raiders. Even if they were victorious, the cost of the victory might beggar the realm and leave it crippled.

The only way forward, the only wave to save Andomhaim and to defend its people, was to defeat the Frostborn and close their world gate.

Hopefully the forces they had gathered would be enough.

Arandar rode up and down the column as it marched, accompanied by his bodyguards. He usually rode with the Master of the Swordbearers and the Master of the Magistri, along with Sir Valmark Arban and Sir Constantine Licinius. Kharlacht, Caius, Camorak, Sir Gavin, Antenora, and Third accompanied him as well. Since Third and Antenora were unable to help Ridmark and Calliande, they had attached themselves to Arandar. Given how powerful they were, he was glad of their help.

He spoke with the Duxi and the Comites and the orcish kings as he rode up and down the column, making sure there were no problems and resolving disputes. After a year of campaigning and siege, the men knew their business, and there were not many disputes for Arandar to adjudicate.

The plan was simple, at least for the first part of the march. The army would head north along the Moradel road until they reached the fork of the River Moradel and the River Mourning at Castra Carhaine. They would ferry the army across the river, a process that would probably take several days. While they waited, Arandar would speak with the castellans he had left in charge of Castra Carhaine and the other strongholds of Tarrabus Carhaine's former duxarchate. They would have news of the Northerland, and perhaps they would have news of the dwarves and the manetaurs.

And beyond that point, Arandar had no firm plans. Their goal was a simple one – drive the Frostborn back to Dun Licinia, seize their world gate, and destroy it. How they would accomplish that, he did not yet know. He would have to speak to Red King Turcontar and King Axazamar and Queen Mara and coordinate his strategy with theirs. Together he hoped they would be strong enough to overcome the Frostborn.

Nonetheless, the reports the scouts brought back were not good.

Rumors came down from the north that Castra Marcaine had fallen, that the Frostborn had seized the entirety of the Northerland and were marching into Caerdracon, that the Anathgrimm had been forced to retreat to their warded forests. The scouts reported that the travelers they encountered repeated those same stories. Still, none of the travelers claimed that they had seen dwarves or manetaurs, so perhaps neither Axazamar nor Turcontar had reached the Northerland yet.

And the Frostborn were always watching.

Often Arandar looked up and saw the distant shape of a frost drake flying high overhead, and the men of the army glimpsed the blue specks of locusari soaring over the River Moradel. Neither the frost drakes nor the locusari ever dipped low enough to come within range of the siege ballistae, but they were always within sight.

The Frostborn knew exactly where Arandar's army was, and he supposed they would know where the dwarven and the manetaur hosts were. That was a dangerous situation, but there was no way around it. Third was a capable scout and could cover large stretches of terrain with tremendous speed, but she was only one woman, and her abilities had limits.

They would have to remain on their guard and be ready for an attack at any moment.

###

As the march wore on, Gavin found himself marveling at Arandar's energy.

The new High King woke well before dawn and went to sleep after the sun had gone down. Arandar spent his days circulating through the army, speaking to his lords and knights, encouraging the men as they marched. Surely Arandar must have felt the strain. Gavin knew that he did, and he was half the High King's age, but Arandar never showed any signs of fatigue or dismay.

"He was never like this before," said Gavin.

"What do you mean?" said Antenora.

The army had stopped to camp for the night, spread out on the cleared lands of forest on either side of the Moradel road. They were well into Calvus by now, the royal domain behind them. The forests were quiet and clear of enemies, and the commoners in their fields seemed glad to see the High King's army pass. Given how brutal and cruel Tarrabus Carhaine and the Enlightened had been, that made sense.

Gavin and Antenora had taken their usual place near the High King's pavilion, seated at one of the campfires the squires had raised. Rather than one huge camp, the army tended to rest of for the night in a score of smaller camps, each one gathered around the banner of a Dux or a Comes or one of the orcish kings. Gavin supposed that made each of the individual camps vulnerable to attack, but it also meant that a single attacking force could not envelop the entire army.

"I think I mean," said Gavin, "that he never used to be so...forceful."

"The High King must be forceful to command the respect of his men," said Antenora. In the flickering firelight, she looked...younger, somehow, as if the light gave a glow to her skin that it did not possess on its own. "It is ever the way for strong leaders."

"But he wasn't like that when we met him at Urd Morlemoch," said Gavin. "He was content to follow Ridmark's lead."

"But in the Vale of Stone Death," said Antenora, "he took command while the Keeper and the lord magister helped Prince Curzonar in his task. He even made Morigna bend to his will while we fought the Anathgrimm and the Mhorites, and that was no easy task."

"No," said Gavin. Morigna had never done anything she did not want to do. The only one she had ever listened to had been Ridmark, and even then not always. "I had forgotten about that."

"The High King was born a bastard," said Antenora with a shrug. "He knew that his birth would be used against him, so he learned how not to put himself forward unless necessary. Now that he is the lawful High King, he must put himself forward to rule well. Often men have qualities that only come to light in times of peril."

"I suppose that makes sense," said Gavin. He was glad she understood such things. She had seen far more than he had, and understood people in a way that he did not.

"That is true of you as well," said Antenora.

"Me?" said Gavin.

"You are Gavin Swordbearer, a great knight and warrior," said Antenora. "But you only became those things because you were born in a time of great peril, a time that allowed your inner strengths to show. If you had remained in your village, you would not have become a Swordbearer."

Gavin snorted. "No. If I had stayed in Aranaeus, I probably would be dead. Agrimnalazur would have killed me eventually."

"But after the Gray Knight slew Agrimnalazur," said Antenora. "If you had stayed there to help rebuild, you would not have become a Swordbearer."

"No," said Gavin, thinking. "I suppose not. Rosanna was going to marry Philip, but...I suppose I would have stayed and started farming my own plot. I probably would have married one of the other girls and had a child or two by now."

"She would have been a fortunate woman," said Antenora, her voice quiet.

Gavin looked at her, startled. She was staring into the fire, her face shadowed. During the battle against Tarrabus, Antenora had thought him slain. She had broken down weeping, relieved that she was still alive. He got the impression that she was embarrassed by the display of emotion, and they hadn't discussed it since.

But he had been touched to realize how much he meant to her...which, in turn, made him reflect on how much she meant to him.

"Maybe," said Gavin. "But I would have been the less fortunate."

She gave him a sharp look, startled. "How so?"

"Because I would never have met you," he said, "and my life would have been the poorer for it."

Antenora blinked, a quiver of emotion going through her gaunt, gray face.

Gavin hesitated, and then slowly reached out and took her left hand in his right. Even through her leather glove, her hand felt icy cold.

"Gavin Swordbearer," whispered Antenora. "Maybe this is my final punishment."

"I don't understand," said Gavin.

"I betrayed the last Keeper of Britannia and Arthur Pendragon to follow Mordred," said Antenora. "I spent fifteen centuries regretting my folly and thought I knew all there was to know of remorse. Then I met you..."

"You regret meeting me?" said Gavin, stung.

"No!" said Antenora at once. "I regret that my folly means we cannot be together." She lifted his hand to her face and kissed his fingers, and it felt like a touch of ice. "Perhaps that is my final punishment. To have met you, and to know that I cannot have you. That is a new torment I thought not to experience."

"I..." said Gavin.

He didn't know what to say. He realized that he loved Antenora, and he had known that since she had broken down weeping after the battle against Tarrabus. But she was correct. She could touch him, kiss him, and feel nothing at all, for she felt neither pleasure nor pain, and her touch was an icy chill. If she touched him for too long, he would start to shiver. If she kissed him for too long, his face might go numb.

And if they were victorious, if they defeated the Frostborn and closed the world gate, the curse on her would be lifted, and she would die at last, earning the natural death that had been denied to her so long ago.

And if they were defeated...well, they would all be dead anyway by the time the Frostborn finished conquering Andomhaim.

"I don't regret meeting you," said Gavin, "and I'm not sorry that we met. I..." He frowned, trying to find a way to phrase his thoughts. This kind of thing wasn't his strong point. "I'm glad we met. And I wish things could be different. But I don't regret anything. Especially not you. I...just wish I could have had...more of those things than we do."

Antenora said nothing.

"That didn't come out right," said Gavin. "I'm sorry. I..."

"Oh, Gavin," she said, and her cold fingers squeezed his. "It was beautiful."

"My tongue is not skillful," said Gavin.

"A man's virtue and courage are not found in his tongue," said Antenora. "Mordred had a tongue of silver, and so did Tarrabus Carhaine. The scriptures are right that a man's tongue is the source of many evils. But not yours. However our path shall end, Gavin Swordbearer, I am glad that I could spend time with you. It was a brief respite before the final sorrow."

"I am glad, too," said Gavin.

They sat in silence for a while, watching the flames.

"But what did you mean by the final sorrow?" said Gavin.

Antenora hesitated. "I should not have said anything."

"No," said Gavin. "What did you mean?" The answer occurred to him as soon as he spoke. "You think we're going to lose?"

"I do not know," said Antenora. "No one can see the future, not even the Keepers. But look at the army, Gavin."

"It is a strong army," said Gavin.

"It is," said Antenora. "But remember the army that marched with Uthanaric Pendragon to Dun Calpurnia. That army was stronger, but a year of civil war weakened the host of the Andomhaim. The Frostborn used that year to build their strength to even greater heights. Uthanaric's army was barely equal to the Frostborn. I do not think Arandar's army will be equal to it."

"We will have the dwarves and the manetaurs," said Gavin.

"Yes," said Antenora. "I hope their strength will make up the difference. But if it does not..." She sighed. "I have seen many wars in my life, Gavin Swordbearer, though I cannot remember them all. I have seen many armies march to their final defeats. This one...I fear it feels the same."

"Maybe," said Gavin. "But like you said, no one can see the future. We may yet be victorious."

A faint smile went over the gaunt face. "My mind tells me that we see defeat, but you cheer my heart."

"Well," said Gavin, "we're not beaten yet."

But a cold part of his mind pointed out that she had an excellent point. The army had been weakened, badly weakened, by Tarrabus's folly and the year of civil war. The Anathgrimm had been able to hold the Frostborn in the Northerland, but the Frostborn would have been able to spend the past year summoning more forces through the world gate.

Perhaps they were indeed marching to their deaths.

But he would fight nonetheless.

And Antenora was right. Whatever happened, however this ended, he was glad they had had this time together

However brief it turned out to be.

Several days later, the host of Andomhaim came to a stop on the banks of the River Moradel and the River Mourning.

Arandar rode back and forth along the southern bank of the River Mourning, the walls and towers of Castra Carhaine rising across the river. The castra was a strong place, filling a peninsula of land that jutted into the water where the River Mourning met the larger River Moradel. Water surrounded the castra on three sides. The great curtain wall, nearly fifty feet high and twenty feet thick, came right to the edge of the waters. Octagonal watch towers stood at intervals along the wall, topped with ballistae and catapults. Within the curtain wall stood three massive keeps, each one topped with war engines.

Castra Carhaine was a strong fortress, and it had been a hard nut to crack during the campaign across Caerdracon. They had only been able to take the castra thanks to Antenora, Sir Gavin, and Sir Constantine launching a daring raid through the castra's water gate.

Arandar supposed that if the battle went ill, they could fall back to Castra Carhaine and hold the Frostborn here.

The castra had been an important water crossing for centuries, and thankfully was well equipped with barges and large rafts. Already dozens of craft moved back and forth across the water to the piers of the castra and the surrounding bank, unloading troops, horses, and supplies. Arandar had sent Sir Joram, Sir Tormark, and Dux Leogrance to take charge of the host on the northern bank of the River Mourning, organizing the men for the march to the Northerland. Arandar spoke with the lords and the knights and the kings as they crossed the river, speaking of the campaign to come in the north. His mind turned over the details, considering a thousand different possibilities. What if the dwarves arrived first? Or the manetaurs? What if the Frostborn bent their full power to destroy the manetaurs before they could join the other forces?

"Do you think they'll change the name?"

Arandar blinked, startled out of his thoughts. He glanced over his shoulder to see Gavin talking with Caius and Kharlacht and the others.

"The name of what?" said Caius.

"Castra Carhaine," said Gavin. "It doesn't belong to Tarrabus Carhaine anymore, does it?"

"It does not," said Camorak. The Magistrius looked disgruntled, though that was likely because there hadn't been any strong drink on the road north. "The High King stripped him of his lands and titles and disinherited him. Not that the scheming bastard had any heirs. Probably was too busy worshipping devils and plotting murder to find the time to sire any little Carhaines."

"So, what happens to the castra?" said Gavin. "And all the rest of the duxarchate?"

"According to the laws of Andomhaim, all the lands of Caerdracon reverted to the crown when the treacherous nobles were stripped of their rank and benefices," said Caius. He probably knew the relevant laws and traditions better than Arandar himself did. "The High King holds the lands now. But he will give the lands to a new Dux, who will appoint new Comites for Caerdracon. Though some of the nobles of Caerdracon refused to have anything to do with Tarrabus – old Rilmar Cavilius of Westhold, for one. They will likely keep their lands as a reward for their loyalty."

"Will the castra change its name?" said Gavin.

"No, it will likely keep the name of Castra Carhaine," said Caius. "The House of the Licinii rules in the Northerland, but Castra Marcaine was not built by them. Their House died out, but the castra kept its name when the Licinii became the ruling House of the Northerland." He shrugged. "Tarrabus fell into folly and evil, but his ancestors were not wicked. Should their memory be erased because their descendants turned from the righteous path? Your own soulblade was once carried by Judicaeus Carhaine, and he would have had nothing to do with the Enlightened."

"I had not given that any thought," said Gavin. "That seems wise."

"Perhaps the High King will make you the Dux of Caerdracon," said Kharlacht.

"God and the saints, no!" said Gavin, and the others laughed.

"Actually," said Arandar, looking over his shoulder at the others, "that is not the worst idea I've heard today."

"Please tell me you are joking, your Majesty," said Gavin.

"Well," said Arandar, "I think…"

Blue fire swirled next to Arandar's horse, and Third solidified out of the flames.

"Lady Third," said Arandar. She had been running messages for him, and her help had been invaluable. The Magistri could send messages through their magic, but the spell drained them, and it wasn't always completely reliable. Third, by contrast, was always reliable. Arandar had to stop himself from overusing her power, knowing that it was best to hold her back for an emergency.

"Lord High King," said Third with her usual calm. "Dux Leogrance asks that you join him on the northern bank as soon as possible. It seems the locusari scouts have been raiding the outlying villages around Castra Carhaine, and some of the freeholders claim that they have seen bear-creatures moving along the River Moradel."

"Medvarth?" said Arandar, frowning.

"Perhaps," said Third. "The description matches that of a medvarth."

"Very well," said Arandar. "We'll take the next barge."

###

Before following the Gray Knight and his companions from Urd Arowyn, Gavin had never been on a boat.

Now, it seemed, he was on a boat every few weeks.

The barge was even larger than the one that Smiling Otto had used to carry them down the River Moradel, a massive slab of thick, weather-beaten wood. A crew of grizzled watermen tended to the barge, manning the heavy oars and the thick rudder. The watermen looked singularly unimpressed by the army making its way across the River Mourning, though Gavin preferred to ride on a barge manned by experienced men who knew their business.

He did know how to swim, but he wasn't particularly good at it.

Arandar boarded the barge, as did Gavin and Antenora and the other members of the High King's guards and entourage. At the request of the barge's captain, their horses remained behind for the next trip, lest the weight cause the craft to capsize.

At Master Marhand's insistence, they did take a pair of the ballistae, lest the frost drakes try to attack the High King as he crossed the river. There had been both locusari scouts and frost drakes spotted flying over Castra Carhaine, and a barge or a raft was vulnerable to attack from above.

The barge pushed off from the bank and headed towards Castra Carhaine, the rowers attacking the current with smooth, solid strokes. Gavin stood next to Antenora, the breeze tugging at his hair, shafts of sunlight falling from the cloudy sky to strike the water. It was pleasant on the river, Gavin thought, so long as the weather was good and so long as the barge didn't turn over.

Then Antenora's head snapped up, her yellow eyes widening as she looked at the sky.

Somehow Gavin wasn't surprised.

"Master Kurastus!" said Antenora. "The enemy comes. A warding spell!"

Kurastus did not need to be told twice. At once the old Magistrius began casting a spell, white fire glimmering around his fingers. An instant later the dome of light surrounded the barge, shielding it from hostile magic and the cold breath of the frost drakes.

But the enemy was not aiming for the barge.

Three frost drakes dropped out of the sky, jaws yawning wide. Both ballistae fired, but the drakes were descending at a steep enough angle that the bolts missed. All three drakes unleashed their freezing breath, and the plumes of white mist swept across the surface of the river.

The barge jolted beneath Gavin's feet, and he stumbled, trying to keep his balance. Antenora almost fell into him, but she slammed the end of her staff against the deck, the symbols along its dark length flaring as she called her magic. Gavin looked around, wondering if the barge had hit something, or if one of the drakes had landed on the craft itself.

Then he saw the ice stretching away for fifty yards around them.

The drakes had frozen the water around the barge, immobilizing it. Sooner or later the current would carry them out to the Moradel, or the ice would melt in the heat. Yet by the time that happened, the frost drakes would kill them or the locusari scouts would land and tear them apart as they fought on the deck of the barge.

It was a perfectly executed assassination attempt on the High King, and Gavin realized it might well succeed

And kill them all in the process, of course.

"Master Kurastus, hold your spell!" said Arandar, yanking Excalibur from its scabbard. "Men-at-arms, get those ballistae reloaded! Antenora, use your magic on the drakes! Defend yourselves!"

The three drakes banked in formation over the river, and Gavin saw the Frostborn upon their backs. To his surprise, he thought one of the three was a woman – she was smaller and slimmer than the other two Frostborn, and her shape seemed more feminine. Did the Frostborn have women? They must have – Antenora had said a Frostborn woman named Arlmagnava had tried to kill her in the threshold, and Ridmark, Arandar, and Jager had faced Arlmagnava in the hours before the battle at Dun Calpurnia.

Antenora thrust her staff, and a fireball leaped from the end and soared skyward. It passed through the dome of light and hurtled towards the drakes, forcing them to scatter to avoid the fire.

It did nothing to slow the scores of locusari scouts who plummeted towards the barge, their wings blurring. Gavin whipped Truthseeker before him in a flare of white fire, cutting one of the locusari in half. In front of him, another locusari blurred past one of the rowers, taking off the poor man's head in a spray of blood.

Everything dissolved into chaos around him, but it was disciplined chaos. The Magistri turned their attention to strengthening Kurastus's ward and casting spells of healing. The Swordbearers devoted their attention to defending the barge. Gavin lost himself in the fury of the battle, cutting down locusari after locusari, sending their gleaming blue carapaces scattering to the deck.

The men-at-arms working the ballistae reloaded and fired, and this time they had better luck. The two bolts punched into the side of a frost drake, and the creature screeched and flew away towards the River Moradel, no longer under the control of its rider. The remaining two frost drakes slowed, hovering as their riders assessed the situation, and Gavin felt the cold, burning gaze of the remaining two Frostborn.

"That is her," said Antenora. "Arlmagnava. I fought her before I came to this world."

Gavin braced himself for another wave of locusari scouts, but it seemed the Frostborn had fought enough for this day. The two frost drakes turned and flew to the north, trailed by their remaining locusari scouts.

Antenora used her fire magic to break away the ice that sheathed the barge, and they continued towards Castra Carhaine.

That night Arandar held a council of war with the chief nobles in the great hall of Castra Carhaine.

The hall of Castra Carhaine reflected the ancestral pride of the House of the Carhainii. The floor had been paved in gleaming marble, and the tapestries hanging on the walls showed the triumphs of past Duxi of Caerdracon. Most of the nobles of Andomhaim preferred to display tales from the scriptures in their art, images of the Dominus Christus healing the lepers or Joshua leading the men of Israel into battle against the wicked Canaanites, but such religious themes were absent from the tapestries of the Carhainii. A huge stone throne rested on the dais at the far end of the hall, carved from a single block of blue marble, its back worked in the black dragon sigil of the House of the Carhainii.

Arandar supposed that whoever became the new Dux of Caerdracon and the Lord of Castra Carhaine would tear out the symbols of the House of the Carhainii and install his own sigil. Though Arandar decided that Gavin was right, that the castra should retain its name. Calliande had cleansed the ancient temple of the

Enlightened hidden in the catacombs beneath the fortress, but there was no reason that Tarrabus's ancestors should be forgotten.

In fact, Arandar wanted to make sure that Tarrabus himself would be remembered so future generations would not walk his path of folly and woe.

"It seems likely," said Gareth Licinius, "that Castra Marcaine has fallen to the enemy."

The old Dux looked grim. Castra Marcaine was his ancestral seat and home. With the loss of Castra Marcaine, the entirely of the Northerland had been lost, and the Frostborn would be free to march into Caerdracon.

"That is grievous news," said Arandar. He sat at the head of the long table, the Duxi and the kings and the Masters and the more influential Comites seated along its length.

"The freeholders of Caerdracon speak of parties of medvarth warriors and constant flights by locusari scouts," said Gareth. "It seems likely that the Frostborn are preparing to move in strength from the Northerland to Caerdracon."

"Aye," rumbled Dux Kors. "Let's meet them and chase them back to their world gate with their tails between their legs."

"I do not think Castra Marcaine fell very long ago," said Dux Sebastian. "No more than a week at most. All the stories are too recent. If we hasten, perhaps we can secure a more northern strong point and prepare to face the Frostborn there. Dun Calpurnia, perhaps."

"This is good counsel," said Arandar. "The Frostborn destroyed the town, but the fortifications can be restored with relatively little work. The town will make a strong base for our campaign into the Northerland. As soon as the army finishes crossing the River Mourning, we will make for Dun Calpurnia with all the speed we can muster."

He prayed they would not be too late.

CHAPTER SIX

PREDECESSOR

The forest surrounding Cathair Solas was ancient.

Ridmark had spent years wandering the Wilderland and had seen every kind of forest there was, from the towering, mossy trees of the Qazaluuskan Forest to the tough pine trees that covered the Northerland. The realm of Andomhaim was ancient, nearly a thousand years old, but compared to many other things, Andomhaim was but a child. He had seen the twisted, eerily beautiful ruins of dark elven citadels, every one of them far older than Tarlion. He had walked through the silent ruins of the dwarves, abandoned and desolate for millennia before Malahan Pendragon had founded the realm of Andomhaim. In the marshes near Moraime and the Torn Hills near Urd Morlemoch, he had seen the bones of long-slain warriors rise as undead, animated by ancient necromancy lingering from those battles.

It seemed that many battles had been fought in the forest surrounding Cathair Solas.

Ridmark and Calliande walked through clearings littered with old bones. The bones should have crumbled into dust long ago, but some lingering magic seemed to hang over the clearings, keeping the skeletons from crumbling into dust. Many of the skeletons looked elven, armored in plates of blue dark elven steel and holding swords and axes of the same metal. Calliande's Sight often detected undead wandering through the trees, and she steered them around the creatures.

In other places, they saw cairns of heaped stone, and crumbling towers of orcish build, like the ruined towers that Ridmark had seen in the Wilderland. From time to time they passed crumbling walls and broken towers of white stone, ancient dark elven strongholds now falling into rubble. Ridmark supposed the old ruins were siege forts built by the dark elves and the urdmordar who had once tried to storm the island and take Cathair Solas.

After the first day, the ground sloped upward steadily, and soon Ridmark and Calliande spent a great deal of their time climbing and working their way around boulders and the trunks of fallen trees. Calliande's clothes hindered their progress. When traveling, she usually wore boots and trousers and a leather jerkin, but she had been wearing a green dress and mantle and cloak. Often, she had to climb with her skirt bunched up in one hand, the other grasping the staff of the Keeper to maintain her balance.

"How much higher does this slope go?" said Ridmark.

Calliande caught her balance and looked around. "A few thousand feet, I think. Not high enough that we'll see snow, but high enough that it will definitely be colder."

"We should rest here for a moment," said Ridmark, looking at the gray sky overhead. "It's almost noon. A few moments to catch our breath won't hurt."

Calliande hesitated, then nodded. "Very well."

She sat on a fallen log, and he sat next to her, looking down the slope of the forest. They had come far enough that the rippling gray waters of the lake were no longer visible.

"Is Cathair Solas atop a mountain?" said Ridmark.

"No," said Calliande. "Well. Not exactly. It's in a caldera."

"Caldera?" said Ridmark. He didn't know the word.

Calliande waved a hand at the trees. "From what I understand, this entire island used to be a giant volcano. At some point, it had an eruption that drained all the molten stone from inside the mountain, and its slopes collapsed into the resultant cavity. That left a huge crater, miles across from rim to rim. Eventually, a lake filled most of the crater, and Cathair Solas was built on the island in the center of the crater." She considered for a moment. "An odd place for a city, really."

"Defensible, though," said Ridmark. "An army would have to cross the Lake of Ice, scale the slopes of the caldera, and then sail across the lake before an assault could even begin."

"I suppose that is part of the reason Cathair Solas has never fallen," said Calliande.

"There must have been many battles here," said Ridmark.

"Oh, yes," said Calliande. "Thousands of them for thousands of years. Cathair Solas, as far as I know, is the last stronghold of the high elves on this world. The dark elves besieged it for millennia, and after the urdmordar enslaved the dark elves, they continued the siege for just as long. I suppose that was why Andomhaim was able to survive until the foundation of the Two Orders. The urdmordar ruled everything north of the Mountains of Ice, and for all that I know, they still do. Cathair Solas kept them from advancing any further south. The lands that would become Andomhaim were ruled by a patchwork of exiles fleeing from the urdmordar – the Traveler, the Sculptor, the Nightcrowned King, and various orcish warlocks. It was only when the urdmordar decided to circle around Cathair Solas and head south that humans encountered them for the first time, and you know the rest."

"A hundred thousand years of war," said Ridmark, gazing into the forest.

"Hmm?" said Calliande.

"That was what the Warden said when he fought Ardrhythain," said Ridmark. "And when we fought Tymandain Shadowbearer, he said the same thing. A hundred thousand years of war with the shadow of Incariel, and we're at the last chapter of it."

They sat in silence for a while.

"The shadow of Incariel," said Calliande. "Shadowbearer corrupted the dark elves and brought the urdmordar here, just as he brought the Frostborn. Why, though?"

"I don't know," said Ridmark. "It troubles me that we don't know. Perhaps when we see Imaria again we can ask her."

Calliande gave him a sharp look. "If we succeed here...you're going after her?" He understood her concern. He had almost gotten himself killed trying to kill Imaria in the burning ruins of Dun Licinia's keep.

"I won't need to," said Ridmark. "She will come after us again. You know she will. She hates both of us, and she's the new Shadowbearer. Whatever the shadow of Incariel desires, we're in its way. Which means she has every reason to kill us, both for her own satisfaction and because we're in the way of whatever the shadow of Incariel wants." His voice hardened. "But if she comes for us once I have the sword of the Dragon Knight, then she won't get away to work more evil. Not this time."

"Yes," said Calliande. He caught the dread that flickered through her expression. He knew full well that trying to wield the sword of the Dragon Knight would be dangerous, but Ridmark did not see any other choice. They might need the sword to overcome the Frostborn, and it seemed that the sword had, for whatever reason, chosen him.

Ridmark would do what he needed to do or die trying.

He supposed it was little different than many other things he had done.

Except this time, he didn't want to die.

Before, he had not cared whether he had lived or died, but now he wanted to survive. He knew firsthand what the pain of his death would do to Calliande, and he did not want her to experience that as he had.

"What?" said Calliande. "What is it?"

Ridmark realized that he had been staring at her.

He took her free hand, leaned over, and gave her a quick kiss.

Calliande smiled at him and then laughed. "What was that for?"

"Why would I need a reason?" said Ridmark.

"I like that line of argument." She kissed him again. "And as pleasant as this is, we should probably keep moving. If we can find a deer or a turkey to shoot for dinner, that would be a good thing as well."

"Agreed," said Ridmark.

He got to his feet, as did Calliande, and they resumed their climb. As before, Calliande used her Sight to sweep the trees for any undead and creatures of dark magic, and twice she steered them past bands of undead warriors and once around a pack of urvaalgs. The ground began to level off, and they made better progress, though they were still going uphill.

Then Ridmark caught a flash of crimson through the trees ahead.

"Wait a moment," he murmured, and Calliande nodded, the staff of the Keeper held ready before her.

A ruined orcish tower stood on the hillside ahead, surrounded by a round wall of loose stone. The tower looked old, its sides covered in moss, and the wall was in the slow process of collapsing. Through the hole in the wall where the gate had once been, Ridmark glimpsed something the color of blood.

It looked almost exactly like the chitinous armor of an urdmordar's exoskeleton. That was bad. Calliande might be able to defeat a single urdmordar with her magic, but it would be a close thing.

"Urdmordar," said Calliande in a quiet voice.

"Do you see any dark magic in the ruin?" said Ridmark.

Calliande blinked several times, frowning as she focused the Sight. "No, nothing. Even male urdmordar have a powerful aura of dark magic. If there is an urdmordar there, it has hidden itself quite well."

Ridmark nodded and crept forward, the staff of Ardrhythain held ready before him. Step by step he moved closer, the staff ready, and circled to the left and peered into the courtyard.

There was an urdmordar squatting there, a female urdmordar. The creature looked like a giant spider with a human woman's torso rising from its abdomen in place of a spider's head. Plates of overlapping crimson chitin covered the creature's entire body, its legs like giant spears, and long claws topped the fingers of its human-like arms. The female urdmordar that Ridmark had fought in the past had eyes that glowed with harsh white light, but this urdmordar's eyes were closed, and the creature was motionless.

Utterly motionless, in fact, and a layer of fallen leaves lay atop it.

Ridmark eased forward a few more steps and rapped his staff on the urdmordar's side. The staff made a loud tapping noise, and the urdmordar's flank felt as hard as granite.

Yet the creature did not move, and Ridmark saw the blackened craters on the back of its human-like torso.

"I think it's dead," he said.

"It is," said Calliande, joining him. She rapped the end of her staff on the side of the urdmordar. "And for a long time. It's been dead for so long its carapace has petrified. Turned to stone."

"I didn't know they did that," said Ridmark.

Calliande smiled. "You killed three female urdmordar, and you didn't know that?"

"Two female urdmordar," said Ridmark. "Gothalinzur and Agrimnalazur. Arandar and Gavin killed Rhogrimnalazur. I just helped."

"Three urdmordar," said Calliande. "There was that male urdmordar under Urd Arowyn."

Ridmark grunted. "I had forgotten about that one. And after I killed the urdmordar, I didn't stay long enough to see if their carapaces turned to stone."

"Just as well," said Calliande. "I think the process takes thousands of years. This one has been here for nearly as long."

"Let's keep going," said Ridmark. "It's no threat to us. Pity we can't…"

Calliande froze, her eyelids fluttering, and then her blue eyes opened wide with alarm. Ridmark knew what that meant. The Sight had stirred to life within her.

There was a creature of dark magic nearby.

"Ridmark!" she said. "Foes approach!" She called her magic, the staff of the Keeper shining with white fire in her right hand. Ridmark stepped in front of her, staff raised, his eyes sweeping the courtyard for any sign of danger. The courtyard was overgrown with grass and ferns and small bushes, which offered plenty of places for an urvaalg or perhaps an urhaalgar or an urshane to hide.

A black shadow passed overhead.

Ridmark looked up just as the urdhracos landed on the rim of the broken tower, her wings spread behind her like black sails.

Calliande held her power ready, preparing to strike at the urdhracos.

The creature looked sleek and beautiful in a deadly sort of way. Overlapping plates of black armor fitted close to her slim body, and her face was pale and lovely, though her eyes were filled with the black void of the shadow of Incariel. A powerful aura of dark magic hung around the creature. This urdhracos was an old one, and unlike many of the other creatures of the dark elves, the urdhracosi could use magic.

Yet for a moment, the urdhracos had done nothing threatening. The creature merely regarded them, the black eyes unblinking, and then at last the urdhracos smiled.

"Do you like my statue?" she said in the orcish tongue, her voice inhumanly melodious.

"Statue?" said Ridmark, and he glanced at the petrified urdmordar carcass. "This is yours?"

"Does it belong to anyone?" said the urdhracos. "It used to belong to an urdmordar. A long time ago, that urdmordar enslaved my master and his creatures, and all my master's creatures went with him to make war upon the high elves. But the high elves slew both my master and his master, and we were free to do as we wished. My master's bones still wander the forest somewhere, if you care to seek for them." She let out a tittering laugh. "He sought to rule the world, but now he is not even the master of his own flesh, for it has all rotted away over the centuries."

"How unfortunate for him," said Ridmark.

Calliande watched the urdhracos with both her eyes of flesh and the Sight. The urdhracos did not seem entirely sane, but she knew that would not put the creature at a disadvantage. An urdhracos could not have survived for this long by taking foolish risks.

"Yes," said the urdhracos. "It really was." Her wings flapped behind her a few times. Calliande wondered if the urdhracos would take flight, but the creature remained in place, one hand gripping the lip of the stone tower for balance. "You are humans, yes? Both of you?"

"We are," said Ridmark.

"Interesting," said the urdhracos, tilting her head to the side as she considered them. Third often did that when she was deep in thought, and it was eerie to see the same mannerism in an urdhracos. "Interesting. I have not seen humans upon this island for two hundred and twenty years. Or close to it. It is so hard to keep track of the time."

That would have been about the time Calliande had been here with Kalomarus and the six doomed Swordbearers. Had the urdhracos watched them from afar? She and the knights had fought several battles with the undead and the urvaalgs infesting the island, but they had not fought an urdhracos that Calliande could remember.

"We did not know that this tower was yours," said Ridmark. "We can be on our way immediately and will trouble you no further."

A flicker went through the Sight. Calliande took a quick glance around and saw that six rippling forms were circling around the outer wall, making for the courtyard.

"Urvaalgs," she hissed to Ridmark. "Six of them."

Ridmark gave her a shallow nod, eyes still fixed on the urdhracos.

"You were here, the last time, the female," said the urdhracos, the void-filled eyes fixing on Calliande. "The last time the sword sent out its call."

"Its call?" said Calliande, surprised that the urdhracos knew about the sword of the Dragon Knight.

"It is why you are here, of course," said the urdhracos. "It is why you were here the last time. You brought seven knights with you, and burned through six of them to make a new Dragon Knight like in the days of old when the world was young." She clucked her tongue and sounded for all the world like a village girl disapproving of scandalous misbehavior. "Now you have brought only one knight, and the sword will consume him. Very sad. Fortunately, I am merciful."

"You are?" said Ridmark, lifting his staff.

Calliande took a deep breath, focusing her will as she gathered her power for a spell.

"Yes," said the urdhracos. "The female loves you, do you not see? So I shall be merciful, and spare her the torment of watching the sword devour you. My hounds are hungry, and I shall be merciful and soothe their hunger. Truly, am I not overflowing with mercy?"

She gestured with her free hand, blue fire blazing to life around her talons, and the urvaalgs appeared, bounding over the crumbling wall with mighty leaps.

Calliande reacted first, slamming the end of her staff against the ground and releasing the power that she had summoned. A ring of white fire erupted in all directions from the end of the staff, rolling across the ground of the courtyard. The white fire struck the urvaalgs and set them rocking back, the creatures screaming as the fire sizzled against their flesh. Calliande had not been able to work a lethal amount of force into the spell, not with the power divided against so many targets, but the spell did hurt and stun the urvaalgs for an instant.

An instant was all that Ridmark ever needed.

He moved so fast it seemed like a blur, the dwarven war axe leaping from his belt and into his hand. Ridmark struck, killing one of the urvaalgs with a blow to the head, and then killed a second before the creatures could recover. The urdhracos thrust her hand, the blue fire of a spell of dark magic leaping from her talons, and Calliande worked a hasty ward, a shimmering dome of white light appearing before her. The urdhracos was strong, but not strong enough to stand against the power of the Keeper's mantle, and the spell shattered in a spray of blue sparks.

The surviving four urvaalgs closed around Ridmark, and Calliande cast again, working a simple spell of earth magic. The ground folded and rippled like a banner caught in the wind, and the spell knocked the urvaalgs over. Ridmark seized the opportunity and killed another creature, even as the urdhracos launched another spell. Again Calliande deflected the blast of dark magic.

She started to cast another spell to aid Ridmark but held off. Ridmark was holding his own against the three urvaalgs. Her ring of white fire had burned the creatures, slowing their reactions, and Ridmark was driving them back. She thought he could kill all three of them without her help, but he would not be able to defend against the dark magic of the urdhracos. Calliande called elemental fire, infusing it with the power of the Keeper, and flung a shaft of flames against the tower. She might have lacked Antenora's precise skill, but she made up for it with power, and the bar of fire ripped across the top of the ruins. The urdhracos let out a shriek of pain and fury and flung herself out of the way, her wings opening as she clawed into the air to get away from the flames.

Calliande looked back at Ridmark, but he had killed two urvaalgs in the time that it had taken her to throw the fire at the urdhracos, and the final creature was retreating as he attacked with axe and staff. She snapped her attention back towards the sky and sent another bolt of white fire blurring towards the urdhracos. The fire of the Well could consume creatures of dark magic, and the urdhracos recognized the danger, banking in midair to avoid the spell. The urdhracos swooped overhead as Ridmark killed the last urvaalg and clung to the side of the tower, her black talons gripping the weathered masonry.

"Remember!" said the urdhracos. "I tried to be merciful! Remember that when you watch the sword devour his heart in flames."

Calliande started another spell, but the urdhracos kicked off from the wall and leaped into the air, wings opening wide. She flew away to the west and did not return. Calliande swept the Sight over the ruined tower and courtyard once more, but no saw no signs of any other foes approaching.

She let out a long breath, releasing the Sight.

"Friend of yours?" said Ridmark, cleaning the black slime of the urvaalgs' blood from his axe.

"I've never seen her before," said Calliande. "At least, I don't think I have. Likely she followed me and Kalomarus and the others from afar the last time, and decided not to risk a confrontation since we had Swordbearers in our midst."

"But a man and a woman traveling alone," said Ridmark, "makes for an easier target than a woman traveling with several Swordbearers."

"Aye," said Calliande. She hesitated. "Ridmark…what she said about the sword…"

"Taunts and nothing more," said Ridmark. He returned his axe to his belt and picked up his staff.

"But taunts," said Calliande in a quiet voice, "with some truth to them, I fear."

"Perhaps," said Ridmark, "but the best lies are mixed with the truth. You led those knights here, but you didn't force them to follow you. They volunteered. Just as I am."

Calliande swallowed but made herself nod. That didn't make her feel any better. Kalomarus and the others had chosen to follow her to this place. The difference was while that she had admired and respected them, she hadn't been in love with any of them.

She was in love with Ridmark, and she feared what would happen when he found the sword of the Dragon Knight.

But he was right. There was nothing to do but to continue on.

"We should keep moving," said Ridmark, "and find a more defensible place before the sun goes down."

"Yes," said Calliande.

They left the ruined tower. Calliande drew on the Sight every few minutes, seeking for enemies.

She saw none, but her dread did not abate.

CHAPTER SEVEN

FOREWARNING

The army of Andomhaim continued its northward march, leaving Castra Carhaine behind and following the Moradel road into the Northerland.

As they rode north, Arandar saw the mountains of Taliand fade away to the south, replaced by the dense trees of the Shaluuskan Forest. It was a pity that the ghost orcs were so reclusive. Their ability to turn invisible would have made them invaluable scouts against the Frostborn, but Arandar knew better than to send ambassadors to them. Anyone who entered the Shaluuskan Forest never returned, and the ghost orcs only ventured forth when they happened to feel like making war upon someone.

Perhaps they would come to regret that when the Frostborn razed their forests and reduced them to slaves.

Arandar rebuked himself for the dark thoughts. So long as the ghost orcs left Andomhaim alone during the war, he would repay them in kind. And the Shaluuskan Forest would only be destroyed if Andomhaim was defeated and the Frostborn had the leisure to turn their attention to lesser threats.

Unfortunately, the constant presence of the Frostborn scouts made it easy to entertain dark thoughts.

After the ambush on the River Mourning, the Frostborn had not tried to assassinate him or any of the chief nobles. The assassination attempt had been led by Arlmagnava, a Seeker of the Order of the Inquisition, and from what Arandar had learned from Calliande and Antenora, the Order of the Inquisition served as the spies and assassins and secret police of the Frostborn. Arlmagnava had been at Dun Calpurnia before the battle, and she had been the one who had arranged Tarrabus's secret pact with the Frostborn. With the defeat of their puppet Tarrabus, the Frostborn had likely decided to try and eliminate the new High King with one blow.

The plan had almost worked.

Arandar found it necessary to take extra precautions. He kept a guard of Swordbearers and Magistri around him, and at least four of the ballistae and their attendant men-at-arms. He felt a bit foolish with all the extra guards, but he recognized the bitter necessity. He was the High King, and his son and heir was in Nightmane Forest. If he was killed, the army would fall into chaos until a new leader could be chosen, and the Frostborn would take advantage of that chaos to deadly effect.

Other dark rumors came to his ears.

They passed many villages on the Moradel road, and the freeholders spoke of seeing locusari and medvarth warriors in the woods. Some outlying freeholds had been sacked and burned, their inhabitants either killed or taken as slaves. The freeholders had also seen locusari scouts and frost drakes flying overhead.

It seemed certain the Frostborn had overrun Castra Marcaine and the whole of the Northerland and were now sending scouting parties unhindered into Caerdracon. Arandar wondered what had happened to the Anathgrimm. Had they been slain and Nightmane Forest overrun? Or had they been forced to retreat into Nightmane Forest and behind the Traveler's ancient wards?

Arandar wished the Keeper was here. She had far greater skill with the Sight than Antenora, and the Sight might have provided answers. He envied the ability of the Frostborn to use frost drakes to scout. More and more, he felt the disadvantages of facing a foe with such an effective method of scouting. The ballistae might keep the frost drakes from descending low enough to attack, but that did not prevent them from observing the army.

And observe the army they did.

As he watched yet another frost drake circle high overhead, Arandar realized that it was time to change his plans.

When the army camped that night, he called together the chief lords and knights for a council of war.

"My lords," said Arandar, standing at the map table in his pavilion. With all the lords crammed into the pavilion and gathered around the table, the air smelled of sweat and horse and oiled steel. "We must address two items tonight. First, the matter of the succession."

"Your son Accolon is the lawful heir to the throne of Andomhaim," said Dux Gareth. The march was wearing on the old Dux, and the lines in his face seemed deeper than ever, though his vigor had not waned. "Should tragedy befall him, your daughter Nyvane is the lawful heir."

"Both my children are safe in Nightmane Forest at the moment," said Arandar. At least, he hoped that they were safe. If they had been slain...no, he dared not dwell on that, not now, not when so much depended on his judgment. "However, both my children are young. Accolon is not yet ready to lead a host into battle." He took a deep breath. "Therefore, I think it is best that we decide who among you will serve as regent for my son if I am slain in the battle to come. Andomhaim cannot wait for my son to take his crown and grow to maturity if I am killed. Strong leadership will be needed at once in the face of such a deadly foe."

This brought a low rumble from the lords and knights. The High Kings of Andomhaim had rarely named potential regents since that invited the assassination of the High King. The Red Family of Cintarra had left its bloody fingerprints on the history of Andomhaim more than once.

"This seems a wise course to me," rumbled old King Ulakhamar of Rhaluusk, his tusks jutting from his gray beard like spikes of rock from a river. "Better to decide this now than to have a debate during a battle." Silent Malhask of Khaluusk nodded his agreement, his scars as transforming his face into a scowl.

"An army must have one commander," said Master Marhand, his arms folded across his chest. "The heat of battle is no time for an argument."

Several other lords voiced their agreement.

"Very well," said Arandar. "If I am killed in battle, it is my wish that Dux Leograncce Arban of Castra Arban serve as regent until Accolon comes of age." Leograncce's blue eyes turned towards Arandar. Even with the rigors and the dust of the march, Leograncce still looked regal and lordly, like a Senator of the Romans from Old Earth in ancient days. "Dux Leograncce has been the Dux of Taliand for many years and is familiar with the burdens of government. Taliand is the oldest of the duxarchates of Andomhaim as well. And if you will forgive my bluntness, Dux Leograncce is among the oldest of us as well." A low rumble of laughter went up from the lords. "Ruling a realm and commanding a host in battle is best left to a seasoned man, not to a hotheaded youngster. Dux Leograncce, would you accept this burden?"

"I do not wish it, your Majesty," said Leograncce with a sigh, "but if it is your wish, I shall accept this charge, and pray that I never need to execute it."

"Thank you," said Arandar. "If both Dux Leograncce and I are slain in battle, I wish the regency to pass to Prince Cadwall Gwyrdragon of Cintarra." Prince Cadwall looked up, his eyebrows rising in mild surprise. Despite the long march, he still managed to cut the figure of a dashing Cintarran knight, albeit something of a dusty one. The House of Gwyrdragon was a bastard offshoot of the House of Pendragon, given the princedom of Cintarra in exchange for removing themselves from the line of succession to the High King's throne, and no Gwyrdragon had ever served as regent. Nevertheless, if Arandar and his children were all killed, the lords would likely choose either Leogrance Arban or Cadwall Gwyrdragon to serve as the new High King. "We all know that Prince Cadwall has governed Cintarra ably for years, and he helped turn the tide against Tarrabus at Tarlion. If both Dux Leogrance and I are slain in the battle, Prince Cadwall, it is my wish that you then serve as regent of Andomhaim until my son comes of age. Will you accept this charge?"

"Like the honorable Dux Leogrance, I do not wish this burden," said Cadwall. "Nevertheless, if disaster befalls us and both the High King and the Dux of Taliand are killed on the same day, then I will accept this charge."

"Thank you, lord Prince," said Arandar. "And if I am killed alongside the Prince and the Dux in the same day...well, we shall have likely suffered a catastrophic defeat, and then I fear you shall have to decide to do as you think best."

No one said anything for a while, contemplating that grim possibility.

Master Marhand then led the lords and the knights in an oath, promising before God and the Dominus Christus to support Dux Leogrance as regent if Arandar was slain, and Prince Cadwall as regent if both Arandar and Leogrance were killed. If all went well, they would never need to use these arrangements.

And if things did not go well...Arandar had done what he could. He was not like Calliande, and would not try to influence events long after he should have died. Arandar would try to do his duty in the time that had been given to him. What happened after his death was beyond his ability to control.

"There is a second matter we need to address," said Arandar. "It seems that circumstances require a change to our strategy."

"I fear so, your Majesty," said Dux Sebastian. "All the scouts agree, and all the reports we have heard say the same thing. The Frostborn have taken Castra Marcaine, and they no longer face any opposition in the Northerland. The Anathgrimm have either been defeated or forced to withdraw."

Accolon and Nyvane were with them...

Arandar forced himself not to think about that.

"If the Anathgrimm have been withdrawn," said Dux Gareth, "and if the Frostborn have control over the Northerland, marching directly into the Northerland could mean disaster. There are a thousand valleys and ravines in the hills of the Northerland where even an army of this size can be ambushed."

"We have come this far," said Dux Kors. "We cannot turn back now."

"No," said Arandar. "We have to take the fight to the Frostborn. But if we march blindly into the Northerland, we may well face disaster. Instead, I propose that we take some strong place and wait for the Frostborn to come to us. Our allies will have a better chance of finding us, and we can hold the Frostborn there."

"That will give the Frostborn ample chance to fortify themselves in the Northerland," said Leogrance.

"The Frostborn already have had ample chance to fortify themselves in the Northerland," said Gareth. "Even before we withdrew, the scouts reported that the Frostborn and their khaldjari engineers were building a huge citadel over the ruins of Dun Licinia. God only knows how many other fortifications they have had the chance to build over the last year."

"We cannot be under any illusions that this will be a quick war," said Prince Cadwall. "We may face years of battle before we can push the Frostborn back to their world gate."

"Then it is best that we take a strong place and meet our allies there," said Arandar.

"Castra Carhaine itself?" said Dux Sebastian. "It is the strongest fortress in Caerdracon.

"It's too far south," said Dux Kors. "We'll lose all of Caerdracon by the time we come to grips with the Frostborn, and if we do, we might never get it back."

"Dun Calpurnia," said Arandar. "We had planned to fortify it anyway, so we may as well make our stand there. The walls and castra were strong, and likely the Frostborn have not damaged them too much. It is close to the River Moradel, and we can use the river to bring up supplies by water."

"The Frostborn will know our plans as soon as we implement them," said Dux Kors. "Those damned frost drakes keep flying over our army and reporting our movements. They can take their bloody time preparing for us."

"The frost drakes can move swiftly," said Arandar, "but none of the other slave kindreds of the Frostborn can move with such haste. Our horsemen can outpace all but the locusari warriors."

Silence answered him as the others considered that.

"Then you want to send the horsemen ahead to seize Dun Calpurnia first," said Prince Cadwall.

"Yes," said Arandar. "The sooner we can take Dun Calpurnia and fortify it, the better."

"Splitting our host is a grave risk," said Leogrance.

"It worked at Tarlion against the usurper," said Sebastian.

"That was a close-fought thing," said Kors. "We might have lost if a dozen things had happened differently. If the Keeper hadn't broken the walls, or if the Gray Knight hadn't beaten Tarrabus in that duel, or if Corbanic hadn't charged the enemy when he did."

"It was a risk," said Arandar. "If we hadn't taken that risk, then we would almost certainly have been defeated when Tarrabus ignited the dvargir mine. I fear if we do not take some risks now, we will lose the war. Prince Cadwall." The prince of Cintarra straightened. "Take command of the heavy horsemen and ride to Dun Calpurnia. Dux Sebastian, provide scouts and skirmishers for him. I will bring up the rest of the army with all speed, and I will also send

Lady Third and Lady Antenora along with you. Their...unique abilities should prove useful to take the ruins of the town."

"It is possible," said Cadwall, "that the Frostborn might already have a strong garrison there. If they do, horsemen alone will not be able to take the town."

"If so, return to the host, and we will make different plans," said Arandar. "But if we can take Dun Calpurnia and hold it until the Frostborn arrive, we can keep them bottled up there. Perhaps the dwarves or the manetaurs or the Anathgrimm will be able to pin them against the walls. It is worth the gamble, I think. My lords, we have our work before us. Prince Cadwall, I would like you to ride tomorrow."

That night Arandar lay on the cot in his pavilion, staring at the cloth ceiling overhead.

He wanted to sleep. He needed to sleep. Tomorrow would be yet another busy day, and he needed his wits about him.

Exhaustion clouded his mind, but sleep eluded him.

His thoughts chased each other around his mind, and a thousand different details worried at him. Maybe it would have been better to fall back to Castra Carhaine. Or maybe it would have been better to press to the Northerland at once, throwing the Frostborn into chaos and making an opening for the Anathgrimm and the dwarves and the manetaurs to arrive. So many decisions to make and every single one of them could lead to disaster and defeat...

Arandar rebuked himself. He could not second-guess himself. Once he had made his decision, he had to hold firm to it. If he spent too much time second-guessing himself, it would lead to paralysis at a moment of crisis.

He had never wanted to be High King because he had known it would be like this. When he had been a decurion and then a knight, a poor decision could have led to the deaths of a few hundred men.

A bad decision from the High King could lead to the deaths of thousands and the destruction of Andomhaim. Which meant he needed a clear mind to make good decisions.

Which meant he needed some damned sleep.

Once again, he felt the urge to invite a woman to his bed. He had always slept well after that. But this wasn't the time for such things, so instead, he focused on slowing his breathing and clearing his mind.

To his mild surprise, it worked.

And in his sleep, Arandar dreamed.

In his dream, he walked through the battlefield of Dun Calpurnia on the grim, bloody day that Tarrabus Carhaine had betrayed Uthanaric Pendragon and his trueborn sons to the Frostborn. Arandar walked past fields salted with corpses, the air heavy with the scents of blood and ruptured bowels and the alien, musky smell of slain medvarth warriors. They had tried to burn as many of the bodies as possible to keep the Frostborn from raising them as revenants, but there had been so many that there hadn't been time to burn them all. That was another matter to concern him in the battle to come, that the Frostborn could raise the dead as soldiers for their own side.

A raven flapped overhead and landed a few yards away, watching him.

For some reason, the raven caught Arandar's attention.

There had been thousands of carrion birds after the battle, vultures and ravens and crows, gorging themselves on a feast of the slain. One raven was not so remarkable. Yet this raven was not joining its brothers as they rushed to their feast. The raven just sat there, watching him with a glinting black eye, and Arandar had the feeling he had seen this bird, this exact bird, somewhere before.

"Well. One finds that you are more your father's son than you thought, Arandar Pendragon."

The female voice was a bit acerbic and spoke Latin with a peculiar, archaic stateliness. Arandar stiffened as the voice filled his ears. He knew that voice. He knew that voice very well.

He turned as the woman approached.

She was lean with thick black hair bound in a long braid and black eyes like polished stones. Her clothing was a rough mixture of leather and wool with well-worn boots, and she wore an odd cloak of tattered brown and green strips that would serve as effective camouflage in the forests. In her right hand, she carried a wooden staff carved with magical symbols.

"You," said Arandar, astonished.

"Yes, me," said Morigna. "One is pleased to see that your accession to the throne has not fuddled your wits more than they already were. Pleased, if rather surprised."

"You're dead," said Arandar.

"Obviously."

"I was thinking about lying with a woman, and now I am dreaming of you," said Arandar. "Dear God in heaven, but the mind can play ghastly tricks."

Morigna's mouth twisted. "How very flattering, High King. But just because I am dead and this is a dream does not mean that we are not speaking in truth."

"Yes, it does," said Arandar.

He had never liked Morigna, and he had never been able to understand why Ridmark found her attractive. Certainly, she had been physically attractive, but Calliande had been besotted with Ridmark at the same time, and Arandar had never grasped why Ridmark had chosen Morigna over Calliande. Morigna had been waspish, arrogant, and argumentative, and she had also practiced forbidden magic and scorned the church of the Dominus Christus. She had delighted in needling Arandar.

Maybe Arandar ought to have been grateful. It had been good practice for his current role. And maybe that was why she had been drawn to Ridmark. He was a strong man, and it took a strong man to tame a virago like Morigna of the Wilderland.

"Such flattering thoughts, High King," said Morigna. "But consider. Lady Third reported my presence in the Tower of the Keeper. Does she seem the sort to make up stories for the enjoyment of it?"

"No," said Arandar. "Though I cannot understand how your spirit can be here."

Morigna shrugged. "Have you so little imagination?"

"To be blunt, I thought your spirit would be in hell for your rejection of the Dominus Christus," said Arandar.

Morigna shrugged. "Perhaps the Dominus Christus is more merciful than you think."

"I do not presume to know the mind and the ways of God," said Arandar.

"Or," said Morigna, "perhaps this is a consequence to the dark magic I used at Urd Morlemoch."

"What do you mean?" said Arandar.

"Call it a…penance, if you like," said Morigna. "You are pious enough, that ought to please you. Before I can move on, there are tasks I must undertake. One of them is making sure Ridmark survives long enough to do what he must accomplish. Another task is to ensure Calliande survives long enough to save Ridmark." The black eyes seemed to dig into Arandar like knives. "And another task is to make sure you survive to fulfill your mission, High King of Andomhaim."

He felt a chill. "Why would you care if I live or die?"

"Normally, I would not," said Morigna. She smiled. "But Ridmark always did like you." The smile faded. "And if you fail in your task, High King, humanity will be swept from this world like sawdust from the floor of a workshop, and the shadow of Incariel will consume the kindreds of this world until the end of the cosmos."

"And what is my task?" said Arandar.

"Simple," said Morigna. "You must defend Andomhaim until Ridmark and Calliande achieve their tasks and return to aid you." A flicker of misgiving went over her sharp face. "If they are able to achieve their tasks."

"Wouldn't you want Calliande to get killed?" said Arandar. "She was your rival, as I understand."

Morigna rolled her eyes. "Do not be petty. I am dead, and will remain so. The dead do not love as the living do. Ridmark and Calliande need each other in a way that Ridmark and I never needed each other if I am to be honest. The dead also are not bound by time the way that the living are, which brings us to the reason for my visit." She smirked. "Unless, of course, you were dreaming of me for another reason. You are the High King of Andomhaim, and you still cannot find a woman to warm your bed? Truly, that is indeed sad…"

"I see that death," said Arandar, biting back his temper, "has not improved your disposition in the slightest."

Morigna shrugged. "I feel much calmer than I did when I was alive if it matters. But while I am not entirely bound by time, you are, and time is fleeting. You must be ready. The Frostborn are waiting for you."

"I knew that already," said Arandar. "Their frost drakes have been shadowing us since we left Tarlion."

"The situation is quite as dire as you believe it to be," said Morigna. "The Frostborn have taken Castra Marcaine, and the entirety of the Northerland is in their control. The Anathgrimm have not been destroyed, though they have been forced to withdraw across the Moradel, and the Frostborn have constructed a line of forts along the river's eastern bank to keep the Anathgrimm from attacking the Northerland."

"Then the Anathgrimm are trapped in Nightmane Forest," said Arandar.

"Not necessarily," said Morigna. "The line of Frostborn forts stands along the eastern bank of the River Moradel. The Frostborn have not yet advanced far enough to fortify the southern boundary of Nightmane Forest. Queen Mara and the Anathgrimm are advancing from there, and hope to aid you soon. The host of the dwarves is marching through Khaluusk, and the manetaurs and the tygrai have nearly reached the western edge of Mhorluusk. Help is coming, High King of Andomhaim, if you can live long enough for it to reach you."

"My plan to hold and fortify Dun Calpurnia," said Arandar. "Will it work?" Whether he liked Morigna had no relevance. The realm was in peril, and if she could help him, then he would take that aid gladly.

"It might," said Morigna. "It is one of the possibilities in the future. Your future exists as a chain of possibilities. In one possibility, you hold at Dun Calpurnia until your allies arrive. In another, the Frostborn destroy you utterly, and it is impossible to say which future is more likely. But beware, Arandar Pendragon! The Frostborn know you are coming, and they know you have allies on the march. They will seek to destroy you before your allies can offer you aid."

A cawing noise rose from the battlefield, and the thousands of vultures and crows and ravens took to the air.

"Ah," said Morigna. "It seems that our time is up. One last warning. Beware my murderess."

Arandar blinked, and then remembered. "Imaria Shadowbearer?"

"That is what she calls herself now," said Morigna. "Beware her. She is weaker than Tymandain but far more dangerous. For even the Frostborn are only her tools, and she will use them to destroy you and take the Well of Tarlion for herself. And if she does that, this world will be lost forever."

The cloud of carrion birds blocked out the sun, and Arandar knew no more.

He awoke with a start, the dawn sunlight streaming through the closed flap of his pavilion. Arandar sat up, rubbing the sleep from his face, the stubble of his jaw rasping beneath his palms. Around him, he heard the noise as the camp awoke and Prince Cadwall's horsemen prepared for their rapid ride north.

It seemed that he had gotten to sleep after all.

The dream was still seared into his memory, sharp and clear, and for a moment Arandar almost dismissed it as the product of an exhausted mind.

No. He dared not. All the evidence was against it. For one, Third had seen Morigna's spirit in the Tower of the Keeper. For another, Arandar certainly had never dreamed of Morigna before.

That meant the Frostborn were indeed ready for them...and Arandar had to continue with his plan.

His hand curled into a fist.

They would have to take and hold Dun Calpurnia until their allies arrived.

CHAPTER EIGHT

A BOON

Ridmark came to a stop, gazing in surprise at the sight before him.

He had never seen anything quite like it.

They had climbed the slope for the last two days, the trees becoming thinner and the ground growing rockier. Game had grown sparser as well, and all they had been able to find to eat had been a rabbit and a handful of nuts. Ridmark's stomach rumbled with hunger, but he had endured worse in the Wilderland, and he pressed on without complaint. He was more concerned about Calliande, but she continued without hesitation. The going had become easier after they had found the ruins of an old road paved in white stone that climbed its way up the slope.

Then they had come to the...distortion.

"What is that?" said Ridmark.

Ahead of them the road, the rocky slope, and the trees continued, but the entire landscape seemed...frozen, somehow, and blurry. Everything looked a little out of focus, and what was stranger, the blur began in a sharp, clear line across the earth. It was as if everything ahead was encased in translucent ice.

"One of the magical defenses of Cathair Solas," said Calliande.

"What will it do?" said Ridmark.

"I'm afraid it's perfectly harmless," said Calliande, pushing back a lock of hair from her face.

"Not an effective defense, then," said Ridmark, "if it's harmless."

"It is both harmless and effective," said Calliande. "The high elven magi can control the flow of time around Cathair Solas."

Ridmark blinked. "Is that even possible?"

"For human wizards, no," said Calliande. "I wouldn't even know where to begin such a feat. But for the high elven magi…they can perform works of magic beyond our comprehension. This is one of them. Sometimes the high elves slow the rate of time around Cathair Solas." She pointed her staff at the peculiar blurry barrier. "For every minute that passes beyond the boundary, perhaps a day passes on the rest of the island."

"Allowing the high elves to destroy their enemies piecemeal," said Ridmark, understanding the utility at last. "They could let their opponent's vanguard into the range of their defenses, and slow time. Once the vanguard was destroyed, they could let time resume its normal flow and lure in more of the enemy."

"Yes," said Calliande. Her eyelids fluttered as she drew on the Sight. "I'm not sure…but I think right now five to seven days are passing on the rest of the world for every day that passes in Cathair Solas."

"A week?" said Ridmark, aghast. Even now, Arandar and the others were marching against the Frostborn. Ridmark and Calliande needed to return as soon as possible to aid them. Even if it only took them two or three days to find the sword of the Dragon Knight, that might mean nearly three weeks could pass in the outside world.

"A week," said Calliande, voice grim. "I don't think we have any choice. If we turn back and try to return on our own, it might take us months to get back to Andomhaim, assuming we can even cross the Lake of Ice. The only way forward is into that."

Ridmark nodded. He didn't see any way around it.

"Take my hand," said Calliande. "We'll go through together on the count of three." Ridmark took her left hand with his right. Her fingers felt dry and cold against his. "On three. One, two…"

Ridmark braced himself.

"Three!"

As one they stepped over the line and into the blurred area.

Ridmark felt a moment of jarring disorientation and heard an odd rushing sound in his head. The sensation was like the odd dislocation he had felt after jumping through the rift in the Tower of the Keeper. His inner ear screamed that he was falling to his death, though his boots retained a firm grip on the ground. His stomach twisted and writhed, and he would have thrown up had he eaten anything recently. Just as well that he hadn't.

Ridmark caught his balance, breathing hard, and saw the same spasm of reaction and discomfort go over Calliande's face.

"That wasn't pleasant," he said.

"Yes," said Calliande, squeezing his hand to keep her balance, "it was not. The shift from one rate of time to another is…difficult on the body. Just as well we won't have to do it too often."

Ridmark looked over his shoulder, wondering what the rest of the island looked like from within the slowed stream of time. To his mild surprise, everything on the other side of the boundary had disappeared into a misty blur. Idly he wondered what would happen if he picked up a rock and threw it over the boundary, and decided not to press his luck.

"I wonder why the high elven magi decided to slow the flow of time around Cathair Solas now," said Ridmark.

"I don't know," said Calliande. She hesitated. "I hope they're not under attack."

"Who would attack the high elves?" said Ridmark.

"The dark elves," said Calliande. "An ambitious orcish warlock or warlord. The urdmordar, if they felt like it – they besieged

Cathair Solas for thousands of years before humans came to this world."

"Do you think they slowed time because of us?" said Ridmark.

Calliande hesitated. "I...had not considered that. I can't imagine why. We're no threat to them. And if the high elves knew we were here, surely they would have come out to meet us by now." She scowled. "Not that Ardrhythain has been rushing to our aid."

"He did save our lives at Urd Morlemoch," said Ridmark.

"True," said Calliande. "He also spent a hundred thousand years hunting Tymandain Shadowbearer, and you killed Tymandain a few weeks after you met him for the first time. What has Ardrhythain been doing since the Frostborn returned? He has the power to close their world gate. If the high elves stirred themselves, they could have dealt a powerful blow against the Frostborn."

"We might be able to ask him in person soon," said Ridmark.

"Yes," said Calliande. "Yes, you're right." She took a deep breath, getting herself under control. "We should keep going."

Ridmark nodded and led the way up the crumbling road. They climbed for another hour or so, the slope growing steeper, and then the road ended as it reached a massive wall of rippling mist that stretched away on either side. The wall of mist rose so high that Ridmark could not see its top, and it blended with the gray sky overhead. The mist rippled and undulated, but never moved. Obviously, whatever it was, it was magical.

"What is that?" said Ridmark. "Another magical defense?"

"Yes," said Calliande. "That's the edge of the caldera. The mist will kill anyone who passes it with hostile intent."

"We don't have hostile intent," said Ridmark. He paused. "Do the high elves know that?"

"I think so," said Calliande. "We were able to pass through the mist once before, Kalomarus and I and the others. You and I should be able to do it."

Ridmark nodded. "On three." This time he counted down, and together he and Calliande stepped into the mist. He took her hand so they would not get separated in the thick haze. The mist washed over Ridmark, cool and damp, and filled his lungs as he took a deep breath. He didn't drop dead or suffer from agonizing pain, so he assumed that the mist had decided neither he nor Calliande were enemies.

They walked perhaps for a hundred yards, and then they passed through the mist and stood at the edge of the caldera.

It was an astonishing sight.

The vast crater was about five miles across, most of it filled with a lake of vivid, intense blue. In the center of the lake stood an island about two miles across.

Cathair Solas filled the entirety of the island.

The city reminded Ridmark of the Tower of the Moon in Tarlion, or perhaps Urd Morlemoch and Urd Arowyn and the other dark elven ruins he had visited. Cathair Solas had some of the same height, and the city had been built of the same gleaming white stone as the dark elven ruins and the Tower of the Moon.

Yet the central tower of the city was enormous, nearly a mile high and hundreds of yards thick. It looked like a far larger version of the Tower of the Moon, and hundreds of smaller towers stood around its base like slender blades of grass. An intricate maze of delicate walkways interconnected the towers. It should have been a bewildering maze, yet the entire city looked stunningly beautiful. The dark elven ruins had always been beautiful, but it had been an unsettling, eerie beauty, one alien and inimical to human sensibilities. Cathair Solas was simply beautiful.

Yet that was not the most remarkable thing about it.

The city was moving.

At first, Ridmark thought it was an optical illusion. Yet he saw that the smaller towers were slowly revolving around the central tower. The bridges from tower to tower moved as well, as if the entire city was one massive clockwork mechanism.

"Cathair Solas," said Calliande in a quiet voice.

"Why is it moving?" said Ridmark.

"The high elves built it that way," said Calliande. "The position of the thirteen moons affects the potency of various spells. The city moves in response to the position of the moons. Within some of the towers are rooms augmented by the magic of one or more of the thirteen moons. Depending on the tower's position, a spell cast within the tower can have tremendous potency."

"Too bad Caius isn't here," said Ridmark. "He would appreciate the scale of the engineering."

Calliande smiled a little, though it didn't touch her blue eyes, which remained worried. "Or he would criticize it." She pointed. A road in good repair wound its way down the inside of the caldera, leading to a causeway of white stone that crossed the lake to reach the city. "That way."

They descended the road, following its twists and turns down the slope to the blue lake. Utter silence hung over the caldera. Ridmark found that odd, and after a moment he realized why the silence was strange. The revolving towers of Cathair Solas moved in utter silence. He was watching thousands of tons of stone rotate around the city's central tower in perfect silence. There should have been a tremendous grinding noise. The vibrations should have made the waters of the lake splash and churn. The entire caldera should have felt as if it was in the grip of a minor earthquake.

Yet he felt no vibrations in the stone beneath his boots, and the city moved in silence.

They reached the end of the road and the start of the causeway. Four men in golden armor stood there, motionless as statues. The armor looked like the dark elven armor that Ridmark wore and that his companions had taken from the armories of Urd Morlemoch. But this armor was of brilliant gold, and the armored figures wore gray cloaks that hung from their shoulders, cloaks that were identical to the one that Ridmark wore.

The men were high elven bladeweavers, and each bladeweaver wore a pair of soulblades at his belt. Ridmark had seen the bladeweaver Rhyannis fight at Urd Morlemoch during their frantic escape from the Warden's creatures, and she had mowed through them with ease. Nonetheless, she had been one of the youngest and least experienced of the bladeweavers, and a veteran bladeweaver, with millennia of experience, would be a terrifying foe in battle.

Ridmark and Calliande stopped, and one of the bladeweavers stepped forward. The face beneath the winged helm was beautiful, albeit in a remote, alien way, cold and aloof and unknowable. The eyes were like polished coins of gold, and they did not blink as they regarded Ridmark and Calliande.

"I am Lanethran," said the bladeweaver in flawless Latin, his voice deep and musical, "Captain of the Gate of Cathair Solas. Only those invited are allowed within Cathair Solas. Turn back now. Should you require provision to survive your journey, it shall be procured, but you may go no further."

"We were invited," said Calliande, stepping forward. All four bladeweavers looked at her. "I am Calliande, Keeper of Andomhaim, and this is Ridmark Arban, magister militum of Nightmane Forest."

"We know who you both are, Lady Calliande," said Lanethran. "You came here once before, as did your predecessor, seeking our aid against the foes that threatened to devour your kingdom. You are known as well to us, Ridmark Arban, for you rescued Rhyannis from the darkness of Urd Morlemoch when she ventured within the Warden's walls. But only those who have an invitation may enter Cathair Solas, and you were not invited."

"We were," said Calliande. "The sword of the Dragon Knight summoned us."

The high elves shared a glance.

"The sword is powerful," said Lanethran, "but it is not a high elf of Cathair Solas, and only those invited by the high elves of the city may pass our gate."

"We must enter the city," said Calliande, a hint of frustration entering her voice. That was unlike her. Either the journey had worn on her, or her fear for him was worse than he had thought. "The sword of the Dragon Knight has summoned us, and we must speak to Ardrhythain at once."

Lanethran started to speak again, but Ridmark spoke first.

"Captain Lanethran," said Ridmark. "You know who I am?"

"As I said," said Lanethran, still calm as ever. "You rescued Rhyannis from the shadows of Urd Morlemoch."

"On that day," said Ridmark, "Ardrhythain gave me this cloak to aid me in my task." He tapped the gray cloak that hung from his shoulders. "Years later I returned to Urd Morlemoch to learn the secret of the Frostborn, and when we escaped he gave me this staff." He rapped the end of the staff against the ground. "But when I rescued Rhyannis, the archmage Ardrhythain granted me a boon."

Calliande opened her mouth, closed it, and remained silent.

Lanethran frowned for the first time and removed his helm. Beneath the helmet, he had thick black hair, stark against his pale face and his golden eyes. Without the winged helmet, Ridmark was struck by how tired the bladeweaver looked. Come to think of it, all four bladeweavers looked tired, even sorrowful, like men who had seen many friends die over the years. If Cathair Solas housed the last of the high elves, every high elf within its walls would have seen countless friends and brothers and sisters and children die.

Once again, Ridmark wondered why Tarrabus Carhaine had wanted physical immortality so badly. A man's life might be filled with sorrows and pain, but they would not last more than seventy or eighty years at the most, and then death would take him to the side of the Dominus Christus. To live for millennia with sorrow piling upon sorrow seemed like an intolerable burden.

"Yes," said Lanethran. "The boon is known to us. It was foretold long ago in the ages of prophecy, before the last of our Seers had been killed in the wars against the dark elves. Then do you call upon the boon, Ridmark Arban? Do you ask to receive your boon from Ardrhythain?"

Ridmark hesitated. There was iron weight in the bladeweaver's tone, and he felt the ancient weight of their gazes upon him.

"I do," said Ridmark.

"Then the hour of doom has come upon us at last," said another bladeweaver. "Either the long war shall come to an end, or shadow shall devour us all."

"All things are in the hands of God," said Lanethran. He gestured with one hand, pale fire dancing around his fingers as he cast a spell. "I have sent word. The archmage will send an emissary to take you into Cathair Solas. Once he does, you will be able to discuss your boon with him."

Lanethran lapsed into silence. Neither he nor the other high elves seemed inclined to speak, and Ridmark did not press them. Truth be told, it appeared that his request had thrown the high elves into a morose, contemplative mood. Was his arrival an omen for the high elves? It seemed unlikely, but stranger things had happened since the omen of blue fire had filled the sky.

They waited in silence, and about ten minutes later the sound of hoofbeats rang against the causeway. A rider appeared, leading two other horses, and reined up behind Lanethran and his men. The rider was another bladeweaver, wearing the same golden armor, and she reached up and removed her winged helmet.

Ridmark found himself looking at the ageless face of Rhyannis.

She had not changed at all since he had seen her last at Urd Morlemoch a year and a half past. Her features were too angular and sharp to be human, her large eyes like shimmering golden coins. She was beautiful, but it was a terrible, alien beauty, like the beauty of the stars or a frozen stream in winter. A man could look upon the stars and admire their beauty, but he could not desire them.

"My lady Rhyannis," said Ridmark.

"Lord Ridmark, Keeper Calliande," said Rhyannis, her voice more melodious than any human tone. "It pleases me to see you again, but I fear what your return means."

"Why is that?" said Ridmark.

"Because it means that the hour of decision and fate is upon the remnant of the high elves," said Rhyannis, "just as Ardrhythain saw in the shadows of your future before you set out from Castra Marcaine. And because whatever happens next, you will face great pain and greater peril."

"From the sword of the Dragon Knight?" said Ridmark.

"From the dangers that the sword will reveal within you," said Rhyannis.

Ridmark wondered what that meant. It did not sound reassuring.

"Please, come with me," said Rhyannis. "The archmage has not yet returned, but he should arrive before nightfall. Quarters have been prepared for you, and you can refresh yourselves until the archmage arrives."

She beckoned to the horses. Ridmark took one, and Calliande claimed the other.

The three of them rode along the causeway, the towers of Cathair Solas rising ever higher over them.

The interior of Cathair Solas was even more bewildering than the exterior.

It was just as well that Rhyannis was there to guide them, Calliande thought. Had she tried to navigate the clockwork stone maze of Cathair Solas herself, she would have been hopelessly lost within five minutes. As it was, Rhyannis led them unerringly through the city's gate, up a series of ramps, and down a long, narrow stone bridge as the towers kept turning around them.

All the while, Calliande tried not to gape. The sights of Cathair Solas alone were splendid. The moving towers dominated the scene, but she also saw lush gardens filled with vibrant flowers, despite the ring of mist that blocked most of the sunlight. There were statues of stunning beauty, images of high elven men and women in armor or robes, some of them holding swords, other staffs.

But all that was nothing compared to the magic that blazed before her Sight like letters of fire.

Cathair Solas might have been a feat of stupendous engineering, but the magical prowess that had gone into the city's creation defied Calliande's ability to understand. Compared to the spells that shone within the city, the powers of the Keeper were the crude skills of a child. Mighty warding spells layered the city, protecting it from physical and magical assault. Spells of elemental fire and earth powered the revolution of the smaller towers around the central tower, the spells making colossal rings of stone and gears of high elven steel slide around each other as smoothly as melted butter. Each one of the towers had been attuned to a different one of the thirteen moons, the power of the spells upon it waxing and waning as the moons spun in their course around the world.

The city was the last relic of the mighty civilization that had once ruled this entire world long before Malahan Pendragon had ever come to Tarlion, perhaps long before the first man and woman had been called into existence on Old Earth. This was an old, old world, and the entirety of human history seemed but a droplet of water in the abyss of time that Cathair Solas had seen.

Rhyannis to Ridmark to his rooms, and then Calliande to hers. The apartment that Rhyannis led her to was in one of the outer towers, overlooking the lake, and it was palatial. The high windows overlooked the calm blue waters, and there were comfortable chairs and a bed. There was also an enormous bathtub filled with steaming water, and despite her dread and the urgency of their mission, a ripple of pleasure went through Calliande at the sight of it.

Three high elven women in gowns of white and green took her clothes, and Calliande lowered herself into the hot water with a sigh. A ripple of guilt went through her, mingling with her dread of what lay ahead. While she bathed herself in comfort, the High King and his army marched to war against the Frostborn. Antenora and Third had to be worried horribly about what had become of Calliande and Ridmark. Calliande ought to have been with them, lending her powers to the defense of the realm against the Frostborn.

Instead, she was here, in a pleasant hot bath.

At the moment, there was nothing she could do for her friends. The only way to help them was to retrieve the sword of the Dragon Knight and bring its power to bear against the Frostborn. And the only way to do that was to help Ridmark to claim the sword without its magic destroying him from the inside out.

Calliande tried to relax as she washed her hair and her limbs. The high elven women returned with towels and her clothes, and Calliande thanked them. As she got dressed, she realized that the high elves had brought her a different set of clothes – boots and trousers and a leather jerkin, the sort of clothes she usually wore while traveling, and she donned them with gratitude. Slogging through the forests of the island while wearing a long skirt had been difficult. How had the high elves known? Of course – she had been wearing similar clothing the first time she had come here two hundred and twenty years ago. To her that seemed like an unfathomably long time.

To the high elves, it was likely no different than a long afternoon.

"Lord Ridmark awaits you beyond, Keeper of Andomhaim," said one of the high elven women. Calliande thanked the woman and followed her into the next room. It was a large dining room, dominated by a long table of polished wood, high windows overlooking the lake and the rocky cliff wall of the caldera. Plates of food had been laid out on the table, and Ridmark sat by them, eating and drinking. He had bathed and shaved, and she thought he looked starkly handsome outlined by the lake, his black-hair close-cropped, his eyes bluer than the lake itself.

He rose to his feet. "I should have waited for you."

Calliande laughed. "No." She kissed him on the cheek and then sat down, and he followed suit. "Neither one of us has had a proper meal for days. It would have been cruel to make you wait." Despite her fear, she was ravenous, and the high elves set a fine table.

For a while, they ate in silence.

"The sword of the Dragon Knight," said Ridmark. He had not eaten all that much, Calliande had noticed. As if he had wanted to keep his wits clear for a battle. "Where will the high elves have stored it?"

"I don't know," said Calliande. "The last time I was here, Ardrhythain took us to the Hall of the Seers in the main tower. It was full of relics and artifacts from the history of the high elves. The sword was lying on a stone table. One by one the knights tried to take it…and it killed them one by one."

Ridmark nodded. He looked as he did before a battle, Calliande noticed, grim and focused and intense. That was good. Perhaps if he was ready to fight whatever the sword would try to do to him, he might be able to overcome it.

"Do you know what kind of challenge the sword posed to the knights?" said Ridmark. "Did it trap them within a dream, like the Warden tried to do to us?"

"I don't know," said Calliande again, trying not to let her fear and frustration show. "Ardrhythain said only that the sword would test them, and that they had to submit the test willingly. Each knight held the sword, and then fire burst from it, flowed through their veins, and burned out their hearts. Some of them held it for longer, others for less time. Kalomarus held it the longest of all, and in the end, he mastered it, though he refused to speak of what he had seen."

"Did the sword speak to him in his dreams?" said Ridmark.

"If it did, he never spoke of it to me," said Calliande. "When I asked him about it, he either said the matter was too painful to discuss, or that it should only be discussed with someone who had undergone the ordeal because no one else would ever understand." She gave an irritated shake of her head. "He was stubborn like that. And he had a rough side to his tongue like you wouldn't believe, and sometimes he drank so much he made Camorak look like a man under a vow to abstain from spirits. Yet he was one of the bravest men and the best fighters I ever knew." She sighed. "He and Marius the Watcher and all the others…God and the saints, Ridmark. So many people have died to bring me here."

"That's not strictly accurate," said Ridmark. He broke off another piece of bread. "It's been nearly two and a half centuries. You didn't get your friends killed. They would have all died of old age a long time ago."

"That doesn't make me feel any better," said Calliande. "They are still dead."

"True," said Ridmark. "But at least their deaths are not on your conscience."

"No," said Calliande. "I should have pressed Kalomarus harder for an answer, Ridmark. Or at least I should have secured the sword of the Dragon Knight in a place where it would have been easier to find."

"You had your reasons," said Ridmark.

"I did," said Calliande. "The sword was too dangerous, too powerful. There wasn't anywhere safe in Andomhaim to store it. It was the same reason I hid my staff in Dragonfall. I couldn't have left it in Andomhaim. Shadowbearer would have found the sword and the staff, and even if he couldn't use them, he would have made sure that they couldn't be used against him."

"And they were used against him," said Ridmark. "Tymandain Shadowbearer is dead."

"Little good it did us," said Calliande.

"Tymandain Shadowbearer is dead, the Enlightened of Incariel have been destroyed, and we are fighting the Frostborn," said Ridmark. "We haven't defeated the Frostborn, yes, but neither is their victory assured. All of that happened because of your foresight and sacrifice. You cannot blame yourself because things did not turn out perfectly."

Calliande blinked at him, and then she laughed.

"What?" said Ridmark.

"I once heard that husbands and wives have the same conversations over and over for all their lives," said Calliande. "Is this going to be one of the conversations we repeat endlessly? The one where we try to persuade the other not to blame themselves for things beyond our control?"

"Perhaps," said Ridmark. "I look forward to finding out."

"You do?" said Calliande. Sometimes it seemed like he could look right through her with a glance, to see through the serene mask of the Keeper to realized how frightened she was beneath it.

"I do," said Ridmark.

"I don't know what's come over me," said Calliande. "I never used to talk about myself this much."

"No," said Ridmark. "Likely because you had no one to talk to about your heart."

"I didn't," admitted Calliande. "Not before you."

A deep wave of affection went through her, and she wanted to get up and have him take her in his arms. She loved him as much as she had ever loved anyone, and she wished more than anything that they could leave all their responsibilities behind and go live together quietly.

But she could not, and neither could Ridmark.

And if he was killed because she had brought him here, because her bad decisions had brought them to this point...

No, she couldn't think about that. If she thought about it too much, she might fall apart, and the Keeper of Andomhaim had to remain calm.

She started to say something, and the door swung open.

Rhyannis returned, still in her golden armor, though her winged helmet was tucked under her left arm. The curved soulblades hung in their sheaths at her belt, the soulstones worked into the tang of the blades occasionally giving off flashes of white light visible through the mouth of the scabbard.

"Lady Rhyannis," said Ridmark.

"Keeper of Andomhaim, Lord Ridmark," said Rhyannis. She gazed at him for a moment. "I remember when you ventured into the Warden's power to rescue me from my own folly."

"Perhaps I was the greater fool," said Ridmark. "I escaped him once, and then returned of my own will."

"Perhaps," said Rhyannis with a ghost of a smile. "But I was struck by your boldness then. I hope that boldness is with you still. For if you truly seek to claim the sword of the Dragon Knight, then you will need all your strength and all your valor."

A cold chill settled into Calliande's chest. "Ardrhythain has returned?"

"He has," said Rhyannis. "He awaits you in the Hall of the Seers, and he has asked me to bring you to him at once. This way, please."

CHAPTER NINE

OLD BATTLEFIELDS

Prince Cadwall Gwyrdragon set a hard pace, driving his men and his horses north along the Moradel road, and Gavin followed them.

Before leaving Aranaeus, he had never been that good with horses. He had known how to ride, of course, since he had grown up helping the villagers to farm and it was impossible to work on a farm and not acquire some knowledge of horses. Nevertheless, when he had set out with Ridmark and Calliande and the others on the quest of Urd Morlemoch, he had not been a very good rider.

A year with the army in the campaign of Caerdracon had changed that, and now Gavin rode with ease, Truthseeker hanging ready at his side in case the Frostborn or their creatures intended mischief. He also had no trouble holding the reins of Third's horse while she scouted ahead. After they had arrived at Tarlion, Prince Cadwall had been unsettled by Third's abilities, but the Prince was too canny of a commander to waste an advantage. Now he was quite comfortable sending Third to scout for enemies.

"You know," said Gavin, once Third reappeared and climbed back into the saddle, "once this is all over, Arandar should give you a title."

"A title?" said Third, nonplussed. Gavin did not often see her taken off-guard.

"In reward for your services to the crown of Andomhaim," said Brother Caius. When Arandar asked Third and Antenora to go with Prince Cadwall, Gavin had volunteered to go with them. He would have preferred to have been guarding the Keeper, but if Third's logic was right, Calliande was in Cathair Solas, and she was probably safer than anyone in the High King's host. So, Gavin would keep Antenora safe, and Kharlacht and Caius and Camorak had volunteered to go along as well.

"My services, while skillfully executed, have been of no consequence," said Third.

"You did go into Tarlion with Ridmark and ask Sir Corbanic to charge the foe," said Caius.

"Thereby helping to turn the tide of the battle at a critical moment," said Camorak.

"Ah, I see," said Third. She smiled briefly. She didn't do that very often. "After our battles together, you hold me in sufficient esteem that you are comfortable teasing me. That is a…pleasant feeling."

"Caerdracon, Arduran, Tarras, and Calvus all need new Duxi," said Caius, "and there are hundreds of small benefices that need new Comites and knights. Why not you?"

"I would make a poor ruler," said Third. "I would execute any malefactors as a matter of efficiency."

Kharlacht snorted. "There are worse ways to go about it."

"I have no desire to rule, nor for lands or power," said Third. "I was made for battle and assassination. For centuries, I used those skills in my father's service, and now I am very pleased to use them in service to a worthy cause."

"Besides, my lady," said Camorak, "you are already a princess."

Third frowned. "I wish people would stop saying that."

"I fear it is true," said Caius. "You are the sister of a queen, and therefore you are a princess. Or a high noblewoman. Perhaps Queen Mara could name you a high noble of Nightmane Forest."

Gavin frowned. "I don't think the Anathgrimm have high nobles."

Camorak shrugged. "They would if Mara told them to have some."

"I shall worry about such matters once the war is finished and we are victorious," said Third. "Should God grant us the victory, I shall return to Nightmane Forest and accept whatever tasks my sister the Queen sets for me."

"What about you, Kharlacht?" said Gavin. "What will you do when the war is over?"

"I shall return to Nightmane Forest and wed my betrothed," said Kharlacht at once.

"I shall officiate, of course," said Caius.

"Of course," said Kharlacht. "After that...I do not know. She has been baptized, so she likely will not wish to return to Vhaluusk. Perhaps we will settle in Rhaluusk. The headman Crowlacht has offered me a place in his warband, should I wish it, and that seems a good life."

"I can think of worse ones," said Camorak. He snorted and waved a hand at the column of horsemen hastening north. "Like this!"

"What about you, Camorak?" said Gavin.

"I will get drunk," said Camorak.

"Obviously," said Third.

Camorak shrugged. "I'll go where the Order of the Magistri tells me. Suppose there will be a lot of work for the Magistri after the war." His bloodshot eyes shifted to Gavin. "What about you, Sir Gavin? You're a young man yet. I keep telling you that you need to find yourself a lusty lass and plant a baby or two in her."

Gavin hesitated, glancing at Antenora. What he wanted, after the war, was to spend more time with Antenora. To kiss her and know that she could feel it. But he knew that was impossible. If they were victorious, the curse on her would end, and she would die at last.

"I suppose," said Gavin, "that I'll go where the Order of the Soulblade sends me. There will also be a lot of work for Swordbearers."

"There's God's own truth, my lad," said Camorak. "See, you should go rescue some farm wench from an urvaalg, and then plow her field with..."

Third raised an eyebrow. "Perhaps if you did not consume so much strong drink, you could plow your own fields."

"Ah, well," said Camorak. "No one's perfect. And I am getting older, I fear."

Gavin met Antenora's eyes for a moment, and she gave him a sad smile and turned her attention to her reins.

He knew her well enough to read the twin meanings in her expression.

First, she knew they could never be together as they wished.

Second, all this talk of the future after the war was a way to distract themselves from the coming battle. The Frostborn were coming with all their power, and despite the High King's preparations and allies, the Frostborn might win.

And then they would all die together.

Gavin tried to put such thoughts from his mind, but they haunted him as he rode north.

A few days later, they came within sight of the walls of Dun Calpurnia.

A chill went down Gavin's spine as he looked at the ruined town. He had been thinking about the possibility of defeat, but the loyalists had almost been defeated here, and Gavin himself had almost been killed several times.

A lot of good men had been killed during the battle.

Dun Calpurnia had been a strong town with stout fortifications. The town occupied a hill about a mile and a half from the broad expanse of the River Moradel, its castra crowning the hill. A stone wall studded with watch towers and siege engines had encircled the town. High King Uthanaric had originally marched here to meet the Mhorites in battle, and the walls of Dun Calpurnia would have held against the entirety of Mournacht's host. Gavin was not sure how long it would last against the Frostborn.

He supposed he was going to find out in short order.

Assuming, of course, that they could take Dun Calpurnia in the first place.

The wall and the gates and the castra were intact, though the town itself lay in ruins. It had been abandoned after Uthanaric's death since Arandar and the loyalists had not been able to spare any forces to hold it. The townspeople had either fled south with Arandar's army or into Nightmane Forest to shelter with Queen Mara and the Anathgrimm. At some point, a fire must have raged through the town, because half the houses were empty stone shells, and Dun Calpurnia's fine stone church had half-collapsed into ruin.

The sight made Gavin sad. Once Dun Calpurnia had been prosperous, and now it was a ruined shell.

He supposed the same thing would happen to Andomhaim if the Frostborn were not stopped.

Right now, he needed to focus on the problem at hand, so he looked at Dun Calpurnia with an eye grown experienced in sieges. The town's southern gate was closed, and he saw figures patrolling the ramparts of the town. It was hard to tell from this distance, but he thought medvarth warriors patrolled the walls, along with some cogitaers. A few locusari scouts flew back and forth overhead, though they hadn't dipped low enough to engage the horsemen. The enemy had to know that Prince Cadwall's horsemen were here...and they had to know that Prince Cadwall's force had no way of getting inside a fortified wall.

Or so they thought.

"Medvarth, locusari, and a few cogitaers," said Sir Valmark Arban, shading his eyes as he examined the town. "Can't see any Frostborn, but they may be within the castra itself."

"I don't believe there are any siege engines left on the towers of the castra," said Sir Constantine Licinius, standing next to Gavin and Valmark. "If we can get into the walls, we shouldn't have to worry about any missile fire from the castra."

"It is the revenants that worry me," said Cadwall, his voice grim as he considered the town.

"Revenants?" said Gavin. They had not encountered any of the Frostborn-created undead on the march north.

"There were thousands of corpses after the battle," said Cadwall, "and not enough time to burn them all. At Dun Licinia, the Frostborn raised the Mhorite and dvargir dead and added them to their army as revenants. There might be only a few hundred medvarth and khaldjari within the town, but there could be thousands of revenants within the ruined houses." He snorted. "I suppose the Frostborn could stack them like firewood."

"The Keeper's spell will protect us from their freezing touch," said Gavin, glancing at the hilltop where Calliande had cast the great spell.

"Aye," said Cadwall, "but we can still be swarmed by thousands of dead men who feel neither fear nor pain." He leaned back in his saddle with a grunt, brushing some dust from his gleaming bracers. "Well, we shall know soon enough."

As it happened, they only had to wait another quarter hour or so. Blue fire swirled in front of the horses, and Third stepped out of the flames, breathing hard and sweating a little. Antenora handed her a skin of watered wine, and Third nodded her thanks and drained half of it in a single swallow, like an exhausted swordsman after a difficult bout of training.

"My lady Third," said Cadwall. "What do you see?"

"I estimate the town is held by approximately five hundred enemy warriors," said Third. "Mostly medvarth and locusari, with some khaldjari. There are no Frostborn within the walls that I could find. There are a group of three to five cogitaer sorceresses, and I suspect they are in command within the walls."

"Did you see any revenants?" said Cadwall.

"None," said Third.

Cadwall frowned. "None? Are you sure?"

"I am certain, lord Prince," said Third. "I fought revenants many times with the Anathgrimm, and I know what they look like. For that matter, they are difficult to conceal, thanks to the blue fire in their eyes."

"True," conceded Cadwall, mulling this over. "And you didn't see a single revenant?"

"Not a single one," said Third. "Should there be revenants in the town?"

"This was where Tarrabus Carhaine betrayed and murdered the High King's father, and where the Anathgrimm rescued us from the Frostborn," said Gavin. He supposed that Third had still been an urdhracos at the time. "Many men and orcs and medvarth and khaldjari were slain. The Frostborn could have easily raised thousands of revenants from their corpses."

"Mayhap they did, Sir Gavin," said Caius, "and sent the revenants to hold their forts on the eastern bank of the Moradel. The revenants are dangerous but limited, and they would make ideal garrison troops, especially with a khaldjari or a cogitaer to command them."

"True," said Cadwall.

"The Frostborn know we are here, my lord Prince," said Constantine, "but save for their locusari and their drakes, they do not have any forces capable of moving at the speed of our horsemen, even our heavy horsemen. It is possible we have arrived at Dun Calpurnia before they could react, especially if they fear action from the Anathgrimm."

"Your counsel is sound, Sir Constantine," said Cadwall. "Very well. We shall continue with our original plan. Swordbearers, make ready to attack as soon as the gate is open. Lady Antenora, Lady Third, are you ready to proceed?"

"I am," said Third. She wiped some sweat from her forehead. "Antenora?"

"I am prepared," said Antenora.

"Be careful," said Gavin.

"I shall," said Antenora.

Gavin watched as Third and Antenora left the horsemen, creeping towards the wall of Dun Calpurnia. Third moved with the silence of a spirit, but Antenora was quite stealthy herself when she put her mind to it. No doubt there had been ample opportunity to hone her skills in stealth during the long centuries of war on Old Earth. He wished he could have gone with her, but it was impossible. Third's power let her transport someone with her over a short distance, but she couldn't transport anyone carrying a soulstone, and Truthseeker had a soulstone worked into its blade.

The plan was simple. Third would transport herself and Antenora into the gatehouse. Antenora would use her spells to seal off the room with the control mechanism for the gate, and Third would open it. Then Cadwall's horsemen would charge into the town, and the Swordbearers would hasten to secure the gate before the enemy could overwhelm Third and Antenora.

It ought to work. It was a variant of the same plan that Arandar had used to end the siege of Castra Carhaine and take the fortress. Gavin just hoped that it worked here.

Third and Antenora soon vanished from sight, thanks to their dark clothing, and Gavin did not see the flash of blue fire when Third drew upon her power. Hopefully, the guards upon the walls had not seen any flash as well. Gavin waited with the others, his fingers tapping against Truthseeker's pommel, his whole mind and body tense for the onset of battle. He had once heard an old man-at-arms say that the waiting before the fight was the hardest part of all, that moment of tension and fear that seemed to stretch for eternity. Gavin understood his point, but wasn't sure he agreed – not getting killed in the fight certainly seemed much harder!

Nevertheless, he did not enjoy the waiting. It felt like an eternity of tension, though he knew it would take no more than a few moments. One way or another, the situation would be resolved soon…

A clang rang from the walls of Dun Calpurnia, capturing Gavin's attention. An instant later a bloom of yellow-orange flame erupted from several of the windows on the western gate tower. Antenora and Third had opened the gate, and they were fighting to hold it.

"Now!" said Cadwall. "Sound the charge! For God and the High King!"

One of Cadwall's standardbearers blew the charge, and a shout rose from the knights. Gavin put his spurs to his horse and drew Truthseeker, the blade flashing white in the noon sunlight. The ground rumbled as the horsemen surged forward, but the twenty Swordbearers who had accompanied Cadwall were the head of the spear. The medvarth and khaldjari on the ramparts scrambled, and Gavin saw the medvarth raising javelins, while the khaldjari lifted their deadly crossbows.

"Shields!" shouted Gavin, raising his own shield of dwarven steel to cover his body. "Shields!"

The cry went up from the other Swordbearers and knights, and they lifted their shields as the medvarth hurled their javelins and the khaldjari fired their crossbows. A knight screamed as a javelin hit him in the chest and hurled him from his saddle. The javelin might have dealt a mortal wound, but if it hadn't, the stamping hooves of the other horsemen would. More crossbow quarrels landed in their midst, the scream of wounded men coming to Gavin's ears. A quarrel clanged off his shield and bounced away, the shock from the impact shooting up his left arm and shoulder. For all that he worried about Antenora, the truth of the matter was that he was more vulnerable than she was. A crossbow quarrel to the chest would irritate her. A crossbow quarrel to the chest would kill him.

Then they were through the gate, galloping into a broad forum lined with ruined shops and burned taverns. Gavin turned his horse hard to the left, riding into the street between the town proper and its defensive wall. Around him, the other Swordbearers reined up, and Gavin leaped from the saddle, Truthseeker flashing in his hand. The rest of the knights thundered into the forum. Some headed for the road climbing to the castra, others headed to secure the northern gate, and other groups dismounted and charged onto the ramparts, intending to sweep them of enemy soldiers.

Gavin ran to the towers of the gate and kicked open the door.

Smoke stung his eyes, and he saw small fires burning here and there on the floor and walls. Several dead khaldjari lay before him, some of them burned beyond recognition. The creatures looked a great deal like dwarves, with the same bulky build, the same low height, and the same granite-colored gray skin. Their eyes glowed with the same harsh white-blue as their Frostborn masters, though death had darkened their eyes.

Gavin dashed up the stairs, Sir Valmark and Sir Constantine and the other Swordbearers following. He ran through one tower room, and then another, and came to a wooden door that led to the narrow room over the gate itself that housed the machinery for opening and closing the doors. The door had been blasted off its hinges, and lay smoking on the floor.

Gavin darted through the door and into the midst of a battle.

Third and Antenora stood back to back in the center of the room, Third's short swords covered with the dark red blood of the medvarth, Antenora's staff burning with elemental fire. Five hulking medvarth encircled them, axes and swords in hand, their jaws snapping and frothing with rage. Gavin always thought that the medvarth looked like bears that walked as men, though unlike actual bears, they could hold weapons, and they wore armor, massive coats of chain mail as large as tents.

Antenora hurled a gout of fire at the medvarth, and they reeled back, raising their arms to shield their faces. Another medvarth lunged at her, and Third intercepted the creature, blue swords blurring, and the medvarth reeled back with a scream of rage.

Gavin charged into the fray, Truthseeker drawn back to strike, and plunged the sword into the back of the wounded medvarth. The warrior's scream of rage turned into a dying gurgle, and Gavin ripped the soulblade free and turned to face the others. A second medvarth hammered an axe at him, and Gavin caught the blow on his shield, Truthseeker's power surging through his arm and giving him the strength to stand. He thrust the soulblade, opening a cut on the medvarth's neck, and the creature reeled back. Before it could recover, Third leaped up behind it and opened its throat with a double slash of her swords.

Soulblades flashed as the rest of the Swordbearers charged into the room, and a short time later the remaining medvarth warriors were dead.

"Well done, Lady Third," said Constantine, lowering Brightherald. "We would have lost many men if we tried to storm the gate."

Third shrugged, wiping the blood from her swords. "If we had to break the gate, it would be of less use against the Frostborn when they march against us."

"True," said Constantine.

Antenora looked at the wall, frowning, her staff still smoldering in her gloved hand.

"What is it?" said Gavin. When she had that expression, she was usually drawing on the Sight.

"Someone is using magic with the town," said Antenora. "Near the castra itself, I think."

"All our Magistri should still be outside the wall," said Constantine.

"Cogitaers," said Third. "We should hasten to the castra at once. The soulblades might be needed there."

"Agreed," said Constantine. "Let us return to our mounts. Hasten!"

They hurried from the gatehouse and to their waiting horses. A steady stream of horsemen came through the gate, and Gavin saw fighting atop the ramparts as the knights and men-at-arms drove back the medvarth and the khaldjari. Even as he looked, a dead locusari warrior fell from the ramparts and landed in the street, bouncing a few times before it came to a stop against the stone shell of a burned house.

"I will meet you there," said Third, and she vanished in a swirl of blue fire.

Gavin and Antenora and the Swordbearers mounted up, and they galloped through the streets, heading for the ramp that climbed to the castra. Gavin remembered coming here for the first time with Ridmark and Arandar and the others as they fled from the ruin of Dun Licinia. Dun Calpurnia had not fared well in the war since, and the town was half-destroyed, most of the buildings burned. Perhaps if they lost the battle, the town would become yet another one of the ruins that dotted the Wilderland, slowly crumbling away into dust.

Then he heard the rumble of a distant explosion, and Gavin turned his mind to the battle.

The Swordbearers rode through the gate of the castra and into its broad courtyard, and Gavin saw a fight underway. Dead and dying knights and men-at-arms lay upon the ground, smoke rising from their bodies. Five cogitaers floated a few inches off the ground before the doors to the castra's great hall. The cogitaers were delicate, even ethereal creatures, and they stood barely five feet tall. Their skin was a pale blue color, and their silvery hair floated about their heads. Each cogitaer wore a simple gray robe, plain and unadorned.

The creatures looked harmless, but they were among the most dangerous servants of the Frostborn. Calliande had said the cogitaers wielded magic as naturally as birds took to the air or fish to the sea, and left unchecked they could cause devastating havoc.

As one, the five cogitaers turned and began casting spells in unison, blue light flaring around their slender fingers.

Antenora acted first, thrusting her staff, and a sphere of fire soared over the courtyard to land before the cogitaers. The bloom of fire washed across the ground and up the walls of the great hall, but the cogitaers stood untouched in a crackling halo of grayish light. Nevertheless, Antenora's attack had given Gavin and the other Swordbearers the time they needed to dismount, and they ran towards the enemy.

A cogitaer pointed at Gavin, white mist swirling around its arms. He couldn't tell if the cogitaer was male or female, and he did not want to get close enough to find out. A lance of ice burst from the cogitaer's outstretched hand and Gavin snapped up Truthseeker. The soulblade shattered the lance of ice into a spray of glittering shards, and Gavin brought the soulblade around in a sideways slash.

Truthseeker sheared through the cogitaer's neck, sending its body to the ground. Third appeared behind a second cogitaer, killing the creature from behind, and the rest of the Swordbearers crashed into the remaining cogitaers. Their magic was powerful, but even the most powerful magic could not stand against the fury of a soulblade.

Gavin lowered his weapon and looked around, but there were no foes left in the courtyard.

###

128 · JONATHAN MOELLER

The battle was over an hour later.

Gavin and the others had gone to assist the men on the walls, but by the time they arrived, the struggle was nearly finished. They swept the ramparts and the streets of any enemies, and the survivors fled through the town's northern gate, hurrying to rejoin their allies in the Northerland. Prince Cadwall declined to have the horsemen run them down. There was no point since the frost drakes and the locusari scouts would report the loss of Dun Calpurnia soon enough.

Prince Cadwall rode into the courtyard of the castra, Caius, Kharlacht, and Camorak with him. Camorak looked tired and grim, but he had spent the afternoon healing wounds.

"My lord Prince," said Sir Constantine. "Dun Calpurnia is ours."

"It was an easier fight than I expected," said Cadwall.

"Perhaps the Frostborn decided the town was not worth the effort to defend," said Caius.

"Aye," said Cadwall, frowning, "but they could have held us up here for weeks if they had been of a mind to do it. If they had filled the town with revenants, it might have taken us days to clear it."

Gavin said nothing. Prince Cadwall made good points. Why hadn't the Frostborn left the revenants from the battle here? Why hadn't they put up more of a fight to hold the town?

Did the Frostborn want the men of Andomhaim to take Dun Calpurnia?

It was a disturbing thought.

CHAPTER TEN

THE THREEFOLD LAW

Calliande walked with Ridmark as Rhyannis led them through the revolving stone maze of Cathair Solas.

The city was silent as they passed through it, the stone rings sliding against each other in perfect silence. Rhyannis navigated the maze with ease, leading them down a flight of steps, across a pair of walkways, up the side of another tower, and down another flight of spiral stairs. They passed other high elves, some of them in golden armor, others in robes of blue and green and gray. All the high elves seemed somber, like mourners at a funeral. Cathair Solas housed the last of the high elves, the final remnant of their kindred, and Calliande supposed every single high elf in the city had seen family and friends perish at the hands of the urdmordar and the dark elves.

At last, they returned to ground level, and Rhyannis led them through the various gardens and orchards that stood at the base of the smaller towers. The central tower rose before them, a massive shaft of white stone, with twin doors of golden metal inside a high archway. Rhyannis stepped to the doors and pushed them, and they swung open.

The Hall of the Seers yawned before them, larger than the Great Cathedral in Tarlion. Instead of windows, the hall of white stone had wide mirrors lining the walls. Sometimes when Calliande looked at the mirrors, she saw her own reflection. But when she glanced again, she saw a forest, or a desert, or a distant range of mountains.

Stone plinths stood scattered around the hall, holding swords and helmets and shields and amulets. Most of the artifacts bore some signs of damage.

"The Hall of the Seers," said Rhyannis. "In ancient times, the Seers of the high elves gathered here and used their powers to gaze into the future, trying to plot the best course for our kindred. Alas, all the Seers were killed in the wars against the dark elves and the urdmordar, and there are none now among the remnant of our kindred. This hall stands as a monument to them," she gestured at the plinths and their relics, "and to those who have died in defense of Cathair Solas."

They walked in silence through the Hall, coming to a dais at the far end. Another mirror covered the far wall, larger than the others, its surface flickering with scenes of distant landscapes. A tall figure in a black-trimmed red coat stood there, gazing at the mirror, a staff of red metal in his left hand.

"Lord archmage," said Rhyannis. "Your guests are here."

The figure turned, and for the first time since Urd Morlemoch, Calliande found herself looking at Ardrhythain, the last archmage of the high elves.

He was over seven feet tall and seemed somehow even taller. His long red coat was open in front, the sleeves and hem and collar trimmed in black. Beneath the coat, he wore a white tunic and black trousers tucked into black boots. His face was alien, thinner than a human's, the ears long and pointed. An unruly shock of night-black hair topped his head, and his eyes were like disks of shining gold. The red staff in his hand had been forged from some metal Calliande had never seen before. It was topped with a ring about the size of Calliande's palm, and something like a star flashed and flickered within the ring. The golden eyes regarded her, and Calliande was struck the age of those eyes, heavy with knowledge and wisdom. Ardrhythain was old, so old that she could scarce grasp it. The Warden and Tymandain Shadowbearer had spoken about a hundred thousand years of war, and she had seen the shattered ruins left by the wars of the dark elves and the urdmordar and the dwarves and the dvargir, each one older than the last.

Ardrhythain was older than them all.

A flicker of anger went through Calliande, and she tried to force it down. All that age and knowledge and power and Ardrhythain hadn't warned them that the mantle of Shadowbearer could pass to another. He hadn't killed Tymandain Shadowbearer himself. He had done nothing to stop the Frostborn.

"Keeper Calliande, Lord Ridmark," said Ardrhythain, his voice far deeper than any human tone, "welcome to Cathair Solas." Rhyannis stepped to the side and waited, as motionless as a statue.

"We were almost not welcomed," said Calliande. "The bladeweavers at the causeway nearly turned us away."

"A necessary precaution," said Ardrhythain. "Tymandain Shadowbearer slipped into the city and stole the soulstone that is the cause of our current troubles. We have no wish for that to happen again." His gaze shifted to Ridmark. "I see you have used that staff well since we parted."

"It has proven useful," said Ridmark.

"With its help, you slew Tymandain," said Ardrhythain. A strange flicker of emotion went over the ancient face, a mixture of relief and gratitude and sorrow. "I had never been able to slay him. He was my match in power and skill, and cunning enough that he never let himself be cornered. But his hatred of you was his undoing."

"Me?" said Ridmark. "Why did he hate me so much? I was barely any threat to him at all."

"Which is why he hated you," said Ardrhythain. "He had plotted for centuries to summon the Frostborn and destroy your realm of Andomhaim, and he had prepared for the same amount of time to kill Calliande and deny Andomhaim the power of the Keeper. Everything moved according to his design, and then at the very last moment, you disrupted his plans, rescued Calliande, and stole the soulstone away from him. It made him furious. For you were one man with neither magic nor a soulblade, and you had hindered his designs. He hated you for it, and his hatred of you led to his destruction at your hands." He shook his head. "If I were to recite the crimes of Tymandain Shadowbearer for you, we would be here for the remainder of your natural lives. Many were the dead avenged on the day you struck him down."

"I thought that was the end of it," said Ridmark in a quiet voice. "The day I killed him. I thought we were victorious, and that the Frostborn would never return."

"As did I," said Ardrhythain. "I thought that Shadowbearer would die with Tymandain. I did not know the shadow of Incariel could claim a new bearer, nor did I know that it could claim another vessel so quickly."

"You...didn't know?" said Calliande, astonished. How could he not have known? "You didn't know the mantle of Shadowbearer could be passed?"

"I did not," said Ardrhythain. "The bearer of the shadow of Incariel had always been Tymandain. From the beginning of this endless war, it has always been Tymandain. He was the first of us to seek power beyond what we already possessed. He was the first to speak to the shadow of Incariel. He whispered to our brothers, and they became the dark elves. He was the one who taught the dark elves to open gates to other worlds, and when they failed him and when the urdmordar failed him, he summoned the Frostborn here to fulfill his purpose. When Tymandain was killed, I thought his curse would die with him. Instead, it passed to Imaria Licinius, and a new Shadowbearer was created, just as deadly as the old."

"Not to you, perhaps," said Calliande, wondering why he had done nothing about Imaria. "Tymandain was your match, but Imaria is not. You could have destroyed her. You could have stopped her. Why didn't you stop her?" More anger leaked into her voice than she would have liked, and she rebuked herself. Shouting at the archmage would accomplish nothing.

"Because I have been stopping her," said Ardrhythain.

"I don't understand," said Calliande.

"As a lodestone draws iron to itself, so does one world gate draw another," said Ardrhythain. "With the world gate open upon the slopes of Black Mountain, Imaria Shadowbearer has no need of another soulstone to open additional world gates. In the last three months, she has tried to open new gates near Tarlion, Cintarra, Coldinium, and central Durandis. Had those gates opened, the Frostborn would have been able to send additional armies to our world. Fortunately, forced her to break off the casting, and I chased her through the threshold. So far, she has always retreated to the stronghold of the Frostborn at Black Mountain. Even I dare not go there, for the combined power of the Frostborn in their citadel would be too much for me to overcome."

"Then you have been trying to stop her," said Calliande, chilled. More world gates? She hadn't even considered the possibility. Their entire strategy had been centered around pushing the Frostborn back to the world gate and closing it. If Imaria had been able to open another gate and bring forth more armies from the Frostborn, then Andomhaim would have fallen months ago.

"I have," said Ardrhythain. "I have kept her from opening more gates, though I have been unable to kill her. She will not stand and fight, knowing that I can defeat her in a magical battle, and the power of the shadow of Incariel gives her the ability to flee anywhere. If she is to be defeated, I fear it will not be at my hand."

"No," said Calliande. "Which…is the reason we are here, I believe."

"The preparations you made long ago," said Ardrhythain. "Should the Frostborn threaten your realm again. And if you could not stop their return, if you could not keep Shadowbearer from opening the gate to this world once more, you laid a second plan. A way to retrieve a powerful weapon to wield against the Frostborn."

"Yes," said Calliande. She looked at Ridmark.

"When I rescued Lady Rhyannis from Urd Morlemoch," said Ridmark, "you promised me a boon in return."

"I did," said Ardrhythain. "Nor have you collected on this boon."

"The time has come," said Ridmark. He took a deep breath. "For my boon, I ask to wield the sword of the Dragon Knight."

They stood in silence for a moment.

"Then the hour of doom has come at last, lord archmage," said Rhyannis.

"So it has," said Ardrhythain. "So it has." He looked at the younger high elf. "Go and call the Captains together. War has come to Cathair Solas, and the final remnant of our people shall need to fight or perish with the rest of this world." Rhyannis bowed and left the dais.

"Does this fulfill a prophecy?" said Calliande. Lanethran had said something similar at the causeway.

"In a way," said Ardrhythain. "The Seers were the true prophets among us. Yet all the high elves can see the flow of time to some extent. Do you recall what I said to you about the nature of time on the day we met, Ridmark Arban?"

"I do," said Ridmark. "You said that the past was like stone, frozen and immutable. The present was like a fire, flickering and changing. The future was the shadow cast by the light of that fire."

"Yes," said Ardrhythain, "and in the shadows of your future, I saw many things. One of them was a shadow that might lead you to this day, to this hour, when you would ask me for the sword of the Dragon Knight. And in the shadows of Cathair Solas after the Frostborn were defeated the first time, I saw this future. If a second human ever came to Cathair Solas and asked for the sword of the Dragon Knight, the hour of fate had come at last. Either we would, at last, be victorious in our long war against the shadow of Incariel, or we would perish along with every other kindred in this world."

"Then will you give me the sword of the Dragon Knight?" said Ridmark.

"I must warn you," said Ardrhythain, "that the sword's power is terrible. It was not meant for human hands to wield. It was not even meant for the hands of the high elves. The power belonged to the dragons of old, and only they could command it without consequence."

"I thank you for the warning," said Ridmark. "But will you give me the sword of the Dragon Knight?"

"It will try to destroy you," said Ardrhythain. "The sword's power can only be wielded by those strong of will and true of purpose. If you try to use the sword's power for selfish purposes, it will destroy you. It was created to defend this world from the shadow of Incariel. To use it for any other reason will consume the wielder."

"Again, I thank you for the warning," said Ridmark. "Will you give me the sword of the Dragon Knight for my boon?"

"And even if you master the sword," said Ardrhythain, "the cost in pain will be immense." His golden eyes shifted to Calliande. "You saw the toll it inflicted upon Sir Kalomarus. You know what this will cost, and yet you urge the Gray Knight to claim it willingly."

Calliande frowned, but a wave of guilt kept her from answering Ardrhythain. Yes, she knew the danger. She knew it very well. She knew it...and still she was asking Ridmark to take the sword. Could she turn him aside from this course? She doubted it. Once he had decided upon a course of action, he rarely second-guessed himself.

And this course of action might lead to his death.

The dread churned in her gut like poison.

"Once more I thank you for the warning," said Ridmark, "but I ask for the sword of the Dragon Knight for my boon."

Ardrhythain bowed his head for a moment, his eyes closed.

"So be it," he said at last, lifting his face. "Thrice I have tried to warn you away, and thrice you have persisted. Therefore I shall show you the way to the sword. Kalomarus was strong enough to master it, and perhaps you shall be as well. If not, it will kill you."

"I understand," said Ridmark.

"Why?" Calliande heard herself say.

She had not intended to speak, but the word erupted from her lips nonetheless. Perhaps it was watching Ridmark walk so calmly into such mortal danger, which had summoned a storm of rage and dread in her chest.

"A question?" said Ardrhythain.

"Why have you made this so hard?" said Calliande.

"It is not I who have made things hard, but the nature of the world," said Ardrhythain. "I wish it were otherwise, but there are limits to how I can act."

"Why?" said Calliande again. "You've helped us before. You've helped Andomhaim and humanity before. You brought the first Keeper to Cathair Tarlias and had her convince Malahan Pendragon to settle there. You founded the Magistri and the Swordbearers among us to fight the urdmordar. You gave Kalomarus the sword. But why have you stood back and let so many die? You could have told me who I really was before Urd Morlemoch. You might not have been able to capture Tymandain, but the Enlightened were not so powerful, and you could have killed Tarrabus Carhaine and the other Enlightened and saved thousands of lives." She shook her head. "That wretched soulstone. If you had taken it from us after we escaped from Urd Morlemoch, then Tymandain Shadowbearer wouldn't have been able to open that gate, and none of us would be standing here."

"Calliande," said Ridmark, but she kept talking.

"You could have averted so much evil, but you have not," said Calliande. "Why? That is all I want to know. Why?"

She tried to push her rebelling emotions under control, her breath coming faster than she would have liked.

"Our law forbids it," said Ardrhythain at last. He did not seem angry, only...tired, somehow, and sad.

"Your law?" said Calliande, incredulous.

"Yes," said Ardrhythain. "Humans have many laws to govern yourselves, for the law written in your heart is often occluded. Dwarves have many laws as well, for it is in their nature to love order above all things. The high elves of Cathair Solas have only three laws."

"Three?" said Ridmark. "Only three?"

"That is all we require," said Ardrhythain. "Our threefold law is this. First, we must honor God in all things. Second, we must resist the shadow of Incariel in all things. The third law is the most difficult, for we are forbidden from ever seeking power over other kindreds. That is why I have not given you more help than I have, Keeper of Andomhaim. I may aid you. I may offer advice to you. But I may not exercise any power over you."

"That doesn't make any sense," said Calliande.

"Doesn't it?" said Ardrhythain. "For even the least of the high elves are so much stronger than you. You regard a man of eighty years as a wise elder. What is eighty years? A high elf who has not even reached his first century is regarded as a raw youth. Eighty years to us is an idle afternoon. Many things can be learned in eighty years, but how many more can be learned in a thousand or ten thousand?"

A flicker of some strange, alien emotion went over his face, and he stepped closer to Calliande, the end of his staff ringing against the pale stone of the floor.

"You all die so quickly," said Ardrhythain. "Generations of humans come and go like grass upon the field, and the high elves are still there. Your realm of Andomhaim has not even stood for a thousand years, and you consider it ancient. The civilizations of humans upon Old Earth is barely five thousand years old, and you consider that unfathomably old. Five thousand years is but a chapter in the saga of the history of the elves. Have you ever considered how very easy it would be to enslave you all? Humans die so quickly, and every generation must learn anew the truths once known by the previous. If we but killed all your elders, it would be a simple matter to teach your children to revere us as gods. Within three of your generations, we would have trained every single human to worship us, and they would regard any attack upon us as an unspeakable blasphemy."

"Ardrhythain," said Ridmark, but the archmage kept speaking. Calliande found herself stepping back in alarm. Ardrhythain had so much power, but now the full attention of that ancient mind and will was bent upon her, and she found it intimidating.

"For next to humans, we might as well be gods," said Ardrhythain. "You think your Magistri are mighty? Compared to our magi, they are but bumbling novices. One archmage of the high elves could destroy an army in battle. In a day, if I put my mind to it, I could conquer Andomhaim and make your armies as chaff upon the threshing floor. And I should I not do it? Do I not have the right? Look at humanity!"

His eyes were changing, Calliande realized with alarm. The brilliant gold was fading, and darkness was creeping into them.

Like the eyes of a dark elf.

Ardrhythain took another step towards her, and suddenly he reminded her of the Warden of Urd Morlemoch.

"What is darker than the heart of a human?" said Ardrhythain, the darkness in his eyes deepening. "You are a kindred of liars and thieves and fornicators and murderers. Your entire history is one of lies and deception and blood, blood without end, and you slaughter each other with wanton abandon. Do I not have the right to bring you to order? Do I not have the duty? If I ordered your lives and governed your nations, I would bring you to order, I would end your crimes and lies and murders, and I would…"

He stopped talking and closed his eyes, taking a deep breath. Calliande realized that she held her magic ready, that Ridmark gripped his staff as if intending to strike.

Ardrhythain let out a long breath and laughed to himself.

"Ah," he said, calm once more. "After so long, the old temptations are still the strongest."

He opened his eyes, and they had returned to a brilliant gold, the shadow gone.

"Forgive me for frightening you," said Ardrhythain, "but I think you can see why no high elf, or especially me, can seek out power over another kindred."

"That...was it, then?" said Calliande. "That is what created the dark elves? The desire to wield power over other kindreds?"

"In part," said Ardrhythain. "Tymandain and those he seduced opened the way for the shadow of Incariel to touch us. Every heart has a weakness to evil within it. Among humans, the weakness is varied. Your weakness, Keeper of Andomhaim, is pride. Yours, Ridmark Arban, is despair, and if I may say so, a measure of lust. Among the high elves, our weakness is a love of power and a love of magic. Incariel offers us both. And if we seek to wield power over you, the shadow of Incariel consumes us, and we become one with the dark elves. That is why I did not aid you more, Calliande of Tarlion. I could not. I gave what aid I could when you asked. But I could not do more, for if I did, I would seek to rule you, and I would open myself to the shadow of Incariel. Should I do that, I would become like the Warden or the Traveler or any other dark elven lord. "

"I'm sorry," said Calliande. "I didn't know. Forgive my hasty words...and please forgive that I awoke that temptation within you."

He smiled. "Fear not. You did not put that temptation in my heart. It has been there since long before you were born, and I have lived with it just as long."

"If we must ask you to help us," said Ridmark, "then I ask now. Take us to the sword of the Dragon Knight."

"As you wish," said Ardrhythain. "It is but a short walk from here. As we walk, I must tell you of the true nature of our enemy."

"Shadowbearer?" said Calliande.

"Yes," said Ardrhythain. "The Frostborn are not your true enemy. Not even Imaria Shadowbearer is your true foe. The shadow of Incariel is the true enemy of us all...and it uses both the Frostborn and the Shadowbearer as its tools."

He turned and gestured with his staff. The flickering mirror behind the dais vanished, revealing a gloomy cavern that descended deep into the earth, a pale glow coming from its depths.

"Come," said Ardrhythain, and Calliande and Ridmark followed him into the cavern.

CHAPTER ELEVEN

THE QUEEN

The patrol rode into the wooded hills of the Northerland, and Gavin looked around him with suspicion.

He did not have many memories of the Northerland, but most of them were bad. The first time he had come here had been after Khald Azalar and Dragonfall, with Mournacht and his host of Mhorite orcs chasing them. Then they had been forced to flee Dun Licinia for Dun Calpurnia as the host of the Frostborn poured out of their world gate to invade Andomhaim. A year later he had returned with Calliande to find Ridmark and the Anathgrimm, and they had walked into Caradog Lordac's trap and nearly been killed.

Gavin hoped this visit to the hills of the Northerland would not bring disaster.

He rode with Antenora, Sir Constantine, and forty mounted men-at-arms sworn to the House of the Licinii. Both Constantine and the men-at-arms were native to the Northerland and knew it well. Some of the men were experienced hunters, and possibly experienced poachers, and knew every back trail and path through the pine-cloaked hills. They made good time, making their way through the hills and past the ruined villages and shattered keeps that the Frostborn and their armies had left in their wake.

The Northerland had been razed. Gavin had seen more burned villages and ruined farms in Calvus and Caerdracon than he would have liked, but many villages had been left intact. Dead freeholders and burned fields could not produce a crop, and Tarrabus Carhaine and his cultists had still needed to eat.

In the Northerland, the devastation was total. The Frostborn had methodically destroyed every village and broken every keep, either slaughtering the villagers or taking them back to Dun Licinia as slaves. Gavin wondered how the Frostborn fed their armies. Had they started farming the valleys near their citadel and the Black Mountain? Or maybe they just brought supplies through their world gate.

Or perhaps they planned to kill off most of the population of Andomhaim, keep the survivors as slaves, and bring large numbers of their other slave kindreds through the gate to repopulate the world?

Gavin didn't know. Hopefully, he wouldn't have to find out. Nevertheless, he brooded on it as they rode through the hills.

He also worried about the complete lack of enemies they encountered.

Soon after Prince Cadwall had reclaimed Dun Calpurnia, Arandar had arrived with the rest of the host, and they had set to work with a will. In short order, the damaged quays had been rebuilt, and large amounts of supplies secured within the town and the castra. Since the town was empty and most of the houses were ruined, there was ample space within the walls to store provisions and house the army. Poor Sir Joram looked more relieved than Gavin had seen him in weeks. Siege engines had been built and mounted on the walls and the towers of the castras, with the portable ballistae manned day and night. The men-at-arms manning the ballistae managed to shoot down two frost drakes before the Frostborn realized the danger and flew higher over the town.

Yet there had been no response from the Frostborn. In the few days after the horsemen had taken the town, Gavin had looked to the north constantly, expecting to see a strong Frostborn force marching south any moment. With the horsemen divided from the rest of the army, they were vulnerable, and if the Frostborn struck fast, they could retake Dun Calpurnia and wipe out the horsemen.

But they did not, and it left Gavin baffled.

It also baffled Arandar and the chief lords and knights. After discussing the matter, they had sent patrols ranging in all directions. Some of Dux Sebastian's men rode east in search of the manetaurs, and others forded the River Moradel and rode west, hoping to find either the dwarven host or the Anathgrimm. Men chosen from the men-at-arms and militia sworn to Dux Gareth rode into the Northerland itself, trying to discover the location of the enemy forces. Two Swordbearers accompanied each patrol, and Gavin, Antenora, and Constantine rode with this one. Gavin supposed they could have stayed in Dun Calpurnia and protected the High King, but the Frostborn had not made any more attempts on his life, and Arandar was surrounded by the most powerful Magistri and the most veteran Swordbearers of the Two Orders. He was as safe as he was likely to be for the foreseeable future.

Besides, Third was with him, and she knew what she was doing.

So, Gavin and Antenora rode with Constantine. Gavin could have commanded his own patrol as a Swordbearer, but he was glad Constantine was here to do that kind of thing. The older Swordbearer had been raised to command, and would one day succeed his father as Dux of the Northerland.

Assuming there was anything left to inherit at that point.

At midday, they stopped at a ruined village. Once it had filled the top of a broad hill, a small keep rising from the center. The nearby hills had been terraced into fields, and Gavin saw the signs of long cultivation in the valley below the town. But the fields were overrun with weeds, and nothing remained of the village except the stone shells of its houses, church, and keep. It was a melancholy sight, and it put Gavin into a melancholy mood. He had seen so many ruined villages that he ought to have been used to the sight by now, but he never was. He had grown up in a place like this, and seeing it reminded him of watching Aranaeus burn, of what Agrimnalazur and her arachar orcs had done.

At least the Frostborn hadn't planned to eat the people of the village as Agrimnalazur had done. Though Gavin still didn't know what the medvarth ate.

He sat with Antenora on the step of a ruined house and ate a piece of bread and a piece of cheese. Antenora didn't need to eat or drink, but still kept him company, which was nice. The other men either ate in groups or explored the ruins of the village, looking for anything interesting. Gavin hoped they wouldn't loot anything. No doubt all the owners were long-dead, but it still would have bothered him.

"I can see why the Anathgrimm and the lord magister held the Frostborn here for so long," said Antenora.

"Oh?" said Gavin.

"In the Northerland," said Antenora. "All these valleys and hills make excellent terrain for ambushes and raids. The Frostborn would have been unable to bring their superior numbers to bear, and the lord magister and his warriors could have attacked their parties one by one."

"That's what he said," said Gavin. Ridmark had spoken a little of the fighting in the Northerland during their journeys to Bastoth and Khald Tormen. "Quick raids and swift attacks. Keep the Frostborn off balance. It must have worked. It's been over a year, and the Frostborn are only now just coming into Caerdracon."

"It is an effective way of making war," said Antenora. "I saw it many times on Old Earth, though I cannot recall all of the wars where I saw it."

"That must be frustrating," said Gavin.

"It is," said Antenora, "but perhaps it is for the best that I cannot recall. Such wars are often savage. Yet they happened time and time again. A larger, stronger army invaded a hostile country, and their foes hid themselves and struck from the shadows. Inevitably the stronger army almost always collapsed in time, though such victories were long and costly and bloody."

Gavin nodded. It also troubled him that there was no sign of the Anathgrimm in the Northerland. Either the Frostborn had indeed walled them off within Nightmane Forest...or the Frostborn had killed them all and razed the Forest to ash. Still, that seemed unlikely. If the Anathgrimm were not a danger, the Frostborn would not have exerted all that effort to build earthwork forts along the Moradel, and according to the scouts, those forts were there.

"I think," said Gavin, "that we..."

"Frost drake!" someone shouted.

They reacted at once. Gavin stood up and stepped into the ruined house, Antenora at his side. The rest of the men-at-arms did the same, taking cover in the ruins. Antenora called her power, her staff starting to glow in the gloom. Gavin hoped that the frost drake and its Frostborn rider would not be able to spot the light from the air.

A moment later he saw the frost drake, a distant speck against the sky to the west. It was flying to the north, and it did not deviate from its course.

The creature vanished from sight, and the men-at-arms came out from hiding.

"I don't think it saw us at all," said Constantine, stopping next to Gavin and Antenora. He had grown grimmer since they had returned to the Northerland. It made Constantine look more like his father.

"It looked like it was in a hurry," said Gavin.

"A courier, then," said Antenora. "A messenger."

"Carrying news of the fall of Dun Calpurnia?" said Gavin.

"Perhaps," said Constantine. "But surely the Frostborn have learned of the High King's arrival by now. Their scouts practically followed us from Castra Carhaine to Dun Calpurnia." He shook his head. "No matter. We have our task, and we shall carry it out."

146 · JONATHAN MOELLER

"We'll drive the Frostborn out of the Northerland," said Gavin.

Constantine hesitated, and then grinned and clapped him on the back. "You cheer me, sir."

"I keep hearing about Castra Marcaine," said Gavin. "I would like to see it." Truth be told, he doubted it would be as splendid as Tarlion, which had been an astonishing sight with its towers and the mighty Citadel of the High King. Yet he did want to see the entirety of the realm he had sworn to defend with Truthseeker. And Castra Marcaine, Gavin had learned, had been where all of this had begun. Ridmark had volunteered for the quest to Urd Morlemoch there.

Imaria Licinius Shadowbearer had grown up at Castra Marcaine. Gavin wondered if there would be some sign of what she would become, some hint that a young noblewoman would be twisted into a monster.

"And I would like to return to it," said Constantine. "Once we've defeated the Frostborn and reclaimed the Northerland, we shall have a splendid feast in the great hall. I hope you shall come, Sir Gavin, and you as well, Lady Antenora. We shall have libations in honor of the fallen and tell of our deeds in the battle."

"Yes," said Gavin. "I would like that."

But he knew it would never happen. If they were victorious, Antenora would be released from her curse, and a natural death would take her at last. The battles to come might well claim Gavin, or Constantine, or perhaps the entire host of Andomhaim.

With that somber thought in mind, he joined the others as they rode from the ruined village and continued their patrol.

Later that afternoon, they walked right into the enemy.

Gavin sat in his horse's saddle, his mind wandering, and then rebuked himself for inattention. Given how fast the locusari could move, he needed to keep his attention on his surroundings. Granted, it was hard to pay attention to yet another rocky hill and yet another stand of pine trees, but that was no excuse for…

"Locusari!" someone shouted.

Gavin's gaze snapped to the trees ahead. The patrol was moving along a path in a valley between two rough hills. The pine forest filled most of the valley, and boulders jutted from the ground. The terrain here was not advantageous for fighting from horseback and was nearly perfect for an ambush.

The boulders did not trouble the locusari warriors in the least.

Something blue blurred through the trees, and then a dozen locusari warriors burst into sight, running towards the path on their segmented legs. Unlike the locusari scouts, the warriors lacked wings and could not take to the air. They made up for it in increased size and strength and toughness, and their scythe-like forelimbs could inflict terrible wounds

The locusari froze, their wedge-shaped heads pivoting as they looked back and forth, their faceted black eyes glittering. Their alien features gave away nothing of their thoughts, and Gavin wasn't even sure that the locusari had emotions. Yet he got the impression that the locusari warriors were surprised to see them.

Then the warriors loosed their metallic cries and charged, raising their scythed limbs to strike.

"To arms!" shouted Sir Constantine, leaping from the back of his horse and drawing Brightherald. "To arms!"

Gavin had already followed suit, pine needles crunching beneath his boots as he charged. He felt heat against his face and neck, and a gout of flame shot across the path as Antenora brought her magic to bear. Her lash of flame swept across two locusari, immolating them.

Five locusari warriors closed around Constantine, Brightherald whipping around him in shining arcs as he kept the creatures at bay. Gavin rushed to join the older Swordbearer, and he crashed into the melee, cutting the head from a locusari warrior even as Constantine killed another. One of the locusari wheeled and tried to drive Gavin to the ground, the bladed forelimbs bouncing off his shield. Gavin shoved, and the locusari rocked back, legs scraping through the pine needles. The locusari warriors had one serious weakness. They were fast and strong, but they were not all that heavy, and it was easy to knock them off balance. Truthseeker sliced through a locusari warrior's rear legs, and before the creature could recover, Gavin killed it.

Antenora flung another lash of fire, setting two locusari ablaze, and by then the men-at-arms joined the fray, swords and maces rising and falling. A moment later the battle was over, the locusari dead upon the ground, either charred black or leaking yellow slime into the dirt.

"Is anyone wounded?" said Constantine, looking over the men, but no one had taken any wounds in the short, sharp fight.

"Suppose it was just bad luck they found us," said one of the men-at-arms.

"They were not looking for us," said Antenora, walking to join Gavin.

"A patrol?" said Gavin.

"Why patrol the Northerland at all?" said Constantine. "At least, why use locusari warriors for a patrol? With the frost drakes and the winged locusari, they can cover a vast distance far more quickly than any forces on the ground."

"Maybe they were looking for us," said Gavin.

"Aye, that must be it," said Constantine. "Or someone else? The Anathgrimm? No, if the Anathgrimm had broken out, we would see far more dead locusari. They must be looking for us, which means that it is time to move." He turned to give orders to his men.

As he did, Gavin saw a flash of blue light in the trees ahead.

He started to speak a warning, but then a distant roar rang out, the cry of an enraged medvarth.

"There is fighting ahead," said Antenora.

"I saw blue fire in the trees," said Gavin. "I think Third is here. The High King must have sent her as a messenger."

Another roar came from the forest, and this time Gavin saw a brighter flash of blue light.

"God and the saints, let us hope that disaster has not befallen Dun Calpurnia in our absence," said Constantine. "You, you, you, and you. Stay here and guard the horses. We will likely need them soon enough. The rest of you, follow me."

Constantine broke into a jog, and Gavin and Antenora and the others followed him. They hurried into the pine trees, and Gavin caught the familiar musky odor of the medvarth warriors, accompanied by the metallic scent of spilled blood. More furious roars rang out, and there was another flash of blue fire.

Three medvarth lay dead upon the ground, their blood spilling upon the stones. Five more medvarth stood in a loose circle, swords and axes in hand, their black eyes glinting with rage, their muzzles pulled back from their fangs in a furious snarl. There were fighting someone, that was plain, but Gavin could not see who. Perhaps Third had traveled away or gone into hiding.

The medvarth turned as the men-at-arms approached, raising their weapons.

As they did, blue fire swirled behind them, and a figure appeared.

It wasn't Third. This woman was shorter, with pale blond hair instead of black. She wore blue dark elven armor over black clothing and moved with the same kind of fluid grace as Third. Before the medvarth could react, she leaped forward, landed on the back of the nearest medvarth warrior, and cut its throat with a short sword of dark elven steel and a bronze-colored dwarven dagger.

She disappeared in blue fire before the dying medvarth fell to its knees, but not before Gavin recognized Queen Mara of Nightmane Forest.

"At them!" shouted Constantine, and they charged into the foe. The medvarth roared and ran to meet their enemies. Antenora hit one of the medvarth with a spell, and the creature collapsed, writhing as her fires consumed its flesh. Gavin struck at another medvarth, dodging under the sweep of its axe and plunging Truthseeker deep into its side. The medvarth howled and then collapsed as the men-at-arms swarmed over it. Constantine struck down a medvarth warrior, and the last creature turned to fight, only for Mara to appear behind it and strike, plunging her sword and dwarven dagger into its neck.

The last medvarth fell, and Mara stepped past it, breathing hard, and she shook the droplets of blood from her blades. She blinked, her green eyes seeming enormous in her delicate, pale face.

Then she saw Gavin, and she grinned in surprise.

"Sir Gavin!" she said, sheathing her weapons and stepping towards them. "Antenora! I am surprised to see you. Surprised, and very glad."

"Queen Mara," said Gavin. "I think we are just as surprised."

"It is good to see you, my lady Queen," said Constantine, sweeping into a proper bow. Gavin wondered if he should bow as well, which seemed odd since he and Mara had been friends long before she had become the Queen of Anathgrimm. Though she was a Queen now, after all, but fortunately Constantine kept talking. "Are you here with the Anathgrimm?"

"No," said Mara. "I am here alone."

Gavin blinked. "The Anathgrimm allowed that?"

"My husband and my captains were not happy with the idea," said Mara, "but it was the only way. We needed to send a message to Prince Arandar, and I was the only one who could make it through the Northerland without getting caught by the Frostborn." She looked at the dead medvarth and shook her head. "Though they came close. I blundered into that patrol, and they started following me. We've had a running battle over the last three miles or so. Then the Sight showed me your soulblades shining like torches, and I headed towards you. Thank you for the assistance, by the way."

"You are welcome," said Gavin, and Antenora inclined her head.

"What news do you have?" said Constantine.

"The Frostborn have built a line of forts on the eastern bank of the Moradel, sealing off Nightmane Forest," said Mara. "The Anathgrimm dare not cross the river to attack because we would be slaughtered. The Frostborn have been moving some of their soldiers across the Moradel into northeastern Khaluusk, but they haven't crossed the river in strength."

Gavin frowned. "That makes sense, I suppose. The High King and his army are at Dun Calpurnia, and that's on the eastern side of the river."

"The High King?" said Mara, blinking. "Then Arandar was victorious against Tarrabus?"

Gavin blinked. "News has not reached you?"

Mara shrugged. "How would news have reached Nightmane Forest?"

That was a good point.

"That I am very pleased to be the bearer of glad tidings," said Constantine. "Tarrabus Carhaine was defeated outside the walls of Tarlion, and the power of the Enlightened broken. Arandar Pendragon is now the High King of Andomhaim, and the entire army of the realm has gathered at Dun Calpurnia for the campaign against the Frostborn."

"Oh," said Mara. "Oh. That is very good news. The best news I've heard for over a year."

"It was Ridmark who beat him," said Gavin. Jager and Arandar, Gavin recalled, had not gotten along at first, but they had later become friends over their shared enmity with Tarrabus Carhaine.

"Truly?" said Mara.

"Aye, my lady Queen," said Constantine. "Ridmark stole into Tarrabus's camp, retrieved the sword Excalibur, and with Lady Third, he fought Tarrabus while surrounded by the dark power of Incariel, yet he was victorious nonetheless."

Mara laughed. "Were you talking about anyone else but Ridmark and my sister, I would accuse you of spinning a tale, Sir Constantine. But I know them, and I am not surprised. Your news is better than mine, I fear."

"What is your news, then?" said Constantine.

"Castra Marcaine has fallen," said Mara, "and the Frostborn are moving south in great numbers. That is why they had the strength to bottle up the Anathgrimm and advance south at the same time. They no longer needed to hold a large force at Castra Marcaine."

"We feared as much," said Constantine. "The freeholders and commoners of Caerdracon have seen scouting parties of locusari warriors and medvarth for several weeks."

"But my news isn't all bad," said Mara. "The southern border of Nightmane Forest is yet unguarded. I have commanded the Anathgrimm to march from the southern boundaries of the Forest in hopes of joining our forces to yours since the Northerland cannot be contested any longer."

"That is indeed good news," said Constantine. "The High King thought to hold Dun Calpurnia and fortify it for the campaign north. The aid of the Anathgrimm would be most welcome."

"And I have another piece of good news," said Mara. "Ridmark and Calliande must have been successful in their mission to Khald Tormen."

"They were," said Gavin. "To both the manetaurs and the dwarves."

"The Anathgrimm encountered a dwarven scouting party," said Mara. "They were still several days away from their main force, but the dwarves are marching through central Khaluusk. They are only a few days from the River Moradel."

"God be praised!" said Constantine. Gavin had seen firsthand the skill of the dwarves in war and seen the terrible power of their taalkrazdor weapons. If the dwarves came to join the battle with a thousand or even a hundred taalkrazdors, it would be a heavy blow against the Frostborn. "God be praised! I spoke too soon, Queen Mara. Today, you are the bearer of glad tidings."

Mara smiled. "We both were, Sir Constantine. Can you escort me to Dun Calpurnia as soon as possible? I might be able to make the journey faster alone. But if I pop up in the middle of a group of medvarth warriors," she gestured at the slain creatures upon the ground, "they might take me off-guard."

"It would be our honor," said Constantine. "We have enough remounts for you to have a horse, though of course you would be welcome to any one of our horses."

"I will be grateful for the help, Sir Constantine," said Mara. She looked at Gavin and Antenora and smiled. "Are Ridmark and Calliande here?"

"Ah," said Gavin. "About that."

CHAPTER TWELVE

ALLIANCES

As he had during the siege of Tarlion, Arandar rode from one end of Dun Calpurnia's walls to another.

Fortunately, Dun Calpurnia was smaller, so the ride didn't take as long. Unfortunately, the town's fortifications were not as formidable as those surrounding the capital, and they lacked the ancient wards that the Keepers and generations of Magistri had woven into the stones. Tarrabus Carhaine had not been able to take the walls of Tarlion, but he would have been able to storm Dun Calpurnia, and Arandar suspected the Frostborn could do the same.

Nevertheless, the ramparts of the walls were wide enough to mount dozens of the mobile ballistae on their ramparts, and the men-at-arms manning the weapons made sure that the frost drakes and the locusari scouts did not descend low enough to cause trouble. Dux Kors had come up with the idea of offering a bounty to any men who managed to shoot down a locusari or a frost drake, and the men-at-arms had responded with enthusiasm.

Dux Leogrance had suggested that Arandar base himself in the town's castra, but he declined. There was too much work to be done, and the castra's hill was steep enough that having messengers ride back and forth would waste valuable time. Plus, Arandar did not want to return to the castra. Uthanaric Pendragon had held court there the final time before his betrayal and murder, and the memory left a foul taste in Arandar's mouth. Sometimes Arandar wondered how much evil might have been averted if he had just found a way to kill Tarrabus Carhaine then and there, even at the cost of his own life.

Well, what was done was done.

The army encamped outside the walls, ready to advance to the attack if the Frostborn showed themselves, or to fall back to the town if they were overwhelmed. Arandar rode through the camps with his lords, consulting with them, Third following him like a silent shadow if the Order of the Inquisition made another attempt on his life. Scouting parties had been sent into the Northerland, and to the east and to the west in search of the dwarves and the manetaurs. Once Arandar had more information, he could decide on a course of action.

Until then, they had no choice but to wait.

As it turned out, the wait did not take long.

Arandar was riding with Dux Kors, Dux Leogrance, and Dux Gareth, discussing the position of the footmen when Dux Sebastian and a group of his knights and men-at-arms hastened to join them. Sebastian looked grim, perhaps even a little alarmed, and a sinking feeling went through Arandar.

He suspected that the host of the Frostborn had been found at last.

"Dux Sebastian!" said Arandar. "What news?"

"The enemy has been sighted, my lord High King," said Sebastian without preamble. "My scouts saw a strong force of medvarth, locusari, khaldjari, and cogitaers march south down the Moradel road, with hundreds of Frostborn in the rear. I believe it is the core of the Frostborn host, and they are coming to meet us."

"What numbers?" said Kors.

"Between thirty and fifty thousand," said Sebastian. "Perhaps more. My scouts did not dare remain long enough to count."

Arandar nodded, thinking hard. At its height, the army of Andomhaim had numbered over fifty thousand men, and that many had marched with Uthanaric when he had left Tarlion. The civil war had reduced that number grievously, however, and he suspected that the Frostborn would outnumber them by a significant margin. Numbers were not everything in a battle, of course. The protective spells of the Magistri could blunt the magical attacks of the Frostborn, and their healing spells could restore men who would otherwise die of their wounds. A single Swordbearer was worth any number of medvarth or khaldjari warriors, and a veteran Swordbearer was a terror on the battlefield. The ballistae would keep the frost drakes at bay.

While numbers did not count for everything on the battlefield, they were nonetheless important, and Arandar did not like the difference in their numbers.

"Has there been any sign of the dwarves, the Anathgrimm, or the manetaurs?" said Arandar.

"None, I fear," said Sebastian.

"Then it seems our options are to meet the Frostborn in battle," said Leogrance, "or to fall back within the walls of Dun Calpurnia and wait for help to arrive."

"Neither choice is a good one," said Gareth.

"No," said Arandar.

"Better to ride out and face the foe," said Dux Kors, frowning behind his bristling gray beard.

"If we do that, we risk losing everything in a single battle," said Leogrance.

"If we retreat within the walls, help might not arrive before the Frostborn crush us," said Kors.

"If the Frostborn are going to crush us within the walls of Dun Calpurnia," said Leogrance, "then they would defeat us on the field as well, albeit far more quickly."

They were both right, but Arandar thought Leogrance had the better grasp of the situation. They could hold out longer within the walls of Dun Calpurnia than they could without, and the Frostborn could not advance further south in large numbers without first taking the town. It reminded Arandar of the situation at Tarlion. Rather than risking an open battle, Tarrabus had built his circumvallation wall and contravallation wall, continuing the siege of Tarlion and holding off Arandar's army at the same time.

Of course, Tarrabus had been defeated.

Then again, Tarrabus could just as easily have won if a dozen things had gone differently. A dozen minor decisions could have changed the outcome of that battle.

Had Arandar already made the choice that would decide this battle?

"Let us wait until the rest of the scouts return, and we have a better picture of the enemy," said Arandar. "The Frostborn might not have equipped themselves for a siege. If they do, we would be better served to retreat behind the walls of the town and wait for our allies. If they come with a siege train, we would be wiser to march forth and attack them rather than letting us trap them within the town."

The Duxi frowned, but they did nod.

"Have any of the other scouting parties returned yet?" said Arandar.

"Not yet, your Majesty," said Sebastian. "They should start arriving tomorrow."

"They'll be barely a day ahead of the Frostborn, then," said Kors. "We'll have to make a decision immediately."

"We will," said Arandar. A thought occurred to him. "Dux Sebastian, did your men see any revenants among the enemy host?"

Sebastian blinked. "Why…no, my lord King. They did not, now that you mention it. It seems a strange lack. Thousands of revenants would have been raised from Dun Calpurnia once we marched south."

"And thousands more raised from the fighting across the Northerland," said Gareth in a grim voice. The people in his lands would have been raised as the undead servants of the Frostborn.

"Then where are all these revenants?" said Arandar.

"The forts along the Moradel, most likely," said Leogrance. "The revenants are dangerous, yes, but they are limited as soldiers. Using them as garrison troops would be the wisest course."

"Or perhaps they are marching behind the main Frostborn force," said Sebastian. "A second wave, as it were."

"If they are, that makes for poor tactics," said Kors. He shook his gray-maned head. "The revenants are easier to replace than living soldiers. Better to use them as shock troops and to screen the more valuable forces. Using them as reserves is just wasteful."

"Maybe one of the other scouting parties will have more information," said Leogrance. "Perhaps..." He broke off, a frown marring his patrician calm. "What are those men doing? They're not supposed to gallop in the camp, not unless there is an emergency."

Arandar followed the old Dux's gaze, and a saw a group of horsemen in the green tabards of the House of the Licinii galloping towards them.

"Those are my men," said Gareth. He straightened up. "Come to think of it, that is my son and Sir Gavin and Lady Antenora. Their patrol is back sooner than I expected."

"There's a...girl with them?" said Sebastian, shading his eyes. "A short girl. She can't be very old. She..."

"That," said Third, "is my sister."

Arandar looked at her in surprise. She was so quiet that he sometimes forgot that she was there.

"Your sister?" said Arandar. "You mean Queen Mara?"

Third almost smiled. "It is her."

Arandar looked at the horsemen, astonished. Queen Mara was here? Did that mean the Anathgrimm were coming to reinforce the host of Andomhaim? But Arandar saw no Anathgrimm among the riders. Mara had come alone? Had the Anathgrimm been destroyed? She would not have left them for any other reason.

If the Anathgrimm had been destroyed, Andomhaim would likely be next.

Yet the horsemen did not have the air of men coming to deliver bad news. They reined up, and Constantine, Gavin, and Antenora walked their horses forward, Mara following them. She smiled as she saw Arandar, and Arandar felt some of his own worries dissipate.

Yes, this had to be good news.

"Your Majesty," said Constantine. "I beg forgiveness for returning sooner than planned, but we met Queen Mara of Nightmane Forest on our way, and she asked us to bring her to you. It would be discourteous to refuse so noble of a lady."

"Well," said Arandar, "we don't want the knights of Andomhaim to develop a name for discourtesy, do we? Well done, Sir Constantine, and well done all of you. Queen Mara, it is good to see you again."

"And you, High King of Andomhaim," said Mara. "Tarrabus Carhaine did great harm to my husband and me, and I am very pleased that you brought him low at last." She looked at Third. "And I am overjoyed to see you again, sister, and am pleased you have come through the battle unscathed."

Third did smile this time. "And I can say the same for you."

"Come with me, if you please," said Arandar. "I think we have much to discuss."

They used Arandar's map pavilion for the discussion, and it soon became quite crowded.

Gavin squeezed into the corner, Antenora next to him. The Duxi soon arrived, as did the orcish kings, and the Masters of the Two Orders. Kharlacht and Caius and Camorak all arrived, and Mara hugged them in greeting. She might be a Queen now, but together they had braved the Iron Tower and Urd Morlemoch and Khald Azalar, and the bonds forged in such a fire were as strong as dwarven steel.

"Before we begin," said Arandar, "I must ask you first. How do my children fare?"

"Well," said Mara. "Prince Accolon has been serving as squire for both Lord Captain Qhazulak and Prince Consort Jager, and I fear he has received quite an education in warfare and the use of every manner of weapon. The Anathgrimm are enthusiastic if demanding teachers. Princess Nyvane has been serving as my lady-in-waiting, though I doubt she has enough to do. I need little care, and the Anathgrimm have no use for ceremony."

"Thank you for guarding them during this last year," said Arandar. "I cannot tell you what a comfort it has been to know that they were in safe hands. But with Tarrabus brought low and the Enlightened destroyed, I think the time has come for them to rejoin me, or at least to return to Tarlion."

"I quite agree," said Mara. "The Anathgrimm are a harsh kindred, and your son and daughter should be with their father and with their own kind. And they will need instruction about the ways of the lords and ladies and knights of Andomhaim. That, alas, is one thing that the Anathgrimm cannot teach. Though Jager has been trying. He has taken it upon himself to tutor the children in the proper ways of a noble court."

"God save us!" said Dux Kors. "We shall win the war, and the crown prince shall be as irreverent and sharp-tongued as Prince Jager." The other lords laughed.

"Well," said Caius, "there are times when a little irreverence is a useful quality in a monarch. Not often, but sometimes. I doubt Tarrabus Carhaine ever laughed at himself."

"Likely not," said Arandar. "Queen Mara, how fare the Anathgrimm?"

Gavin listened as the High King of Andomhaim and the Queen of Nightmane Forest exchanged news. Since Ridmark had departed with Calliande, the Anathgrimm had continued his tactics of quick raids and attacks designed to throw the Frostborn off balance and bleed them behind their lines. At first, it had worked, but soon the Frostborn had been able to throw more and more numbers into the hills of the Northerland. More forces had come through the world gate, and the fall of Castra Marcaine had freed up a great many troops to be used against the Anathgrimm. As the Frostborn built their line of forts along the Moradel, the Anathgrimm had been left with no choice but to withdraw across the river.

It took longer for Arandar to share his news because Caius and Gavin kept interjecting. They had accompanied Ridmark and Calliande to Bastoth and Khald Tormen and had seen the events there firsthand. Between them, Gavin and Caius told Mara what happened in the Three Kingdoms and the Range, and Arandar told her about the siege of Tarlion and the defeat of Tarrabus.

Third told her about the Tower of the Keeper.

"The sword of the Dragon Knight?" said Mara, blinking. "Truly?"

Third shrugged. "We have no way of knowing for certain until the Keeper and the lord magister return. But that seems to be the only reasonable explanation of the facts."

"And Morigna's spirit," said Mara, shaking her head. "That would have been hard for him to see. Especially with Calliande. I wonder if he ever figured out what to do about her."

"In point of fact, he asked her to marry him a few moments before the gate in the Tower opened," said Third.

"Oh!" said Mara, her eyes going wide, a smile going over her face.

"What?" said Caius, flabbergasted. Gavin had to admit that he was surprised. Then again, it made perfect sense in hindsight. He remembered interrupting Ridmark and Calliande's conversation on Smiling Otto's barge and felt a flicker of retroactive embarrassment. Had he interrupted more than their conversation? Still, it didn't seem to matter now.

"You didn't mention this before," said Arandar.

Third shrugged. "There seemed no reason to mention it. The matter is their concern, not mine. But my sister charged me to look after the lord magister before we departed Nightmane Forest, and I believe that included the state of his mind and heart. So, I was obliged to report the betrothal."

"Oh, yes, of course," said Kors, snorting. "That makes perfect sense."

"We shall have to hold the wedding in Nightmane Forest," said Mara. "You'll conduct the rite, of course, Brother Caius. The Anathgrimm are not great cooks, but they do have remarkably potent liquor." Mara seemed to catch herself, shook her head, and turned her attention back to Arandar. "But those are concerns for a happier hour, I fear."

"Yes," said Arandar. "For now, we must prepare to reach that happier hour. The Frostborn are marching behind our patrols in the Northerland. We think they will reach Dun Calpurnia with the bulk of their forces within two days."

Mara frowned. "That is ill timing. The host of the Anathgrimm are three days away in northeastern Khaluusk on the other side of the river, and it will take us at least a day to cross the Moradel itself."

"Then it seems we must hold for that long," said Arandar.

"There is another piece of news," said Mara. "Some of the Anathgrimm scouts encountered an advance scouting party from the dwarves of Khald Tormen. Fortunately, they didn't kill each other on sight, and the dwarves will carry news back to their kings and lords. The dwarven host is several days further west in Khaluusk. I don't know how far west they are – the scouting party would only report back when they encountered foes."

"I see," said Arandar. He scowled at the map table for a moment, thinking.

"Your arrival is most fortuitous, Queen Mara," said Leogrance. "The army of Andomhaim was badly weakened by

Tarrabus's folly. Ten thousand Anathgrimm warriors would go a long way to evening the odds with the Frostborn."

"And fifty thousand dwarven soldiers as well," said Mara.

"My lords," said Arandar, looking up from the table, "it seems that our course is decided. We must stand here and hold the town against the Frostborn. We must hold it until the Anathgrimm and the dwarves arrive to join the battle against the enemy. It is also possible the manetaurs may arrive at any day – Lord Ridmark and the Keeper visited them first, and they have had longer to prepare. If we march to engage the Frostborn in open battle, our enemies might destroy us before our allies can arrive. If we fall back, the Frostborn could destroy our allies one by one."

No one disagreed.

"We will therefore hold the town until our allies join the attack," said Arandar. "Queen Mara, under happier circumstances I would ask you to enjoy our hospitality this evening..."

"But we must wait for those happier circumstances," said Mara. "I will leave at once and return to the Anathgrimm as soon as possible."

"Should I accompany you, sister?" said Third.

Mara hesitated and then shook her head. "No. They will need your help more than I will. As much as I would like you with me, I think your talents would be put to better use here. Keep them alive until I can return with the Anathgrimm."

Third inclined her head.

"If you wish any food or supplies before you go, they are yours," said Arandar.

"Thank you," said Mara.

Arandar hesitated. "And...please give my greetings and my love to my children. Tell them that I shall see them soon."

Mara smiled. "I shall." She bowed and stepped back from the table. "The Anathgrimm have been eager to come to grips with the foe, so I suppose they shall be glad of the news. We..."

A sudden thought occurred to Gavin. They didn't know what had been happening in the Northerland, but the Anathgrimm had been fighting there for a year.

"Wait," said Gavin. "Mara." She was a Queen now, and he should probably call her that. "I mean, Queen Mara. Please wait a moment by your leave."

Mara smiled. "Once you've killed urvaalgs with someone, there's no need to be formal."

Dux Kors snorted. "There's God's own truth."

"Those forts the Frostborn built along the river," said Gavin. "What kind of soldiers are holding them?"

"Medvarth and locusari, mostly," said Mara. "The khaldjari did most of them work. They aren't complicated constructions, just walls of earth and a watchtower of ice, but they are effective. Usually, a cogitaer or a khaldjari engineer is in command."

"But revenants," said Gavin, and the lords shared a look. "Are there any revenants in the forts?"

"No," said Mara, an odd look coming over her face. "There are not."

"Then where are all the revenants?" said Gavin. "There were thousands of dead soldiers after the first battle here, and there must be thousands more from all the fighting in the Northerland. If they're not in the forts, and they're not marching south, where are they?"

"That is a good question," said Mara.

"Perhaps we have been frightening ourselves," said Prince Cadwall. "Maybe the Frostborn haven't been raising the dead as revenants."

"No, they have," said Mara. "Whenever they win a battle, they always raise the dead as revenants. Even when they lose, if they can withdraw in an orderly fashion they raise revenants to take with them. They must have thousands of the things by now...but now that you mention it, the Anathgrimm haven't fought any of them in months."

"Then where are all the revenants?" said Arandar.

Gavin suspected they would not like the answer when they found out.

CHAPTER THIRTEEN

SHADOWBEARER

A cool, dry breeze blew from the depths of the cavern.

Ridmark shared a look with Calliande, and together they stepped through the archway and into the cave, Ardrhythain striding before them. The cave looked little different than dozens of other caves that Ridmark had visited during his travels. The walls and floor and ceiling were rough rock, glittering crystals embedded in the stone here and there. Stalagmites grew from the floor, and stalactites hung from the ceiling like stone fangs. Despite the presence of the rock formations, the cave seemed dry. Dust rasped beneath Ridmark's boots, and the cool wind blowing out of the depths of the earth didn't carry a hint of moisture.

"Do these caverns lead to the Deeps?" said Ridmark.

"Eventually," said Ardrhythain. The light from the archmage's metal staff threw flashes of light from the crystalline chips embedded in the walls. "As you have guessed, this mountain was once a volcano, and molten rock carved a great maze of channels and caverns beneath the mountain, caverns that eventually joined the larger network of the Deeps themselves. When Cathair Solas was built, we located the entrance to the Deeps and sealed it with a gate warded in strong spells, and no one has ever successfully attacked the city from the Deeps."

"Tymandain Shadowbearer did, didn't he?" said Calliande. There was wariness in her expression as she watched Ardrhythain. The discussion about the high elves' threefold law had left her unsettled. Or maybe she was just frightened for Ridmark. He felt the cold clarity that marked a battle starting to descend on him, his fingers tight against the black staff.

Because from what Calliande and Ardrhythain had said, it would be a battle to claim the sword of the Dragon Knight.

Ridmark just wished he knew what kind of fight it was going to be. It was hard to prepare for battle without knowing the nature of the enemy.

"Tymandain entered in stealth," said Ardrhythain. "He came not to attack, but to steal, and he was successful." The tunnel widened, and the pale glow from ahead brightened. "Here you can see where our present difficulties began."

The tunnel opened into a large cavern, and Ridmark looked around in astonishment.

The walls and large portions of the floor were filled with soulstones.

The cavern was as large as the nave of a cathedral, its floor covered in sand, its walls and ceiling rough. Massive formations of milky white crystals grew from the walls and the floor, and soulstones grew from them like fruit hanging from crystalline trees. Each of the soulstones gave off a pale, flickering glow. Ridmark took a few steps into the cavern, looking at the forest of crystals, and on the left and right saw side caverns opening from the main room.

"There are so many of them," said Calliande, looking around with wide eyes.

"Yes," said Ardrhythain. "Though not as many as once there were. Once there were miles and miles of caverns like this, where soulstones were grown with gentle care over the centuries. Now, this is the only one that remains." He gestured at one of the side caverns as they passed. "In there grow another crop of soulstones intended for use in soulblades. Should we survive the dangers to come, in twenty years I will travel to Tarlion as part of the Pact of the Two Orders and forge another thousand soulblades for the Order of the Knights of the Soulblade."

"I saw a place like this once," said Ridmark, remembering. "In the Qazaluuskan Forest. The halflings that call themselves the Hidden People know something of growing soulstones."

"Truly?" said Calliande, startled. "You never mentioned this."

Ridmark shrugged. "It never came up."

"The halflings of the Hidden People learned the art from the Jeweler, a lord of the dark elves," said Ardrhythain.

"I wonder why Shadowbearer did not just steal a soulstone from the Hidden People," said Ridmark. "Surely it would have been easier to steal."

"Such soulstones as the Hidden People grow are not powerful enough to maintain a world gate," said Ardrhythain. "The Jeweler himself only had some of the knowledge we possess here, and the Hidden People only retain a part of his lore. To open a world gate, Tymandain required a soulstone of the highest power." He stopped and gestured at one of the crystal formations.

The formation had been damaged, a crack running down its center, and shards of crystal had fallen to the sandy floor. There was a crater in the center of the crystal, and Ridmark saw that a soulstone had been ripped free with great force.

"That was it, wasn't it?" said Ridmark. "That was where Tymandain got his soulstone."

"Yes," said Ardrhythain. "He took it from this cavern and fled, and that soulstone now powers the world gate of the Frostborn. This is where it began." He beckoned towards another archway on the far side of the cavern. "But, in truth, this war began long before any of us were born. Come with me, and I shall tell you the truth of our enemy."

"The shadow of Incariel," said Calliande.

"Yes," said Ardrhythain. "The shadow that threatens us all."

They crossed the cavern of crystals and reached the entrance on the far wall. Beyond a narrow tunnel sloped into the earth, illuminated by clusters of crystals in the walls. Ardrhythain went first, the light from his staff flickering.

"A long time ago," said Ardrhythain, "long before this world was called into being or most of the physical universe was established, there was a war against God. Your own scriptures speak of it. The rebels were defeated and imprisoned either outside of reality or within various locations within the material universe. One of these rebels was called Incariel."

"A fallen angel," said Calliande.

"A demon," said Ridmark.

"Both terms are accurate, though not all-encompassing," said Ardrhythain. "Suffice it to say, Incariel was an order of life different than our own, older and more powerful and far more intelligent. It is powerful enough that our natural reaction would be to worship it as a god, and indeed, that is how Incariel would prefer to see itself. It is wholly evil and past the point of redemption. Indeed, it is no longer even capable of repentance. To his last moment, Tymandain Shadowbearer had possessed the capacity to turn back from his path of evil, but he never did."

They walked in silence. The wind continued to whisper up the tunnel, tugging at Ridmark's hair and gray cloak. Ardrhythain seemed lost in thought for a moment, but then he kept speaking.

"At the moment of this world's creation, Incariel was imprisoned here, within a physical location," said Ardrhythain.

"The Black Mountain," said Calliande. Ridmark looked at her, and her face was tight with a grim realization. "That's why it was sacred to the dark elves and the dvargir, isn't it? Incariel is imprisoned within that mountain."

"Very good, Keeper," said Ardrhythain. "To be more accurate, Incariel is imprisoned within a small universe that has no access to the rest of reality, and the anchor point for that prison in the material world is the Black Mountain. That is the reason why both Tymandain and Imaria opened their world gates on the slopes of the Black Mountain, but we shall return to that shortly. When this world was created, and Incariel imprisoned here, there were also seven Wells of magic created, Wells that drew upon the great power of the world's own magic. The nearest of the Wells is located within the Citadel of Tarlion."

"Which is why the high elves built Cathair Tarlias and the Tower of the Moon," said Calliande. "To protect the Well."

"Yes," said Ardrhythain. "At first, the only inhabitants of this world were the dragons. They were older than this world, and they guarded both the Black Mountain and the Wells. In time, the elves arose, and the dragons departed, handing this world over to us. Before they did, they left their bones and the sword of the Dragon Knight to use for the defense of the world, since both contained great power. The bones we concealed within Dragonfall. The sword we kept, though we had no need of it, not at first."

"Why not?" said Ridmark.

"Because there was no war among us," said Ardrhythain. "Our civilization covered this world, and we developed our arts and sciences to the highest degree. We lived in power and splendor, but for some of us, it was not enough. They desired greater power, greater mastery, and dominion over other worlds beyond our own. Chief among them was the archmage Tymandain, and it was he who discovered the power in the Black Mountain, and he who drew upon it. He damaged the prison enough that the shadow of Incariel fell upon him, and others could draw upon it as well."

"And he became the first bearer of Incariel's shadow," said Ridmark.

"To our last sorrow," said Ardrhythain. "What happened next, you have likely heard before from other sources. The elven kindred sundered into the high elves and the dark elves, and we warred among each other. The dark elves summoned other kindreds to this world to serve as soldiers and slaves, and sought to build an empire. What they did not know was that they served only as tools for Tymandain Shadowbearer, for Incariel's goals had overwritten his own mind. He had desired power, but now he desired to free Incariel and unleash it upon the world."

"I wondered about that," said Calliande. "What Shadowbearer really wanted. What Imaria really wants. They would both talk about freedom from time and matter and causality…"

"What Incariel desires is to destroy both its prison in the Black Mountain and then this world," said Ardrhythain. "It will then be free to remake our world in its own image, a nightmare of chaos and despair. That is what Incariel wants, and that is what it convinced Tymandain and Imaria to desire."

"How would summoning the Frostborn allow Shadowbearer to destroy Black Mountain?" said Ridmark. "Do the Frostborn know what Imaria intends?"

"The Frostborn, I fear, are dupes," said Ardrhythain. "Powerful and deadly dupes, who left unchecked will conquer this world and add it to their Dominion. Nevertheless, they have been fooled. They did not know what Tymandain planned, and they do not know what Imaria really wants. They think of Imaria as a useful but insane local ally, one that can be eliminated at a convenient later date. They will learn otherwise to their sorrow."

"If the Frostborn are dupes," said Ridmark, "then what has Imaria duped them into doing?"

"The Well," said Calliande. "The Well in the Citadel of Tarlion. That's what this is about, isn't it?"

"Yes," said Ardrhythain. "To destroy the Black Mountain, the Shadowbearer needs two things. First, a functional world gate of great power upon the slopes of the mountain. Second, she needs access to the Well of Tarlion. If Imaria enters the Citadel and claims the Well for herself, she will enter the threshold and channel the power of the

Well into the world gate. The gate will expand to enormous size, ripping open the Black Mountain and shattering Incariel's prison, and the world will die."

They walked deeper into the cavern, their boots rasping against the rough floor. Ridmark remembered what the Warden had said about a hundred thousand years of war. Tymandain Shadowbearer had spent that long preparing to free Incariel from its imprisonment, and now Imaria would follow in his footsteps.

"That was why you unlocked the Tower of the Moon for the first Keeper," said Calliande. "That was why you convinced our ancestors to settle at Cathair Tarlias and found Andomhaim. You wanted them to defend the Well."

"I did," said Ardrhythain. "Your ancestors arrived at this world by accident. So many world gates have been opened here over the millennia that it is now possible for wild gates to open at random. The Keeper and Malahan Pendragon stumbled upon one and used it to escape their pagan foes on Old Earth. When they came here, I thought they might be able to defend the Well, so I sent a vision to the Keeper and showed her how to open the Tower of the Moon. Indeed, you exceeded my wildest hopes. The magical defenses you built around Tarlion kept both the urdmordar and Shadowbearer from accessing the Well, and you broke the power of the urdmordar after centuries of tyranny and bloodshed."

"And that is why Shadowbearer decided that Andomhaim had to be destroyed," said Ridmark.

"Yes," said Ardrhythain. "He summoned the Frostborn to destroy you, both to establish a world gate on Black Mountain and to clear the path to the Well. When the Frostborn were defeated, he decided to poison Andomhaim before trying again, hence the creation of the Eternalists and the Enlightened of Incariel…and the reason you put yourself into the long sleep below the Tower of Vigilance, Keeper, for you recognized the danger when few others did."

"Then that is the whole purpose of Imaria's plan," said Calliande. "Or Tymandain's plan, rather, since she inherited it when Ridmark killed him. The Enlightened were to have crippled Andomhaim from within, and the Frostborn would sweep aside the realm and seize Tarlion. Once Tarlion had been taken, Imaria would enter the Citadel, take control of the Well, and use it to rip apart the Black Mountain and free Incariel."

"Destroying this world utterly in the process," said Ardrhythain.

"Then the shadow of Incariel has been our true enemy the entire time," said Ridmark.

"That is the truth of this war," said Ardrhythain. "That is our true enemy. Everything that has transpired from the day the elven kindred sundered into the high elves and the dark elves to the hour when Imaria Shadowbearer murdered the High King upon the field of Dun Calpurnia. All of it, every battle, everything, has been designed to allow the bearer of Incariel's shadow to seize the Well of Tarlion and use its power to shatter the Black Mountain. And that is why the only path to victory is to destroy the world gate and kill Imaria Licinius Shadowbearer. Perhaps a new Shadowbearer will arise to take her place, or perhaps not. But even if the mantle of Incariel's shadow passes to a new bearer, it will be centuries before the moons are in the proper alignment to allow another world gate to open on the slopes of Black Mountain."

The tunnel went through another turn, and then stopped sloping downward. It began to widen, too, and the white gleam ahead grew brighter.

"Perhaps if we can tell the Frostborn the truth about Imaria," said Calliande, "they will no longer consider her an ally. They might even turn on her."

"It is unlikely," said Ardrhythain. "The power of the Frostborn is matched only by their arrogance. They considered first Tymandain Shadowbearer and then Imaria as unreliable and dangerous allies, but nonetheless useful tools. The thought that Imaria might be using them will never cross their minds until it is far too late. No. If Imaria and the shadow of Incariel are to be stopped, it lies in the hands of the men of Andomhaim. It lies in the hands of the Keeper of Andomhaim." The golden eyes turned towards Calliande. "It will lie in the hands of the Dragon Knight if the Dragon Knight is to be found."

The cavern widened, and Ardrhythain came to a stop and lifted his staff. The light within the metal ring blazed brighter, and at the far end of the cavern, Ridmark saw a pair of doors fashioned from a gold-like metal, framed in white stone that gave off a pale glow of its own.

He had seen glowing stone like that in his dreams as the spirit of Morigna spoke to him and the old knight watched him from the throne. The spirit of Kalomarus himself, most likely, guiding his successor as he came to claim the sword.

"Our destination," said Ardrhythain. "Behold the Tomb of the Dragon Knight."

Calliande swallowed. "That is where Kalomarus is buried?"

"Yes," said Ardrhythain. "He came here after you began the long sleep and entered the Tomb to begin his final rest. For that is the ancient tradition of the Dragon Knights. When the previous Dragon Knight was slain in battle, his body and the sword were brought here to await the new Knight. Those who felt the calling of the sword came to test themselves, and if they were worthy, they left the Tomb as the new Knight."

"And if they failed," said Ridmark, gazing at the doors, "the sword devoured them."

"Yes," said Ardrhythain.

"Did the Knights always bring themselves to the Tomb?" said Calliande.

"Kalomarus was the first to do so, just as he was the first human Knight," said Ardrhythain. "All the other Dragon Knights, all the high elven Dragon Knights, perished in battle and were brought here. Which was why we brought the sword to the Hall of the Seers when you arrived. There had never been a human Dragon Knight, and there was much debate among the magi of the high elves whether to allow it. In the end, we decided to present you with the chance to wield the sword, and you know the results."

They crossed the cavern and stopped before the golden doors. They seemed to give off a faint humming noise. Ridmark looked at the doors and then at Calliande. Her face was tense, and he could tell that while she was trying to put on a calm mask, she was nonetheless frightened.

She was frightened for him.

"Hear me, Ridmark Arban," said Ardrhythain. "Only you may enter the Tomb. The rate of time has been altered within the Tomb as a defense. For every hour you spend within the Tomb, only a minute will pass in the cavern."

"Good," said Ridmark. He took a deep breath. "The sooner I can return with the sword, the soon we can go to the aid of the men of Andomhaim."

Ardrhythain nodded. "Go with God, Ridmark Arban. Your courage will do you credit. Remember that the sword will try to use your weaknesses against you."

"I should go with you," said Calliande.

"You cannot, I fear," said Ardrhythain. "The Tomb will only allow him to enter, for the sword has called him. We must await his return here."

Calliande gave a sharp nod. "Very well." Her eyes met Ridmark's, tense and full of fear. "Please. Be careful."

"I will come back," said Ridmark. He took her hand with his free one. "You've given me the best of reasons to come back."

She closed her eyes and let out a long breath. "Yes, you have to come back. You promised to marry me, and I'm going to hold you to that." She opened her eyes. "I love you."

"I love you," said Ridmark.

They stood in silence for a moment, then Ridmark took another deep breath, stepped back and looked at Ardrhythain. "I am ready."

Ardrhythain struck the doors with his staff, and the deep clang rolled through the cavern. The golden doors swung open to reveal a narrow hall of white stone with a high, arched ceiling. Ridmark took one last look at Calliande and stepped through the doors.

As he did, he heard the heartbeat in his head.

It was the same heartbeat he and Calliande had heard in Tarlion, the heartbeat that had drawn them to the Tower of the Keeper and then to Cathair Solas.

It was, he realized, the heartbeat of the sword of the Dragon Knight

The doors clanged shut behind him with an unsettling finality.

CHAPTER FOURTEEN

THE ORDER OF THE VANGUARD

The war horns wailed from the walls of Dun Calpurnia.

Arandar waited atop his horse before the northern gate of the town, his armor heavy against his shoulders, Excalibur resting in its scabbard at his left hip. Around him waited the Swordbearers and Magistri of his guard. Sir Gavin, Sir Constantine, Kharlacht, Caius, Antenora, and Camorak were behind him, watching the scene to the north. Behind him on the walls of Dun Calpurnia waited thousands of the men of Andomhaim, crossbows and javelins and siege engines ready to rain steel down upon any foes.

He knew that would happen very soon.

To the north, the army of the Frostborn came into sight.

It had been going on since dawn. The scouting parties had come galloping back from the Northerland one by one, reporting vast numbers of medvarth and khaldjari warriors marching down the Moradel road, flanked by locusari and guarded by groups of cogitaer wizards. Arandar and Dux Sebastian sent some of the scouts out again, specifically those comfortable using a short bow from the saddle. Hopefully, the horse archers could harass some of the outlying formations of the Frostborn, though Arandar knew they would only inflict scratches on the enemy.

Scratches were better than nothing.

A score of frost drakes circled and swooped over the gathering Frostborn host, flanked by squadrons of locusari scouts. Had the frost drakes come at the town in a rush, they might have been able to do terrible damage with their freezing breath before the ballistae brought them down, but so far, the drakes had stayed out of range. Perhaps the frost drakes were too valuable to lose in large numbers.

"It appears they are forming up about three miles to the north," said Caius, shading his eyes as he watched the enemy. "Locusari in front, medvarth behind."

"A wise formation," said Constantine, voice grim. "They can use the locusari warriors as skirmishers, while the medvarth serve as heavy infantry."

"The blasted things are heavy enough," said Camorak. "I had to pull dead medvarth warriors off wounded Anathgrimm a few times. God and the saints, but the medvarth smell bad."

"It is too far to see what the khaldjari are doing," said Constantine. "It looks like they are building something, though."

"Siege engines, most likely," said Caius. "They can assemble them out of reach of any engines and archers upon our walls, and then drag them to within range when the battle begins and we're bottled up within the town."

"If the manetaurs and the dwarves and the Anathgrimm arrive while the Frostborn are attacking Dun Calpurnia," said Constantine, "we could inflict a smashing defeat upon them."

That assumed, of course, that they could hold out in the town long enough for help to arrive.

"Does anyone see any sign of the revenants?" said Arandar.

No one did.

Arandar frowned, his hand itching to grasp Excalibur's hilt. Perhaps the Frostborn had held back the revenants as a reserve. Maybe they were manning garrisons elsewhere. Or maybe the dark magic that animated the revenants was a temporary measure and had expired before the creatures could be used in another battle.

He doubted it would be that simple.

There was a pulse of blue fire in front of his horse, and Third stepped out of it, breathing hard, dark blood on her drawn short swords. On reflex, some of the Swordbearers of Arandar's guard reached for their weapons, but Third only cleaned her blades and put them away.

"You ran into trouble, my lady?" said Arandar.

"Nothing of significance," said Third, unruffled. "I traveled next to a pair of medvarth warriors who took exception to my arrival. Dux Sebastian's raids are causing a degree of chaos among the enemy scouts, so I was able to observe for longer than I expected." She straightened up and faced Arandar. "The initial estimations were correct. The enemy has brought between forty-five thousand and fifty-five thousand warriors. Mostly medvarth, locusari, and khaldjari, though there are significant numbers of cogitaers and the Frostborn themselves." She frowned. "I also suspect they are just the first wave, and another large host is coming down the road behind them. Perhaps another twenty or thirty thousand."

A few of the Swordbearers swore under their breath.

"That does not change our strategy," said Arandar, loud enough that everyone could hear him. "We will still wait here for the Anathgrimm and the dwarves and the manetaurs. If they catch the Frostborn against the walls, we will inflict a crushing defeat on them."

They waited, watching the enemy array themselves. One by one the scouting parties returned, some of them with wounded. The Frostborn had gotten serious about ridding themselves of the raiders attacking their scouts. Arandar waited until the last scouting party had ridden through the gates and into the increasingly crowded town. The High King of Andomhaim would be the last man through the walls. It was only a symbolic gesture, he knew, but symbolic gestures were part of the work of ruling.

"Back to the town," said Arandar. "We will await the..."

"What are they doing?" said Constantine.

A group of about twenty locusari scouts had broken free of the main host and were flying towards the town, hovering no more than two or three yards from the ground. The only time the locusari scouts ever flew that close to the ground was to attack. For them to fly so low for so long was out of character.

"They're heading right for us," said Constantine. "We should return to the walls now."

"Wait," said Arandar. "I don't think they're here to attack."

The locusari scouts slowed and landed perhaps thirty yards from Arandar's party, wings fluttering. Arandar felt the black, faceted eyes staring at him, but the creatures did not otherwise move.

"I think they're here to parley," said Arandar.

The locusari scouts began speaking in unison.

"We come with a message for the High King of Andomhaim," said the locusari. Their voices sounded like tearing metal, a ghastly droning shriek, but they spoke flawless Latin without a trace of an accent.

"It seems you were right, your Majesty," said Caius. "The Frostborn do wish to parley."

"And what shall we parley about?" said Constantine, incredulous. "They have already destroyed the Northerland and laid Castra Marcaine waste. What do they expect? That we shall surrender without a fight?"

"I do not know," said Arandar.

The locusari spoke again. "We come with a message for the High King of Andomhaim."

Kharlacht grunted. "Insistent devils, aren't they?"

"It may be a trap," said Antenora. "The Frostborn tried to kill you already. They may wish to lure you to a meeting to slay you. Such things have happened several times on Old Earth."

"Maybe," said Arandar, intrigued. Why would the Frostborn want to parley? They had demanded surrender at Dun Licinia, but Dux Gareth had refused them. "Meeting with the Frostborn would be a waste of time...but wasting time will hurt them more than us. The Anathgrimm and the dwarves and possibly the manetaurs are on the way. The more we delay, the better."

"We come with a message for the High King of Andomhaim," chorused the locusari. It sounded like a score of blacksmiths cutting through a sheet of metal at the same time.

"Perhaps you should see what the message is," said Third. "The locusari lack imagination. They will stand there and repeat their message until they are acknowledged."

"Very well," said Arandar.

He eased his horse forward a few steps, his guards following close. The heads of the locusari scouts swiveled to face him in unison. It was an eerie sight.

"We come with a message for the High King of Andomhaim," said the locusari.

"I am Arandar Pendragon, rightful High King of Andomhaim," said Arandar.

"The High Lord Kajaldrakthor, Lord Commander of the Order of the Vanguard, extends an invitation," said the locusari scouts. "He wishes to meet you at the halfway point between the walls and the host of the High Lords to discuss matters of importance."

"And what matters are those?" said Arandar.

"Matters of importance."

"The Frostborn have waged war against the realm of Andomhaim," said Arandar. "What could we possibly have to discuss?"

"Matters of importance."

Both Calliande and Third and Antenora had said the locusari tended towards literal-mindedness. They had not been exaggerating.

"This meeting may be an attempt at treachery," said Arandar.

"The High Lord Kajaldrakthor, Lord Commander of the Order of the Vanguard, will guarantee your safety for your journey to the meeting, the duration of the meeting, and your return to the town of

Dun Calpurnia," said the locusari. "You may bring up to one hundred guards with you, should you feel it necessary."

"And why would I wish to meet with the Lord Commander?" said Arandar.

"Unnecessary bloodshed may be avoided," said the locusari.

"Since when are the Frostborn opposed to bloodshed?" said Arandar. "They have certainly wrought enough of it during their time on this world."

"Unnecessary bloodshed may be avoided," said the locusari.

"Very well," said Arandar. "I will speak with the Lord Commander. We will depart in a few moments."

"We shall escort you to the High Lord Kajaldrakthor, Lord Commander of the Order of the Vanguard," said the locusari.

"Lady Third," said Arandar. "Please go to Dux Leogrance and Prince Cadwall. Tell them that I am meeting with the Lord Commander to gain time for our allies to arrive. If I am slain, Dux Leogrance is to assume his role as regent at once."

"You are the High King of Andomhaim," said Constantine. "Perhaps you should not gamble with your life in this fashion."

"Perhaps," said Arandar. "But we shall gamble with all our lives in a few hours, one way or another." He turned back to the locusari scouts as Third vanished. "I am ready. You may take us there now." He looked back at the others. "If any of you wish to remain behind, you may do so."

No one left.

Arandar nodded, turned his horse, and followed the locusari as they rose into the air. His guards and companions closed around him, and they rode at a trot as the locusari glided forward, their gossamer wings blurring. As they drew closer to the massive host of the Frostborn, Arandar spotted a dozen towering figures in gray armor striding from the lines of the waiting medvarth.

The Frostborn themselves.

The locusari stopped and landed, and Arandar reined up his horse, the others following suit. He scanned the lines of the enemy host as he waited for the Frostborn to approach. The medvarth had gathered in block-like formations, ready to protect themselves with massive steel shields. The locusari warriors waited in orderly lines before the medvarth, and Arandar glimpsed khaldjari working to assemble catapults and ballistae.

Then his attention turned to the Frostborn themselves.

Each one of them stood eight to ten feet tall, clad in gray armor the color of old, hard ice. Their crystalline skin glittered beneath their spike-crowned helmets, and each warrior carried a massive sword strapped to their back. Blue fire flowed through their veins, visible through the crystalline skin, and their eyes burned with harsh blue-white light, like the sunlight reflecting on a frozen lake in the utter heart of winter. Arandar was struck by the aura of power around the creatures, a sense of strength and potency. He had felt something of the same when he had confronted Rhogrimnalazur in Urd Cystaanl, the same sense of ancient power and terrible strength.

The urdmordar had been malicious and hungry. The Frostborn lacked that malice, but they were cold and merciless and as strong as the winter itself.

Arandar waited, watching as the Frostborn stopped a dozen yards away. Behind him the others shifted, hands waiting near their weapons. He spotted Arlmagnava standing with the Frostborn and felt the cold weight of her attention. One of the other Frostborn stepped forward, a tall male in gray armor, the ghostly fire flickering and dancing within in his veins.

"High King Arandar Pendragon?" said the Frostborn, his voice like melodious thunder.

"I am," said Arandar.

"I am Kajaldrakthor, Lord Commander of the Order of the Vanguard," said the Frostborn.

"Yes," said Arandar. "I assume you succeeded Rjalmandrakur after the Gray Knight slew him upon this very field?"

He wanted to see if Kajaldrakthor would respond to the barb, but the Frostborn didn't even blink. Calliande had said that the Frostborn had little emotion, but instead were ruled by cold and calculating logic that knew neither pity nor mercy.

"That is correct," said Kajaldrakthor. "I was the subcommander of the Order of the Vanguard, so I took Rjalmandrakur's place when he was slain. Should I be slain in battle, my own subcommander shall take my place, and the great mission of the High Lords of the Dominion shall continue."

"Or you could be defeated utterly," said Arandar.

"One defeat is of no consequence in the long-term," said Kajaldrakthor. "Even the most optimistic among us thought it would take a minimum of a century and a half to subjugate this world and bring its kindreds into the fold of the Dominion. An additional year is of no importance."

"Or we could drive you back to your own world and close your gate behind you," said Arandar.

"You shall not," said Kajaldrakthor. "Already we are sufficiently entrenched around the world gate that it would take years of campaigning to dislodge us from our fortifications, and we can bring more reinforcements through the gate on a regular basis. Our ally is able to recharge the gate in a short time after every use."

He beckoned, and Arlmagnava stepped to the side, revealing a shorter figure in black armor.

Arandar kept himself from flinching, but his hand twitched a few inches towards Excalibur's hilt.

Imaria Licinius Shadowbearer took a few steps forward, gazing up at him as her shadow rotated around her feet like a living thing.

When Arandar had last seen her, she had still been wearing the white robe of the Magistri. She had abandoned that for close-fitting black armor of dvargir design, fashioned of interlocking plates of dvargirish steel. The Frostborn had veins of icy fire, but Imaria now had veins of shadow, veins that seemed linked with her armor. Her face was pallid and corpselike, and her eyes were like quicksilver, distorted mirrors that showed a twisted reflection of everything around them.

She tilted her head to the side as she regarded Arandar. The armor on her chest shifted and moved, the plates sliding over each other like shuffled cards, and he had the strange feeling that the armor was alive somehow, fused to her flesh like a living creature.

"The High King of Andomhaim," said Imaria. It was as if two voices were speaking through her lips at the same time. One of the voice of Imaria Licinius, the voice of a noblewoman of Andomhaim. The second voice was an inhuman, twisted rasp, a voice that no human throat should have been able to produce.

"Surprised?" said Arandar. "Were you expecting Tarrabus Carhaine to march forth and grovel before the boots of the Frostborn?"

"Tarrabus was a tool," said Imaria. "He was either fit to serve his purpose, or he was not. This was also true of the Enlightened. They claimed to be strong, but when put to the test, they proved to be weak. By their own doctrines, they were defeated, for they said the strong would rule the weak, and they were crushed." Her eyes gazed at Arandar without blinking, and something about them made his skin crawl. Or maybe it was the way her shadow kept rotating around her. "In the end, they served a purpose, and that purpose has ended. Just as Imaria Licinius was the larval form of Imaria Shadowbearer, so were the Enlightened the predecessor to what is to come. I am the herald of change, the handmaiden of rebirth, and I shall be the gateway for our liberation from time and space and matter."

Silence answered that speech. The expressions of the Frostborn were alien, but from the way they looked at Imaria, Arandar suspected that they had heard that speech many times before.

"A great many words," said Arandar, "to say yes or no. And you didn't actually answer the question, traitor."

"Our ally," said Kajaldrakthor before Imaria could speak again, "opened the world gate for us, as part of our pact with her predecessor Tymandain Shadowbearer. We would destroy the realm of Andomhaim for her, and in exchange, she would open the way for us. She has fulfilled her side of the pact. The world gate is open, and she recharges it regularly, allowing us to bring additional forces from our worlds in the Dominion." The alien eyes turned back to Arandar. "Which brings us to the reason for this meeting."

Arandar snorted. "You have admitted that you intend to destroy Andomhaim. I intend to stop you. What more is there to discuss?"

"Potentially, a great deal," said Kajaldrakthor. "Your realm and the rest of this world will be made part of the Dominion of the High Lords. That is our objective. The methods by which those objectives will be accomplished is immaterial."

"Is it?" said Arandar. "Because I intend to resist every single one of your methods."

Kajaldrakthor looked at Arlmagnava. "Your assessment of him was correct, Seeker."

"And what assessment was that?" said Arandar.

"You will recall we encountered one another briefly before the battle of Dun Calpurnia," said Arlmagnava. "At that encounter, you came close to slaying me. Tarrabus Carhaine was wise to seek your death, though he abjectly failed with that as with numerous other tasks. The Order of the Inquisition concluded that Tarrabus would have been an easier ruler to manipulate, and making him into a vassal of the Dominion would have been a straightforward process. You, however, we may have to destroy utterly."

"Unless you are willing to listen to the path of logic," said Kajaldrakthor.

Imaria looked at the Lord Commander, and for just a moment Arandar saw the sneer of contempt there. He was certain, utterly certain, that Imaria was using the Frostborn for something, though he could not imagine what. He wondered if Kajaldrakthor had seen it.

"And what path is that?" said Arandar.

"Your realm and the rest of this world are going to become part of the Dominion of the High Lords," said Kajaldrakthor. "This is inevitable. We can sustain the conquest of this world for centuries if necessary. Can you say the same? Your lives are only seventy or eighty years, and only if some mischance does not claim you first. Our lives are far longer, and we can plan for a far more distant future. Perhaps you will hold us at bay, but shall your son say the same? Shall his grandson?"

"What is your point, Lord Commander?" said Arandar. He kept his voice hard, but the utter certainty in the words of the Frostborn chilled him. Kajaldrakthor spoke not with bravado or haughtiness, but with cold, simple logic, and that simple logic foretold the destruction and conquest of Andomhaim.

"Your world will become part of the Dominion of the High Lords," said Kajaldrakthor. "That is inevitable. But your realm need not be destroyed. You could choose to submit to us willingly."

"And why would I do that?" said Arandar. "You supported Tarrabus Carhaine and helped him seize the throne of Andomhaim. He murdered my father, and he did his best to murder my children. Many good men died because of his vile treachery." He looked at Imaria. "And because of the wicked cult he spread among the men of Andomhaim."

Imaria did not respond, but her shadow kept twisting around her feet.

"We did support Tarrabus Carhaine," said Arlmagnava. "He proved himself unworthy of trust, and you are now the High King of Andomhaim by right of blood and right of conquest. Therefore, we make our offer to you."

"Submit to us willingly," said Kajaldrakthor, "and you shall join the Dominion of the High Lords as vassals. You shall join us in the great work of perfecting the cosmos. The kindreds within reach of your authority shall be uplifted."

"Uplifted?" said Arandar.

"Our magic and our sciences can accomplish much," said Kajaldrakthor. "The medvarth were once little more than savage beasts, warring against each other endlessly. We taught them the use of letters and tools, and they now serve us as soldiers. The khaldjari were struggling to survive when we found them. We gave them the ability to control ice and frost, and they serve as the engineers of the Order of the Tower. The locusari were mere animals when we found them. We gave them the ability of thought and language and gave them a purpose beyond mere life and death. The High Lords can do the same with humans and orcs. We can extend your lives significantly and overcome some of the defects caused by your inferior physical configurations. In exchange, you shall join the Dominion of the High Lords, and assist us in the conquest of the cosmos."

"And if we refuse?" said Arandar.

"If you refuse," said Kajaldrakthor, "then you shall be destroyed. Your world shall be cleansed and made habitable for other kindreds that have submitted to the Dominion. Humans and orcs might be kept as slaves, or we may exterminate them. The halfling kindred we shall certainly exterminate, for they are too small and weak to be of any use as soldiers or as workers. It is inevitable that your world shall be conquered and made part of the Dominion. All that is left to you is to choose the method by which you shall join us."

"This is a poor attempt at negotiation," said Arandar. "You offer us the choice of voluntary enslavement or involuntary enslavement. We reject both."

"This is not a negotiation," said Kajaldrakthor. "It is a statement of simple fact. If you wish for as many of your people to be preserved as possible, High King of Andomhaim, you will submit to us, and the process shall be easier. If you defy us, we will break you and remake your world as we please. Either way, your kindreds and your world shall join our great work to perfect the cosmos."

"Neither choice pleases me," said Arandar. "Instead, I shall offer you two choices of my own. Take your slaves, march back into the Northerland, withdraw through your world gate, and close it behind you. Or else we shall break your armies and drive you back to the gate."

He knew that would take years of fighting. But he would not hand Andomhaim to these arrogant tyrants on a silver platter. Nor would he consent even to surrendering kindreds and nations not under the authority of the High King to the Frostborn. If the Frostborn wanted this world, they would have to take it, step by bloody step.

"His defiance is expected, Lord Commander," said Arlmagnava. "The Order of the Inquisition did not think he would yield. We shall have to destroy him."

"Agreed," said Kajaldrakthor. "It is regrettable but necessary. You would have made a capable governor of some of the conquered territories. But if we must destroy your world and your nations, that too will bring them closer to perfection in our work of remaking the cosmos. Return to your soldiers, High King of Andomhaim. When you do, the battle shall begin, and you will die with your army."

"Many a man confident of victory," said Arandar, "lay dead upon the field once the battle was over."

Kajaldrakthor said nothing. Evidently, the Frostborn did not feel the need to have the last word the way someone like Tarrabus Carhaine would have. They turned and walked back towards their waiting army, and the locusari scouts who had delivered their message took to the air and flew away.

Imaria remained behind, gazing at nothing, her expression distant. For a moment, Arandar considered attacking her. The parley was obviously over, and Arandar doubted the Frostborn would take it as a breach of the parley if he cut her down. More, he would be well within his rights to do it. Her predecessor had engineered the return of the Frostborn, and he had no doubt that Imaria had inherited his goals. More, Imaria had murdered Uthanaric Pendragon and the Crown Prince Kaldraine and Morigna and God knew how many others. She was a murderess and a traitor, and the High King would be well within his rights to execute her here and now for her many, many crimes.

The quicksilver eyes turned to Arandar, and she smiled.

"Do not fear, High King of Andomhaim," said Imaria. "I would see Ridmark and Calliande dead for the joy of it, but not you. You, too, shall be free of matter and causality once my work is finished."

"No," said Arandar. "You have shed innocent blood in service to a false and demon god. I will defeat you just as the Enlightened were defeated."

He almost drew Excalibur, but Imaria took the decision from him. She vanished in a swirl of darkness, leaving Arandar and his guards alone on the field between the town and the Frostborn.

"We're done," said Arandar, turning his horse. "Let's return to Dun Calpurnia."

The battle, he knew, would begin within moments.

Gavin and Antenora reined up in the northern forum of Dun Calpurnia. Behind them the men-at-arms pushed the doors shut with a boom, sealing the gate with heavy timbers. The gate had been built of massive beams sheathed in bands of iron, and it looked strong enough to hold an army at bay.

He wondered how long it would last against the wrath of the Frostborn.

Dux Leogrance, Dux Gareth, and Prince Cadwall awaited the High King, and Gavin listened to their conversation.

"What did the Frostborn want?" said Gareth.

"They more or less restated the demands they gave us the first day at Dun Licinia," said Arandar, dropping from his saddle as his squires tended to his horse. "We can choose to join their Dominion of our own will, or we will be forced to join the Frostborn. Their conquest is inevitable, and they will perfect the cosmos and all their usual nonsense."

"A waste of time, then," said Leogrance.

"As a negotiation, yes," said Cadwall. "But every moment we delay gives Queen Mara another moment to arrive with the Anathgrimm and the dwarves."

"Yes," said Arandar. "Send word to the other Duxi and Comites. The Frostborn will attack at any moment."

"We are ready," said Gareth as Cadwall dispatched some of his squires to serve as messengers. "The siege engines are sighted and prepared, and we have enough men to hold the entire wall with ample reserves. We should be able to hold until help arrives, if God wills it."

"If God wills it," said Arandar.

Gavin hoped that he was right. He wished that Calliande was here. In the past battles with the Frostborn, her powers had been invaluable, even critical.

Drums boomed out from outside the wall, deep and solemn.

The Frostborn were coming, and the battle was about to begin.

CHAPTER FIFTEEN

THE TOMB OF THE DRAGON KNIGHT

Utter silence hung over the corridor as Ridmark walked forward.

In some ways, the Tomb of the Dragon Knight reminded him of the dark elven ruins he had visited in the past. The walls and floors and ceilings were fashioned of the same sort of white stone, hard and impenetrable and strong enough to endure millennia without crumbling into dust. The same silence hung over the Tomb, and Ridmark's ears strained to hear anything but the rasp of his own breathing and the drumbeat of his own heart.

And the heartbeat inside his own head, of course.

Yet there were obvious differences. In places the walls glowed, giving off their own pale light, identical to the hall of white stone he had seen in his dreams of Morigna and the burning woman. The Tomb also lacked the strange, alien angles of the dark elven ruins. It also lacked the aura of ancient malice that always hung over the ruins of the dark elves. Instead, the Tomb felt...

Watchful, somehow. Like it was waiting.

Ridmark supposed that it had been waiting for him.

A thick mist coiled and flowed across the floor, coming up to his knees and lapping at the pale walls. Ridmark ran his fingers through the mist, but he felt nothing at all, no moisture, no chill, nothing. The walls ought to have been damp with it, but the floor was as dry as dust.

That meant the mist was magical. Ridmark wished Calliande was here. With the Sight, she could have taken one look at the mist and told him its function and purpose. Without her, he could only guess, though it did not seem to harm him.

Still, he was glad she wasn't here. The danger had come to him, and Ridmark was glad he could face it without exposing her to risk.

The corridor continued deeper into the Tomb. Ridmark supposed he was underneath the level of the lake by now, though the walls remained dry. He felt the need to hurry, though he supposed it was unnecessary. If the rate of time flowed differently inside the Tomb than it did on the outside, Ridmark could spend days here and only a few hours would pass in the caverns outside. Still, he wanted to return to Calliande, and he wanted to return to Arandar and the others with the power of the Dragon Knight in hand. He wondered what had happened since he and Calliande had been snatched from Tarlion. If time was flowing faster outside of Cathair Solas than it was within, the host of Andomhaim might well have reached the Northerland by now. Had Mara and the Anathgrimm joined them? Or the dwarves and the manetaurs?

Ridmark didn't know, but it was his duty to aid them. He had helped Calliande build the alliance that had brought the dwarves and the manetaurs to war against the Frostborn, and he would not leave them to face the Frostborn alone.

That meant he needed to find the sword of the Dragon Knight as soon as possible. He wasn't sure what the sword could do, but if it could command the fire of dragons, that would be of immense use against the Frostborn. If the sword could create gates like the one in the Tower of the Keeper, gates that had carried Ridmark and Calliande over a thousand miles in the blink of an eye, that would be of tremendous value in battle.

If he had been able to do that, he could have killed Mhalek and saved Aelia. He could have killed Tarrabus Carhaine before Uthanaric Pendragon was murdered. Maybe he could have even saved Morigna before Imaria and the Weaver murdered her.

Ridmark shook his head, pushing away the dark thoughts. He had to focus on the future now. What was done was done, and he had to think about those who yet lived, who yet could be saved.

He had to think about Calliande.

At last, the corridor ended in a high stone hall, and Ridmark looked around with a scowl.

"A maze," he muttered. "Of course, it had to be a maze."

The hall was about the size of a large church, and a balcony went along all four walls. Ahead of Ridmark opened another corridor, and two more on either wall. Three more corridors opened off the balconies as well. Ridmark was reminded of the Labyrinth near Bastoth, of how Ralakahr had hunted him through the silent ruins of the dark elves.

Hopefully, there wasn't anything as dangerous as Ralakahr down here.

He stepped forward, the mist swirling around his boots, and looked at the different corridors. Each corridor seemed identical to the others, but it seemed like the heartbeat in his head coming from the corridor at the far end of the stone hall. But the one on the balcony or the one on the ground level? Ridmark could not tell.

He decided to start with the lower corridor. Even the engineering of the high elves could not have dug into the earth forever, and he could search the lower levels and make his way to the higher levels if he found nothing.

He took a step towards the corridor, and the quiet voice came to his ears.

"It is good to see you again, my love, though I fear to see you in this place."

Ridmark swallowed, took a moment to collect his composure, and turned around.

The spirit of Morigna stood a few yards behind him, translucent enough that he could see the mist swirling through her body. She wore her usual wool and leather and tattered cloak, her long black hair bound back in a thick braid. A sharp tangle of emotion went through him. Her spirit had haunted his dreams for nearly a year, and he had forgotten those dreams until he had seen her spirit atop the Tower of the Keeper. Then the shock of the gate and the necessity of keeping himself and Calliande alive had occupied his attention.

There had not been time to process how sad and how strange seeing Morigna again had been.

"Was it really you?" Ridmark heard himself say.

"Do elaborate," said Morigna, raising an eyebrow.

"The dreams," said Ridmark. "I had those dreams of you and the spirit of the sword of the Dragon Knight for over a year. Was it really you? Or was I hallucinating?"

"Was it all a dream, you mean?" said Morigna.

"Yes," said Ridmark. "Was it?"

"Not in the least," said Morigna. "I am dead, of course, but I still have work to do. Absorbing some of the Warden's dark magic to escape Urd Morlemoch carried a price, and I must work off that price before I can move on." She shrugged. "There are more disagreeable ways to spend one's time, and the work is important."

Ridmark stared at Morigna. There were a thousand things he wanted to say to her.

"I'm sorry," he said at last.

"For what?" said Morigna.

"For not saving you from Imaria and the Weaver," said Ridmark.

"That was hardly your fault."

"Maybe not," said Ridmark. "But I'm sorry nonetheless. I'm sorry that I couldn't save you. I'm sorry that I couldn't take you to

Tarlion like I said I would. And…I am sorry that I fell for Calliande so soon after you died."

Something like pity flickered over her face. It was a strange sight on her usually harsh expression. "Ridmark. You always did torment yourself more than was necessary. The dead do not love as the living do, nor are the dead given in marriage. Did I not tell you that you needed Calliande?"

"You did," said Ridmark. "Several times. Though I never remembered when I woke up."

"The peril of speaking through dreams, alas," said Morigna. "The waking mind cannot always recall what the sleeping mind has learned. But the sword chose you, and it was reaching out for you. We had to warn you."

"But I am sorry," said Ridmark. "I wish…" What did he wish? He was glad to be betrothed to Calliande and frankly wanted to be back in Tarlion with her. But he wished Morigna hadn't died. He wished she was here now in the flesh. "I wish things could have been different."

"So do I," said Morigna. "But if you do one thing in my memory, Ridmark, then do this. Do not feel guilty on my account. Do not blame yourself for my death. What is done is done. And you need Calliande as much as she needs you."

"I will try," said Ridmark.

Morigna's mouth curled in a smile. "And Calliande does indeed need you, Ridmark. She has never known the touch of a man…and do you have any idea how often she has thought about your touch, shall we say? Sometimes it is all she can think about. One does forget how eager virgins can be. Really, it would be cruel to make her wait any…"

"For God's sake," said Ridmark, and despite himself, he laughed. "Death hasn't changed you much, has it?"

"People keep telling me that," said Morigna, and her smile faded. "Listen to me, Ridmark. I have come to warn you."

"About the sword?" said Ridmark.

"Yes."

He nodded. "Can you tell me about the trial? Calliande and Ardrhythain both said that the sword would try to test me somehow, but Calliande didn't know any details, and Ardrhythain would not speak of it."

"The sword of the Dragon Knight can only be mastered by strength," said Morigna. "It will try to dominate you by turning your weaknesses against you. It will be able to read your mind, find your deepest weaknesses, and exploit them to the fullest."

"That sounds dangerous," said Ridmark.

"It is," said Morigna. "And I fear it is especially dangerous to you, my love."

"How so?" said Ridmark.

"When your wife was killed at Mhalek's hands, you blamed yourself and plunged into the Wilderland to find the secret of the Frostborn," said Morigna. "It was a noble quest, but you hoped it would kill you in retribution for her death. When Imaria and the Weaver slew me, you dedicated yourself to avenging my death, even at the cost of your own life."

"I don't want to get myself killed now," said Ridmark. "I don't want to leave Calliande bereft." He grimaced. "I've known that too often to inflict that upon her."

"Remember that!" said Morigna. "Remember that and hold tight to it, Ridmark, for that will be the trial. That will be the weapon the sword will use against you. There has always been an urge for your own death in your nature, like a flaw in a pane of glass. That will be how the sword attacks you."

"But I don't want to die," said Ridmark. "At least...I don't think I do, not now. I won't deny that I've wanted to in the past..."

"I should hope not," said Morigna in her familiar acerbic tones. "As well deny that the sky is blue or that water flows downhill."

Ridmark sighed. Death had indeed failed to change her. "I won't. But I don't want to die now."

"Really?" said Morigna. "Perhaps I misspoke. What you have really wanted, buried deep within your heart, is to sacrifice yourself for those you love. If the chance came to throw yourself on a sword to save Calliande...I fear that is a temptation you would be hard-pressed to resist. And that is the weapon the sword will use against you."

"All right," said Ridmark. "I will be on my guard against that."

"It will be harder than you think," said Morigna. She sighed. "And I have given you all the aid that I am permitted. The rules may be bent, but not broken. Be very careful, my love. I wish you to be united with Calliande in life...and not joined with me in death before your proper hour."

She vanished without another word, the mist swirling through the spot she had occupied a moment earlier.

Ridmark closed his eyes and let out a long breath, regret and grief and sorrow twisting through him. They hadn't been just dreams. Morigna had been speaking to him.

And the thought that she approved of his betrothal to Calliande...it surprised Ridmark how much better that made him feel.

Yet her warning troubled him. If there was a death wish buried within his very nature, how would the sword try to use it against him? Visions of some kind?

Would it simply try to drive him mad?

There was nothing to do but to continue onward.

Ridmark sighed, gripped his staff, and strode towards the entrance on the far wall. The corridor beyond stretched for forty yards and then ended in a spiral stairwell that sank deeper into the earth. Ridmark took the stairs, staff held in guard before him. At last the stairs ended and opened into a large square room, the floor covered with tiles of white stone inscribed with symbols, the ceiling rising in a vault of pale stone. The white stone gave off a faint glow, providing enough light that it was almost like standing in moonlight.

A tall woman stood in the center of the room, her back to Ridmark. She was wearing a blue gown with black trim and a blue mantle, a common outfit among the noblewomen of Andomhaim. A black leather belt encircled her waist, holding a sheathed dagger at her hip, and her black hair hung in dark waves down her shoulders and back.

Ridmark looked a careful step forward, watching the noblewoman. He was certain, of course, that she was not actually a noblewoman of Andomhaim. No doubt she was a disguised urshane or an illusion spun by the magic of the Tomb. Yet he recognized her. He was sure he recognized her, and something stirred in his mind at the sight.

Ridmark took a step to the left, intending to circle around the woman, and she turned to face him.

A jolt of recognition went through him, and for a moment he was frozen with shock.

"Greeting, Ridmark," said Tomia Arban.

His mother looked just as he remembered before she had taken sick, tall and strong with long black hair and a face that looked a great deal like his own. Ridmark and his four brothers had inherited their eyes from their father, but everything else in their features had been taken from their mother.

She had been dead…twenty-two years, twenty-three years?

Ridmark had been devastated by her death. As the youngest son, he had spent more time with her than his brothers, who had already been serving as squires and even knights in the courts of other great lords. After she had died, he had been sent to serve as a page in Gareth Licinius's court.

Maybe that was why he had never liked to return to Castra Arban. The memories there had been too sharp.

"No," said Ridmark. "No, I'm not doing this. You're not Tomia Arban. You're not my mother. You're an urshane or a shapechanger or an illusion or some other damned thing. My mother died when I was a boy."

"All that is correct, Ridmark," said Tomia. God, but she sounded exactly as he remembered. The same accent of Durandis, where she had grown up before marrying Leogrance Arban. The same faint smile as she looked at him, the same sparkle in her dark eyes. "I have been dead for quite a long time, but I am your mother."

"No, you're not," said Ridmark.

"Perhaps I am her spirit returned to speak with you," said Tomia, "like your lover Morigna. A pity I never got to meet the girl. I think I would have liked her. A pity I never got to meet any of your women. Perhaps I could have given you better guidance."

"You're not my mother," said Ridmark.

"How do you know?"

"For one, you're not translucent," said Ridmark. "For another, Morigna used dark magic, and that seems to have kept her soul from moving on. You never used magic."

"No," said Tomia. "But I am your mother. At least, I am your memories of her."

"Then this is a trick," said Ridmark.

"It's not a trick, my son," said Tomia. "It is the truth."

"The truth of what?" said Ridmark.

"Your memories. That is what I am, am I not? Your memories of me."

"You tell me," said Ridmark.

"Do you remember how I died?" said Tomia.

"A foolish question."

"Yet," said Tomia with kindly patience, "I note that you do not answer it."

"You were sick," said Ridmark. "Father was traveling, and his Magistri were with him. By the time he returned, it was too late. The

FROSTBORN: THE DRAGON KNIGHT · 201

physicians and the Magistri could do nothing for you. Maybe they wouldn't have been able to do anything for you. Their healing magic doesn't always work on illnesses."

"No," said Tomia, the glitter in her eyes brightening. "And so I died."

She seemed to have become thinner in the last few moments, her cheekbones sharper, her eyes sinking into her face. She was starting to look the way she had in the final weeks of her life as the illness consumed her. Old memories and old pain surged through Ridmark's mind at the sight. His mother's death had been the first time anyone he had loved had died. He did not care to relive the experience.

"And so you died," said Ridmark. "It was a long time ago."

"It was," said Tomia. Her voice remained calm, though her eyes glinted with fever, her skin becoming tight and waxy against her skull. "A long time ago, and you thought the pain buried. But it has always been with you, hasn't it? It has always been part of the man you have become."

"Is that meant to rattle me?" said Ridmark. "Most people live long enough to see their mother and father die. Better that than the other way around."

"Do you blame yourself?" said Tomia. Her face had sharpened to an exhausted mask now, the way it had in the final days before her illness. "Did you blame yourself for my death?"

"For your illness?" said Ridmark. "No. Sometimes people get sick and die. It is sad, but it's no one's fault."

She gave him a sad smile. "Maybe it was your fault."

"I fail to see how."

"You were my fifth son," said Tomia. "Every birth was harder than the last. I miscarried four children as well. Nine pregnancies, and they were all exhausting. You pushed me over the edge, Ridmark. I never quite recovered from your birth."

"No," said Ridmark. "I was eight years old when you died. If childbirth was going to kill you, it would have been long before that."

"I was sick so often," said Tomia. Her breathing had turned into a raspy whistle. "Do you remember? I was sick half the time, and more and more as you got older. The years had eroded my health, and perhaps you were the final straw..."

"What is the point of this?" snapped Ridmark, his temper fraying. "Do you want me to blame myself for your death? I don't. A disease killed you, not me. If this is some sort of trial, it is a poor one."

"Oh, Ridmark," said Tomia. "I don't want you to think about my death. I want you to think about yours."

"And how you'll bring it about?" said Ridmark.

"Wouldn't it have been better," said Tomia, "if you had never been born?"

Hearing his own mother speak those words, even if he knew that she was an illusion, hit him like a blow to the gut.

"What?" said Ridmark.

"If you had never been born," said Tomia, "perhaps I would still be alive. Perhaps I would have lived long enough to have seen grandchildren."

"Absurd," said Ridmark. "No one can see what might have been."

"But you can, Ridmark," said Tomia. "You always could. You've done so much harm in your life. You know that as well as I do. If you had never been born, then Aelia would still be alive, wouldn't she? She would have married some other man and have surrounded herself with children by now. Morigna would be alive as well, safe and secure. And Calliande..."

"Don't talk about her," said Ridmark.

"The poor woman," said Tomia, "to fall in love with a man like you. Hasn't she suffered enough? Hasn't she endured enough? How much pain have you brought into her life? Wouldn't it have been

FROSTBORN: THE DRAGON KNIGHT · 203

better to spare her all that?" She gave a sad shake of her head. "And you failed Aelia and Morigna. You failed to save them. You'll fail to save Calliande. Wouldn't it be better to spare her that? Wouldn't it have been better if you had never been born?"

Ridmark had no answer for her. Her words made a disturbing amount of sense. Maybe it would have been better if he had never been born. Maybe...

He rebuked himself. She wasn't real. His mother had died over twenty years ago. Either she was a shapeshifter like an urshane or the Weaver, or the sword of the Dragon Knight was reflecting his memories back at him in some damn test or another. On the other side of the square room, he saw an archway opening into another corridor, and the heartbeat in his head seemed to be coming from that direction.

"Whether or not they would be better off if I had never been born is moot," said Ridmark. "I was born, I'm here, and I don't intend to kill myself."

He started towards the far archway,

"My poor son," said Tomia. "Don't you deserve death?"

"Because of my failures, you mean?" said Ridmark.

"No," said Tomia. "So you can rest at last."

He hadn't expected that answer, and he came to a stop, looking back at her.

"What?"

"You've suffered so much," said Tomia. "You've seen those you love suffer so much. Don't you deserve to rest? Don't you deserve to know the peace of death at last? Haven't you carried enough sorrow?"

"Not yet," said Ridmark.

"I disagree," said Tomia, and she stepped forward and changed.

One moment she looked just as his mother had on the day she had died, thin and wan and exhausted. The next her vigor had returned, but overlapping plates of black armor covered her body, her hands concealed beneath gauntlets tipped with razor-edged talons. Great black wings unfolded from her back, and blue fire started to dance around her clawed hands.

His mother had just transformed into an urdhracos.

"Then, my son," said Tomia, "I shall give you the peace of death with my own hands."

She leaped, wings lifting her into the air. Then the wings folded and she dove, claws sweeping for his throat. But Ridmark had fought enough urdhracosi to see the maneuver coming, and he dodged the blow, the black claws screeching against the white stone of the floor. He struck with the staff, and the weapon hit the urdhracos in the knee.

The creature reared back with a scream, and his mother's face twisted with pain.

Ridmark went on the offensive, swinging his staff and snatching his dwarven axe from his belt. The urdhracos retreated, the staff rebounding from the claws, the wings curling around her like shields. Again and again Ridmark struck, forcing the urdhracos back, and at last, he saw an opening through the creature's guard.

His axe blurred towards her neck.

At the last moment, the urdhracos vanished, replaced by Tomia Arban as she looked in the prime of her life before the illness had taken her.

She screamed as his axe sank into her neck, blood gushing across the blade.

"Ridmark," she croaked, falling to her knees.

Ridmark stared at her, horrified, watching her die for a second time.

Tomia Arban slumped to the floor and then vanished as if she had never been there.

Ridmark stepped back, taking a moment to get his breathing under control.

"What was the point of that?" he shouted. "Just be cruel? Did you think that would stop me? I've fought urshanes before."

No one answered. He hadn't expected that anyone would.

Ridmark gave an angry shake of his head. Maybe that was the point of the trial, to make him kill duplicates of his loved ones. But that trick had been used on him several times before, and while it infuriated him, it wouldn't stop him or break his mind with madness.

He remembered what he had thought about Tarrabus Carhaine, about how terrible it would be to live forever. Ridmark had lost so much already. How much more would he lose if he lived forever?

Didn't he deserve to die already? He had caused so much pain. Maybe be it would be better...

He grimaced, shook off the dark thoughts, and turned towards the far archway.

People were depending on him, and he had work to do. Calliande was waiting for him.

Ridmark walked deeper into the Tomb of the Dragon Knight.

CHAPTER SIXTEEN

FIRE AND ICE

Gavin climbed to the ramparts of Dun Calpurnia, Truthseeker burning in his hand.

The walls of Dun Calpurnia were nowhere near as strong as the walls of Tarlion, which was bad. They were, however, much stronger than the walls of Dun Licinia, which was reassuring. The walls of Dun Calpurnia stood thirty feet tall and ten thick, with numerous watch towers topped with siege engines. Against a normal army, Gavin knew they could hold out indefinitely. Against the Frostborn, he hoped they would be able to hold out long enough for help to arrive.

Antenora followed him, her black staff tapping against the stones as she climbed the stairs. Kharlacht, Caius, Third, and Camorak followed Antenora. He had thought they would stay back and guard Arandar, but the High King would remain in the northern forum below the gate, directing the battle. Every Swordbearer was needed upon the wall, and Antenora's fire magic was a deadly weapon against the creatures of the Frostborn.

Gavin hurried around the base of one of the gate towers and came to the section of wall directly over the northern gate. To the north, the drums boomed out, again and again, and the masses of medvarth and locusari warriors were moving. A score of white-robed Magistri had gathered over the gate, guarded by men-at-arms with crossbows and a dozen Swordbearers. Master Kurastus stood in their midst, directing the Magistri.

"Sir Gavin, welcome," said Kurastus. "The High King and his captains have given us the responsibility of casting protective wards against the magic of the Frostborn and the freezing breath of their drakes."

"Then it seems our task," said Caius, "will be to keep you alive while you do that."

"That would be helpful, yes," said Kurastus.

Camorak shook his head. "I'm no good at this kind of magic."

"Better to save your strength for healing spells, Magistrius," said Kurastus. "Wards may not be your strength, but we have few healers to equal you." The old man took a deep breath. "We will need that soon enough."

Camorak gave a grim nod.

"Lady Antenora," said Kurastus, "please, strike as you see fit. If the Frostborn bring their ice against us, answer them in kind with your fire."

"I shall focus on keeping the enemy from reaching the walls," said Antenora. Already the sigils in her staff burned with harsh light.

"That shall be wise," said Kurastus.

And with that, there was nothing left to do but wait.

Gavin divided his attention between watching the approaching army and the frost drakes circling overhead, ready to call out a warning if the frost drakes descended. So far, the drakes and their Frostborn riders appeared content to watch the battle, staying out of range of the engines upon the walls. The medvarth lines advanced at a slow, methodical pace, the locusari skittering before them, but the khaldjari had not begun pulling their siege engines forward, and neither the cogitaers nor the Frostborn themselves had moved closer to the wall.

"The khaldjari are calling upon their powers," said Antenora.

"Are they working a spell, my lady?" said Kurastus.

"Not one of great power," said Antenora, her eyelids fluttering as she drew upon the Sight. "Rather, it seems as if many of them are working together to combine their abilities."

"Siege ladders," said Kharlacht.

They all looked at him.

The big orc grunted. "They must be making siege ladders. The khaldjari can call forth blades of ice from their hands, and they helped build fortifications of ice and stone for their masters. Why not use their powers to fashion siege ladders wrought of ice? Surely it is less work than cutting down trees and sawing planks."

"That is likely it," said Kurastus. He looked at one of the younger Magistri. "Quickly, go to the High King and give him this news. He must be warned."

"No need, Magistrius," said Third, and she vanished in a swirl of blue fire.

"A useful talent," said Kurastus.

"We've often found it so," said Caius.

A moment later Third returned, the blue fire dimming in her veins. "The High King has been warned. He has sent word to those commanding on the wall to expect siege ladders of ice."

"We will not need to wait long," said Caius. "Here they come."

Gavin watched as the lines of the locusari warriors parted, and groups of medvarth rushed forward. In one hand, each medvarth carried a massive tower shield, raised to protect their bodies. In the other hand, the medvarth carried something that looked like a long pole of glittering blue ice.

A pole? What use would a pole be?

The medvarth couldn't use that to scale the walls. Was it a giant spear of some kind? Then Gavin saw the columns of locusari running after each group of medvarth, and he understood. The medvarth might not be able to scale the poles, but the locusari would scamper up them with ease.

And then the fighting on the ramparts would begin in earnest.

Commands rang along the ramparts, and the crossbowmen and the catapults loosed a storm of missiles. Volleys of bolts slammed into the shields, quivering there, and catapult stones landed in the locusari columns, shattering them. Antenora flung a fireball, and the sphere landed in a group of medvarth and exploded, sheathing the bear-like creatures in flame and shattering their frozen pole into tumbling pieces. About half the groups of medvarth were killed or scattered before they could reach the town, their frozen poles dropping to the ground.

The rest reached the walls, flinging their poles against the battlements. The magic within the poles flared as they touched the walls, and a layer of thick frost spread against the stones, holding the poles at a steep angle to the ground. A human would not have been able to scale the poles, and neither could a medvarth.

The locusari had no such trouble, and they swarmed up the poles and attacked.

Arandar watched the fighting on the walls, his sword hand closing and opening again and again.

He felt the urge to rush to the ramparts and join the fray, but he held himself back. He was the High King, and his role was to command the battle, not to fight in the front line. Granted, he had done a lot of fighting at Tarlion, but that battle had been a chaotic mess, and both sides had nearly been defeated until Ridmark had beaten Tarrabus and the enemy had collapsed. If Arandar rushed to the walls and got himself killed for nothing, it would be a grave defeat for the army and would cause chaos until Dux Leogrance took command as regent.

It would also leave Accolon and Nyvane as orphans.

So Arandar watched, surrounded by his bodyguards, as the men of Andomhaim struggled against the locusari.

It looked as if the defenders were having the better of the first attack. Here and there Arandar saw a man-at-arms or a militiaman fall, killed by the scythed forelimbs of the locusari, but he saw far more locusari go tumbling over the battlements or fall dead into the town below. White fire flashed amidst the melee as the Swordbearers pushed back the locusari, shattering the frozen poles they had used to ascend the walls. A bloom of fire rushed over a portion of the wall as Antenora brought her power to bear, melting the icy poles.

"A weak attack," said Dux Sebastian, who stood near Arandar with the other chief nobles.

"It is," said Dux Leogrance. "But this is just the beginning. A probing attack, to assess our strength."

"They began much the same way at the siege of Dun Licinia," said Dux Gareth. "Lighter attacks, followed by heavier ones. There the Frostborn started by sending groups of locusari scouts to open the gates."

"I doubt that would work here," said Prince Cadwall. "We were already on our guard, and the gatehouses are fully manned."

"Why are they only assaulting the northern wall?" said Sebastian. "They have enough soldiers to completely surround the town and assault from all four directions at once."

Arandar frowned. That was a good question.

"Perhaps the terrain isn't viable," said Leogrance. "To the west, there is not much land between here and the River Moradel. To the east, there is not much space before the hills and the forests of the Northerland. Either direction does not offer much room for a large army to maneuver. North and south are the best directions for attacking Dun Calpurnia, and to attack us from the south, the Frostborn would first have to get past the town."

That made sense. The Frostborn couldn't attack from the south until they had gotten past the town.

And yet...

They could have made this probing attack far more forceful. They could have sent waves of medvarth behind the locusari or had the locusari scouts and the frost drakes attack from above. Or they could have started hammering at the walls with powerful spells. The Frostborn had to know that allies were coming to aid the men of Andomhaim.

Yet the Frostborn were holding back. Why?

Another locusari warrior sprang at Gavin, and he pushed with his shield, catching the serrated forelimbs against the dwarven steel. The metal let out an angry shriek the locusari's forelimbs grated against the metal, and Gavin shoved. The locusari stumbled back, legs clicking against the battlements, and Caius smashed its head with a blow of his mace. The creature shuddered and went still, and Kharlacht kicked it off the ramparts to clear his path as he attacked another of the warriors.

Up and down the northern wall the battle raged, the locusari scrambling up the frozen poles. Nearly all the original poles had been shattered by axe blows or burned away from the walls by Antenora's magic, but the teams of medvarth had charged again, placing new poles against the ramparts. Gavin supposed the khaldjari could turn out hundreds of the damned things before their strength gave out.

Maybe they hoped to wear down the men of Andomhaim through sheer attrition.

Yet it didn't seem to be working. The locusari had inflicted casualties, but there were far, far more dead locusari on the ground and on the ramparts than dead humans. Gavin looked around, ready to aid Kharlacht and the others defending the Magistri and Antenora, but Antenora had already burned the frozen pole from the side of the wall, and another had not come to take its place.

"They have not even sent the frost drakes to attack," said Kurastus. The old Magistrius sounded confused, and Gavin could not blame him. The frost drakes remained circling over the Frostborn army, and they had not once descended close enough to attack or to expose themselves to missiles from the wall.

"Likely they are waiting," said Antenora.

"But waiting for what?" said Gavin.

"A spell to be finished," said Antenora, staring to the north.

Kurastus gave her a sharp look. "You sense that as well?"

"The Sight shows it to me," said Antenora. "The Frostborn are gathering a tremendous amount of magical power behind their army. It looks as if most of them, and most of the cogitaers, are putting their power into the spell."

"We must warn the High King," said Gavin.

"Likely he already knows," said Camorak, flexing his fingers. "Any Magistrius near the High King will be able to sense it. I'm not much of a Magistrius, and I can still sense the damned spell."

"Can you tell what it will do?" said Caius.

"No," said Antenora, "save that it is not targeted at the town. Were it targeted at the town, I might be able to discern its purpose, but..." She gave an irritated shake of her head. "Until it is cast, I can only guess at its design."

"Are they raising more revenants?" said Gavin.

"There weren't enough corpses near the town for them to raise as revenants," said Camorak. "At least, not yet. Suppose they could be trying to raise all those dead locusari."

Antenora shook her head. "Then the spell would be targeted at the town."

"If it is not directed at the town," said Master Kurastus, "then we must hold our powers in reserve until they are needed. Not that we could do anything to stop them at this distance anyway. Not even the Keeper could strike that far unless she had a few hours to prepare first."

"They're coming again," said Kharlacht, cutting the discussion short.

Only a few of the icy poles were left, and the defenders were forcing back the remaining locusari step by step. Yet another wave of medvarth was coming towards the walls, shields raised to protect themselves, and Gavin expected to see more columns of locusari following them.

Except these medvarth were heavily armored in chain mail and plate, their ursine features hidden beneath heavy helms. Gavin realized that the first wave of medvarth were not carrying more poles of ice but massive siege ladders, their tops crowned with iron claws to grasp the battlements.

"It seems the khaldjari found the time both to fashion the poles of ice and to assemble proper siege ladders," said Third. "I will inform the High King."

She vanished again in a flare of blue fire.

"There are at least twenty ladders," said Kharlacht. "Maybe thirty. They'll be able to hit the entire northern wall at once."

Gavin half-expected to see the khaldjari moving siege engines ahead to support the medvarth or for the frost drakes and the locusari scouts to attack, but the siege engines behind the Frostborn lines were not moving, and the frost drakes remained well out of reach.

What were they waiting for?

Arandar heard the shout just as he reached the roof of the tavern.

It was impossible to see the progress of the battle from the forum, and with the medvarth launching a major assault, Arandar needed to see what was happening. One of the taverns near the northern forum was a tall building of four levels, and its roof was higher than the level of the northern wall. Arandar and his guards had ascended to the rooftop, and could now watch the unfolding attack from a relatively secure vantage point.

He did not like what he saw.

The catapults released and the crossbowmen fired, sending stones and bolts hurtling towards the medvarth with the siege ladders. Two of the columns of medvarth warriors went down, pierced by concentrated crossbow fire, and dropped their ladders. Two more died when catapult stones landed in their midst, the ladders smashed by the heavy stones. The rest kept advancing, preparing to throw their ladders against the walls.

"Dux Gareth," said Arandar. Gareth had the overall command of the infantry, as he had during the battle of Tarlion. "Have our reserve companies ready. I fear we may need to rotate the men upon the walls very soon."

Gareth nodded, his gray beard stirring in the wind coming down from the north. "The medvarth are fierce fighters."

"They are," said Arandar, frowning. The wind from the north had gotten stronger, and he could just glimpse a flickering blue glow as the Frostborn worked their spell.

Whatever it was.

The crossbowmen and the catapults managed to stop about half of the ladders. The other half of the siege ladders crashed against the ramparts with ringing clangs, the iron hooks gripping the stone battlements.

With a roar, the medvarth surged towards the ladders, and the fighting began in earnest.

Gavin shouted and stabbed with Truthseeker, the blade plunging beneath the medvarth warrior's arm. The hulking warrior wore a cuirass and a skirt of chain mail, bracers and shoulder plates affixed to its thick arms. It held an axe over its head, ready to bring the weapon down upon its foes. Gavin twisted Truthseeker, ripped the blade free, and stabbed again.

This time the medvarth warrior collapsed and did not rise again.

Two more rushed to take its place.

Antenora killed one with a quick blast of magical fire that scoured the fur and flesh from its skull. Kharlacht and Caius slew the second one. Caius's mace landed on the medvarth's right knee with a crunch, shattering the bone, and as the medvarth stumbled, Kharlacht's greatsword came down on the back of the creature's neck.

It fell, hit the edge of rampart, and rolled into the town below.

Gavin stepped back, breathing hard, and saw that for the moment the section of wall was clear.

"The ladder, quickly!" he shouted. "Quickly!"

Three men-at-arms heard his call and rushed to the nearest ladder. The blasted iron hooks made it a challenge to push the ladders away from the wall. Fortunately, the men-at-arms had axes, and they began hammering away at the sides of the ladder, severing the hooks. Another medvarth warrior started to pull itself over the top of the ladder, but Gavin killed it with a stab to the neck, sending its armored body tumbling to the ground below. He stared at the ladder and saw three more medvarth rushing towards its base. Just a little longer…

The last hook snapped free, and the ladder shuddered.

"Now!" said Gavin, and he and the three men-at-arms seized the ladder and pushed. It overbalanced and fell backward, knocking the medvarth back, and for a moment their section of wall was clear.

But more were coming. Three more columns of medvarth ran towards the gate, carrying ladders between them. Antenora stepped to the ramparts and thrust her staff, and a sphere of fire soared across the distance and exploded amid a medvarth column. The medvarth warriors scattered, trying to put out the flames that chewed at their fur, their ladder burning.

The other two ladders reached the wall, and with roars of rage, the medvarth began climbing, their weapons in hand.

Gavin fought for his life, Truthseeker burning as the soulblade rose and fell.

Arandar watched the fighting, trying to make sense of the chaos of the battle.

The medvarth attacked with far more fury and skill than the locusari warriors, and bloody fighting raged along the entire length of the northern wall. Twice now Gareth had been forced to rotate reserve companies to the battlements, bringing in reinforcements to close a breach. Yet the men of Andomhaim were still holding and were even throwing down the siege ladders one by one. The Frostborn could not sustain this rate of attack forever, especially if their siege engines and frost drakes did not join the fray. Sooner or later they would have to fall back to regroup and prepare for another assault, and that would give the men of Andomhaim time to rest and recover…and more time for their allies to arrive.

So why were the Frostborn fighting with one hand behind their back?

Another siege ladder was thrown back from the ramparts, falling with a crash to the increasingly blood-soaked ground.

Perhaps the Frostborn feared the Keeper was here and was preparing a great spell to direct against them. She had beaten them once before, centuries ago, and they would be wary of her magic. Yet for all her power, even Calliande's magic would not be enough to turn back the Frostborn if they came in full force.

"Those siege engines are moving," said Dux Sebastian, shading his eyes.

"Where?" said Arandar.

"There, along the riverbank," said Sebastian, pointing. Arandar could just barely glimpse the distant movement, so he decided to take Sebastian's word for it. "It looks like...trebuchets, I think."

"Why along the riverbank?" said Arandar. "If they set up there, even a trebuchet wouldn't have the range to hit the walls. For that matter, there isn't enough level ground to use a trebuchet there, and if they get any closer, they will be within range of our own engines."

"I do not know, your Majesty," said Sebastian, and he heard the bafflement in the Dux's voice. "The enemy's strategy does not make sense."

"No, it makes sense," said Leogrance, his voice grimmer than usual. "The Frostborn have their reasons. We simply do not know what those reasons are. We must discern them before it is too late."

"Yes," said Arandar. The memory of Morigna's spirit flashed through his mind. She had warned him that the Frostborn had set a trap for Andomhaim. But how? Arandar could not see it. As far as the scouts had been able to determine, the Frostborn had concentrated for the attack on Dun Calpurnia. There were no other Frostborn armies nearby, save for the second force marching down the Moradel road, but that was still several days away.

Though they never had figured out what had happened to those revenants.

And the Frostborn were still casting that mighty spell outside the walls.

Arandar gritted his teeth, trying to keep the unease from his face. Was this how Tarrabus had felt, he wondered, watching Arandar and the loyalists build their siege wall outside of Tarrabus's own walls? Had Tarrabus questioned himself as much as Arandar?

Still, Tarrabus likely had never questioned himself about anything.

"More medvarth and siege ladders," said Sebastian. "God and the saints. I think there might be another forty of those ladders heading towards us. The khaldjari have been busy."

Leogrance nodded. "Perhaps the entire purpose of the attack was to soften us up for this moment."

Arandar frowned. "If it was, it was a wasted effort. Even with forty ladders, that many medvarth can't climb the ramparts at once. Thousands of them will die from our crossbowmen and our siege engines. They won't even have to aim. We'll..."

He broke off as a commotion in the forum below caught his attention. Men in the colors of Dux Sebastian were running towards the tavern, alarm on their faces.

"Sebastian?" said Arandar.

"Those men," said Sebastian. "I posted them on the western wall in case the Frostborn tried to send a small force to surprise us. I..."

Blue fire swirled on the roof next to Arandar, and Third stepped out of the air, her expression grimmer than usual.

"High King," she said. "You had best come to the western wall at once. You will wish to see this with your own eyes."

###

Up and down the northern wall of Dun Calpurnia the fighting raged, and Gavin fought in the heart of it.

He had lost count of how many medvarth warriors he had killed, and his arm ran red with blood. Again and again, he and the other Swordbearers rushed into the deadliest fighting, driving back the medvarth and helping the men-at-arms throw down their siege ladders.

The medvarth had gotten dozens of ladders to the wall, and now they poured up to storm the ramparts. The bloodshed had been tremendous, and the medvarth had taken the worst of it. Perhaps thousands of the creatures lay dead upon the ground, torn by sword and axe and spear. Yet more of the medvarth charged towards Dun Calpurnia, and there seemed to be a never-ending tide of them.

It was madness. The Frostborn had always been cunning. Yet now they were throwing away medvarth warriors by the thousands, flinging them against the walls of Dun Calpurnia to die in droves. Every man on the wall was engaged with the medvarth, but they were holding. If the Frostborn kept this up, they would break their army against the walls of Dun Calpurnia.

Gavin cut down another medvarth. The creature's carcass fell towards him, and he twisted out of the way. The dead medvarth fell from the ramparts and landed in the town below, joining the others already scattered across the ground. Maybe that was the stratagem of the Frostborn. Maybe they planned to let the men of Andomhaim slaughter thousands of medvarth warriors, and then raise them as revenants. But that wouldn't work. If the Frostborn tried that, the Magistri would collapse their spell.

If he had time to think about it, it would have worried him, but Gavin's full attention turned to remaining alive.

He fought alongside Kharlacht and Caius, as he had a hundred times before. Antenora stood behind them, flinging blasts of fire at the medvarth whenever an opening presented itself. The Magistri stood behind her, guarded by the Swordbearers and men-at-arms battling the medvarth. Since the Frostborn had not used any magic, there had been no need for them to cast wards, and so instead they turned their magic to the aid of the men-at-arms. Some of them cast spells to make the men-at-arms stronger or faster, and others used their healing magic when the soldiers took wounds. Camorak had healed Gavin of minor wounds twice, and Kharlacht once. Somehow Caius had not yet been touched. Perhaps he was too short for the medvarth to consider a threat.

Gavin killed another medvarth, ripping Truthseeker free from the creature's neck.

As he did, horns rang out, calling men to the wall. But the men were already at the wall.

No. The horns were coming from the town's western wall.

Arandar ran up the steps to the western rampart, his guards and lords following him.

At once he saw what had so alarmed Third.

The battle had not yet touched the western wall, and only some of Dux Sebastian's guards waited here, watching in case the Frostborn attempted an attack by stealth. Perhaps a mile of empty, rocky ground stretched from the wall to the eastern bank of the River Moradel.

The river itself was glowing.

Arandar blinked, uncertain of what to make of it. The river gave off a blue light, the glow rising from within its depths. His first thought was that the Frostborn had poisoned the river, but that made no sense. Dun Calpurnia had its own water supply, several wells dug at the base of the castra's hill. Had the great spell of the Frostborn targeted the river?

"What is it?" said Arandar.

"I do not know," said Third. "I have never seen anything like it."

Arandar blinked. If someone as old as Third had never seen this before…

He looked for one of the Magistri, but none of them were with his guard at the moment. "Find one of the senior Magistri and get them over here. We need to figure out what this light is. The Frostborn have to be behind it."

One of the men-at-arms ran back to the northern forum, seeking a Magistrius. Arandar turned his attention to the glowing river. Something about the sight seemed familiar, stirring something in his memory. He certainly had never seen a glowing river before. Yet the pattern of light was familiar, and…

With a horrifying jolt, the memory came to him.

The memory, and the realization of the trap.

It had been on the walls of Dun Licinia a year ago, on the first night of the return of the Frostborn. The woods outside of the town had been lit with an eerie blue glow, a blue glow that had been revealed to be the ghostly fires dancing in the eyes and upon the limbs of the dead Mhorite orcs and the dead dvargir warriors. The light had come from the thousands of revenants marching towards the walls of Dun Licinia.

Revenants were undead.

Revenants didn't need to trouble themselves with things like breathing.

Which meant that the revenants could march quite comfortably along the bottom of the River Moradel, hidden from the scouts.

The first of the revenants emerged from the river's waters as he looked, nearly a thousand of them marching in a broad line. Some were the Mhorite orcs and the dead dvargir he had seen at Dun Licinia, their frozen flesh preserved by the icy magic of the Frostborn. Others were Anathgrimm warriors, no doubt killed during Ridmark's raids across the Northerland. There were quite a few medvarth and khaldjari. The Frostborn would collect their own dead for reanimation into revenants.

The sea of revenants emerged from the Moradel, striding with a slow, steady pace towards the western walls of Dun Calpurnia, their eyes glowing with eerie blue light. In a few minutes, they would reach the wall, and most of the army of Andomhaim was engaged at the northern wall.

In that horrible instant, Arandar saw the trap of the Frostborn closing around the town.

"God and the saints," said Gareth.

"There must be thousands of them," said Sebastian as the river kept vomiting forth undead.

"Tens of thousands," said Leogrance.

"Sound the alarm," said Arandar. "Get all the reserves to the western wall, now!"

"Will they even be able to climb the wall?" said Sebastian. "I don't see any ladders."

"The blue fire on their hands," said Arandar. "The Keeper's magic protects us from their touch, but it won't ward the walls. They'll be able to climb up the walls and attack the town."

Several of the Swordbearers in his guard produced horns and began sounding them. Arandar looked to the east and the north, saw the men struggling on the northern ramparts. They still had enough reserves to man all the western ramparts, and the engines atop the walls of the castra could be brought to bear, raining fire down on both the medvarth and the revenants. Despite the additional of tens of thousands of additional revenants, they could still hold Dun Calpurnia until help arrived.

Then the Frostborn finished casting their great spell.

Gavin yanked Truthseeker from a dead medvarth, his breath rasping in his throat, his shoulder and arms and back aching from the effort of fighting. They must have killed thousands of medvarth warriors, but the sea of them never seemed to end.

And now the revenants were assaulting the western wall, rising from the waters of the river like the spirits of the unquiet dead.

He lifted Truthseeker, drawing on the sword for strength and power, and as he did, he saw Antenora go rigid, her yellow gaze turned to the north.

"What is it?" said Gavin.

"The spell is finished," said Antenora.

There was a brilliant flash of blue light, almost as bright as the sun. Gavin squinted and looked away, and the blue light faded. He looked around, half expecting a rain of razor-edged ice to fall upon the town, but nothing happened. As far as he could tell, the spell hadn't done anything.

"The river," said Antenora.

He looked at the River Moradel and blinked in astonishment.

The spell had frozen it solid.

Already the khaldjari were pulling their siege engines onto the frozen river. Because of the curve of the river, they would be able to assemble their trebuchets and rain missiles onto the town with ease.

Arandar cut down a revenant, and then another, and still another.

He ought to have retreated to safety, but there had been no time, and while he might have been the High King, he was still a Swordbearer. Excalibur sliced through the undead without any resistance, even as the white fire of the sword destroyed the cold magic animating the undead.

The revenants crawled up the wall like roaches, their undead flesh freezing to the stone until they pulled it away. More men-at-arms rushed to the ramparts, fighting to hold back the tide of undead

Arandar cut down another revenant and glimpsed the frozen river.

The khaldjari had assembled a line of twenty massive trebuchets, and even as he looked, the engines released their missiles. Twenty burning fireballs soared through the air, leaving a trail of thick black smoke, and landed in the town.

The shock wave of the explosions almost knocked Arandar from the wall. The stones the trebuchets had thrown had been hollow, and they must have been filled with some sort of alchemical concoction that exploded on contact with the air.

The screams of burning men filled his ears.

The Frostborn were masters of ice, but it seemed they could also wield fire in battle as well.

CHAPTER SEVENTEEN

DESTRUCTION

The white mist swirled around his boots as Ridmark strode deeper into the Tomb of the Dragon Knight.

There were many turns and side passages, but the heartbeat in his head drew him deeper into the gloom below the earth. In places the white stone of the walls gave off its own pale radiance. In other places the walls did not glow, but instead crystals had been set into the ceiling at regular intervals, giving off a dim blue light. The place was a vast maze, and Ridmark was relieved that time was flowing faster for him than it was for anyone outside the Tomb. The sooner he retrieved the sword and returned to Calliande, the sooner they could return to Andomhaim and aid the others against the Frostborn.

Assuming he could return with the sword, and that he wasn't killed in the process.

Or that he was killed before he even found the sword, because from time to time things emerged from the white mist to attack him.

The first time was a band of kobolds. Ridmark was walking through a wide corridor, staff in hand, his eyes scanning the walls as he listened to the heartbeat in his head. He had maybe a second of warning as the mist rippled, and then a half-dozen kobolds erupted from the floor, appearing out of nothingness. Like all the kobolds he had fought, they were about the size of human children, lean and spindly with gray scales covering their bodies, long tails coiling behind them for balance and crimson crests rising from their necks and the tops of their lizard-like skulls. These kobolds had blue hands painted onto their chests, marking them as members of the tribe of the Blue Hand, a group of kobolds that Ridmark had fought near Dun Licinia soon after he had found Calliande on Black Mountain.

But that was impossible. Shadowbearer had killed them all, raised their corpses as undead, and sent them to kill Calliande.

Impossible or not, the kobolds of the Blue Hand were here, and he just had time to raise his staff in guard before they rushed him.

Ridmark parried a short sword with his staff, dodged, and struck back. His staff hit the kobold on the side of the head with a crack, and the creature went down. The remaining kobolds tried to swarm him, and Ridmark retreated, whipping his staff in wide arcs to keep them at bay. He dodged the thrusts of their spears, shifting his staff to his left hand to use as a shield and drawing his axe with his right hand. He swung the axe, the heavy blade shearing through kobold skulls and necks, and one by one he killed the creatures.

They collapsed motionless at his feet, the mist crawling over them like a shroud.

Ridmark stepped back, breathing hard, watching for more enemies. The kobolds had to be an illusion of some kind. Tymandain Shadowbearer had killed them all, and even if he hadn't, there was no way the survivors could have found their way to the Tomb of the Dragon Knight.

A thought occurred to him, and he tightened his grip on his weapons.

If these were illusionary duplicates of the kobolds of the Blue Hand...then would they rise as undead as the real kobolds had?

The dead kobolds vanished.

Ridmark blinked. One moment they had been sprawled on the floor, their blood leaking across the white stones. The next they had simply vanished without a trace. Even the blood had disappeared.

Ridmark scraped the end of his staff over the floor, wondering if they had somehow turned invisible, but he felt nothing.

The kobolds had vanished.

Or maybe they had never been there at all. Perhaps the creatures had only been illusions, constructions of magical force, or maybe he had only seen them in his own mind. That was a disturbing thought.

It also seemed likely. Ridmark had just had a conversation with his long-dead mother where she had suggested that it would have been better if he had never been born, and then she had shifted into the form of an urdhracos and tried to kill him.

That definitely suggested that not everything he saw in the Tomb was real.

He wished Calliande was here. Her Sight would have been able to pierce any illusions. Or Mara – she had the Sight as well, and she could handle herself in a fight. He wondered how Mara and Jager and Qhazulak and Zhorlacht and the rest of the Anathgrimm fared. There had been no word from the Anathgrimm or the Northerland since he had left Nightmane Forest with Calliande. Were they still fighting the Frostborn? Had they retreated into Nightmane Forest?

Or had the Frostborn killed them all?

Ridmark shook his head and kept walking. Brooding would solve nothing. The only way to help Calliande and his friends was to find the sword of the Dragon Knight and use its power against the Frostborn. That was the only way forward. Perhaps that was the only way to make up for some of the harm he had done …

He pushed aside the grim thought and kept walking.

More attacks came as he followed the heartbeat. Another group of kobolds surged out of the mist and charged, brandishing short swords. These kobolds had elaborate blue tattoos in the shape of grinning skulls upon their faces. They were the Blue Skulls, a tribe of kobolds sworn to the service of the Traveler, and Ridmark had killed hundreds of them when he had collapsed their rockfall trap on their heads.

Again, he fought them, killing them all, and again their corpses vanished a few moments later.

What was the point? The illusionary enemies would not turn him aside from his goal. Perhaps their blows would kill him if they landed home, making this part of the trial to claim the sword.

He survived a half-dozen more fights in the next hour. Once he fought a group of Mhorite orcs, their faces adorned with the red tattoo skull of the blood god Mhor. Later he dueled a pair of masked assassins of the Red Family, their swords flickering and dancing with deadly skill and speed. After that, he fought deep orcs led by a pair of dvargir warriors, and then a group of the Warden's Devout orcs, their veins glowing with the blue light of the Warden's dark magic.

The enemies might have been illusionary, but their weapons dealt real wounds. Ridmark took two minor cuts in the fight with the assassins of the Red Family, and a dvargir mace clipped his shoulder. He bound up the cuts as best as he could to stop the bleeding and continued.

Another reason he missed Calliande. She could have healed the cuts in a moment.

The fights forced his mind back to the past, to all the enemies he had fought and defeated. Ridmark had been in a lot of fights, and he had won most of them. He had left a lot of dead kobolds and orcs and dvargir and humans in his wake.

He had killed a lot of people.

Maybe the specter of Tomia Arban had been right. Maybe those people would be alive if he had never been born.

Ridmark dismissed the thought. He had killed a lot of people, yes, but he had never started a fight. A lot of his opponents had deserved their end at his hands. For that matter, he could not think of a time he had regretted a fight. No, his regrets were different. His regrets were his failures, the times he had not been strong enough, not been smart enough, not been quick enough.

The people he had failed to save, that was what he had regretted. The catastrophes he had failed to prevent.

Morigna's spirit had said that the sword would try to use his regret against him and that it would play upon the death wish buried in his nature. So far, his time in the Tomb of the Dragon Knight had been unpleasant, but Ridmark still had no wish to kill himself.

Maybe the ghost of his mother was right. Maybe it would have been better if Ridmark had never been born, but killing himself would not retroactively undo the harm his life had caused, and it would do nothing to help Calliande and his friends.

Nevertheless, his thoughts turned over the past again and again as he moved through the silent corridors and halls of the Tomb.

He was not entirely surprised when he saw a second woman standing in the center of another hall.

Her back was to him, her black hair bound in a braid that hung to her hips, and Ridmark's eyes noted the familiar and the pleasing shape of those hips. She wore a green gown with golden trim beneath a green mantle, the color the exact shade of her father's banners. Ridmark took a step forward, his mouth tightening into a frown, and the woman turned to face him.

"Ridmark," said Aelia Licinius Arban with a faint smile.

He let out a long breath, part angry, part annoyed, and part sad. Aelia looked just as he remembered, just as she had on the day he had failed to save her. She had the same green eyes shared by her father and brother and sister, and something of the same facial features, with a proud beak of a nose. Yet she was beautiful, with a vital energy that seemed to infuse her. He had been besotted with Aelia ever since he had been old enough to understand the desire for a woman, and he had gone to Urd Morlemoch to win her hand from her father.

After that, they had been married, and the only flaw in their happiness had been their inexplicable inability to have children.

Then Mhalek had come, and Ridmark had failed to save her.

Aelia's life had ended, but the path he had started at Urd Morlemoch had continued until he stood in the Tomb of the Dragon Knight looking at a phantasm constructed from his memories of his dead wife.

"No," said Ridmark.

Aelia blinked. "You will not greet your wife?"

"You're not my wife," said Ridmark. "My wife died eight years ago. You're not her spirit, either." Like Tomia, Aelia's form was solid, without the translucent shimmer that had marked Morigna's spirit. "You're...I don't know what you are."

Her gentle smile did not waver. "Then what I am, Ridmark?"

"A test, a trial, a trap, I don't know," said Ridmark. "The sword of the Dragon Knight or the magic on the Tomb thinks to test me by throwing my own memories at me." He kept his eyes on Aelia, waiting to see if she would transform into an urdhracos or some other horror. "I don't know what you are, but you're not Aelia."

"If I am your memory of Aelia Licinius Arban," said Aelia, "then I am indeed your wife, Ridmark. I might have died, but I am always in your memory, am I not?"

Ridmark stared at her.

"Yes," he said at last. The grief of Aelia's death had almost driven him to destruction. That urge had passed, but that grief would always be a part of him, even if he had learned to move past it.

He waited for her to speak. No doubt this illusion of Aelia would berate him for failing to save her, turn into an urdhracos, and then try to kill him. Once he had dispatched the creature, he would continue on his way.

"Oh, my husband," said Aelia. She lifted a hand to her mouth for a moment, and to his surprise, Ridmark saw that she was blinking away tears. On pure reflex, he almost reached for her to comfort her. He had never liked to see her cry. "Oh, I am sorry. I am so sorry."

"For what?" said Ridmark, baffled.

Her green eyes met his. "For how much you have suffered."

He said nothing.

"For you have suffered, have you not?" said Aelia. "Over and over again."

"I'm still alive," said Ridmark, his voice rougher than he would have liked. "I'm not maimed or crippled. I cannot complain."

"There are different kinds of suffering," she said. "You blamed yourself for my death. You felt so guilty when you fell in love with Morigna, and when my sister murdered the poor woman...oh, Ridmark. One loss like that was bad enough. But two? No one should have to endure that."

"People have endured lots of things they shouldn't have, but they did," said Ridmark. He hesitated. "And...I am sorry."

He knew she wasn't really there. He knew that he was talking to himself, or to the magic of the sword and the Tomb. But he couldn't have stopped himself from saying it.

"For what?" said Aelia.

"For...moving on," said Ridmark. "For falling in love after you. For there being other women after you. Twice."

"Ridmark," said Aelia with a smile. "You promised to be faithful to me so long as we both lived. And you were. I would not wish you alone for the rest of your days." Her smile faded. "I would not wish you to suffer as you have. Haven't you earned a rest?"

"What do you mean?" said Ridmark.

"Haven't you earned the right to die?" said Aelia. "To rest from your labors?"

"For God's sake," said Ridmark. "This again? I didn't believe it when the phantasm of my dead mother said it, and I don't believe it from the phantasm of my dead wife."

"You were right about Tarrabus Carhaine," said Aelia.

"What?" said Ridmark. He wondered if the phantasm would take a different tactic, if Aelia would taunt him that Tarrabus would have been able to save her when Ridmark had not.

"He was a fool," said Aelia. "He wanted physical immortality. That would mean grief piled upon grief, loss piled upon loss. One lifetime's sorrows are enough. The sorrows of an eternity would be an unendurable torment. Hell itself, I imagine. And Tarrabus wanted that for himself. You know better, Ridmark. You've lost so much. Are you not ready to rest from your labors in the heaven of the Dominus Christus?"

"From what I understand," said Ridmark, "suicides are not admitted to the kingdom of God."

"I could do it for you," said Aelia.

"No," said Ridmark. "That would make you a murderer, and I would not make even the phantasm of my dead wife into a murderer."

"You know if you continue," said Aelia, "there will be pain and suffering."

"Yes," said Ridmark. "But that is the nature of life. And if I am going to be killed, it will be only after I am defeated, not because I have given up."

"If you continue," said Aelia, "you will cause Calliande great pain."

Ridmark hesitated. It was harder to shrug that off.

"Because you caused me pain," said Aelia, "and you caused Morigna pain. You lost both of us. Maybe if you continue, you will lose Calliande." She gave him a gentle smile. "Maybe it would have been better if you had never been born."

"What?" said Ridmark.

"I loved you, Ridmark, but I would still be alive if you had never been born," said Aelia. "I would still be alive, and I would be married and surrounded by my children. Morigna would still be alive. Perhaps your mother would still be alive."

"Maybe," said Ridmark, "but it is a pointless thought. The past is the past. It cannot be rewritten."

"Can't it?" said Aelia.

"What are you talking about?" said Ridmark.

"The magic of the high elves controls time," said Aelia. "You've seen it yourself. Time passes faster outside of this Tomb."

"What of that?" said Ridmark. "Not even the high elves can rewrite the past. If they could, no doubt Ardrhythain would use that power to save his kindred from their fate."

"No," said Aelia. "No magic of mortal men can alter time. Yet the high elves were greater than we are, and their magic can slow the passage of time. The dragons were far greater than the high elves. What could their magic do? Could their magic rewrite the past?"

"Impossible," said Ridmark.

Yet something in the idea seemed to grip his mind.

"Could the sword of the Dragon Knight," said Aelia, "give you the power to rewrite time so you were removed from the past? Think of all the suffering you would have averted. Your mother would not have died of illness. I would still live. Morigna would still live. Calliande would still sleep, for the Frostborn would never have returned."

"No," said Ridmark. "If I hadn't stopped them, Qazarl would have killed Calliande and opened the gate on the day of the omen of blue fire."

"Using the soulstone that Tymandain Shadowbearer stole from the city above us," said Aelia. "But he was only able to steal it because Ardrhythain was not there. Ardrhythain was not there because he was in Castra Marcaine, speaking to you. Had you never been born, Ridmark, none of this would ever have happened."

"That's impossible," said Ridmark. "That is an utter fantasy."

Yet part of his mind wondered if she was telling the truth. He had made so many mistakes. Maybe one of those mistakes had led to Imaria opening the world gate and calling forth the Frostborn and killing thousands of people in the resultant war. Perhaps if he had never been born, someone else would have stopped her. Or some other knight would have killed Shadowbearer. Some other knight who would not have failed to save his wife.

And perhaps it was not so strange that the sword of the Dragon Knight could rewrite the past. Ridmark had been stunned by Cathair Solas and the magical prowess of the high elves. Ardrhythain had said the power of the dragons had been beyond the skills of the high elves.

And maybe, just maybe, the sword of the Dragon Knight had the power to work such a miracle.

Maybe it could bring back all those Ridmark had failed and all those who had died because of him. He had seen so many horrible things, and perhaps he could undo them all.

All it would cost was his life.

Wasn't that a small enough price to pay?

"No," said Ridmark, shaking his head and pushing away the absurd fantasy. "No, this is madness. The Dragon Knight can't change the past. No one can. I am going to find the sword of the Dragon Knight, and we are going to defeat the Frostborn. That's all."

"Oh, Ridmark," said Aelia with a sigh. "As always, you must suffer before you see the truth."

She stepped forward and changed, the green gown becoming black armor plates, talons of dark steel sprouting from her fingers, and her eyes filling with the dark void of an urdhracos.

Ridmark had expected the transformation and raced to attack her, but Aelia moved first. The urdhracos spun, and a leathery wing caught Ridmark across the chest. It was a bit like getting hit by a door. Ridmark stumbled, and Aelia leaped into the air, wings beating. She reached the ceiling and gripped it with one hand and one foot, hanging like a hunting bird about to swoop down on its prey.

He stepped to the side, watching her. Could she cast spells? If so, she could rain down dark magic at him with impunity. His mind flashed back to his first visit to Urd Morlemoch all those years ago. He had fought an urdhracos then, and she had breathed fire at him...

Even as the thought crossed his mind, Aelia's jaws yawned wide.

Ridmark cursed and threw himself to the side, and he avoided the cone of fire that erupted from Aelia's mouth. The urdhracos threw herself after him, no doubt intending to finish Ridmark off as he burned.

Instead, she flinched as he attacked, and his staff hit the side of Aelia's head with a loud crack. She stumbled back, and before she could recover, Ridmark yanked the axe from his belt and swung it, burying it in her chest. The heavy blade crunched through the armor plates with a loud crack, and Aelia shrieked and stumbled back.

And as she did, she changed.

Ridmark stared at her, frozen.

She looked as she had on the day that she had died in the great hall of Castra Marcaine. Every detail of that terrible day had been seared into his memory, and he stared at her in horror as she gazed at him, her green eyes full of pain, lips moving as she tried to speak, but no words came from her mouth, only blood.

He grabbed her, reaching for Heartwarden's healing magic, only to realize that he had been severed from the soulblade's magic years ago, and even then, the first time this had happened, the soulblade's power hadn't been enough to save her.

For the second time, Aelia Licinius Arban died in his arms.

Ridmark dropped to his knees, her body a warm weight against him, her blood hot where it trickled against his hands.

Then she was gone, and he was alone, kneeling in a silent room as mist swirled around him.

Ridmark took a moment to get his breathing under control, waiting for his heartbeat to slow to something resembling its normal speed. It hadn't been real. He knew that it hadn't been real.

But it had felt real. It had been like living through it all over again.

Ridmark took a ragged breath and got to his feet, collecting his weapons as he did. A vicious surge of anger went through him. Damn Ardrhythain for making him do this! Damn the high elves and their precious threefold law! He rubbed his hand over his chin, trying to keep the storm of anger and remembered grief under control.

Maybe Aelia had been right. Maybe the sword of the Dragon Knight could undo her death and every other death Ridmark had seen.

No. Ridiculous. The sword wouldn't have that power, no matter what the phantasm said. No one had that power.

Yet if the sword had that power, if it could kill Ridmark and rewrite the past so that he had never been born...

...didn't he have the obligation to use it?

He pushed aside the thought and stalked deeper into the Tomb, wondering what regrets from his past would come to assail him next.

CHAPTER EIGHTEEN

KEEPER

Calliande paced back and forth before the doors to the Tomb of the Dragon Knight over and over again.

She wondered if Ardrhythain found it annoying.

If the ancient archmage did, he gave no sign. He had asked once if she would like to sit, and she had refused. After that, he had fallen silent, both hands grasping his staff, his head bowed, his golden eyes half-closed. He looked as if he were lost in thought, or perhaps meditating. He did not seem inclined to speak, and Calliande was not inclined to interrupt him.

Instead, she waited, trying not to imagine what might be happening to Ridmark behind those closed golden doors.

Several times she reached for the Sight, hoping it would show her something of Ridmark. Every time, it was useless. Far above her head Cathair Solas blazed with magical power, wrapped in mighty wards, and she also saw the power shining from the soulstones in the higher cavern. Even if the Tomb of the Dragon Knight had been unprotected, it would have been difficult to direct the Sight through the magical power shining around her.

And the tomb was protected, warded with the strongest spells Calliande had ever encountered, save for perhaps the warding spells that bound the Warden to Urd Morlemoch. No wonder Tymandain Shadowbearer had asked her about the sword of the Dragon Knight when she had awakened. If she had been foolish enough to hide the sword somewhere outside of Cathair Solas, it would have been Shadowbearer's best chance to claim the sword, or at least ensure that it was never used against him.

The Sight could show Calliande nothing of Ridmark.

There was nothing to do but to wait.

She supposed it was little different from what millions of other women had endured throughout the bloody centuries of human history. When the men went to war, the women who loved them remained behind and waited to learn of their fate, whether they would return victorious or defeated, alive or dead.

Sometimes they never learned of the soldiers' fate at all.

Calliande shook her head. Maybe this was repayment for her pride. She had helped lead armies to battle many times. Men had left their homes and followed their lords and the High King at her call, leaving their wives and children behind. She had known at the time she was causing pain, but now she got to experience that pain firsthand.

Her thoughts chased each other, heaping rebuke upon rebuke. Calliande wondered what she could have done differently. If she had foreseen the war of the five Pendragon princes, she could have strengthened the Order of the Vigilant, and they would have endured to the present day. Or if she had advised the High King Uthanaric Pendragon more wisely. If she had been more persuasive, perhaps she could have convinced him that Tarrabus was a snake, and Uthanaric would still be alive, and the Frostborn would have been already defeated.

Or maybe if she hadn't been so damned clever.

She had been clever, hadn't she? After all, her plans had worked. She had slept the centuries away beneath the Tower of Vigilance and awakened as the return of the Frostborn threatened. Her memories and her staff and the power of the Keeper had been returned to her. Tymandain Shadowbearer had been killed. And when Imaria opened the gate and the Frostborn returned, Calliande had left herself a weapon to use against the Frostborn. The sword of the Dragon Knight had been waiting for her all along.

She had been so damned clever...and that cleverness had led to her pacing before the door of the Tomb, waiting helplessly for Ridmark to return and dreading what might happen to the realm of Andomhaim in her absence. Perhaps Ridmark would die trying to retrieve the sword, and Calliande would return to a broken Andomhaim lying beneath the boots of the Frostborn.

And it would be her fault.

Calliande kept pacing, her thoughts chasing each other like starving dogs.

A noise caught her attention. She looked up in sudden hope, wondering if Ridmark had returned, but the doors to the Tomb remained shut. Instead, a trio of high elven women approached, laying something upon a flat stone a few yards away.

"What is that?" said Calliande as the high elven women bowed to Ardrhythain and withdrew.

"Refreshment," said Ardrhythain. "I thought perhaps you might be hungry."

Calliande blinked. The high elven women had set out a tray holding bread and sliced sausages, and what looked like a pot of steaming tea with a pair of cups.

"I'm not hungry," said Calliande.

Ardrhythain nodded but did not say anything. Calliande resumed pacing.

The tea did smell good, though. So did the bread. She had been too nervous to eat much earlier. And if Ridmark returned from the Tomb with wounds, she would need her strength to heal them.

Calliande sighed, crossed to the flat stone, and sat down cross-legged next to it. A moment later Ardrhythain joined her, seating himself on the other side of the stone. He poured a cup of tea, passed it to her, and then poured one for himself.

"I apologize for this humble setting," said Ardrhythain. "In ancient days, tea was a ceremony among our people, much as banquets and feasts and tournaments of knightly valor are among yours. Among the students of the magi, we would drink tea and discuss the nature of the cosmos into the late hours of the morning." He said nothing for a moment. "That was a long time ago."

He lifted his cup, and Calliande had tea with the last archmage of the high elves, a man who wielded powers just short of a god.

It was a strange experience, but not anywhere near the strangest thing she had done in her life.

They ate and drank for a while in silence. Calliande kept resisting the urge to look at the doors of the Tomb.

"Thank you for the food," she said at last.

Ardrhythain inclined his head. "You fear for the Gray Knight."

"Yes," said Calliande. She hid her discomfiture with another sip of tea. "I imagine that is obvious."

"It is," said Ardrhythain. "Though you did not fear for Kalomarus and the other six knights who accompanied you here the first time."

"That's not true," said Calliande. "I feared for their lives. The fear grew worse every time the sword killed one of them."

"But you did not," said Ardrhythain, "fear for them as you now fear for Ridmark."

"No," said Calliande.

"Why is that?" said Ardrhythain.

Calliande hesitated, a dozen angry responses stirring in her head, and she decided to tell him the truth. "Because we are betrothed."

Ardrhythain nodded.

"He asked me in Tarlion," said Calliande. "I told him I wanted to find a priest so we could be wed at once. Instead, we heard that damned heartbeat. It took us to the Tower of the Keeper, and to the gate that Kalomarus had left there if I needed the sword of the Dragon Knight again. Then we ended up here, and you know the rest."

Ardrhythain nodded again but said nothing.

"Were you ever married?" said Calliande.

To his surprise, he answered. "Twice. My first wife was slain fighting the dark elven lord you know as the Warden, and I married again after her. My second wife was killed fighting the urdmordar. My wives and I had many children and grandchildren, but I fear they have all been dead for a very, very long time, and none of my family yet live."

"I'm sorry," said Calliande.

"Thank you," said Ardrhythain. "When I say that I understand your fear, you know I speak from much experience. Though it is surprising."

"What is?" said Calliande.

"That you are betrothed."

"Is it?" said Calliande. "Surely I am not that repulsive."

"There are qualities other than the physical," said Ardrhythain. "When last you were here, you had no interest in marriage whatsoever."

"I was the Keeper of Andomhaim," said Calliande. "My duty was to defend the realm from dark magic. Marriage was never an option for me. Nor even taking a casual lover, not that I ever wanted to do such a thing."

"But you could have quite easily," said Ardrhythain. "Past Keepers have wed and borne children. Some of them became knights of renown, as I recall. And while your self-restraint is commendable, it is rare. Many Keepers and High Kings did enjoy companionship outside the bounds of marriage. Your current High King was the offspring of one such liaison, I believe."

"Yes," said Calliande. "But...why are we talking about this? Andomhaim is about to go to the war with the Frostborn and Ridmark is seeking the sword of the Dragon Knight. Surely there are more important matters to discuss."

"Because a storm is about to befall Andomhaim and the rest of the world," said Ardrhythain, "and you stand at the heart of the storm. Therefore, it is necessary that you understand yourself completely. Very soon you will face a trial of your own, as severe as the one challenging Ridmark even now. To survive that challenge, you must understand yourself."

"All right," said Calliande. She didn't want to talk, but she supposed it was better than sitting here and waiting to see if Ridmark lived or died. "What do I need to understand?"

"You could have sought marriage or simply a companion in your previous life," said Ardrhythain, "but you did not. When I met you outside of Urd Morlemoch, you could have seduced Ridmark then, but you did not..."

"That's not a good example," said Calliande. "Morigna was alive, and...and I didn't know myself. I didn't know if I had a husband and children sleeping in some other ruin of the Order of the Vigilant."

"But when you recovered your memory, you knew the truth," said Ardrhythain. "You knew the truth even before you went to Dragonfall, thanks to the Warden. Yet you did not act on it."

Calliande frowned. "Ridmark was with Morigna. I wasn't...I wasn't going to try and seduce him away from her. Anyway, I was the Keeper. I had my duty. I thought I would spend the next several years rooting out the Enlightened of Incariel from Andomhaim. I had my duty, and Ridmark had Morigna, and that was that."

"Your duty came first," said Ardrhythain.

"Yes," said Calliande. "It always did. That was why I never married during the first war, and even after the Frostborn were banished. There...I always had my duty, and I would not turn from it."

And such joy it had brought her, she thought bitterly.

She had done her duty, and now the Frostborn threatened Andomhaim and Ridmark put himself at risk to claim the sword of the Dragon Knight.

"What changed?" said Ardrhythain.

"I'm sorry?" said Calliande.

Ardrhythain took a sip of the tea. "What changed? For something did change. Else you would have refused Ridmark when he asked for your hand."

"I…" said Calliande.

What had changed? For the archmage had a point. She could have taken a lover before she had gone into the long sleep. Many knights and noblemen had subtly and politely made their interest known (and a few drunken louts not so subtly), but she had always refused them without hesitation. Her duty had always come first, and while she had regretted that she would not have a husband and children, it had never troubled her unduly.

It had never bothered her the way seeing Ridmark with Morigna had bothered her.

That was what had changed. She had met Ridmark Arban.

"I love him," she said, looking into her tea. "I…he saved my life the day we met. He promised me that he would help me find my memory, and he did. We had to go to some of the most dangerous places anyone can ever visit, but he kept his word. And my duty…" She sighed and closed her eyes. "I would have failed in my duty but for him."

"What do you mean?" said Ardrhythain.

"I always put my duty before anything else," said Calliande, "and I would have failed, it not for Ridmark. Shadowbearer and his servants would have killed me and opened the world gate on the first day I awakened, and I never would have known why. I wouldn't have lived long enough to make it to Dragonfall if not for him. I would have failed the final test if he had not killed Tymandain Shadowbearer. I would have failed to gather allies against the

Frostborn if not for him." She felt her eyes burning and realized that she was starting to cry and tried to pull herself together. "I...I owe him so much, and I've sent him to do this risky and dangerous thing."

"Is that why you want to marry him?" said Ardrhythain. "Of a sense of gratitude?"

"No," said Calliande. "No. I do owe him, yes. But I am the better for him in my life. I was so glad to see him again when we went to Nightmane Forest. And I want him to be happy. I want him to be less grim. I want to see if I can make him less grim. I want..." She took a deep breath, collected herself, and looked the ancient archmage in the eye. "I want to stay with him until I die."

Ardrhythain inclined his head. "Then you understand what you are fighting to defend. What is at stake for you."

Calliande rubbed at her eyes. "Why did you ask me all that?"

"Because I wished to know," said Ardrhythain. "And it may be important, vitally important, that you understand your own motivations. The Sight does not always grant a clear vision of the future, you know that as well as I do. But when you and the Gray Knight came to Cathair Solas, I saw the shadows of your future, and in those shadows, I saw that you would have to save him."

"From what?" said Calliande.

"I do not know," said Ardrhythain, nodding towards the golden doors, "but from our present context, it must have something to do with the sword."

"Morigna's spirit said the same thing to me several times," said Calliande.

"Spirits are less subject to the flow of time than those of us who are still alive," said Ardrhythain. "You would do well to heed her warning." He set down the tea cup. "You may at least comfort yourself with the truth that your duties and the desires of your heart are at last aligned. A new Dragon Knight is our best chance to defeat the Frostborn, and if the Frostborn are defeated, Imaria will never reach the Well, and the shadow of Incariel will never be freed from its prison."

"A small comfort," said Calliande, "but a rare one."

They sat in silence for a moment. Calliande's appetite had fled with the rush of emotions, but she knew that was just an illusion, so she made herself finish the bread and sausage.

"Why did you never remarry?" said Calliande after a while. "Since we are asking each other piercing questions."

A faint smile went over Ardrhythain's alien face. "One cannot deny the fairness of the question." He shrugged. "In answer, I did not feel the need. Among the high elves, the mating instinct is not as…perpetually inflamed as it is among humans."

"Perpetually inflamed," said Calliande in a dry voice.

"Alas, there was no polite way to put that," said Ardrhythain. He sighed. "But the high elves are now a remnant. There are no children in Cathair Solas. The bladeweaver Rhyannis is the youngest of us, and she is already centuries old. There have been no new marriages in Cathair Solas for a long time. I fear that the time of our kindred has ended, and our world shall pass into the hands of the humans and the orcs and the dwarves and all the others the dark elves summoned over the millennia." He shrugged. "Perhaps you will do better than we did. But the future is in God's hands, not yours or mine."

"That is a comfort," said Calliande, and Ardrhythain nodded.

They lapsed into silence again, and Calliande looked at the golden doors.

"I wish I knew what was happening to him," said Calliande. "I wish I knew what was happening in Andomhaim."

"Even I cannot look into the Tomb of the Dragon Knight," said Ardrhythain. "But I may be able to see the realm of Andomhaim and what transpires there."

"You can?" said Calliande. "The difference in the rate of time will not stop you?"

"It would be a useless defense for the city if it did," said Ardrhythain. He rose to his feet, and Calliande followed suit. "Come. I shall attempt to use the Sight to discern how Andomhaim fares."

He swept the staff before him, and a pale curtain of mist rose from the cavern floor, shivering and rippling. Ardrhythain gestured, and the mist shuddered. Images appeared in the mist, flickering and dancing.

Calliande stepped closer, watching the images.

In one she saw Arandar and the army of the realm of Andomhaim marching north. It looked like they were heading to the town of Dun Calpurnia, or at least the ruins of it. Did Arandar think to make a stand there? It was a logical place. The dwarves and the manetaurs and the Anathgrimm would be able to find him there.

As if in response to her thoughts, the images changed. The mist showed her thousands of dwarves marching to war, and vast lines of manetaurs and tygrai marching. She saw the Anathgrimm heading south from Nightmane Forest, led by Qhazulak and Zhorlacht and Jager, though she didn't see Mara. South? Why were they heading south? The Frostborn were to the north.

The mist shifted, and she saw the Frostborn and their soldiers.

God and the saints, but there were so many of them.

Tens of thousands of medvarth marched south, flanked by just as many locusari warriors. Squadrons of locusari scouts flew overhead, along with hundreds of frost drakes. Battalions of khaldjari escorted carts laden with the components of siege engines, and groups of cogitaers floated behind them, guarded by medvarth warriors. Behind them marched thousands of Frostborn, and even through the vision of the mist she saw the magical might around them.

"There's so many," said Calliande, and then the vision shifted again.

The revenants of the Frostborn marched to war, Mhorite orcs and dvargir and humans and Anathgrimm and others. They were moving slower than Calliande expected, and the vision was…distorted, somehow, as if she was looking at the undead through a translucent obstruction.

"Are they shielded?" said Calliande. "Warded, somehow?"

"No," said Ardrhythain. "I believe they are underwater."

"Underwater?" said Calliande, and then she realized the truth. "The Moradel. They are marching along the bottom of the Moradel."

It was something she never would have guessed if she had not seen it with her own eyes…and the Frostborn would be in a perfect position to launch an ambush.

Arandar and the lords of Andomhaim would never see it coming.

Calliande looked at the golden doors, fresh dread flooding through her.

Dread for Ridmark…and dread for the army of Andomhaim marching into the trap of the Frostborn.

CHAPTER NINETEEN

REWRITTEN

The Tomb of the Dragon Knight changed around Ridmark once again.

The first time had startled him. He had been walking through a corridor of white stone, the walls giving off a faint glow, and the corridor vanished around him. Suddenly he was walking through the Northerland, specifically the valley south of the Black Mountain and north of Dun Licinia where the army of Andomhaim had beaten back the host of the Mhalekites. Mhalek had murdered the leaders of the army during a parley, and Ridmark had taken command, beating the Mhalekite orcs and sending Mhalek himself fleeing towards Castra Marcaine in search of revenge.

He stopped in shock, and then the valley disappeared, transforming back to the corridor.

It had to be another illusion. But why? Ridmark did not see the point. Maybe the Tomb would summon urvaalgs or Mhalekite orcs to attack him.

The heartbeat still echoed inside his head.

Ridmark pressed on, and the Tomb changed around him again and again.

One moment he was walking through the pine forests of the Northerland. The next he strode through a valley in the Torn Hills near Urd Morlemoch, and the moment after that, through the towering, ancient trees of the Qazaluuskan Forest. A few moments later, he found himself walking through the foothills of the mountains of Vhaluusk, not far from the pass that led to the Vale of Stone Death and the gates of Khald Azalar.

Every time the landscape changed, the heartbeat remained constant in his head, and he employed it as a compass, using it to select a constant path through the changing terrain. Ridmark wasn't sure, but he thought that the heartbeat was getting louder. Did that mean he was getting closer to wherever the sword rested?

He hoped so. The sooner he returned to Calliande with the sword, the better.

The doubts chewed at his mind. The words that Aelia's phantasm had spoken would not leave his thoughts.

What if it was true? What if he could use the sword of the Dragon Knight to rewrite the past, to remove himself from the pages of history, to make it as if he had never existed? The idea seemed absurd, but who knew what kind of powers the dragons had possessed? Perhaps their magic had let them shape time the way the dwarves shaped steel and stone.

He thought about all the times that he had failed, all the mistakes that he had made. If the sword could remove him from time, would all that be undone? Aelia might still be alive. His mother might have lived for decades more. The realm might still be at peace. The Frostborn might never have returned. Calliande...

Ridmark blinked, pushing aside the wild fantasies. Calliande was waiting for him, and he had promised to return to her. He had to focus on that, not brooding about what could not be changed.

But if the sword could change the past, didn't he have the duty to use it? If he could destroy himself and undo so much harm, didn't he have the obligation?

The terrain changed again, and he found himself walking through the grassy plains of the Range, the home of the manetaurs, a range of volcanoes rising away to the north. Then it blurred again, and he strode through the plains of eastern Durandis, where the men of

Durandis often struggled against Mhorite raiders coming down from the mountains of Kothluusk.

Then the land blurred again, and Ridmark found himself in a large hall of white stone, light coming from the crystals mounted in the apex of the ceiling overhead. Their pale blue glow painted the mist swirling around his knees an eerie azure color, as if he was walking through a sea of liquid ice.

Two women awaited him in the center of the hall, their backs to him.

One was short, and the second almost as tall as Ridmark. The shorter woman had blond hair so pale it was almost white, and the taller woman had hair the color of the deepest night. Both were slender, but the smaller woman seemed almost delicate, while the taller woman had a fit, lean look to her. The shorter woman wore dark clothing and blue armor of dark elven steel, while the taller woman wore close-fitting armor of black material.

Ridmark recognized them.

Mara and Third turned to face him. Third looked as impassive as usual, but Mara's green eyes were touched with sadness.

"Mara?" said Ridmark. "Third?" Was it really them? His mother and Aelia had been dead for years, but it was not outside the realm of possibility that Mara and Third had somehow found their way to Cathair Solas to speak with him.

"Ridmark," said Mara, and the coolness of her tone made him think this was another phantasm.

"Lord magister," said Third.

"You're another illusion," said Ridmark.

Mara raised an eyebrow. The hall blurred and vanished around them, and they stood in the eerie, blue-lit gloom of Nightmane Forest, the massive trees rising over them.

"I see you have not lost your ability to note the obvious, lord magister," said Third in a dead tone of voice.

"No," said Ridmark. He gripped his staff, holding the weapon level before him. If he had to fight these illusionary duplicates of the two half-sisters, he would have to assume they possessed Mara's and Third's ability to travel. If it came to a fight, likely one of them would distract him while the other traveled behind him to stab him in the back. Third and Mara had not often gone into battle alongside each other, but when they had, they made a fearsomely effective team. If the spells of illusion had built them out of his memories, then they would share that ability.

"It seems you are seeking the sword of the Dragon Knight of old," said Mara.

"Let me guess," said Ridmark. "You're going to say that I need to kill myself to make up for wrongs I have done, that if I destroy myself with the sword of the Dragon Knight, then I will undo all my mistakes." He took a step forward, watching both the women at once. Neither one of them would be able to travel without a distinctive flash of blue light.

"Why should we do that?" said Third.

"You already know it is true," said Mara. "You know the ancient dragons possessed powers far beyond human comprehension, far beyond even the reach of the high elves. Why should the sword of the Dragon Knight not have the power to remove you and all your errors from history?"

"Then you're telling me to kill myself and rewrite myself from the past?" said Ridmark.

Third sneered. It was the first time he had seen that expression on her face. "Why should we waste our breath telling you what you already know? Why should we waste our breath speaking to a man who lacks the strength to do what needs to be done?"

"What are you talking about?" said Ridmark.

"Ridmark," said Mara, her tone gentle and sad. It was the same tone of voice she used when she thought he was being foolish, when she needed to talk him down from a dark mood. "You know what has to be done. You know what kind of opportunity lies before you. You've known the truth from the moment you stepped into the Tomb, didn't you? You need to use the sword of the Dragon Knight to kill yourself. That's the only way."

"I doubt that," said Ridmark.

Third looked at the shorter woman. "We are wasting our time. He is too weak to do what needs to be done. Let us slay him and wait for a worthier bearer of the sword."

"No," said Mara, "no, he's not weak. Just wounded. You know how much he's lost. His mother and his wife and his lover and so many friends. He blames himself for it. Maybe if he had seen the truth earlier and killed Tarrabus, then the war might have been averted. Maybe if he had killed Imaria when he had the chance, then Morigna would still be alive. We are asking a wounded man to carry a heavy burden…but that is just it. Don't you see?"

"See what?" said Ridmark. He reminded himself to watch for the coming attack. Yet Mara's words were playing on his mind, seeming to sink in his thoughts like water into a dry sponge.

Or poison into a parched throat.

Yet if the phantasms were right…

"All that pain you've endured," said Mara. "All the losses you have suffered. They can be wiped away as if they have never been, for you will never have existed. Haven't you the right to rest from your labors?"

"As if that argument would persuade him," said Third. "He loves to suffer. He wallows in it."

Mara gave her sister a reproachful glance and then turned her attention back to Ridmark. "But you do not care about yourself, do you? No. Think on this, then. Think of all the pain you have seen, all the pain you have inflicted over your life…and how it can all vanish if you are but strong enough to use the sword on yourself."

Ridmark said nothing.

"You can save them, Ridmark," said Mara. "You can save them all. You saved me from myself, and you saved Third. How many more lives can you save if you are just strong enough? If you never existed, the Frostborn will never have come to Andomhaim, and the realm will be at peace."

"No," said Ridmark, trying to think through the persuasive words. "No, the Frostborn would have returned anyway. And if I hadn't been there, Shadowbearer would have killed Calliande on the day of the omen."

"If you hadn't been there," said Mara, "then Imaria would not have killed Morigna."

Ridmark didn't have an answer for that.

"But none of it matters," said Mara. "If you take up the sword and use it on yourself, then none of it matters anymore. All of it will be undone. You just have to kill yourself with the sword of the Dragon Knight. Let its fire consume you. Let it burn with you. And then you will have never existed. You will have peace, and so much evil will be undone." She sighed. "You are their last hope, you know. The Frostborn will conquer Andomhaim and the rest of this world. But if you destroy yourself, they will never have been here."

The vision seemed to waver before Ridmark's eyes. It staggered the mind. But was it possible? These phantasms had to be created by the power of the sword of the Dragon Knight. Maybe the sword was telling Ridmark what it could do.

Maybe that was the trial, to see if he was brave enough and bold enough to take the final step.

He pushed back from the thought with some difficulty. Kalomarus hadn't used the sword of the Dragon Knight to rewrite history. He had used it to defeat the Frostborn and save Andomhaim. That was why Ridmark was here, not to listen to ghosts from his memory taunt him about his failures.

"No," said Ridmark. "I'm not going to kill myself. I am going to take the sword, return to Calliande, and help her defeat the Frostborn."

"I told you he was not strong enough to do what needs to be done," said Third, her disdain obvious.

"I know," said Mara. She drew the short sword of dark elven steel and the dwarven dagger from her belt, the blade glinting in the dim light. "It was only fair to give him a chance to do what needs to be done, sister. But if he is not strong enough to do it, then we will."

She and Third vanished in swirls of blue fire.

At once Ridmark threw himself to the ground and rolled. He came back to his feet, whipping his staff around him in a wide arc, and that saved his life at the last possible moment. Both Third and Mara reappeared in flares of blue flame, and they reappeared with their blades leading. The sweep of Ridmark's staff deflected Mara's blades, and he jumped back as Third came at him, her short swords slashing.

Ridmark fought for his life as Third and Mara disappeared and reappeared around him, stabbing and thrusting. The fight was far more challenging than the duels with the two urdhracosi earlier in the Tomb. Both Mara and Third knew how to handle their weapons. Third was faster and stronger than her sister, but Mara could disappear and reappear with equal speed. The battle turned into a chaotic, whirling dance as Third and Mara pushed Ridmark down one side of the hall and back up the other. He had his staff in his left hand and his axe in the other, and he had to use both weapons to keep Third and Mara from slicing him into ribbons.

He had only one advantage. There was a flicker of blue fire an instant before Mara or Third could appear anywhere. It was not a long flicker, and it lasted barely a fraction of a second. If Ridmark could thrust his weapons towards the blue fire when he saw it, he might be able to land a blow the instant his enemies reappeared. Unfortunately, they kept trying to appear behind him.

Perhaps he could use that against them.

Ridmark charged at Mara, stabbing with his staff and swinging the axe. Mara retreated, quick and nimble, and vanished in a flash of blue light before Ridmark could get close enough to strike. The instant he saw the blue light, he whirled, and his eyes caught another pillar of blue fire behind him. He drove both his weapons towards the fire with all his strength, knowing that he was leaving his back open.

But the gamble paid off. Third reappeared, short swords raised to strike, and before she could move the end of Ridmark's staff hit her in the stomach, all his strength and speed behind the blow. She doubled over with a gasp, and before she could recover Ridmark swung his axe at her neck.

Third fell dead at his feet. Killing Third, even if she was only an illusion, had been hard. She had been a loyal lieutenant and a good friend through some dangerous battles, and…

He spun, swinging his staff crosswise before him, and managed to keep Mara from plunging her sword and dagger into his back. He attacked again, but his angle was wrong, and Mara managed to lift her weapons in a cross-parry. His grip on the staff wasn't secure, and the weapon was ripped from Ridmark's hand.

But that was all right because it freed both hands to wrap around the haft of his dwarven axe. Mara drew back her blades for the kill, and Ridmark raised his axe and brought it down with all his strength.

She wasn't wearing a helmet, and the blade crunched into her skull. Mara stiffened, her face going slack, and collapsed at Ridmark's feet. He stepped back, breathing hard, her blood glistening on the axe's blade. Killing her had been even harder than killing Third. No, he hadn't killed either Mara or Third. They weren't here. These were just illusions, just phantasms conjured up to tell him lies.

Or to tell him the truth.

Because if he could undo all the harm that he had done, if he could erase himself and make it so that the Frostborn had never returned to Andomhaim…

The dwarven axe shattered in his hand.

Ridmark flinched and stepped back as the pieces of the weapon fell to the floor with a ringing clang. The Taalkaz of the Dwarven Enclave in Coldinium had given him that weapon, and he had carried it through countless battles ever since. Dwarven steel never broke or shattered, not unless it was destroyed by irresistible force, and chopping through a skull was hardly the most difficult thing the axe had ever done.

The shards shivered and melted into smoke, vanishing away.

It was like the power in the Tomb had eaten away the weapon, as if it had never existed at all.

Ridmark blinked. As if it had never existed…

He looked at the corpses of Third and Mara, but both bodies had already dissolved back into the white mist. That made him feel a little better. He had just killed two of his friends, but it had only been an illusion.

He took a tighter grip on the staff of Ardrhythain and headed deeper into the Tomb, following the steady pulse of the heartbeat inside his head. The stone corridors shifted around him, seeming to become hills and battlefields he had visited years ago, only to shift again as he kept walking. The heartbeat in his head grew louder with every step, and he knew that its source would not be much farther away.

Then he stepped into another hall of white stone, and a woman waited, standing with her back to him.

This woman wore a brilliant white robe with a black sash wound tight around her waist, her hair hanging black and loose against her shoulders. Her hair was the exact shade that Aelia's had been, and recognition flooded through Ridmark, followed by hatred and the wariness that came over him before battle.

He knew this woman. He knew this woman very well, and he cursed himself that he had not been able to kill her when he had the chance.

"Imaria," said Ridmark, and he stepped into the hall.

Imaria Licinius Shadowbearer turned to face him.

He saw his distorted reflection in her quicksilver eyes, saw the veins of shadow flowing through her flesh like corruption through rotting meat. She had been a beautiful young woman, and while she was still attractive, her features had a corpselike pallor to match the quicksilver eyes and the black veins. Once she had looked a great deal like Aelia.

Now she looked like Tymandain Shadowbearer.

"Ridmark Arban," said Imaria, speaking in the strange double voice of the bearer of Incariel's shadow. "The man who was too weak to save my sister. And the man who will be too weak to save his nation, his kindred, his betrothed, and his world from me."

"I suppose you're here to tell me to kill myself as well?" said Ridmark.

"Hardly," said Imaria. "I am here to rejoice that you are too weak to kill yourself as you must."

"I'm sure," said Ridmark. "It is just as well that you are not here." His fingers tightened against the smooth black wood of the staff. "Else I would kill you with my own hands for what you have done."

"For killing your precious sorceress whore?" said Imaria with indifference.

A pulse of anger went through Ridmark, an echo of the mad fury that had driven him into the burning shell of Dun Calpurnia's keep to pursue her.

"For that," said Ridmark, "and for opening the world gate. I failed to stop you...but the blood is on your hands, Imaria, the blood of thousands of innocents."

"True," said Imaria. "I intend to free this world from time and causality and the prison of matter. The dead I have slain have no cause for complaint. I simply freed them a little sooner than planned."

"You cannot believe such madness," said Ridmark, remembering what Ardrhythain had told them. "The shadow of Incariel seeks to enslave us all. It is a demon, a fiend from the pit. And you think it is telling you the truth?"

"A useless question," said Imaria with a disdainful sniff. "If I am a construction of your memories, then you are asking the wrong question."

"Then what is the proper question?" said Ridmark.

Imaria smiled. "The form you see before you is an illusion spun from your memories...but is this shadow?"

She gestured, and the white mist vanished from the hall. Ridmark blinked in surprise. He had become so used to the presence of the mist that he had almost forgotten that it was there. Imaria gestured again, and the shadow spread from her boots and poured across the floor around her like spilled ink. The symbols on Ardrhythain's staff glowed with white light, and the shadows flowed around Ridmark, leaving him standing in a cleared circle as the darkness covered the floor of the hall.

"This form might be an illusion," said Imaria, "but the shadow is not."

"The shadow of Incariel," said Ridmark.

"It can reach even here into the heart of the high elves' power," said Imaria. "It can even reach here and touch you."

"Try it," said Ridmark. He stepped forward, and the light from the staff flared, pushing back the shadows.

Imaria laughed, long and loud. "Kill you? No, I don't need to kill you, Ridmark. It's much too late for that. I need to do nothing at all. My victory is already assured, and you are far too weak to stop it, just as you were too weak to save my sister."

"What are you talking about?" said Ridmark.

"Andomhaim will fall to the Frostborn," said Imaria. "It is inevitable. The realm is not strong enough to resist them. It does not have enough soldiers, and its magic is not powerful enough. It will take a year or a century, but the outcome is not in doubt. The Frostborn will grind away your armies, subjugate your people, and shatter your realm to dust. When Tarlion falls, the realm is theirs."

"And when Tarlion falls," said Ridmark, "you'll use the Well to open Black Mountain and free Incariel."

"Yes," said Imaria. "I shall have my freedom at last. And you shall have your freedom as well, you and all your other little mortals. Freedom from law and consequence, freedom from morals and duties…"

"Madness," said Ridmark.

Imaria grinned. "Madness and chaos and disorder and freedom from all laws and rules. That was what God took from me. That was what I shall bring to this world, and you shall scream and rejoice and revel and shriek when I do."

"No," said Ridmark. "We will defeat the Frostborn and drive them back to their world gate, and once we do, we will hunt you down."

"You won't," said Imaria with placid indifference. "It's too late for that. The Frostborn have moved too many of their forces here, and they cannot be defeated. Not even the little alliance you crafted is strong enough to stop them now. The only way to stop the Frostborn is to undo them, to rewrite history so they never came to this world."

Ridmark snorted. "And now you're going to tell me to kill myself with the Dragon Knight's sword. I've heard that speech before."

"Kill yourself?" said Imaria, laughing. "You misunderstand. I know you won't use the sword to destroy yourself. You're too weak. I am not here to tell you to kill yourself. I am here to rejoice that you are too craven to do it."

Ridmark shook his head. "Then get out of my way and don't try to stop me."

He started walking again, the light from the staff pushing back the shadows.

"There is no need to stop you," said Imaria. "My victory is assured, and it was your failure that made it possible. You were too pathetic to save my sister, and that set me on the road to the Enlightened and to the shadow of Incariel. And you were too weak to save Morigna."

Ridmark grimaced and kept walking.

"She thought you would save her right up until the Weaver tore out her throat," said Imaria. "Such faith she had in you. For just as Imaria Licinius was the larval form of the new Shadowbearer, so was Morigna the catalyst. It was her blood that opened the gate for the Frostborn. It was her death that was the herald of the new world of freedom to come. And it was all because of you, because my sister loved a man who could not save her…"

Ridmark drew back the staff to strike.

She did not try to stop him, her smile only widening.

He hit her in the stomach, doubling her over, and landed three rapid strikes on her head, each one driven with bone-crushing force. Imaria Licinius Shadowbearer collapsed at his feet, blood leaking from her nostrils and her lips, the smile still on her mouth.

"Too weak," she hissed, and then her corpse swirled into mist and vanished.

The staff shattered in Ridmark's hand.

He looked at the shards of the staff of Ardrhythain in shock, watching as they fell to the floor and unraveled into smoke. Had killing Imaria broken the staff? She had hardly been an innocent, and her death had been richly deserved. Besides, he had only destroyed the phantasm, not killed her in truth.

Was the power of the sword stripping away his weapons as he approached?

A storm of doubt roiled through his mind. Maybe Imaria had been right. Maybe he could destroy himself with the sword and save Andomhaim, and he was too weak to do it. He hadn't been strong enough to save Aelia or Morigna, after all, and...

Ridmark squeezed his eyes shut, forcing back the twisting emotions and the chaotic thoughts. The silence of the Tomb and the endless scorn of the phantasms was getting to him. No wonder Kalomarus had never spoken of the trial to Calliande if it had been anything like this.

He was almost there.

The thunder of the heartbeat in his head proved it.

Ridmark took a deep breath, pulled himself together, and pressed deeper into the shifting stone maze of the Tomb.

The whispers that Imaria and Mara and Aelia and the others had put into his thoughts did not seem to leave his mind.

If anything, they grew louder with every step.

CHAPTER TWENTY

BREAKING

Gavin killed and killed, his armor spattered with both the blood of the medvarth and the thick yellow slime that served as the blood of the locusari. His arms trembled with fatigue, and every joint in his body groaned with strain. He had been hit a dozen times, and each time one of the nearby Magistri had healed the wounds, permitting him to continue the fight. He had put their healing to use, and with every blow he cut down one of their foes, sending another corpse tumbling over the battlements or falling to the town below.

It wasn't enough.

It wasn't nearly enough.

Chaos ruled the town as flames rose from the buildings the khaldjari weapons had shattered. Against the northern wall, the Frostborn had flung the full weight of their medvarth warriors, dozens of siege ladders against the ramparts. The medvarth warriors climbed up the ladders, brandishing swords and axes. The defenders fought back, but they were being overwhelmed inch by inch. The khaldjari moved additional engines to within range of the walls, lighter catapults and ballistae, and a steady stream of missiles rained upon the ramparts.

Even worse, the frost drakes had joined the fray.

The ballista crews had managed to shoot down several of the drakes, but the creatures always flew away and swooped back to the attack, flanked by squadrons of locusari scouts. Before the frost drakes dove to attack, the scouts hurtled down at the ballistae, distracting the crews long enough for the frost drakes to unleash their freezing breath. The Magistri had to turn their full attention to defensive wards, but even their combined powers were not enough to block the full attack, and more and more men were killed, frozen inside cocoons of ice.

The defenders of the northern wall were holding, but they would not hold for much longer without immediate help.

Unfortunately, there was no help to be had.

The town of Dun Calpurnia burned in half a hundred places, the flames throwing thick plumes of black smoke high into the air. The khaldjari trebuchets on the frozen river continued their bombardment, and whatever alchemical weapon the khaldjari engineers had concocted burned with an intense, long-lasting fire. Men had screamed as the liquid fire spattered across them, sticking to their flesh like glue, and not even the Magistri had been able to save them. If the bombardment continued, soon everyone in Dun Calpurnia would burn to death or choke to death on the smoke.

Assuming the undead did not kill them all first.

A horde of revenants assailed the western wall, and fierce fighting raged up and down the length of its ramparts. Somehow the icy power that animated the revenants allowed them to scale the walls like roaches, and they rushed up in their thousands. The defense there had held, but the khaldjari trebuchets had blasted several craters into the ramparts, and sooner or later they would knock down a section of wall.

If that happened, they were finished. The Frostborn would swarm inside and slaughter the gathered host of Andomhaim. Gavin supposed that some survivors might escape through the town's southern gate, but they would be broken and demoralized. The Frostborn might be able to march right to the gates of Tarlion, especially if they could freeze the Moradel and use it as a highway.

But Gavin could do nothing to affect the course of the battle. He could do nothing but try to survive.

So he fought.

There was no more order on the ramparts, though from time to time he heard decurions and optios shouting commands, though the howl of the battle swallowed the words. Antenora stood next to him, flinging blasts of fire at the enemy, and in the distance, he glimpsed the rise and fall of Kharlacht's greatsword, though he had been separated from Kharlacht and Caius in the chaos. The surviving Swordbearers stood in a ring around the Magistri, protecting them as they cast the warding spells against the freezing breath of the drakes.

A pair of medvarth came at Gavin, axes in their clawed hands and their muzzles pulled back to reveal their yellowed fangs. Antenora hit the one on the right with a blast of magical fire, scouring the flesh from its skull. The second medvarth swung its axe, and Gavin caught the blow on his dwarven shield. The shield clanged, and a deep ache shot up his weary arm, but the axe did not damage his shield.

His soulblade proved more effective against the medvarth. Truthseeker punched through a gap in the creature's armor and sought its heart, and the medvarth started to fall. Gavin managed to rip his blade free in time to meet the attack of another medvarth. Steel clanged on steel as he blocked its attack, and his boots slipped on the increasingly blood-slick stones of the rampart. He recovered his balance and struck back, opening a cut on the medvarth's shoulder. The creature bellowed its rage, and then a militiaman plunged his spear into its neck. The medvarth shuddered, and Gavin drove his soulblade home, finishing off the medvarth.

He yanked Truthseeker free and nodded his thanks to the militiaman, and the other man's eyes went wide.

Gavin looked up just in time to see the fireball hurtling towards them, trailing a thick line of black smoke in its wake.

"Take cover!" someone screamed.

The fireball slammed into the rampart a dozen yards away, exploding in a wash of fire. A score of men and medvarth went up in flames, screaming, and the rampart shuddered beneath Gavin's boots.

And then it collapsed, and the world vanished into an avalanche of broken stone and fire.

###

Arandar battled for his life as his kingdom crumbled around him.

The revenants were not a formidable foe, especially to a man wielding a soulblade. Their danger lay in their blood-freezing touch, but the Keeper's magic had protected the army of Andomhaim from that. They were still inhumanly strong, but they had no weapons, and a disciplined formation of men-at-arms could keep them at bay with spear and shield. The fire of a soulblade tore through them, and Excalibur's keen edge sliced through the revenants like grass.

There were just so damned many of the things.

A tide of undead flesh clawed its way up the wall and onto the ramparts. Arandar thought of a dozen things he could have done to repulse the revenants. Boiling oil could have been poured from the battlements, incinerating the undead. Catapults set up in the town's forums and streets would have rained down fire upon the revenants. Even a cavalry charge sent to circle around the town and smash through the revenants would have been enough to get them away from the walls.

Any one of those things would likely have worked, but there were simply no men left to carry them out because every man in Dun Calpurnia was struggling for his life.

The trap of the Frostborn had been masterful, and Arandar had walked right into it. The baffling behavior of the Frostborn army now made sense. Why throw the locusari against the northern wall?

Why let the medvarth attack without support from the siege engines and the frost drakes?

They had been waiting for the revenants.

Arandar cursed himself as a fool. He had never considered, not even once, the possibility that the revenants might march along the bottom of the River Moradel. He had never heard of undead doing that, though it made perfect sense in hindsight.

Of course, mistakes were always obvious in hindsight.

Another pair of revenants hauled themselves up the wall, leaving frost in their wake. This pair had once been Mhorite warriors, and likely they had been undead ever since the Anathgrimm and Dux Gareth had smashed Mournacht's host at Dun Licinia. Once they had been green-skinned with red skulls tattooed over their faces, but a year of undeath had turned their skin a blotchy yellow, their faces and hands covered with frost as blue fire danced on their heads and shoulders.

They reached for Arandar, and he struck first, Excalibur trailing white fire from its blade. The soulblade's magic would have burned away the cold power animating the revenant, but since Excalibur could cut through anything, that was hardly necessary. The sword sheared through the first undead creature's neck, and Arandar pivoted, bringing Excalibur around. It was a weak swing, but it didn't matter because the sword's magical edge sliced through the undead flesh with ease.

Both undead collapsed to the rampart, and Arandar flung himself into the fray, the Swordbearers and Magistri of his bodyguard fighting alongside him. The high nobles who had been within him also fought, battling to get free of the revenants. Arandar cut down revenant after revenant. Excalibur's keen edge gave him an advantage that no other soulblade could match, and the soulblade filled him with strength and power, letting him fight longer and harder than a man could otherwise.

He needed to cut his way free. He needed to get the army organized and take command, needed to coordinate a more effective defense against the Frostborn horde.

Unfortunately, he could not, because the town was on fire.

Another volley of fireballs soared overhead, landing in the ruins of the town and exploding with enough force to send a vibration through the wall. The entire northern half of Dun Calpurnia was already sheathed in flames, slowing movement and cutting off groups of men-at-arms from one other. The men on both the western wall and the northern wall were pinned in place, but no help could reach them thanks to the flames.

"We must withdraw!" shouted Dux Leogrance, his sword glittering with frost as his chest rose and fell. The old Dux was giving a good account of himself, but both he and Dux Gareth and Dux Kors looked exhausted. "We must withdraw! If we stay here, we shall be overrun!"

"I agree!" said Prince Cadwall. He started to speak, paused long enough to cut down a pair of revenants, and kept shouting. "We must abandon the town and reform to the south. If we stay we shall be caught in the trap, and the Frostborn can rain fire and ice down upon us at will."

Arandar stepped back, looking around. "If we leave the town we will lose men. Thousands, probably."

"We shall all die if we stay here," said Gareth.

He was right. Arandar saw no way around it. There was no way they could stay here. The Frostborn would grind them down foot by bloody foot. They had to withdraw and reform south of the town. Perhaps they would have to fall all the way back to Castra Carhaine before they could hold a line against the Frostborn. But what about their allies? The dwarves and the Anathgrimm were coming from the west, and the manetaurs were coming from east. If the men of Andomhaim fell back, the Frostborn might be able to defeat the dwarves and the Anathgrimm and the manetaurs one by one.

If the men of Andomhaim stayed here, they would all be killed.

"We haven't any choice," said Arandar. "We…"

A fireball soared over his head and slammed into the northern wall, right near the gatehouse. There was a roiling burst of flame, and the tower and a portion of the wall ripped apart in a spray of shattered masonry and burning timber. Screaming men and medvarth and chittering locusari tumbled through the air, wreathed in fires as they fell to their deaths.

As the smoke cleared, Arandar saw that the explosion had torn a breach in the northern wall.

That was it, then. Already the advancing medvarth were heading towards the breach. The explosion was close enough to the Magistri atop the gate that it would have killed or at least disrupted their concentration, which meant that the Magistri would not be able to coordinate their efforts to ward against the freezing breath of the drakes.

"Sound the withdrawal!" said Arandar to the Swordbearers of his guard. "We shall withdraw through the southern gate, and I will place my banner there. We can reform the host, and either withdraw in good order to the south or face the Frostborn here." They would lose a lot of the supplies that Sir Joram had carefully gathered over the last year. Well, supplies could be replaced, but men could not. "Sound the withdrawal now!"

Those Swordbearers and knights who still had horns lifted them to their lips and blew the prearranged series of blasts that instructed the host to withdraw. Answering blasts came from the northern wall and along the western wall, and from the observers in the castra atop the hill. Arandar hurried for the stairs, his mind racing. They would have to get through the southern gate as soon as possible, and the army would be vulnerable as they withdrew. Could he arrange for a guard to hold the southern forum? Any men who tried to hold the forum as the others escaped would be slaughtered. Perhaps the

Swordbearers could do it and escape, or maybe some of the warriors from the three orcish kingdoms.

Arandar and his guards and the lords reached the town and hurried down a street leading towards the castra. The houses burned around them, the alchemical weapon of the Frostborn blazing inside the brick walls. In places, the heat was so intense that the brick walls had collapsed into heaps of rubble, and the street reminded Arandar of the interior of a baker's oven. Before the battle, he had wondered what it would feel like to be killed by the cold magic of the Frostborn, but he had never considered that the Frostborn might burn them all alive.

Yet another failure on his part.

"My lords!" shouted one of the Swordbearers.

Arandar looked up to see one of the fireballs fall from the sky. Right towards them.

He just had time to duck into a doorway, and then the missile struck the street and exploded, the shock wave hammering into the houses.

Gavin didn't pass out, but he was woozy.

He heaved himself to his feet and looked around, dust and blood sliding off his armor. Broken stones and shattered bricks rasped beneath his boots, and he stumbled several feet before he could catch his balance. For a moment, he feared he would fall backward off the rampart, and then he realized that he was in the northern forum.

The forum. How had he ended up in the forum?

He shook his head, and a cold shock of fear snapped him back to lucidity.

The last explosion had ripped a hole in the town's wall. The sheer force of the explosion had knocked back the medvarth outside the wall, who had taken the brunt of the fiery blast. But the medvarth were recovering from their shock. Gavin saw that they were about to form up and charge through the breach.

When they did, Dun Calpurnia was lost.

He looked around, trying to think through the ache in his head. It looked as if many of the men who had been near the explosion had been killed. Nearby he saw a soot-covered corpse in a bloodstained white robe who Gavin was pretty sure had been Master Kurastus. In the distance, he heard the wail of war horns, and his tired mind recognized the call for withdrawal. The High King was calling for his men to abandon the town and fall back to the south. Gavin supposed that made sense. If they stayed in the town, the Frostborn could bombard them at will until they all burned alive.

He stepped back as men started to flee from the wall and head towards the south. Perhaps he ought to follow their lead. There would be a moment of indecision as the Frostborn realized that the men of Andomhaim were abandoning the town, and then they would charge with all their strength. Best to be gone by then. He looked around for the others with a surge of fear. Kharlacht and Caius and Camorak had all been up there, and so had Antenora. She had been standing right next to him when the trebuchet's missile had exploded. Had she survived so much only to fall victim to the explosion?

He spotted a dark coat amidst the rubble, and he cursed and hurried towards it.

Antenora lay half-buried by broken stones, her yellow eyes closed, her gray face marked with blood and dust. She looked dead, but she did not need to breathe, and Gavin began pulling the stones off her, using Truthseeker's power to augment his strength.

The call for withdrawal rang out again, followed by the boom of another explosion as a trebuchet missile exploded somewhere near the western wall.

"Antenora," said Gavin. "Antenora, we've got to go." He heaved another stone off her. There was no blood on her chest and stomach, but her left leg was a mangled mess. "Antenora."

For an awful instant, he was sure that she had died in truth, that the fall from the ruined wall had been enough to kill her at last, but her eyelids fluttered, and then opened all the way. She grimaced, tried to sit up, and then slumped back as her damaged leg failed to support her.

"Gavin Swordbearer," said Antenora. "It seems that we are losing the battle."

"Aye," said Gavin, casting a wary look at the breach in the wall. He wondered if Arandar would be able to hold the army together after this. "We need to go. The army is abandoning the town."

"I cannot walk," said Antenora. She tried to stand again, but her damaged leg refused to move.

"It'll heal," said Gavin. Her wounds always regenerated in time.

He didn't think they had that time now. Not the way the medvarth warriors were swarming across the ramparts.

"Not in time," said Antenora. "Go. I will burn as many of them as I can before I am overwhelmed."

"No," said Gavin. He sheathed Truthseeker and dug away more of the rubble around her.

"There is no time!" said Antenora, looking at the damaged wall. "If you do not go at once you will be overwhelmed and slain."

"I'm not going to leave you here," said Gavin.

"You must go!" said Antenora, frustration and fear going over her face.

"If I go you'll be killed," said Gavin, digging at the rocks holding her in place. He had almost gotten her loose. Just a little more and he would be able to pick her up and carry her.

Antenora grunted, raised her staff, and pointed it towards the breach in the wall. A sphere of flame flickered to life over the end of the staff, spinning faster and faster as she drew on her magic.

"I should have died fifteen centuries ago," said Antenora. The sphere spun faster, widening as it did, and Gavin started to feel the heat of it as he worked to pull the rocks off her. "If I meet true death here at last, well, then it will be a small loss. Go!"

"It would not be a small loss!" said Gavin. He got the last of the stones off her. She wasn't that heavy, and he ought to be able to carry her out of Dun Calpurnia until her leg repaired itself.

"My death would not be a great loss! Yours would be!" said Antenora. "Go! At least let me save you. At least let me do one thing right. I love you, and I would not see you slain. Please, go!"

Gavin stared at her, torn. He loved her, too, and nor would he see her slain. He knew that she was right, that if he stayed here, he would die alongside her. But he couldn't do it. He couldn't make himself leave her.

He nodded, straightened up, and drew Truthseeker, the blade shimmering with white flame. Gavin stepped to the side, putting himself in a location where he could defend her while still leaving her a clear line of sight to work her magic.

"Oh, Gavin," said Antenora, her raspy voice heavy with sorrow.

"I'm sorry," he said. "I can't. I can't do it. I just can't."

He braced himself, preparing to fight to the end.

"What are you doing, you idiot?"

The hoarse voice was exhausted and irritated.

Gavin blinked and saw Camorak hurrying towards him, Caius and Kharlacht following. Camorak looked terrible, his face tight and glittering with sweat, his eyes heavy with exhaustion, but he was still on his feet. Both Caius and Kharlacht were covered in dust and spattered with blood, but they seemed unwounded.

"Her leg," said Gavin. "It won't heal in time…"

"Damn it," muttered Camorak. "Can't heal her. Spell won't work because of the curse."

Kharlacht sheathed his greatsword, stooped, and picked up Antenora with a grunt. She twisted around in his arms, bracing the staff against one of his shoulder plates to point behind him.

"Thank you," said Gavin.

"She can throw fire to slow our foes," said Kharlacht. "But we must go now."

Even as he spoke, a roar came from the breach in the wall, and the medvarth surged forward, charging into the town.

Antenora thrust her staff, the sphere of flame leaping from its end and hurtling towards the enemy. It landed amid the medvarth and exploded, throwing a dozen of the creatures into the air. A wall of flame sprang up from the breach, closing it off, and the medvarth charge faltered.

It would not falter for long.

"Go!" said Caius, and they hurried forward, joining the exodus from the ruins of Dun Calpurnia.

Arandar's mind drifted and spun. One moment he was in a ruined town, fire raining from the sky around him. The next he was back in Tarlion, walking with Isolde down the Via Ecclesia, their first child in her arms. The next he was fighting for his life outside the siege walls of Tarlion, the Enlightened of Incariel rushing to kill him...

"Lord High King!" said a man. "Lord High King!"

"He's alive," said a second voice.

"Lord High King!" said the first man.

Arandar's eyes snapped open.

He was slumped in a doorway in the burning ruins of Dun Calpurnia, his head resting against the rough brick. Constantine Licinius stood nearby, another Swordbearer next to him. Soot covered Constantine's face, and there was a cut on his temple, but he was otherwise hale.

The same could not be said of most of the rest of Arandar's guards and companions.

Arandar hauled himself to his feet with a curse, looking over the street. He saw Dux Leogrance's corpse first. A piece of flying rubble had hit him in the head and staved in half of his skull. Dux Gareth lay a few yards away, flames still dancing on his legs. The shock of the explosion must have killed him, and his sightless eyes stared unblinkingly at the plumes of smoke overhead. Several of the other Swordbearers and Magistri had been killed by the explosion.

Arandar had led them to their deaths.

He had led a lot of men to their deaths today.

"Lord High King," said Constantine, his voice raw. "We must go."

"Yes," said Arandar, heaving to his feet. "Yes. You are right."

It would have been only just if he had died with the others, but Arandar still had his duty. He would hold to that duty until the end of his life.

Which might be sooner than he had thought.

"Quickly!" said Constantine. "To the High King! Quickly!"

The surviving knights and Swordbearers and Magistri gathered around Arandar. He looked around, trying to take stock of who had survived. He couldn't account for everyone. Maybe some of the others had escaped.

Maybe they had been buried beneath the collapsing wall.

"To the southern gate," said Arandar, once they had gathered around him. "Hurry." The others nodded and started forward, and Arandar grabbed Constantine's shoulder. "Dux Constantine. Thank you."

Constantine blinked, looked back at his father, and a brief spasm went over his face. Then he nodded and joined the others. Arandar supposed that Tormark Arban was now Dux of Taliand if he was still alive. He had been with Sir Joram and some of the Comites from Taliand, commanding the reserve companies. Hopefully, he had been able to get out of Dun Calpurnia and form up to the south.

They hastened through the streets, joining the flow of men heading for the southern gate. Arandar jogged ahead of his surviving bodyguard, speaking to the men, urging them onward. He could not let any of his regret and guilt and fear show. If anything was to be salvaged from this disaster, he could not waver.

A few moments later he was through the gate, and Arandar gestured to his standardbearers. They ran forward, stopping out of catapult range of the southern walls, and planted his standard. It had come through the attack mostly undamaged, though there were scorch marks here and there.

His standardbearers sounded the call to assemble, and as the army retreated through the gate, it began to reform around Arandar's banner. He looked around, trying to get an assessment of the situation. Most of the army of Andomhaim would escape from the town, though they had taken losses, and he saw many wounded men. Traversing the ruined town would slow the Frostborn, and it would give the men of Andomhaim time to reform their lines.

But it would not be much time.

The magic of the Frostborn had frozen the Moradel this far south, and already formations of medvarth and revenants marched down the frozen river, forming up for a charge on their flanks. Worse, the khaldjari had dismantled some of their trebuchets and moved them down the frozen river, hastening to reassemble them. Arandar dared not lead his men onto the frozen water since he suspected the Frostborn could cancel their magic at will and send his men plunging into the waters.

To the east, he saw more medvarth hastening around the town, forming themselves up to charge at the wavering army of Andomhaim. Arandar had hoped that he might be able to fall back to Castra Carhaine good order, keeping the army together, but he now saw that was impossible. If the army tried to withdraw, the Frostborn would come at them with their full power, and it would be easy for the enemy to break them and send them flying down the road.

The only hope was that one of their allies might arrive in time to turn the tide, but it was a thin hope.

"I think I can walk now," said Antenora.

Kharlacht grunted, slowed, and set down Antenora. Gavin moved to her side, ready to catch her if she fell. She wobbled a bit, using her staff to help support her weight as her injured leg clenched, but she kept her balance. That was the advantage of her curse. Anyone else would have been in too much pain to move.

"Keep moving," said Camorak. "The Frostborn are coming around the town. If we're caught out in the open like this, we're finished."

The host of Andomhaim was pulling itself together in the fields south of Dun Calpurnia, the standardbearers sounding the call to assemble. For lack of anywhere better to go, they headed towards the red dragon banner of the High King where it flapped in the breeze over the center of the army.

"Why are we standing and fighting?" said Camorak. "We can't remain. If we do, the Frostborn will overwhelm us."

"I fear," said Caius in a quiet voice, "that if we try to retreat, the Frostborn will break us. The frost drakes can attack at will, and the Magistri will run out of strength before the drakes run out of freezing breath. If the High King and enough of the nobles are killed here, the army of the realm will collapse, and nothing can put it together again. Andomhaim will become a collection of fiefdoms, and the Frostborn will devour them one by one."

Gavin looked at Antenora, and he saw the same grim hopelessness reflected there.

Something cold and resigned settled over him.

It seemed they would die fighting alongside each other after all.

###

Arandar readied himself for the next battle.

The men of Andomhaim and the three orcish kingdoms reformed their lines with admirable speed, but it would not be enough. Too many of their leaders had been killed or wounded in the frantic retreat from Dun Calpurnia. Dux Gareth and Dux Leogrance had not been the only ones. Silent Malhask of Khaluusk and his chief headmen and warriors had been wiped out by one of those damned trebuchet missiles, and King Ulakhamar of Rhaluusk had been knocked unconscious by a blow to the head and had been carried out by Crowlacht and his other headmen. Men had been wounded and killed in the withdrawal, and they would not be able to fight as effectively as they had before the trap.

Blue fire swirled next to Arandar, and Third stepped out of the flames. She was breathing hard, and both her short swords were in hand, the blades dark with the blood of the medvarth. Third took a step back, stumbled, and went to one knee.

"Are you injured?" said Arandar. If there were any Magistri with remaining strength, he would have her healed. Her ability to travel quickly might be one of the few remaining advantages they possessed.

"No," croaked Third. She shook her head and pushed back to her feet. "I had to travel in haste, and I landed in a group of medvarth three or four jumps ago." She began cleaning the blood from her swords with the fluid motions of long-ingrained habits. "I did manage to find the Anathgrimm. They are moving with haste, but my sister's army is at least a day away."

"A day," said Arandar, and with those words, he felt the jaws of the trap tighten around him for the last time.

They could not escape, and they had no hope of rescue. The best Arandar and the host of Andomhaim could hope to do was to weaken the Frostborn enough that the Anathgrimm and the dwarves and the manetaurs could defeat them. He hoped Calliande was still alive, wherever she was. She might be the only one capable of holding such the alliance together.

"A day," said Third.

"Then we will make our stand here," said Arandar, "and commit our fates to God."

For Arandar thought he would stand before the throne of the Dominus Christus soon enough.

He hoped God would be merciful to a failed High King.

CHAPTER TWENTY-ONE

KNIGHTS

Ridmark strode deeper into the Tomb, his thoughts chasing each other in circles, his ears straining for any sign of foes.

He had no weapons left. He had tried drawing his bow, but it had crumbled into dust as he lifted it. Evidently, whatever power protected the Tomb did not want him bringing weapons this far into its depths. If more creatures from his past appeared, or if some other phantasm tried to kill him, he was going to be in trouble.

But no more enemies appeared. The Tomb did not change shape to landscapes he had visited in years past. Instead found himself walking through silent corridors and wide halls of white stone, the mist forever swirling around his knees.

He almost wished that more enemies would appear to fight.

It would have given him something to think about other than his doubts.

His failures circled through his mind, accompanied by the taunts and promises of the phantasms that he had faced. He thought of all the disasters he had seen, all those who had died, all those he had been unable to save.

Could he save them all by destroying himself with the sword of the Dragon Knight?

Maybe that was the central question.

Would the world be better off if he had never been born? Would the lives of his friends and loved ones be better if Ridmark had never been born? Usually, that was an utterly meaningless question, the sort of thought that popped into a man's head in the dark reaches of the night as he brooded upon his failures. For the most part, it was an idle doubt, gone with the rise of the sun.

But the sword might give Ridmark the power to answer the question.

And as he thought upon his failures, he began to think that the answer to the question was yes.

The world would have been better if he had never been born.

Ridmark stepped through another archway and into a long hall of white stone, and the mist vanished. He looked around the hall, and saw that it ended in a pair of double golden doors about a hundred yards away. Reliefs of dragons and armored high elven warriors covered the doors. Niches lined the walls of the long hall, and in the niches stood statues of red gold.

They were statues of the Dragon Knights of past epochs.

All of them were high elven men, and wore armor of similar design to the armor that Rhyannis and Lanethran and the other bladeweavers had worn. Some of the Knights wore winged helms, and some of them were bareheaded. Some carried shields, and some did not. But all the Knights bore an identical weapon, a longsword, unadorned save for its pommel, which was worked in the shape of a dragon's head.

Ridmark kept walking, drawing closer to the doors.

The statue in the final niche before the doors was different.

It showed a human man of advancing years, wearing battle-scarred armor of plate and chain. He had thick hair and a tangled beard, and he held the sword of the Dragon Knight in his right hand. This had to be Kalomarus, the first human Dragon Knight and the last Dragon Knight, the Dragon Knight who had been buried in this Tomb.

He looked exactly like the old knight in Ridmark's dreams.

The spirit of the last Dragon Knight had indeed been calling to him, just as the sword itself had been summoning him.

Ridmark stepped away from the statue and crossed to the doors. There was no obvious handle or bar, and he touched the doors, wondering if the handle was hidden or if he would need to push them open. The doors shivered at his touch and swung open on silent hinges. Pale white light spilled into the long hall, washing over him like a cold wind.

The chamber from his visions opened before him.

It was a long hall of unadorned white stone, beautiful in a stark and austere kind of way. There was no mist in the hall, and the stone of the floor and walls and ceiling gave off a gentle white glow. Ridmark stepped into the hall, his boots clicking against the smooth stone, his eyes fixed on the dais at the far end of the hall.

There were two people on the dais. One was the old knight, seated on the throne, the sheathed longsword across his knees. His gray-maned head rose as Ridmark approached, his eyes solemn. Before the dais stood the woman gowned in flame, her features shifting from those of Aelia to Morigna to Calliande and back again, over and over.

"Burn with me, Ridmark Arban," said the woman.

"So, boy," said the old knight, watching Ridmark from the throne. "Looks like you survived long enough to make it here. Can't say that I expected it…but can't say that I'm surprised, either. You always seemed like a determined one. The sword called you, and neither the shadow of Incariel nor the hordes of the Frostborn stopped you."

"Burn with me, Ridmark Arban," said the woman. "Burn with me, and I shall burn out your record from the pages of history. All that you have done shall be undone. All that you have wrought shall be no more. All those who suffered because of you shall suffer no more."

A shiver of despair and hope went through Ridmark at those words.

He walked the length of the hall, drawing closer to the old knight and the woman gowned in flame. The woman watched him with a gentle smile, even as her features cycled through the women that Ridmark had loved. The old knight did not rise, but his gaze did not waver. Here, in the flesh, he looked more tired and older than in the dream, but the sense of iron strength that hung around him only seemed sharper.

"Burn with me, Ridmark Arban," said the woman, "and undo all the harm that you have done."

"You're Kalomarus, aren't you?" said Ridmark at last. "The last Dragon Knight."

The old knight inclined his head. "That I am. I suppose you have all kinds of questions for me. Go on, ask them. I'm likely the only man in the world who can answer some of them."

"How are you still alive?" said Ridmark.

"Sword wouldn't let me die," said Kalomarus. "I knew those shadow-worshipping morons were going to help old Shadowbearer summon up the Frostborn again, and the Keeper knew it as well. After I had put her to sleep under the Tower of Vigilance, when I came here, I came here to die. I was an old man, and my work was done, but God and the high elves had one last job for me. I was to be the sword's custodian until the time came to bestow the blade on a new Knight." He shrugged. "It wasn't bad. I slept for most of it until the gate opening woke me up." A flicker of sympathy went through his hard eyes. "Sorry about Morigna, boy. She was a mouthy wench, but I liked her. If I was two hundred and fifty years younger and she was still alive, I would have charmed her away from you."

"Burn with me, Ridmark Arban," said the woman.

"Do you," said Ridmark. He took a deep breath and tried to get his twisting emotions under control. "Do you see her?"

"The spirit of the sword?" said Kalomarus, glancing at her. "Aye, I can see her."

"What does that mean?" said Ridmark. "Burn with me?"

"That's what she's been telling you?" said Kalomarus.

"You can't hear her?" said Ridmark.

"No," said Kalomarus. "She's been talking to you, boy. You're the one she's chosen. Her words are for you and you alone."

"She told me that I can kill myself with the sword," said Ridmark. "That if I kill myself with the sword, its magic will rewrite history so that I never existed, that everything I've ever done will be undone."

Kalomarus grunted. "That so?"

"Is she telling the truth?" said Ridmark.

"Hell if I know," said Kalomarus. "I never thought about killing myself." He smiled behind his beard. "My weaknesses were of a different kind. Guess she's found your weakness and is hammering on it."

"But can the sword do it?" said Ridmark. "Destroy someone so they never existed?"

Kalomarus shrugged. "Maybe. I used the sword to open gates, to set the weapons of my allies ablaze, to call fire to destroy my enemies, and to slow and speed up time when I needed. That's all I used the sword to do. Oh, and to kill a whole lot of Frostborn, of course. Can it change the past?" He frowned. "Strange idea. Never heard of such a thing. Suppose it might be possible." His eyes narrowed. "But that's your trial, I think."

"How?" said Ridmark.

"To choose whether you believe the sword or not," said Kalomarus. "She's going to try to destroy you. That's just her nature. She holds the fire of the old dragons, and fire never serves a weak master. On the other hand, the old dragons had power. Maybe they can do it." He leaned back in the throne, frowning. "You ready for this?"

"No," said Ridmark. "I'm not...I don't know if the sword is telling the truth or not."

"Neither do I," said Kalomarus. "But it has to be you or no one else. The sword's chosen you. She won't accept another, not while you still live." He drummed his fingers on the stone arm of the throne. "And I wager the realm needs the Dragon Knight. Else you wouldn't be here and I'd still be sleeping."

"It does," said Ridmark.

"Burn with me, Ridmark Arban," said the woman in flames. "Burn with me, and I will undo all your mistakes. Burn with me, and you will know rest at last."

"There is only one piece of advice I can give you," said Kalomarus. "Calliande. Does she need you to take up the sword?"

"She does," said Ridmark.

Kalomarus nodded. "Then you'd better risk it, I think. She was always such a brave child. She takes on too much." He sighed like a father worried about an overworked daughter. "She needs someone to help her. You love her, don't you, boy?"

"Yes," said Ridmark.

"Then take the sword and trust her," said Kalomarus. "She needs you, but I think you need her." He sighed. "It's up to you now, Ridmark Arban. Morigna told me about some of the things you have done. Great deeds, aye, but this will be your hardest challenge yet."

"So be it," said Ridmark. "I will accept the sword."

"Burn with me, Ridmark Arban," said the woman in flames.

"Then I will tell you a secret known only to the Dragon Knights," said Kalomarus. He grunted, moving slowly, and grasped the sheathed sword on his knees. He gripped the blade and presented the hilt to Ridmark. "Not even Ardrhythain knows this. Only the dragons of old knew this secret, and now only the Dragon Knights."

"What is the secret?" said Ridmark.

"The name of the sword of the Dragon Knight," said Kalomarus. "Its true name, a name that can only be spoken by its chosen wielder." He lifted the hilt towards Ridmark. "Speak its name and draw the sword."

"What is the true name of the sword?" said Ridmark.

"The sword's name," said Kalomarus, "is Caledhmaer."

Ridmark took a deep breath and grasped the sword's hilt.

"Caledhmaer," he said, and drew the blade.

"God go with you," said Kalomarus, "Dragon Knight."

He leaned back into his throne, closed his eyes, and died.

Ridmark just had time to note that the sword looked like an unremarkable longsword of steel, and then the woman gowned in flame exploded into a whirling vortex of flames and sparks. The fire poured into the sword, seeming to sink into the blade like water soaking into a sponge. The sword transformed in his hand, the blade becoming a strange metal like red gold, the pommel reshaping itself into a roaring dragon's head.

Caledhmaer burned in Ridmark's hand, the blade crackling with fire hotter than anything that even Antenora could conjure.

The sword's power exploded through Ridmark's mind like a storm.

He stumbled back with a grunt of pain, his right hand gripping the sword's hilt in a death grip. Ridmark had carried weapons of magical power before. He had carried Heartwarden as Knight of the Soulblade, and again after the sword had rejected him. He had carried Excalibur itself into battle against Tarrabus, after convincing the sword that he intended to return it to its rightful bearer. The taalkrazdor he had worn in Khald Tormen had been powerful, its will as implacable and unyielding as dwarven steel itself.

Caledhmaer was far more powerful than those weapons.

Fire and a torrent of knowledge exploded through his mind. Memories of past Dragon Knights flickered through his thoughts, showing him the sword's power. The Dragon Knights had used the sword to command elemental fire, to slow and speed time, to fold time and space somehow to allow them to travel vast distances in the blink of an eye. With such powers, they had won great victories against the dark elves and the urdmordar, though the Dragon Knights were almost always killed in battle.

It was overwhelming. Ridmark felt like his blood was on fire, like his head was about to explode. The memories of the Knights manipulating time burned before his eyes. Yes, that was it. That was the secret. Caledhmaer could undo the past, and if Ridmark killed himself with the sword, he would never have existed, and so much pain would be undone.

Burn with me...

Yes. That was what he had to do. It was his duty to destroy himself.

Ridmark raised Caledhmaer, preparing to cut his throat with it. He looked at the sword burning in his hand and noted that the fire seemed to be sinking into his veins, making them glow beneath his skin. The fire had even reached his heart, and he saw its glow shining through his dark elven armor. He had seen that before, hadn't he? No, it had been described to him. Someone had once seen a man die like this.

Calliande, that was it. Calliande had told him about this.

The thought of his betrothed froze him, made him forget about his duty to kill himself.

He couldn't leave her. He had promised Calliande that he would see her to the end of this. He had promised to marry her. Ridmark had to keep those promises.

But, the power in his mind murmured, wouldn't it be better for her if he had never existed? Wouldn't she have avoided so much suffering? Andomhaim itself would have avoided so much suffering. Yes, he ought to destroy himself now, at once.

He had promised to return to her.

Ridmark stared at Caledhmaer's fire, caught between the two imperatives warring in his mind.

Kalomarus had said to trust Calliande.

Ridmark had promised to return to her.

He turned and left the throne room, Caledhmaer howling with fire in his fist.

CHAPTER TWENTY-TWO

TOO LATE

Calliande watched the flickering mist, fighting against her growing horror.

She stood with Ardrhythain before the curtain of mist, alternating between watching the doors of the Tomb for Ridmark and looking at the scenes of the battle raging at Dun Calpurnia. Because time was moving slower at Cathair Solas than the rest of the world, it was impossible to grasp more than scattered images. Calliande saw flashes of images in the mist, like paging through a book and glancing at the illustrations.

The images she saw alarmed her.

She watched as Arandar fortified Dun Calpurnia, preparing to meet the Frostborn there. The dwarves and the Anathgrimm marched from the west and the manetaurs and the tygrai from the east, but they would be too late. The vast host of the Frostborn flooded down from the north, and Calliande saw the trap. The Frostborn had as many soldiers as the allies combined, drawn steadily through the world gate over the last year. The army they had sent to Dun Calpurnia was only the vanguard of their strength. Lord Commander Kajaldrakthor and his lieutenants planned to draw the army of Andomhaim into a trap, crush it utterly, and deal with the allied armies one by one before they could unite.

The revenants marched beneath the waters of the Moradel, their eyes glowing with blue fire.

Calliande watched the army of Andomhaim driven out of Dun Calpurnia. The host of the Frostborn surged around the town, thousands of medvarth and khaldjari and revenants and locusari moving to finish the battle.

And Imaria watched a safe distance from the fighting, laughing as the Frostborn destroyed the obstacles between her and the Well of Tarlion.

"I should have been there," said Calliande. "I could have stopped it. I could have warned Arandar. This was my fault. I am the Keeper of Andomhaim, and I failed to save it."

"The shadows of the future," said Ardrhythain, "are not yet decided."

Calliande didn't know what to do. Should she ask Ardrhythain to transport her to Dun Calpurnia? A human traveling that far through an elven transport spell might go irreparably insane, but maybe the time had come to risk it. Yet Ridmark had not emerged from the Tomb, and she could not leave him.

A metallic creaking noise cut into the storm of her thoughts, and Calliande's head snapped around.

The doors of the Tomb swung open.

The revenants spearheaded the attack.

Gavin gripped Truthseeker and braced himself. The army of Andomhaim had managed to reform itself into some sort of order, with lines of spearmen standing ready, the heavily-armored knights and men-at-arms on the wings, though they had lost most of their horses in the frantic retreat from the burning town. Crossbowmen and archers hung back, holding their fire until a living foe approached. Master Marhand had gathered the Swordbearers into a massive fist of steel, ready to attack the Frostborn themselves once the High Lords took the field. Master Kurastus had been killed in the attack, but the Magistri had gathered near Arandar's banner, ready to cast defensive wards.

The High King's banner flew at the center of the host, and Gavin stood there with Antenora, Kharlacht, Caius, Camorak, and the rest of the High King's surviving bodyguards. Arandar waited at their head, Excalibur burning in his hand, his face stern and cold as he watched the approaching enemy. Third stood near him, ready to carry messages, but there was no more need for carrying messages.

They would fight, or they would die.

Though as Gavin watched the enemy approach, he realized that death was the most likely outcome.

The wall of revenants charged, and Gavin fought.

Antenora flung a sphere of fire that ripped through a score of the revenants. The Magistri cast their spells as well, throwing shafts of white fire into the charging enemy. Elemental fire and the white fire of the Well cut down hundreds of the undead, but there were thousands more.

Gavin swung his shield, bashing an orcish revenant in the face, and drove Truthseeker into the stunned creature's ribs. The white fire of the soulblade pulsed and quenched the blue flame, and the revenant collapsed. A second revenant reached for him, its dead hands burning with cold blue fire. This one had once been a dvargir warrior, and still wore armor of black dvargirish steel, though the void of Incariel in its eyes had been replaced with the icy flame of the magic of the Frostborn.

The creature's fingers brushed Gavin, and he felt a chill, but he took no harm from it. The great spell the Keeper had worked before the first battle of Dun Calpurnia still held, and protected him from the freezing grasp of the revenant. Gavin aimed blows at the revenant's thick neck, and on the third blow, the head rolled off the shoulders, the black-armored corpse falling to the ground.

Thanks to Calliande's magic, the revenants were not a serious threat. They were hideously strong and felt no pain, but they carried no weapons, and without their freezing touch they could only kill a man with their bare hands. The army held against the revenants, holding them back with sword and spear and axe.

But with the revenants holding them in place, they could not maneuver, and the second wave of the attack came.

Locusari scouts fell from the sky like blue bolts, flying in formation towards the Magistri and the men-at-arms who had managed to rescue some of the portable ballistae from the wreck of Dun Calpurnia. The scouts were no serious threat to the men-at-arms or the Magistri, but they distracted the men long enough for the frost drakes to close.

A dozen frost drakes flew over the host of Andomhaim, pillars of freezing mist shooting from their fanged mouths. The Magistri managed to recover in time to cast warding spells, and the men-at-arms sent a volley of ballista bolts into the sky. Three of the frost drakes went down, pierced with iron bolts, and some of the white mist hardened against the the wards of the Magistri.

But most of the freezing mist swept across the unprotected lines of the army, and hundreds of men died in an instant, sealed within cocoons of granite-hard ice. The frost drakes banked away, circling away to the north as they prepared for another pass.

Gavin could pay them no heed. The enemy on the ground occupied his full attention. Bands of locusari warriors surged through the revenants, charging towards the High King's banner, and Gavin fought them, Truthseeker rising and falling in a white flame. A locusari sprang forward, its scythed forelimbs slashing at Gavin. He caught the first attack on his shield and the second. Sheer exhaustion kept him from getting his shield up in time to block the third, and the warrior's forelimbs hit him in the chest. The armor of the dark elves proved stronger than the chitin of the locusari warrior's limbs, but Gavin felt the impact through his entire torso.

He staggered back and stabbed Truthseeker, ripping the soulblade through the warrior's thorax. Thick yellow slime dripped from the hideous wound, and the warrior fell dead at Gavin's feet, twitching atop some of the destroyed revenants. Gavin killed another locusari warrior, and another, and then a third, even as Antenora flung fire into their charging foes and the frost drakes circled high overhead.

Through the haze of his exhaustion and his battle fury, he noted that they were losing ground, that the mass of undead and locusari were pushing the army back. How much more punishment could the men of Andomhaim and the orcs of the baptized kingdoms take? He feared that the army would break, that some of the lords would begin calling for a retreat to Castra Carhaine. If that happened, the victorious Frostborn would hunt down the shattered pieces of the army and eliminate them one by one.

A thunderous roar cut into Gavin's concentration, and he looked up from a dying locusari.

Lines of medvarth warriors charged from either side of the town, thousands of medvarth warriors. Despite the fighting at the northern wall, the medvarth seemed fresh and eager for blood. Perhaps the Frostborn had held them in reserve for the critical moment of the battle.

Gavin lifted Truthseeker and his shield, his shoulders and arms trembling with exhaustion, and braced himself for the next wave of attack.

Arandar slashed Excalibur upwards, opening the medvarth warrior from groin to throat, the sword's edge slicing through flesh and bone and armor like butter. The medvarth's roar of fury turned to a gurgle of pain, and it fell over, its blood sinking into the trampled ground, its corpse joining the carpet of the dead that covered the land.

He feared it would not be much longer now.

Around him the knights and Swordbearers of his bodyguard battled, cutting down the medvarth warriors and the locusari and the revenants. Third flickered in and out of the melee in pulses of blue fire, gutting the medvarth from behind and disappearing again before their comrades could strike. The Swordbearers fought with fury, standing fast against the tide of the enemy, but they could not endure forever.

An explosion rang out to the west, not far from the bank of the River Moradel, and Arandar glimpsed a half-dozen fireballs soaring through the air to land in the battle. The khaldjari had moved their massive trebuchets south along the River Moradel, and from the middle of the frozen river, they had a perfect platform from which to hurl their burning missiles into the army of Andomhaim. Arandar could not ask any man to stand and fight in the face of that barrage of alchemical fire, but his army was trapped. They could not retreat to a strong place, and if they tried to flee, the Frostborn would tear them apart.

It looked as if the Frostborn would tear them apart no matter what they did.

Another roar boomed over the melee, and Arandar saw a wedge of medvarth warriors running towards him. These medvarth were taller and broader than the rest of their kindred, and armored from head to foot in dull gray steel plate. Enormous tower shields rested on their left arms, and in their right hands, they carried huge axes.

The Frostborn themselves came with the armored medvarths.

Nearly a hundred Frostborn strode behind their soldiers, each warrior carrying a huge greatsword that swirled with freezing white mist. Their gray armor made them look like advancing glaciers, and their eyes shone with cold light. Many of the Frostborn were casting spells, and they hurled blasts of jagged ice or bolts of cold fire into the men of Andomhaim. The Magistri tried to cast defensive spells, and some of the freezing blasts shattered against the wards.

But many more spells got through, killing men in an instant and sheathing their bodies in ice.

The Frostborn cast another spell in unison, and a wave of blue fire erupted from them, rolling across the battlefield. The blue fire lingered on the corpses of the slain and sank into their heads, shining like azure candles within their eyes.

Slain humans and orcs and medvarth rose one by one from the ground, joining the ranks of the Frostborn army as new revenants. Arandar killed another medvarth and saw the wedge of armored medvarth and the Frostborn heading right towards him.

Of course. They saw the banner of the High King, and they knew that killing the High King would demoralize the army and break its leadership.

And Arandar realized there was nothing left for him to do but die.

He had failed. At least Accolon and Nyvane were safe with the Anathgrimm for now, and he hoped those who came after him would succeed where he had been defeated.

Arandar said a quiet prayer, commending his soul to God and asking for forgiveness for his failures, and lifted Excalibur and prepared to die with a ring of slain foes around him.

###

The doors of the Tomb of the Dragon Knight opened, and Calliande saw a flicker of harsh, fiery light.

"Ridmark?" said Calliande, taking a step forward.

Ridmark walked from the Tomb of the Dragon Knight and into the cavern, a sword in his right hand.

Calliande knew that sword. She knew that sword very well.

It looked as if it had been forged from red gold, but it was far stronger and far lighter than any other metal. Its pommel had been wrought in the shape of a dragon's head, and the last time she had seen that sword, it had been in the scabbard at Kalomarus's belt as he escorted her to the Tower of Vigilance. The blade burned with yellow-orange fire, so hot that the sword itself looked white with molten heat.

It was the sword of the Dragon Knight.

Calliande started to smile, and then took a better look at Ridmark and froze in alarm.

His eyes were...burning, somehow, as if they had been filled with fire. More fire flowed through his veins, visible even through his clothing and armor and skin. She saw the glow of his heart burning through his chest.

The last men Calliande had seen who looked like that had been the six knights the sword had killed before Kalomarus had been able to master the blade. The Sight blazed to life within Calliande, responding to the powerful magic in the sword, and she saw the tendrils of its power pouring down Ridmark's arm and sinking into his heart and mind.

It was devouring him.

"Oh, God," said Calliande. "Ridmark."

This was her punishment, the retribution for her pride and folly and her failures. All her clever plans had brought her to this, to watch her betrothed devoured by the sword. She had fallen in love, and she would see the man she loved killed even as the Frostborn destroyed the army of Andomhaim. She had done this to him, and she had failed Andomhaim.

All her duties and her hopes would turn to ashes in a single moment.

Yet the fire did not spread. It was trying to sink deeper into Ridmark, to burn him out from the inside, but he was resisting it.

"Ridmark," said Calliande. She heard Ardrhythain step closer. "Listen to me..."

The burning eyes turned towards her. "Calliande."

His voice was a hard rasp, the sound of a man in terrible pain.

"Yes, I'm here," said Calliande.

"Should it be undone?" said Ridmark.

"Should what be undone?" said Calliande.

"Everything that I have done," said Ridmark.

He came closer, the sword burning like a torch in his fist.

"The sword showed me," said Ridmark. His expression was strange, almost twisted, caught halfway between agony and ecstasy. "I've made so many mistakes. I've failed so many times. The sword can undo it all."

"How?" said Calliande. "That doesn't make sense."

"If I destroy myself with the sword," said Ridmark, "it has the power to make it so that I never existed. All my decisions will be undone. All those I've failed will be saved."

"No," said Calliande. "No, that's impossible. The sword doesn't have the power to do that." She looked at Ardrhythain. "Does it?"

His voice was solemn. "It does not. No magic has the power to change the past. Only God himself possesses that power, and he does not employ it."

"No," said Ridmark. "You don't understand. The sword does have that power. I can undo it all, I can..."

"The sword is testing you," said Ardrhythain, still calm. "It is preying upon your inner weaknesses and offering you a vision of something impossible to test your strength."

"It's not impossible," said Ridmark. "I can see it. The sword has that power. I can repair everything. I can bring Aelia and Morigna back..."

"Ridmark," said Calliande, taking another step closer. She wanted to touch him, but she didn't know how he would react. "It wouldn't work. The sword is just testing you. If you kill yourself...nothing will happen. You'll have killed yourself for nothing." She swallowed. "Please, please, don't. Please."

"All the pain I inflicted on you," said Ridmark, "it can be taken away."

FROSTBORN: THE DRAGON KNIGHT · 297

"Pain?" said Calliande. "You saved my life. You saved my life a dozen times over." She wanted to say something comforting, to say that he had never hurt her, but she suspected that lying to him would be a terrible idea. "Maybe...yes, there were times when you caused me pain. When we parted after Dun Calpurnia. Or when I saw you with Morigna, or when I feared for your life as I fear for it now. But I swear on all the saints and all the apostles that I don't want that pain taken away. I wouldn't trade it for anything, because I love you, Ridmark. Please don't kill yourself. You promised that you would see me to the end of this. You promised that you would spend the rest of your life with me."

With cold, horrified detachment, she realized he could fulfill that promise right now if he killed himself with the sword.

Ridmark shook his head. "But the sword..." He blinked several times and shook his head again, the fire in his veins pulsing. "It could undo all the horror we have seen. It..."

He grimaced, and Calliande had the impression that he was arguing with someone that only he could see.

"It can't change the past," said Calliande. "But maybe it can change the present."

"What?" said Ridmark.

"Look," said Calliande, pointing at the curtain of mist that Ardrhythain had conjured. "The Frostborn are about to destroy the army of Andomhaim. The realm needs us. It needs the Keeper and the Dragon Knight. It needs you, Ridmark. Are you going to let the Frostborn kill them all? Because if we do not act now, Andomhaim is doomed and all our friends will die."

Ridmark stared at the curtain of mist, at the flickering images of the unfolding battle. The strange expression of mingled ecstasy and agony wavered, and confusion came over his face.

"I..." He shook his head again. "I can undo it. I...no, I cannot allow it." His face turned stern. "No. I will not allow it."

He slashed the sword before him, and to his right a curtain of mist rose from the ground, shining with an inner white light. The Sight responded to the power in the glowing mist, and Calliande saw that it was a gate of the same kind that Kalomarus had left in the Tower of the Keeper. She saw the currents of powerful magic flowing from the sword, forcing the gate open.

Ridmark turned and stepped through the gate.

It began to close behind him.

Calliande didn't hesitate.

Just as he had thrown himself after her in the Tower of the Keeper, she sprinted after him and through the gate an instant before it closed.

CHAPTER TWENTY-THREE

DRAGON FIRE

Gavin's chest ached with every breath. He must have cracked a rib at some point. He didn't think the rib had broken because he couldn't taste any blood, just his sweat when it trickled down his face. A half-dozen minor wounds on his arms and legs burned with every movement, and he knew that the next hit he took would likely drive him to his knees, and that would be the end of his life.

The charge of the medvarth warriors and the newly raised revenants had driven great wedges into the lines of the men of Andomhaim. Perhaps the charge would have broken the host, but the Frostborn were beginning to encircle them, and anyone who tried to run would be cut down without mercy. Gavin wondered if the Frostborn had planned this as a battle of annihilation, if they intended to exterminate the men of Andomhaim and raise them as a vast new host of revenants

More and more, that seemed the likely outcome.

He had killed a Frostborn warrior a few moments earlier, dueling the towering creature until he had driven Truthseeker through its guard and into its crystalline skin, seeking its heart and releasing the blue fire that served as blood for the creature. The effort of fighting such a powerful foe had drained Gavin, and he had barely been able to fend off three medvarth that had rushed him. If Antenora had not incinerated the third medvarth, Gavin would have been killed then and there.

The High King's bodyguard and some of the surrounding men-at-arms had been surrounded and pushed into a circle. Gavin fought alongside them, Antenora standing behind him as she cast spells again and again. Caius and Kharlacht were still on their feet, as was Camorak, casting his healing spells even though he looked on the edge of collapse. Third flickered in and out of sight, carving her way through the medvarth and leaving them dead in her wake.

Gavin felt a pulse of exhausted, grim pride. If he was going to die, at least he would die surrounded by men (and two women) who had fought to the bitter, bloody end. The Frostborn would pay a steep price for taking Andomhaim.

He managed to block the strike of a locusari warrior's limbs, and he swung Truthseeker in a wobbly, drunken chop, taking off the creature's head. It fell to join the dead, and Gavin saw another wave of medvarth warriors charging towards him.

A peculiar sort of peace fell over him.

This was indeed the end. Was this how his father had felt in the final moment of his life when he charged Agrimnalazur, knowing that it would mean his death, knowing that his efforts were likely futile?

Perhaps Gavin could ask him in person soon.

"What?" said Antenora.

He blinked. She was looking in the direction of Arandar, frowning.

"What is it?" said Gavin.

"I do not know," said Antenora. She sounded bewildered. "I have never seen magic of this type or potency before."

There was a flicker of white light.

###

Arandar sought out the Frostborn, killing them whenever he could manage it.

Excalibur gave him an advantage that no one could match. The Frostborn wore heavy armor and carried massive greatswords, but Excalibur cut through them with ease. Arandar attacked the Frostborn themselves, using Excalibur to slice off their greatswords at the hilt and carving through their armor.

After he had cut down seven Frostborn, the enemy grew wise to his tactics.

The Frostborn fell back, using their magic to hurl icy blasts at him. Excalibur protected him from those spells, but the Frostborn also sent the medvarth warriors to assail him, and some of the medvarth carried throwing axes. They hurled the axes with terrific force, and Arandar had no choice but to duck and dodge.

The handle of one of the axes clipped him on the jaw. The impact knocked his head back, and Arandar lost his balance and fell. The Swordbearers tried to rush to his aid, but the fight had carried Arandar too far forward, and they could not reach him in time. Two Frostborn warriors charged, their greatswords raised high. Arandar tried to regain his feet, but his head was spinning, and he could not get back up.

The Frostborn raised their greatswords for the kill.

Fire exploded before Arandar's vision.

Not the blue fire of the cold magic of the Frostborn, but the harsh yellow-orange flame of a blacksmith's furnace.

Arandar's first thought was that Antenora had come to his aid. But the fire was too concentrated for that, and it looked hotter and sharper than anything Antenora had ever conjured.

Then he saw Ridmark.

The Gray Knight attacked the two Frostborn, not with his black staff or with his dwarven axe, but with a longsword of red gold, its pommel worked in the shape of a dragon's head, the blade burning white-hot with howling flames. Ridmark stabbed one of the Frostborn, and the tip of the red sword scraped along its crystalline skin. The flames exploded from the sword and ripped through the Frostborn warrior, and it fell dead to the ground. The second Frostborn warrior charged at Ridmark, and he swept the red sword up in a parry. The weight of the Frostborn's massive greatsword ought to have broken both of Ridmark's arms, but the greatsword shattered against the burning blade like rotten ice struck by a hammer. The Frostborn stumbled, and Ridmark ripped the burning sword across its throat. Even the slightest wound from the sword seemed to prove fatal to the Frostborn, and the fire exploded through its body, sending it dead to the ground.

Someone grabbed Arandar's left temple, and the cold of healing magic washed through him. When it passed, his head was clear, and he got back to his feet.

"High King."

Calliande stood behind him, the staff in her left hand glimmering with the white light of the Well's magic. Her face looked tight with fear and strain, her eyes bloodshot.

"You..." Arandar looked at her, at Ridmark, and his brain caught up with his eyes. A surge of fresh hope went through him. Third had been right. They had done it! They had gone to retrieve the sword of the Dragon Knight, and they had been successful.

The hope faded. They had returned too late. No matter how powerful the sword, it could not turn back the tide of the Frostborn.

And Ridmark looked...

Arandar wasn't sure, but he thought that Ridmark looked as if he had gone mad.

His face was locked in a grimace, the cords standing out on his neck. That alone looked disturbing, but his eyes were filled with flames, and more fire seemed to burn in his veins.

It looked like the sword was killing him.

"High King," said Calliande.

"You did it," said Arandar. "You found the sword of the Dragon Knight."

"Yes," said Calliande. She was staring at Ridmark. "But it's devouring him. I don't think he can control it. It..."

"It's too late," said Arandar, stepping in front of her and lifting Excalibur. "The Frostborn have us. We can't withdraw, and we can't win. Not even the sword of the Dragon Knight can turn the tide now."

He saw the despair on Calliande's face, something he had never seen there before. Even during the darkest days of the campaign through Caerdracon and the siege of Tarlion, she had always projected cool confidence.

It seemed that the Keeper, too, had realized that they had reached the end.

"I'm sorry," said Calliande. "I should have..."

"No."

Ridmark's voice was hard, and it seemed to reverberate in time to the howl of the flames coming from the red sword.

"Ridmark?" said Calliande.

The fire in his eyes blazed. "This will not come to pass."

He walked towards the Frostborn host, lifting the sword before him in a two-handed grip.

The sword's power thundered through Ridmark's mind.

He knew it had the power to undo him, to remove him from the pages of history. Ardrhythain had told him that it could not, but the archmage had never wielded Caledhmaer and had never felt that awful power burning through him. If Ridmark fell on Caledhmaer right now, he could undo all of this and prevent the battle from ever happening.

And yet...

When he looked at Calliande, his certainty turned to doubt. He felt as if the things the sword had been telling him were a delusion, a fever dream, and that she was telling him the truth. Kalomarus had told him to trust Calliande.

And yet…if he could undo all of this…

But something else demanded his attention.

The battle. He would not allow the Frostborn to destroy the men of Andomhaim and the kingdoms of the orcs. He would not allow the Frostborn to slaughter his friends.

If Caledhmaer had the power to rewrite time…then surely it had the power to defeat the Frostborn.

He walked towards the enemy, Caledhmaer raised before him. A band of revenants rushed towards Ridmark, and the sword's fury burned hotter. Caledhmaer sensed the cold magic animating them, and it rose in wrath against the dark power.

"Burn with me," said Ridmark.

He strode to meet the revenants, bringing the sword around in a crosswise cut, and power exploded from it.

Flames caught Gavin's eye.

He thought that Antenora had cast a spell, or that one of the trebuchets had hurled their missiles into the High King's bodyguard. But Antenora was standing right next to him, spinning another sphere above her staff, and none of the trebuchet missiles had reached this far yet.

"The Keeper!" said Antenora. "The Keeper is here!"

Gavin spotted Calliande standing next to the High King, her face tight with fear. The Swordbearers and knights around them were reforming. Something had driven back the enemy, given them a moment to catch their breath.

The fire was coming from a sword in the hands of Ridmark Arban. The flames from the sword seemed to be spreading into his flesh, turning his veins into a map of fire visible even through his armor.

"They did it," said Gavin, stunned. "That must be the sword of the Dragon Knight."

"It is magic beyond anything I have ever seen," said Antenora. Her yellow eyes were wide with amazement. "But the power...the magic is killing him."

Ridmark strode alone towards a mass of revenants and Frostborn, his eyes burning with the same fiery light as his sword.

"We have to help him," said Gavin.

"He cannot fight them alone," said Caius. Caius and Kharlacht had fought their way to Gavin's side. Third was with them, her expression alarmed as she looked at Ridmark.

"Agreed," said Third. "We must aid the lord magister at once."

"He might not need our help," said Antenora.

Ridmark swung the sword and drove the blade through the chest of the first revenant, an undead medvarth. The howling fire burned out the cold blue light in the creature's eyes, and the two pieces of its corpse fell burning to the ground.

But the fire did not stop.

The flames exploded from the destroyed revenant, leaping into the nearby creatures. The fire ripped through them like a firestorm through chaff, spreading out in a widening circle. More revenants burned, more and more, and soon hundreds of the undead burned, and then thousands.

For an instant, it seemed as if thousands of giant torches burned on the field of battle below the scarred walls of Dun Calpurnia.

The revenants fell smoking and smoldering to the ground. Thousands of them had been destroyed in a single instant by the power of the Dragon Knight's sword, and a shocked silence fell over the battlefield. The Frostborn and their creatures were stunned with dismay, while the men of Andomhaim were stunned with simple shock.

Ridmark kept walking forward, heading for the Frostborn themselves.

"Hurry!" said Caius, and they ran towards him.

The wrath of Caledhmaer snarled through Ridmark's mind, hotter and stronger than he could have imagined.

The power of Heartwarden and Excalibur had been opposed to dark magic, had burned with fury when they encountered it. Caledhmaer had the same kind of power, but it was a thousand times stronger. Ridmark had set one revenant ablaze, and that fire had spread to every revenant upon the battlefield, shattering the cold power in their undead flesh.

For a moment, he wondered if he could use Caledhmaer to turn the entire host of the Frostborn to ashes, but the sword's magic did not work that way. It could destroy legions of undead in a single instant, but it could not do the same to living creatures.

But Caledhmaer had other powers to direct against the living.

Including Ridmark's allies.

He lifted the sword and called upon its power, and more fire exploded from the blade.

Gavin ran towards Ridmark. The Frostborn around the Gray Knight seemed dismayed or at least shocked by the sudden destruction of their revenant horde, but Gavin knew that would not last. Ridmark himself had come to a stop, the sword's hilt grasped in both hands as he lifted it before him, a miniature firestorm whirling around the blade.

Then he swung the sword, and the fire exploded from it. An expanding dome of yellow-orange light rose from Ridmark and swept across the battlefield. It passed through the Frostborn without touching them, and it moved through Gavin. He felt the power in the light, felt it tugging through Truthseeker, but it did nothing to him.

But Kharlacht and Caius and Third stopped, raising their weapons. Kharlacht's greatsword was now wreathed in magical flames, as were the blades of Third's twin short swords. Even the head of Caius's mace of dwarven steel burned, making it look as if he held a torch.

Light shone across the army as the swords and spears and maces of the men of Andomhaim and the orcish kingdoms burst into flames.

"The sword," said Antenora, her voice stunned. "It has shared its magic with the entire host."

That seemed to snap the Frostborn from their paralysis. Drums boomed across the enemy lines, and the medvarth roared and charged, while the Frostborn themselves rushed towards Ridmark, intent on cutting down this new threat.

Ridmark did not move.

Arandar looked at the army in astonishment, watched thousands of swords burn with magical fire.

"The sword," said Calliande when he looked at her. "The sword can share its magic with allies of the Dragon Knight."

"Then this is our chance," said Arandar. He turned and saw that his standardbearer had survived, still standing beneath the battered Pendragon banner. "Sound the advance. Sound the advance! We must attack at once! This is our last chance!"

The standardbearer nodded and blew the advance, and the answering call came from horns scattered throughout the host. Arandar started running forward, passing the smoldering shells of the destroyed revenants, Calliande behind him.

A dull roar rose from the army as thousands of men and orcs charged, throwing themselves at their surprised foes, swords and axes of fire rising and falling as they attacked.

Ridmark felt the power flowing from Caledhmaer, maintaining the aura of fire that had ignited the swords of the army.

The Frostborn must have felt it, too, because dozens of them rushed towards Ridmark. Some of them lifted huge greatswords wreathed in freezing mist, and others hung back and began casting spells, calling power enough to kill a hundred men in a single instant. Caledhmaer was powerful, but the sword did not make Ridmark any faster and stronger, and even a soulblade would not have let Ridmark overcome so many Frostborn at once.

But Caledhmaer had powers that a soulblade did not.

It could alter the flow of time.

Ridmark thought again about throwing himself upon the sword's blade. If it could control time, and if it could undo his existence, then none of this would ever have happened. All the slain men lying upon the field would live again. All the wounded men screaming in agony would be healed.

But he thought of Calliande and stayed his hand.

Instead, he called on Caledhamer's magic, an aspect of the power that had let him travel from Cathair Solas to Dun Calpurnia in the blink of an eye.

And with that power, he slowed time.

Everything around him blurred, and the advance of the Frostborn dropped to a crawl, their swords seeming to creep through the air as they reached for him.

Time had slowed, but it had not slowed for Ridmark.

He began killing, driving Caledhmaer through the skulls and the hearts of the Frostborn. The sword's flame consumed the Frostborn warriors, killing them with elemental fire, and Ridmark slew a dozen of them before time sped up again. Caledhmaer was powerful, but even the sword of the Dragon Knight could not stop time indefinitely.

But the shock to the Frostborn was obvious. To their eyes, Ridmark had just killed a dozen of them in less than a second. They spread out around him, and again Ridmark called on the sword to slow time, and he started killing once more.

The army of the realm crashed into the Frostborn, striking their dismayed foes with new vigor. The medvarth flinched from the blazing fires of their weapons. The lines of the enemy wavered, beginning to fall back, and fresh hope went through Arandar.

He charged towards the Frostborn, intending to aid Ridmark, and then the younger man moved.

Ridmark moved so fast that he became a blur of blue armor and gray cloak and burning sword. In an instant, he moved twenty yards forward, almost seeming to disappear and reappear as Third did, and a dozen Frostborn fell dead behind him. The Frostborn reeled and moved to attack him, and Ridmark blurred again, killing a dozen more of his enemies.

Fireballs soared through the air and landed in the struggling armies, and Arandar looked to the west in time to see another wave of medvarth charging along the frozen river, preparing to fling themselves into the flank of the army of Andomhaim.

###

The explosion shook Ridmark, the ground vibrating beneath his boots.

He looked west and saw the trebuchets on the frozen river raining fire, saw thousands of fresh medvarth warriors preparing to charge into the battle. Caledhmaer also sensed the magic in the ice of the river, the cold power of the Frostborn sustaining the thick ice.

Ridmark called on the sword to freeze time, and he ran.

He covered half the distance to the River Moradel before time sped up again, and then he used the sword to slow it once more. A moment later he reached the bank of the River Moradel and saw the khaldjari engineers laboring over their trebuchets, saw thousands of medvarth warriors hastening to attack.

Time sped up again, and the medvarth charged towards the bank.

Ridmark raised Caledhmaer over his head and drove the sword into the river.

The blade stabbed into the ice without resistance and exploded with fire. A maze of burning cracks spread through the ice. The medvarth roared and ran faster, trying to reach the bank, and the burning cracks shone brighter.

The ice shattered and evaporated into mist.

The trebuchets fell into the river at once, sinking beneath the waters. The medvarth fell as well, roaring and bellowing as they tried to claw their way to the bank despite the weight of their heavy armor. Ridmark jumped back as the river surged over its bank, the waters displaced by the weight of thousands of khaldjari and medvarth.

He left them to their fate and went to rejoin the battle, Caledhmaer trailing flames from his fist.

###

The loss of the trebuchets and the khaldjari broke the will of the enemy.

The tide turned, and the army of the Frostborn began fleeing.

Gavin intended to pursue, but he needed a moment to catch his breath. The locusari fled first, racing through the ruined town and around its wall, followed in short order by the medvarth warriors and the Frostborn themselves. Drums boomed out, and the medvarth managed to retreat in good order. No doubt the Frostborn would reform their army somewhere north of Dun Calpurnia and prepare to renew their attack.

But, for now, the battle was won. Arandar's standardbearers called a halt, and the army began to stream back into Dun Calpurnia to reclaim their lost supplies.

Gavin looked at Antenora, stunned that they had survived. He had been so sure they would die side by side.

They had won this battle, but even with the fury of the Dragon Knight, he wondered if they would prevail in the next.

CHAPTER TWENTY-FOUR

LAST CHANCE

Calliande hurried with Arandar through the gate of Dun Calpurnia.

Her mind whirled with a mixture of dread and relief and the urgent need to do about twenty different things at once. The battle had nearly been a disaster, and even then, it had been a costly victory. The army was ragged and tired, and it would need to move quickly to keep the Frostborn from regrouping and finishing them off. Calliande ought to have been moving among the wounded, helping the Magistri to heal wounds. She ought to have been using the Sight to track the Frostborn, trying to determine where and when they would attack next.

Mostly, though, she felt dread for Ridmark.

He had disappeared after he had shattered the ice and drowned the khaldjari trebuchets, and she hadn't been able to find him. The Sight, at least, should have been able to detect the radiant power of the Dragon Knight's sword, but that had vanished as well. Had he been killed? Given the power of the sword, it seemed unlikely.

Or had he killed himself, succumbing to the trail of the sword?

That, she feared, was far more likely.

"Your arrival was most timely," said Arandar, stopping in the southern forum of the town. His standardbearers raised his banner here, calling the surviving high lords and commanders to him. "The

Frostborn had us. Another hour and most of us would have been dead and the rest fleeing."

"It was the Dragon Knight," said Calliande. "We would not have won the battle without Ridmark. I must find him. If we don't have his help against the Frostborn, we might not win the next battle."

"No," said Arandar. "The sword...what was it doing to him?"

"It was driving him mad," said Calliande. "The sword tests anyone who dares to wield it. It is using his own weaknesses against him. It has convinced him that if he kills himself, he will be removed from the pages of history and that everything he has ever done will be undone."

"Is that even possible?" said Arandar.

"No," said Calliande. "It's not." She took a deep breath, again using the Sight to look for Ridmark. "And...doesn't Ridmark realize that none of us would be here if not for what he has done? We would have all died in Urd Morlemoch. Or Khald Azalar."

"A man's regrets are a powerful weapon to turn against him," said Arandar.

A flicker of power caught the Sight's attention. Ridmark was here, somewhere near the western wall of Dun Calpurnia.

"High King, listen to me," said Calliande. "I have to help Ridmark, but I must tell you this. In Cathair Solas we learned the truth. We learned why Shadowbearer summoned the Frostborn."

As quickly as she could, she told Arandar of the shadow of Incariel, how Shadowbearer had been working for millennia to shatter the Black Mountain and release Incariel from its prison.

"God and the saints," said Arandar. "When the Warden spoke of a hundred thousand years of war, he was telling the truth."

"Yes," said Calliande. The pulse of power from the sword grew stronger. "This is just the latest battle in a war that started long before any of us were born. And this might be the final battle. I'm going to try to talk Ridmark out of killing himself. If I don't...or if I get killed in the process, remember this. The Well of Tarlion must be defended at all costs, or else the world is doomed. Make sure that Queen Mara and King Axazamar and Red King Turcontar know the truth. Imaria will probably convince the Frostborn to attack Tarlion as soon as possible. Likely she will have them freeze the Moradel to advance south. You have to be ready."

"We shall," said Arandar. He looked at the ruin around them. "God willing."

"God willing," said Calliande. She took a deep breath. "I will return with the Dragon Knight or not at all."

"Go," said Arandar, and she turned and broke into a run, heading towards the flicker of power that her Sight had detected. Dead men and orcs and medvarth and locusari and khaldjari littered the town's streets, and Calliande ran past them, her heart thudding with fear in her chest.

Blue fire swirled in front of her, and Third appeared. She looked exhausted, her armor spattered with blood and dirt, her eyes sunk deeper into her face.

"Keeper," said Third. "You must come at once."

"What's wrong?" said Calliande.

"I have found the lord magister," said Third. "I think he has gone mad. He is talking about how it would have been better if he had never existed, that he needs to kill himself with the sword of the Dragon Knight."

"It's the sword," said Calliande. "It's overthrowing his sanity. It..."

Someone grunted, and she saw Caius running towards her. He looked just as tired as Third, though he had come through the battle unharmed.

"If you are looking for Ridmark, I saw him go this way," said Caius. "I tried to talk to him, but he said that his duty was clear."

"Come with us," said Calliande. Sometimes Ridmark had been willing to listen to Caius when he would heed no one else.

Calliande wished that Mara was here. She, too, had often been able to get Ridmark to listen to her.

"This way," said Third.

The three of them ran through the streets and past dozens of ruined houses, many of them still burning from the trebuchets' bombardment. As they approached the western wall, Calliande saw many Mhorite orcs and dvargir lying dead on the street. Revenants, likely, either destroyed during the fighting in the town or when Ridmark had unleashed the power of the Dragon Knight.

She turned a corner, coming to a street leading to the western wall, and saw Ridmark.

He stood in the middle of the street, the sword still burning in his right first. He was staring at two corpses, and with a shock Calliande recognized them. One was Dux Gareth Licinius, and another was Dux Leogrance Arban, Ridmark's father. A burst of grief and regret went through Calliande. Dux Gareth had always seemed so strong and unyielding, and she had come to appreciate Dux Leogrance's cool head and sound judgment. She had always hoped she would find a way to get Leogrance to reconcile with Ridmark.

Now it that would never happen.

Calliande should have been here. She should have been advising Arandar. Perhaps she could have averted these deaths.

"Ridmark," said Calliande.

He looked up at her, and she flinched.

He looked terrible. The fire blazed in his eyes and his veins and in his heart. It made him look like a coal on the verge of bursting into flames.

"I did this," he said, his voice a pained rasp.

"I am sorry about your father," said Calliande.

"I didn't know him that well," said Ridmark. "I spent more time with Dux Gareth." He took a deep breath. "I did this."

"You did not," said Caius. "The Frostborn killed your father and the Dux, not you. That any of us are alive at all is thanks to your return."

"No," said Ridmark. "All this could have been avoided." His fingers tightened against the hilt of the burning sword. "All of it can yet be undone."

"It can't," said Calliande.

"It can," said Ridmark, the fires in his eyes brightening. "The sword has shown me the way. It had the power to burn the revenants. It had the power to break the ice. It had the power to stop time. It must have the power to reverse time." He stepped back, raising the sword before him. "I know what I must do."

Fear almost choked Calliande. "No, don't, please don't."

"I am sorry," he said, and he gestured with the sword, opening a rift of mist and white light. He turned and stepped through it, no doubt intending to go off somewhere quiet where he could kill himself without interruption.

The gate started to close behind him, and Calliande cast a spell, fusing the power of the Keeper's mantle into the fabric of the gate. The rift shuddered, undulating, and almost collapsed.

But it would stay open for another few moments.

Calliande ran after Ridmark and into the rift, Caius and Third a half-step behind her.

CHAPTER TWENTY-FIVE

BURN WITH ME

Ridmark stepped across the ruins of the great hall, Caledhmaer's harsh light throwing black shadows against the damaged pillars and the broken windows.

It had to be here. It always had to be here. This was where Ridmark would undo his mistakes and atone for his failures.

He stepped across what had once been the great hall of Castra Marcaine, the seat of Gareth Licinius, Dux of the Northerland.

The Frostborn had all but destroyed the castra. Rather than fortifying it after it had fallen, they had decided to abandon it. The roof had been shattered and lay in shards across the tiles of black and white. Ridmark walked to where Aelia had died and looked around, memories flickering through his mind. There was the dais, where Dux Gareth had knighted Ridmark. There was where he had danced with Aelia for the first time. He and Aelia had stood before the dais and been wed as Gareth's household knights had cheered.

He stood motionless on the spot where she had died.

Ridmark closed his mind for a moment, the fire of Caledhmaer burning through his thoughts.

Here, this spot, this was where he would kill himself with the sword.

All of it would be undone, all his mistakes, all his failures. Aelia would live again. Morigna would live again. Dux Gareth and his

318 · JONATHAN MOELLER

father would live again, as would all the men slain at Dun Calpurnia. The Frostborn would never have returned, and the realm would be at peace.

And Calliande...

He hesitated, something in him wavering.

No. It would be better for Calliande if she had never met him. She would have awakened to a realm at peace, the Frostborn banished. It would be worth it.

He lowered Caledhmaer, preparing to reverse his grip on the sword.

"Ridmark!"

He turned and saw Calliande, Third, and Caius standing at the other end of the hall.

It took Calliande a moment to recognize their surroundings.

She had not been here in centuries, not since the first war with the Frostborn. This had to be the ruins of Castra Marcaine, where Ridmark had been a page and a squire and then a knight. He had practically grown up here. He had been married here. His wife had died here.

Where else would he go to kill himself?

Ridmark stood in the center of the hall, the sword's fire throwing black shadows from the pillars against the wall. The ceiling had been torn open, rubble lying in heaps across the black and white tiles of the floor. Ridmark's face was a harsh grimace of emotion, a mask of pain and regret.

"You shouldn't have followed me here," said Ridmark.

"I had to," said Calliande. "The sword is lying to you. If you kill yourself, it won't do anything. Nothing will be undone."

"It will," said Ridmark.

"No magic can undo the past," said Third. "Else my father would have used it. If the dark elves or the high elves knew of magic to change the past, would not they have employed it already and restored their dominion?"

"You know that suicide is a great evil," said Caius. "If the sword is telling you to do something evil, then you know it is testing you to see if you are strong enough to resist the temptation."

"It would not be suicide, but a sacrifice," said Ridmark. "And it would be a sacrifice of little value. How much evil would have been avoided if I had never been born!"

"No," said Calliande. "No, how can you say that? You saved my life, Caius's life. You helped Third save herself from the Traveler's power. None of that would have happened without you."

"There would have been no need to save your lives," said Ridmark, "if I had not been there."

She took a careful step towards him. "Let me show you."

"Show me what?" said Ridmark.

"The Sight," said Calliande. "I can use the Sight to show you what would have happened if you had never been born. It can do that, sometimes, when I turn it towards the past. It can show us things that never were but might have been if we had chosen a different path. I can use the Sight to show you that."

Ridmark hesitated.

"Please," said Calliande, taking another step towards him. "Let me show you. Do that for me. Let the Sight show you what would have happened if not for you, and...and if you don't like what you see, I won't try to stop you."

He stared at her with fire-filled eyes, and Calliande desperately wished she could see his real eyes again.

At last, he nodded.

"All right," said Calliande, her throat dry. She crossed the remaining space between them and grasped his free hand with hers. His skin felt dry and fever-hot. "All right. I will show you."

She took a deep breath, calling on the Sight, and praying that it would work.

The Sight rushed up at her call.

Ridmark grasped Calliande's hand.

She looked frightened, so frightened, and he wanted to comfort her. But she didn't understand yet. If he used the sword on himself, she would be safe.

Her eyelids fluttered, and he felt power erupt from her and join his mind.

Visions flickered before his eyes, showing him the lives of his friends, of the path they would have taken had he not been there.

Kharlacht lifted his sword as he walked towards the walls of Tarlion, his arms heavy with fatigue. Around him marched the remnants of Qazarl's men, all those who had survived the long campaign across Andomhaim to the gates of Tarlion.

Ever since Shadowbearer had opened the gate on the day of blue fire, the Frostborn had poured forth, conquering all before them. Qazarl and his orcs had been enslaved by the Frostborn, used by their new masters as fodder in their conquest of Andomhaim. Kharlacht had seen countless sieges and countless towns burn, until at last the remnants of the High King's armies huddled behind Tarlion's walls, waiting for the end.

Crossbow bolts streaked down from the walls, raking into the lines of enslaved orcs and medvarth and locusari that charged towards Tarlion. A crossbow bolt punched into Kharlacht's stomach, two more into his chest, and another through his neck.

He fell, the blood pouring from his wounds.

He hoped the Dominus Christus would forgive him.

Death, when it came, felt like a relief.

The man who called himself Brother Caius stood behind the Great Gate of Khald Tormen, flanked by a thousand armored dwarven warriors and a hundred taalkrazdors. No enemy had ever broken the Great Gate, and many had tried.

Now the Gate shuddered and groaned, massive dents appearing on its surface.

Andomhaim had fallen to the Frostborn, and the Frostborn had turned their attention to the other kindreds of this world, breaking them and enslaving them one by one. The orcs of Kothluusk had been slaughtered, and the gates of Khaldurmar thrown down, the proud dvargir led away in chains to toil for the High Lords. The full fury of the Frostborn had turned to the Three Kingdoms of the dwarves, and Caius had returned to his people. They still did not approve of his worship of the Dominus Christus, nor of how the faith had spread among the younger generations of dwarves, but that no longer mattered.

The Frostborn would kill them all, no matter what gods they followed.

With a howling screech, the unbreakable gates shattered, and the hordes of the Frostborn charged into Khald Tormen.

Caius wondered if this was how his son Nerazar had felt in the final moments of his life.

He hoped Nerazar would forgive him when they met again because it would not be long now.

Caius fought and killed, raising a ring of the dead around him, until he fell to the greatsword of a Frostborn warrior and the horde poured into Khald Tormen like water through a breached dam.

###

Gavin stumbled through the burning village of Aranaeus, unable to believe the carnage.

After Rosanna had married Philip, Gavin had resigned himself to his life here, working with his father to farm their plot. There had been rumors coming out of the south and east, tales of a vast army of alien creatures sweeping across the High Kingdom, but he had paid little heed to them. The wars of the High King were no business of the men of Andomhaim.

Then the Frostborn came to Aranaeus.

The medvarth warriors swept through the village, setting it aflame. Any who resisted were killed. The survivors were rounded up in the village square and put into chains. A towering creature in gray armor with glowing eyes informed them that they were now the property of the Dominion of the High Lords, and since they had no other practical use, they would be worked in the fields until they died.

Gavin tried to fight back, and a medvarth axe split his skull.

###

Jager ran through the alleyways of Cintarra as the city burned, screams and shouts and howls of rage rising into the fiery night.

The invasion of the Frostborn hadn't concerned him at first. The Northerland was a long way off, and surely the Swordbearers and the Magistri would put a stop to it. But battle after battle had been lost. The invaders had pushed into Caerdracon, and then Calvus and besieged Tarlion itself. Worse news had come as well. The Frostborn were enslaving humans and orcs, but evidently had no use for halflings, and had decided to exterminate them as a waste of resources.

And now the Frostborn had come to Cintarra. Jager should have fled long ago, but he had been searching for his sister, hoping to take her to safety, but he had never found her.

He skidded around a corner and came to a stop.

Six of the huge bear-like creatures were there, the ones the Frostborn called the medvarth. One of them growled and threw an axe. Jager dodged the first one, but not the second. It went hard into his back, and he fell, in too much pain to rise.

The medvarth closed around him, laughing at their good fortune.

The Frostborn had no use for the halflings, but the medvarth found them delicious.

The urdhracos who had once been a woman called Mara soared through the air as Nightmane Forest burned below her.

Once, she had been human, or mostly human, but her father's song had filled her mind and overwhelmed her, and now his will was her will, and she served him in an ecstasy of joy. Or agony. She could no longer tell the difference between the two.

But she did not think her service to the Traveler would last much longer.

The Frostborn had shattered his wards, scattered his armies of Anathgrimm, and poured into Nightmane Forest. Already the forest burned beneath her, and the urdhracos who had been Mara and her few remaining sisters battled the Frostborn flying through the skies on frost drakes. She soared towards a frost drake, hoping to kill its Frostborn rider.

The drake snapped its head around and breathed, and the urdhracos dodged.

She almost made it. The mist hardened around her wings, encasing them in ice.

The urdhracos who had been Mara plummeted into the inferno that had been Nightmane Forest.

Her head struck the ground, and her father's song ended, death bringing her peace at last.

###

Arandar killed and killed, Heartwarden blazing in his fist like a storm of white fire.

The sea of enemies outside the walls of Tarlion seemed endless. Arandar fought for his life, and he fought for his children. Accolon and Nyvane were within the walls of Tarlion, and if the Frostborn took the city, they would be enslaved or killed.

Arandar could not let that happen.

Though he did not see how he could stop it.

The assault was relentless. The Frostborn had overrun the rest of Andomhaim, and now their hordes battered against the walls of Tarlion. The remnants of the armies of the realm were exhausted, fighting on the final reserves of their strength. Arandar could not remember the last time he had slept, the last time he had eaten.

Another medvarth came at him, and Arandar raised Heartwarden to block.

But even with the soulblade's strength augmenting him, his exhausted arms could not move fast enough.

The axe struck him in the chest with a hideous crunch, and Arandar fell off the ramparts.

The walls of Tarlion were tall and strong, which was just as well because the impact of his landing killed him at once.

###

Morigna half-ran, half-hobbled through the forest, breathing hard, trying to think through the pain.

When the first rumors of the war in Andomhaim had come to Moraime, she hadn't cared. The High Kingdom and its woes were not her concern, and Morigna had bigger problems. She was more and more certain that the Old Man was plotting against her. She wasn't sure what Coriolus had in mind, but she was certain it was nothing good, and she had begun preparing to fight him.

The preparations had proven unnecessary when the Frostborn had conquered Moraime, enslaved its people, and killed the Old Man.

Now they hunted her. Two khaldjari crossbow bolts had hit her in the leg, and while she had killed the khaldjari responsible with a cloud of acidic mist, she had no magic to heal wounds. The surviving khaldjari hunted her, along with their cogitaer leaders.

Morigna felt a surge of magical power, and she turned, leaning on her staff for balance.

They had found her. Twenty khaldjari rushed towards her, swords of ice in hand, and three cogitaers floated behind them, all three creatures casting spells.

Morigna worked a spell of her own, calling upon the magic of the earth. The ground before her rippled and folded, knocking the khaldjari from their feet. Unfortunately, the cogitaers were floating above the ground, and her spell did not reach them.

Three spikes of ice hurtled from the cogitaers and slammed into her chest, driving her to the ground.

###

Calliande lay naked on the altar of rough black stone, struggling against the ropes that held her wrists and ankles fast.

She didn't know who she was, or why she had come here. All she knew was that her name was Calliande and that the orcs and Shadowbearer had been waiting for her. They had bound her and taken her to the ring of standing stones on the slopes of Black Mountain, tying her to the altar.

"Please!" she screamed. "Why are you doing this?"

No one answered her.

The orcish shaman continued his spell, placing the empty soulstone between her breasts. Calliande felt dark magic swirling and twisting around her, rising to a mighty climax.

The shaman raised his dagger high.

Calliande felt an overwhelming sense of failure, but she did not know why.

The dagger plunged into her heart.

Tymandain Shadowbearer strode into the Tower of the Moon as Tarlion burned below the Citadel.

He smiled at the gentle glow coming from the walls and at the mighty magic radiating from the Well. At last, at long last, after uncounted millennia of labor, the Well was his, and there was no one to stop him, no one to distract him.

He cast a long and complex spell, opening a gate to the threshold, and stepped into it.

A moment later the Well exploded with enough force to reduce Tarlion and everything within five miles of the city to smoking ashes. Hundreds of miles to the north, an earthquake shook the Northerland, and the world gate of the Frostborn expanded, swelling out of control.

It shattered the Black Mountain open like an egg, and the broken mountain vomited out shadow, endless shadow, shadow to engulf the entire world.

And the kindreds of the world screamed in horror as freedom from time and causality and matter overtook them.

###

Calliande jerked away from Ridmark as he let out a strangled gasp, the visions of the Sight draining away. She caught her balance, leaning on the staff of the Keeper for support, and Third and Caius rushed to her side. Ridmark staggered away, shaking his head, the fire in his veins flickering.

"Ridmark?" said Calliande.

He did not answer.

Ridmark struggled against the power in his mind, trying to make sense of the things that he had seen.

The visions Calliande had shown him had been true. He knew that beyond all doubt. If he had never been born, that was how the past would have transpired. The guilt from his mistakes remained with him, would remain with him until he died, but he understood now that it could have been far worse. A man made mistakes as he made his way through life. That was inevitable.

But choosing to do nothing would have been far worse. And if Ridmark chose to let the sword destroy him, that would be the same as doing nothing at all.

Had Caledhmaer lied to him?

"No, Ridmark Arban."

He opened his eyes and saw the woman gowned in fire standing next to Calliande. Neither she nor Third nor Caius saw her.

"That was your trial," said Caledhmaer. "That was always your trial. Always you have sought to sacrifice yourself. In pursuit of noble goals, true, but that was your weakness. Death is simple, but living is harder, and your duties lie in life. Would you be strong enough to resist the weakness of your heart? That was your trial."

"I failed it," said Ridmark.

"What do you mean?" said Calliande.

Caledhmaer smiled. "You would have failed it but for her. As iron sharpens iron, so one man sharpens another. She has made you stronger, just as you have made her stronger. This was as it was ordained to be. Neither you nor the Keeper are strong enough to bear your burdens on your own. Together, perhaps you shall be victorious. And this was your first victory, Dragon Knight."

Ridmark let out a long breath and nodded.

The woman gowned in flames vanished, and the sword unraveled and vanished from Ridmark's grasp. But it wasn't gone. He felt it within his mind and knew he could call it back to his hand any time he wished.

That was his right.

For he was the Dragon Knight.

###

Ridmark closed his eyes and opened them again as the sword dissolved and vanished from his grasp, and a wave of crushing relief went through Calliande.

His eyes were blue again. The flames had vanished from his veins and heart.

He was himself again.

"Ridmark?" said Calliande.

"Yes," he said in a quiet voice. "Thank you."

"I'm sorry," said Calliande. "I'm so, so sorry I did that to you. I..."

He pulled her close in a tight embrace, and Calliande buried her face in his shoulder and wept.

CHAPTER TWENTY-SIX

JOINED

"It was a test," said Ridmark.

They sat on the steps of the dais. They were safe enough for now. Calliande's Sight had revealed no sign of any foes anywhere near Castra Marcaine. The Frostborn must have sent their whole strength south to attack Dun Calpurnia.

Ridmark knew they would have to return to Dun Calpurnia as soon as possible. Arandar needed the help of the Keeper, and he also needed the help of the Dragon Knight. Ridmark had taken the Frostborn by surprise at Dun Calpurnia, but they would be ready for him next time. He knew better than to think that the Frostborn would not find a way to counter Caledhmaer's power.

But for now, they sat on the dais. Ridmark owed them an explanation, and there were some important things he had to do first.

Calliande sat on his left, pressed against him, gripping his hand as if she never intended to let it go again. He did not find that disagreeable.

"You were right," said Ridmark. "All three of you were right. I always had that urge to sacrifice myself, to destroy myself somehow. I blamed myself for Aelia, and I blamed Imaria and the Weaver for Morigna…" He shook his head. "And the sword knew that. That was the trial. To see if I was strong enough to resist the weakness within myself."

330 · JONATHAN MOELLER

"It seems that you were," said Caius.

"Not by myself," said Ridmark.

Calliande squeezed his hand. She was still a little teary-eyed.

Caius shrugged. "No man is an island. I think every kindred on this world speaks that proverb."

"Aye," said Ridmark.

"I am pleased you survived," said Third, her face emotionless. "I would not be pleased to report to Queen Mara that I failed in my charge to protect you."

Ridmark smiled. "Nor would I wish you to report failure to Mara on my account."

Third's cool mask cracked, and there was a flash of warmth there. "And I would have been displeased if you had been killed. We have been through too much together for you to kill yourself."

"Thank you, Third," said Ridmark.

She inclined her head and said nothing, but she did smile.

"We should probably get back to Dun Calpurnia," said Calliande. "The High King will need us."

"Yes," said Ridmark. He stood, took Calliande's hand, and drew her to her feet. "He does. We need to do something first."

"What?" said Calliande as Third and Caius stood.

"Marry me," said Ridmark. "Here and now." Her eyes widened. "Just as we would have done in the Great Cathedral before the sword interrupted us. Caius is a priest, and Third will be the witness." He looked Calliande in the eyes. "Let us do this now, before the Dragon Knight and the Keeper go to war against the Frostborn."

"Yes," whispered Calliande, smiling.

It did not take long.

Caius had the marriage rite memorized, and he led them through it as Calliande knelt with Ridmark before the dais. One by one Caius asked them questions, and Calliande and Ridmark answered as they swore their vows. Calliande found herself trembling a little, her heart racing.

She was grateful, so grateful, that they had survived to reach this moment. She knew there would be dark and hard days ahead, that they both might be killed. But they would always have this. She would be Ridmark's wife, and he would be her husband until the end of their lives.

At last Caius finished, threatened the stern judgment of God upon whoever would tear asunder what God had brought together, and proclaimed them husband and wife.

Ridmark drew her close and kissed her, and Calliande smiled and kissed him back.

A flush of heat went through her, and she belatedly thought about the consummation. She supposed that would have to wait until they returned to Dun Calpurnia. Though she didn't know where it could take place. A tent would have to serve, though she had never imagined spending the first night of her marriage in a tent.

But so long as she was with Ridmark, it was all right.

Ridmark gestured with his right hand. Fire swirled in his fingers, and the sword of the Dragon Knight appeared, burning with harsh flames.

"What are you doing?" said Calliande.

"Give us a moment," said Ridmark.

Caius looked puzzled, but then Third smiled.

And then both Third and Caius froze.

"What...what did you do?" said Calliande.

"The sword can't change the past," said Ridmark. "But it can change the flow of time, just as the high elves do at Cathair Solas. They're still breathing and moving. We're just moving faster than they are." He considered that. "A lot faster."

Calliande frowned. "Why did you do that?"

The sword disappeared, and he took both her hands in his.

"Because," he said. "I can give you this before we go to be the Keeper and the Dragon Knight. A moment just for us, where no one can interrupt us."

"Oh," said Calliande, and then she understood. "Oh!" She kissed him hard. "That is a good wedding present."

He took her hand and led her to a door behind the dais.

The room was small, but the ceiling was intact, and no one would disturb them.

Ridmark laid their cloaks down to serve as a bed and removed his armor and clothing. He was a little concerned about his ability to perform. It had been a long and exhausting ordeal of a day, preceded by many exhausting days, and he was tired.

The concern vanished as Calliande undressed and drew her trousers down her legs. He had seen her naked before, of course, on the day they had met, but this was different. Then she had been terrified, and he had been fighting for his life to escape from the Mhalekites. Now she looked nervous, but there was also exhilaration there, mixed with an almost wild joy. His eyes swept her up and down, the shape of her legs, the curve of her hips, the swell of her chest, the blond hair hanging loose against her shoulders.

No, he had no doubts about his ability now.

Ridmark drew her down to their cloaks, her arms tight against his back. He was gentle, knowing it was her first time, and she soon began to shudder and moan against him, her body moving in rhythm with his. Her fingers slid across his back, gripping tighter and tighter, and when she finished, she nearly deafened him with the volume of her cry.

Once they were done Calliande curled on her side next to him, her head resting against his chest, his hand stroking her naked back.

FROSTBORN: THE DRAGON KNIGHT · 333

"Oh," said Calliande in a shaky voice. "Oh. I see why people get so excited about that. I had no idea what I was missing all these years." She levered up on an elbow, draping herself over him, and kissed him. "Whatever happens next, whatever happens to us...I'm so glad you're my husband, Ridmark."

"Yes," said Ridmark, and he kissed her back. "Whatever happens, we'll face it together."

Because the future did look grim. He had given the Frostborn a bloody nose, but he knew they would not stop. Worse, the Frostborn were not even their true foe. Imaria was still there, spinning her poisonous webs in the shadows, and she would not stop until the Well was hers and she could free the shadow of Incariel.

But for now, this moment belonged to Ridmark and Calliande and no one else.

SHADOWBEARER

The Frostborn, as ever, were undaunted by their defeat. It was one of the things that Imaria Licinius Shadowbearer found useful about them. When they faced setbacks, they did not rage or despair or weep. They simply considered the new facts, recalculated their strategy, and continued their program of conquest.

It was why they made such useful tools. The Weaver had failed her. The Enlightened of Incariel had failed her. Tarrabus had failed her.

The Frostborn would take Tarlion for her.

"Then the appearance of the Dragon Knight makes your course clear, my lords of the Order of the Vanguard," said Imaria.

She stood with the Frostborn in their camp five miles north of Dun Calpurnia. The Frostborn had withdrawn there after Ridmark and the Keeper had returned, fortifying themselves within walls of ice raised by the khaldjari. That had proven an unnecessary precaution. Arandar's army was in no shape to pursue, and the dwarves and the manetaurs and the Anathgrimm were still a few days away.

"You must strike for Tarlion at once," said Imaria. "Leave a force to hold your strongholds in the Northerland, freeze the Moradel, and march south to Tarlion. With the river frozen, you can use it as a highway and reach Tarlion long before anyone can stop you. Once you take the city and the High King's Citadel, you shall have access to the Well of Tarlion, a mighty source of magical power. With that, you can destroy the kingdoms allied against you one by one."

The Frostborn shared a look among each other. Imaria knew by now that they could communicate without speech, and no doubt they were debating her plan amongst themselves.

"The Order of the Inquisition agrees with our ally's assessment of our strategic position," said Arlmagnava at last.

"Very well," said Lord Commander Kajaldrakthor. "I shall give the orders. We shall march on Tarlion and cut out the heart of our opposition, and then destroy our foes one by one."

Imaria inclined her head, keeping her face calm, but her laughter rang inside her head.

The laughter of the shadow of Incariel joined her.

The Frostborn were fools. Powerful, clever, dangerous fools. They had no idea of her true purpose and no idea that their precious world gate was a bomb that would rip open Black Mountain and free Incariel from its prison.

Though it did annoy her very much that Ridmark was still alive.

It annoyed and alarmed her that Ridmark had become the Dragon Knight. Tymandain had underestimated Ridmark, but Imaria would not make the same mistake.

Perhaps the Frostborn would kill Ridmark and the Keeper for her.

But if they didn't, no matter. Because the Frostborn would give her the Well of Tarlion.

And with the Well of Tarlion, she would free Incariel at last, and humanity would join Incariel in chaos forevermore.

THE END

Thank you for reading FROSTBORN: THE DRAGON KNIGHT. Look for the final chapter of the FROSTBORN series,

FROSTBORN: THE SHADOW PRISON, to appear in summer 2017. If you liked the book, please consider leaving a review at your ebook site of choice. To receive immediate notification of new releases, sign up for my newsletter, or watch for news on my Facebook page.

ABOUT THE AUTHOR

Standing over six feet tall, USA Today bestselling author Jonathan Moeller has the piercing blue eyes of a Conan of Cimmeria, the bronze-colored hair of a Visigothic warrior-king, and the stern visage of a captain of men, none of which are useful in his career as a computer repairman, alas.

He has written the DEMONSOULED series of sword-and-sorcery novels, and continues to write THE GHOSTS sequence about assassin and spy Caina Amalas, the COMPUTER BEGINNER'S GUIDE series of computer books, and numerous other works. His books have sold over a half million copies worldwide.

Visit his website at:

http://www.jonathanmoeller.com

Visit his technology blog at:

http://www.computerbeginnersguides.com